OF WICKED BLOOD

OLIVIA WILDENSTEIN
KATIE HAYOZ

OF WICKED BLOOD
BOOK I OF THE QUATREFOIL CHRONICLES

Cover design by *Ampersand Book Covers*
Editing by *Krystal Dehaba*
Proofreading by *Janelle Leonard*

Be kind. Be wise. Or be cursed.

GLOSSARY

FRENCH

allez-y – go on ahead
apéritif – a drink
berceau – cradle
biensûr – of course
bienvenue – welcome
bise – customary French greeting consisting of two kisses, one on each cheek
bon appétit – enjoy your meal
bonsoir – good evening / goodnight
bouchon en bois – wooden cork
bordel de merde – goddammit
chaton – kitten
chérie – darling
chez moi – my place
chouchen – mead (Brittany specialty)
dieu merci – thank god
dieu sait pourquoi – God only knows why
dragon de merde – fucking dragon
enfoiré – bastard
fait chier – damn it

foutu – fucked
galette – a savory crepe
gare – train station
guivre – wyvern
horloger – watchmaker
incroyable – incredible
j'en ai rien à branler – I don't give a shit
Joyeux Noël – Merry Christmas
le mal – evil
magie noire – dark magic
manoir – manor
merci – thank you
Monsieur Le Maire – Mister Mayor
mon dieu – my god
oui – yes
mon amour – my love
non – no
pardon – sorry
peste - pestilence
pouvoir – power
Puit Fleuri – Flowered Well
putain – fuck
putain de merde – fucking hell
quartefeuille – quatrefoil
salidou – salted caramel (Breton specialty)
salut – hey
ta gueule – shut up
tabac – convenience store
voilà – there you have it

(OUR) BRETON

arzoù-kaer – beaux-arts
diaoul – demon
diwallers – guardians
erenez e v'am – bind to me

kelc'h – circle
kelouenn – the scroll
groac'h – shapeshifting water sprite
Istor Breou – History of Magic
dihuner – clock

THE DIHUNER

THE ASTRONOMICAL CLOCK

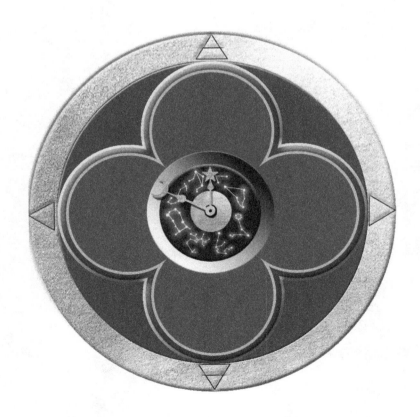

1

SLATE

I step out of the private elevator to find the door to my newly refurbished loft wide open.

I pat down my tuxedo for something I can use as a weapon, but all I come up with is a strand of black Tahitian pearls, six thousand euros in cash, and a Rolex Cosmograph Daytona. The Opéra de Marseille is a profitable place to pick pockets. Swearing under my breath, I pull an umbrella from the stand near the door and lunge into the apartment.

"Well if it isn't Mr. Mary Poppins, my favorite thug." Bastian sits on the leather couch devouring my stash of madeleines.

I toss the umbrella on the kitchen counter, then nudge his sneakers off my expensive coffee table. "Doors are equipped with this magical thing called a latch, little brother. Use it."

He snorts. "Heard your car, so I knew you were on your way up. The engine on that thing is *loud*. I'm surprised the neighbors haven't complained."

Loud and beautiful. "I'd love to see them try."

Bastian and I met in my third foster home, seven years ago. He was a skinny, bookish almost-eleven-year-old, with skin a shade darker than mine and a soul ten times brighter. I was thirteen and two full heads taller. I kept to myself and so did he. But then our foster parents took in two meathead strays with only a scattering of braincells between them. They got their kicks from slamming Bastian's head inside his books, cackling when they bloodied the pages. The day I caught them at it, I broke their noses. For the next year, anytime they gave Bastian a hard time, I broke other body parts. Toes. Fingers. An arm. Finally, I got tossed out of the family. I took Bastian with me to the next homey hellhole, having developed a soft spot for the kid.

The only thing I might love more than larceny is that boy. And madeleines.

"I see you've come into some cash since I last visited." Bastian gestures to the custom fireplace that runs along the bottom of the living room wall, then to the granite kitchen countertop, the *le Corbusier* stools, and the Noguchi glass and maple coffee table he had his dirty sneakers on only a moment ago.

Some is an understatement.

I smile as I appraise all the material beauty that is now mine. "Sold a lost Renoir."

"Lost or stolen?"

"It was lost among a clutter of other masterpieces. Total shame." I snatch the bag of supermarket madeleines from him.

He can eat anything else in the place, but not these. These are mine.

As I bite into one, I spy a thick, creamy envelope on the couch beside him. "What's that?" I ask, my mouth full. "Christmas isn't until tomorrow."

"Yeah, not from me. My gift to you is my visit." He holds the letter out—it's big and square and made of quality vellum. "It was under your door. Found it when I came in."

"Huh."

His thick eyebrows gather over the black plastic frame of his glasses. "It says *Monsieur Rémy Roland*. New underground persona?"

I take the envelope from his hands and swallow a dry clump of madeleine. *Monsieur Rémy Roland a.k.a. Slate Ardoin* is written in a deep-blue ink by an elaborate hand. "What the fuck?"

Bastian hums the *Mission Impossible* theme. "Rémy Roland a.k.a. Slate Ardoin, your mission, should you choose to accept it—"

My murderous glare gives him pause.

"Wait," Bastian's voice breaks. "Is Roland your . . . birth name?"

Ardoin is the family name given to me by the system. My first name was also a gift from the system, although, as far as names go, Slate isn't exactly the easiest on a francophone tongue. Whoever was handing out monikers that day must've smoked one too many blunts.

Bastian knows his birth family's past—Algerian immigrants who came upon life-crushing hard times and thought he'd be better off with someone else. Me, I'm a goddamn ghost. According to social services, I came from nowhere.

I read the fancy script again, then flip the envelope, run my thumb over a navy wax seal bearing an ornamental capital M laced through with a small, curly d. *Pretentious.* I break the flap and yank out a bundle of papers. A key drops out and lands on the tabletop with an alarming clink. Thankfully, the glass doesn't chip.

As Bastian picks up the key, I read the cover sheet, a letter written in the same scrolling hand that penned the address.

Monsieur Roland,
My name is Professor Rainier de Morel. I am Acting Dean at L'Université de Brume. Founded in 1350 by four local families, the university is rich in history and culture...

Blah, blah, blah. I skim until my gaze snags on a sentence that makes my blood turn to ice.

As a descendant of one of the founding families, you are entitled to a full scholarship, room and board included. In the packet of materials I've given you, you'll find your original birth certificate. Before you became Slate Ardoin, you were born a Roland.

Nothing about me is soft, not my body, not my personality, yet my knees suddenly turn to jelly as I flop down onto the couch next to Bastian.

"What?" Bastian snatches the letter from my hands, his eyes going wide behind his rectangular lenses.

I flick through the pages I'm clutching, and ... *putain de merde.*

There it is.

My birth certificate.

Rémy Roland. My birthday: November 18, not October 9, like a social worker told me. My parents' names: Eugenia and Oscar Roland.

It's just a document, one that shouldn't have my heart pounding so hard, but my pulse lances against my skin. I pass the certificate over to Bastian.

He whistles and shakes his head. "You think it's real? If it is, then you're going to have to change your ID."

"I'm not changing anything," I growl. "My name's Ardoin." Why would I associate myself with people who tossed me out like day-old trash?

"But you will take the scholarship, right? I mean, I've heard about that college. It's prestigious. Like, on equal ground with the Sorbonne."

"I don't even have my damn baccalaureate, Bastian."

While I dropped out after ninth grade, Bastian aced his final exams and got into college a year early. The boy could be anything. A rocket scientist. A lawyer. A neurosurgeon. Instead, he's studying to be a social worker to help kids like us in the system. Where my heart has withered and dulled, his has stayed shiny and pure.

"This De Morel dude doesn't seem to care about diplomas. You get in on your family name alone."

"My family name is Ardoin."

"Slate, come on ... Or should I call you Rémy?"

I growl at him, and Bastian holds up his palms. I snatch the letter back and continue reading:

I've been waiting for the right moment to call you back to your birthplace and share some of your family's history, since your parents are no longer here to tell you themselves. That time is now. It is vital that you come to Brume, and soon. Please do not attempt to telephone me. I will only answer questions in person.

A student dorm has been made available to you, and you can find me on campus. Classes start on the 2nd of January. In their will, your parents left you money in an account at the university bank. You will be able to use it for any extracurricular expenses you might have.

I cannot tell you how pleased I am to welcome you...

I wasn't tossed out of the nest.

My nest was pulverized.

My parents are *dead*.

And this De Morel prick knew the entire time.

I stand and tear the letter.

"What the hell?" Bastian collects the pieces like they're bits of a five hundred-euro bill.

Every inch of me boils with rage. "What do you mean, *what the hell*? This professor knew about me! He knew I had a history. Money. *He knew my name*. And he only contacted me *now*? Where was he and this money when I fought off pigeons to eat stale loaves out of the bakery's dumpster? Where was he when I got my face smashed in and went two years without front teeth! Where was he when the two of us were sleeping in that abandoned factory with the damn rats just to have a roof over our heads?"

Bastian looks at the shreds of paper in his hands. "Yeah, money would've been nice."

But it's not even the money that's making me see red. Not really. It's this stupid feeling of relief unwinding the familiar knot in my gut. I've always believed no one wanted me. That maybe I can't be loved. But my parents didn't abandon me; they died.

My relief turns to bitterness, though. Finding out that this man knew this and never told anyone—not even social services—infuriates me even more than his keeping my money. "Where does this *enfoiré* get off thinking he can waltz into my life after all this time and expect me to be grateful? And how does he even know where I live?"

There's no way I'm going to some snooty school in some cold, assbackwards town all the way up in Brittany. I've been part of the shameful dregs of society for far too long to sit in a classroom and listen to philosophical vomit.

Bastian gets up and strides to the kitchen counter. He lays the key on top and pulls open a drawer, rifling through it until he finds a roll of scotch tape. "I know you don't think you're worth a different kind of life—"

"I happen to love my life. Look at this place." I gesture to the expansive loft and its unobstructed sea view. "Besides, I'm damn good at what I do."

Bastian begins piecing the letter back together. "Yeah, you are good at it. And this place is amazing. But deep down, I don't believe it's what you really want. Also, you live day to day, never sure how much you have in your pockets. And do I have to mention that you're in a dangerous business? One slip-up and you're done."

I blow air out one corner of my mouth.

"Here's your chance to do something else. Something other than simply survive. Who knows, you might even be *happy*."

"Happy?" I scoff. "I don't do happy. Besides, I'm not into the college scene. It's not me."

"Except..."

I stare out the bay windows at the harbor. At night, the Mediterranean looks like a black tongue licking the beach. I wait for him to continue. When he doesn't, I turn. "Except what?"

"Except maybe it *is* you. You've never even had the slightest inkling of your origins. What if you descend from a long line of joyful brainiacs? I mean, your ancestors founded a *college*. You could be royalty in Brume. Who knows? Even if you don't attend classes, go there to scratch that itch you've always had."

He's talking about the itch of being *someone*.

Bastian sighs and tips his head to the side, mocking me. "*Or*, you could go to get revenge. Con this guy out of his cash. Sleep with his wife. Seduce his youngest daughter. Loot his home. Would that make you happy?"

I ignore Bastian's sarcastic tone and smile. "Happy is overstating it. But revenge would be . . . *pleasing*."

He rolls his eyes and goes back to his papery puzzle.

I *could* make a short trip, learn about my family from this Rainier guy, empty my trust fund.

Bastian hands me the patched letter and the key. "I'll go with you."

"No way, little bro." If he comes with me, he'll nag me to sign up for classes. He'll want to go sightseeing. Turn my quick in-and-out into a holiday.

"But—"

"Look, I'll still be here for a week. Annoy me all you want until then. On the 31ˢᵗ, I'll take off for Brittany—*without you*—because someone needs to stay behind to care for Spike." Spike's my cactus, a rare Eve's Needle that's over three feet tall and currently sitting in the middle of my cavernous living room.

"Fine. As long as you're going. 'Cause this trip, Slate . . . I have a feeling it'll change your entire life."

A shiver slinks down my spine. "Let's fucking hope not."

2

CADENCE

"**P**apa, we're going to be late. Are you almost ready?" I skim the sleek curls I created using the flat iron Alma gifted me last Christmas and which I only just removed from the packaging.

To my best friend's despair, I'm a big fan of minimal maintenance when it comes to my straightish brown hair. I have to admit, though, as I study my reflection in the glass protecting the Gauguin sketch, I like the effect.

"Sorry, I was finalizing some details for the New Year's party." The tires of Papa's wheelchair squeak against the white marble floor just as Alma arrives.

"Hello, Rainier," my best friend singsongs, leaning over to kiss my father's cheeks, her tamed curls falling around her face like a sheet of copper.

"Your coat, Papa." I hold up the thick navy cashmere.

As he maneuvers his arms through the sleeves, he looks up at me, and his brow pleats. "You look different, *ma* Cadence. Beautiful as always but different."

"It's the hair." Alma grins. "I have two words for you, Cadence. Gor. Geous."

"That's actually one word."

"Not the way I say it."

I roll my eyes. "Gloves are in the pockets, Papa."

He digs them out while I slide mine on. Brume has two seasons: summer and winter. Sadly, they're nowhere near equal. We get blue skies and piping hot air for two months—if we're lucky, three. The rest of the year, we're swallowed by a marrow-congealing fog that makes the air feel raw and icy.

The only person in the entire town who doesn't seem affected by the frigid temperatures is Alma. I don't know how she hasn't gotten frostbite on her legs, considering her closet consists of miniskirts and doll-sized dresses.

Like tonight. "Nice skirt. Very Christmassy."

She pats her scarlet mini, which she's paired with sheer stockings a shade darker. "Right?"

As he wheels himself out of the house, Papa's cricket ringtone chirps. He picks up, then proceeds to talk in muted, cryptic one-word answers. Sometimes, I think he may be having an affair, but is it an affair if there's no wife to cheat on?

I've been motherless since I was a week shy of my first birthday, and although I regret Maman passed away, I don't miss her. You can't miss someone you don't remember.

Alma hangs back with me as I lock up.

"Your ladybits are going to end up freezing and falling off one of these days," I tell her.

She blinks her whiskey-colored eyes at me, and then she wrenches her neck back and releases a bark of laughter that echoes against every old stone in Brume.

"I can't believe the word ladybits just came out of your mouth, Cadence de Morel."

I smile as we walk away from the manor. In seconds, the thick fog, that's densest at the bottom of the hilly town, curls off the lake and swallows my home.

When we reach the cobbled road that winds through Brume like swirled frosting, I grip the handles of Papa's motorized chair. Even though he doesn't really need my help maneuvering, I worry about him skidding on black ice or getting stuck in a patch of deep snow.

"You should ask the mayor to build you a ramp, Rainier. They could add one along the stairs." Alma gestures to one of the staircases cut right into the flank of Brume, which facilitates access to the different *kelc'hs*, or circles.

Unoriginal people have streets, Brumians have circles.

"It'd be way too steep," I say.

Besides, when Papa absolutely needs to be on campus, someone from the fire brigade drives him there with an electric utility vehicle —the only car allowed in our pedestrian town.

Alma's eyes light up. "Ooh. Imagine how fun it'd be to slide down."

"Imagine how dangerous."

"Forever the party pooper."

"You mean, forever the conscientious adult?" I volley back.

Papa shakes his head at us but lets out a brief chuckle.

"I'm still going to suggest adding a ramp to our dear old mayor over dinner tonight."

I snort. "Can't wait to hear you build your case."

"It'll be good for tourism."

"How?" I challenge her.

She raises her hands and draws them apart, creating an imaginary sign. "*Slide down Merlin's Hat.* What do you think, Rainier?"

"I think our town's touristic enough as is, Alma *chérie*, but I admire your enthusiasm."

"I see where Cadence gets her party-pooping from." She pouts, but it's brief and fleeting like all of Alma's reactions.

Soon, she's rambling on about something else, while I'm stuck glancing at the pale façade of Town Hall that stands out like a ghost amidst the soupy fog. Four years ago, we had Christmas dinner there, in the Merciers' private apartment on the top floor. Crisped capon with chestnuts and glazed carrots. I can still recall the taste of that meal, the feel of Camille's arms around my shoulders, the powdery floral scent at the base of her neck.

Perhaps that's why I never missed Maman . . . because I had Camille Mercier.

Now, the town cemetery has both.

Two college kids run past us, laughing as one takes a spill on a patch of ice. He gets up and shakes the wet snow off the back of his coat.

"You okay, son?" Papa asks as he maneuvers his chair around the ice.

The boy—I think his name is Patrice—looks stunned by my father's concern, but then he spots the wheelchair, and recognition makes his brows level out. "*Oui,* Monsieur de Morel. *Merci.*"

"Be careful. We wouldn't want you starting the second semester in one of these." Papa tips his head to the chair.

"I'll be more careful."

Alma wiggles her fingers. "Bye, Patrice."

I can't believe I was right about his name. Unlike Alma, my brain isn't hotwired to remember the finer details about people. Quiz me on history, though, and I'll knock your winter boots off.

"'Night, ladies, Monsieur de Morel." Patrice pats his coat one last time before following his friend into one of Brume's oldest establishments, *La Taverne de Quartefeuille.*

The old inn, turned restaurant centuries ago, slumps on the edge of the square housing the *Puits Fleuri*—a well built during the Middle Ages and rumored to grant wishes to coin throwers. Do I believe this? No. But I like legends and have read *Istor Breou,* an old tome on the history of Brumian magic, from crumbly cover to crumbly cover more times than I care to admit.

My boot catches on a slick cobble, and I grip the wheelchair tighter to avoid faceplanting. Alma elbows me after I've regained my balance. I think she's about to offer to replace me at the helm but nope. She nods to two guys leaning against the well, sipping from hammered copper mugs. It takes me a minute to make out who they are—Paul and Liron.

Liron is Alma's ex. They met over the summer when they both worked as counselors for the university's summer camps, then dated until October, after which they amicably parted ways. They still hook up from time to time, but that has more to do with pickings being slim around these parts than ardent attraction.

"Liron was telling me that Paul wants to ask you out." She says this in a stage-whisper which I pray doesn't carry to the boys.

"Who wants to ask Cadence out?" Papa's legs might not work, but his ears work way too well.

"No one, Papa."

"Paul Martinol."

I shoot Alma a pointed glare, which just makes her smile brighten. I swear, she lives for embarrassing me.

Papa stares poor Paul down, making red blotches appear on his skin. Like me, he's a blusher. He might be worse than I am, actually. Or maybe it just looks more acute, because his hair is red and his skin's bathed in freckles.

"Not interested," I say to both Alma and Papa.

My heart's set on someone else.

Someone completely unattainable and completely uninterested.

Someone whose house we reach a couple minutes later up on Third Kelc'h.

Adrien Mercier.

Camille's son swings open his front door, golden hair slicked back, shirt sleeves rolled up to his elbows. After flashing us a wide smile and chanting *Joyeux Noël*, he seizes Papa's chair and hoists it up the two front steps, muscles bunching inside his long forearms.

"Charlotte couldn't make it I see," she tells Adrien, waggling her brows at me. "What a shame."

"If you weren't my best, and only, friend," I hiss, "I'd toss you into my family's crypt."

"Oh, please." She rolls her eyes. "I'd love it. I'd get to hang out with Viviene."

"Who's dead."

"Not according to the rumor mill. Her ghost's been spotted all over Brume."

"By drunks and tour guides."

Supposedly, I descend from the legendary enchantress who trapped Merlin in a cave under a rock in the neighboring forest of Broceliande. Alma's convinced I also descend from Merlin, but Viviene was reputed to have had many lovers, so who really knows?

"Here." Adrien reaches for my silver puffer jacket, and his fingers graze mine. "Let me get that."

Cheeks blazing, I murmur a rapid-fire *merci* and streak into the living room where Papa and Adrien's father, Geoffrey Keene, are exchanging niceties even though they never have anything nice to say about one another.

Both Geoffrey and Papa married into Brume's founding families. Where Geoffrey kept his own last name, my father took my mother's, something which Geoffrey rails him about at least once a year. In my opinion, I find Papa's gesture generous. Maman wanted me to carry her maiden name, and Papa wanted to make sure no one ever forgot I was his baby girl.

But the root of their hatred runs deeper than taunts about family names. My father's loathed the Mayor of Brume since he tried to seduce Maman, despite both of them being married.

"*Bonsoir*, Cadence." Geoffrey's eyes, which are the same mosaic of brown and green as his son's, stroke up my body, taking in the skinny black pants I've paired with a sleeveless, chunky turtleneck. I don't think he's looking at my outfit as much as the curves around my hips and chest.

"I made some *vin chaud*," Adrien announces. "Can I get you all a glass?"

"Yum." Alma settles on the leather couch. "Bring it on, Professor M."

"Your parents couldn't make it back for the holidays?" Geoffrey asks Alma.

"Oh, you know my parents, Monsieur Keene. They're not big on holidays." She scoops up a handful of cashews from the low table and chomps on them while I go help Adrien ladle the mulled wine into mugs.

Both Alma's parents were professors here at the university. They had Alma late in life, and then, two years ago, they left her under the care of my father and moved to an island off India's coast where they teach English to underprivileged children.

I lean my hip into Adrien's kitchen counter. "Thanks for having us tonight."

He looks away from his saucepan of wine and smiles, which makes his already square jaw look more chiseled. "You think that on my first Christmas back, I wouldn't try to reinstate the tradition?"

My gaze strays to the oil portrait of the woman who'd made the holiday so special, who'd made every day special. How did no one spot her depression beneath her smiles? Sure, Adrien had been away at Cambridge, but Geoffrey was here. Papa was here. *I* was here. How did we all miss the signs? The memory of Papa explaining she wasn't coming back still rattles me, even after four years.

"Thanks for letting me bring Alma," I say, returning my attention to the boy Camille left behind.

The boy who's like her in so many ways—wonderful, smart, kind.

He hands me a mug. "Alma's welcome anytime." He grabs two more and tips his head to the living room.

Unlike his father, his eyes don't stray down my body. They stay perched on my face. I really wish he'd look lower, notice my new curves, notice I'm no longer the little pigtailed girl he considered like a sister.

He has a girlfriend, I remind myself as I walk ahead of him. And he's six years older. Still, disappointment bloats inside me.

As I plop down next to Alma, I take a big, frustrated swill of the spicy wine. It's delicious, so I take another, then lick my lips to catch any fugitive droplets. I'm about to compliment Adrien on having brewed the best beverage I've ever tasted when I catch him staring at my mouth.

His eyes flick up to mine, then away, and he leans back in the sofa, one hand smoothing his hair. He asks Papa something I don't hear because I'm too busy wondering if I imagined him watching my mouth.

And did it mean anything?

3

SLATE

To celebrate the last day of the year, I book myself a seat on the TGV, France's bullet-train.

Direction: bumblefuck Brume.

As we roll past the lush French countryside, I thumb through webpages about the quaint old town, a tourist's wet dream—a perfectly preserved medieval village built on a hill, around an ancient temple, now the college library, housing the oldest astronomical clock known to mankind. Cobbled streets lined with half-timbered houses and gray limestone ripple in concentric circles around the temple all the way down to the *Lac de Nimueh* on one side and the *Forêt de Brocéliande* on the other.

The cemetery at the bottom of the hill is famous. That fairy or witch or whatever from the Arthurian legends is said to be buried in De Morel's family crypt. As for the sorcerer Merlin, he's supposedly trapped for eternity in the forest, Viviene having tricked him into entering some cave which she then blocked with a heavy Carnac stone. Crafty woman.

I have to admit it's smart to add fictional characters to your family tree. Maybe I'll buy a patch of land, stick a few menhirs on it, and declare it the resting place of my long-lost great-great-great-great-great uncles, Obélix and Astérix. Bet I could make a pretty penny off unsuspecting tourists.

I tap my finger on my phone's screen, setting this business

venture aside to focus on my destination and the rare and valuable items I'm bound to find there. I mean, there's the clock, but considering it's the size of a spaceship, I can't exactly stuff it inside my bespoke jacket pocket.

An alert for a new email from Bastian pops up. I click on it, then scan his in-depth research into local lore and odd tales. Some shit about Brume being the birthplace of magic. More shit about how they celebrate this magical history in costume throughout the year. And then . . . the blowfly on top of the pile of steaming manure . . . the stories of cursed artifacts. I find myself chuckling as I read. I mean, come on. How gullible are people?

My laughter attracts the eye of a woman seated across the aisle. She bites her bottom lip, denting the soft flesh. She's got nice ice on her ears, each diamond larger than my pinky nails, but I'm not in the mood to relieve her of her itch *or* her earrings.

I turn toward the window for the remainder of the trip, concentrating on my festering hatred toward this Professor Rainier de Morel. How he ignored me until it suited his purpose. It's not something I can easily forgive. It's not something I *want* to forgive.

And again, how the fuck did he know where I lived? Possibly, that annoys me more than anything because it means he's been tracking me, and I like to be tracked as much as I enjoy getting stabbed in the hand with a steak knife.

Distractedly, I finger the wound, a pale strip that resembles a zipper because of my less than adroit needlework. Not that my tools —gin, nylon fishing line, and a rusted needle—had been ideal for stitching skin. I roll my fingers, which pushes out the white scar. Bastian says I'm lucky my tendon wasn't damaged, lucky I still have use of my thumb.

I don't believe in luck.

I still have a tendon, because I fought to save it.

Fought to save myself from the shitty hand I was dealt.

THE MOMENT I arrive in Brume, there's no doubt the place lives up to its name. A steely gray mist blankets the entire hill, and icy fingers of cold slip under the collar of my wool coat. As I walk from the train station to the fortified entrance of town, I can't help but snort at its quaintness. Bastian's research said this place was sometimes called Merlin's Hat, but in my opinion, the streetlights winding upward look more like candles on a stacked birthday cake than stars on a wizard's hat.

Noise leads me up a set of uneven stone stairs, to a road crawling with people dressed in witch hats and black sorcerer robes. Some tote stuffed black cats, others sport fake beards or press-on warts. Garlands of evergreen boughs and mistletoe adorn façades, and candles sit in frosty windows. A vendor ladles spiced wine from a large cauldron in the middle of what I assume is the town square considering it's *square* and animated.

There's laughter and dancing, but nothing like the debauchery I'm used to. Nothing like Marseille, with clubs pounding bass out into the street, restaurants heaving with happy drunks, motorbikes screeching down passageways. Here, there are no cars, no motorcycles, no fireworks. No neon lights or club music. Only geeks and old geezers waving around LED-activated wands.

I squeeze through the hordes of villagers, shoulders tightening from the crush of bodies. I usually enjoy crowds, enjoy *working* them. Since I'm not working, the contact of so many limbs sets my teeth on edge.

Once I'm free of the throng, I drop my gaze to my map application, following the directions to the dormitories. When I pass the last of the shops, the winding road clears of people but swarms with shadows. A furry black creature streaks across the street, inches from my boots. No wonder people think this town has wicked origins; it looks like something out of a Grimms' fairytale.

The cold humidity pricks my skin as I finally step beneath an illuminated, rectangular bronze panel strung up on a chain between two houses. The words THIRD KELC'H glint as it swings and clanks. How the hell do the people living nearby stand the grating noise? I would've clipped the thing down and melted it.

Huh.

Maybe I *could* clip it. Could be worth something if it's an original. I snap a pic, then go back to studying my map and stroll past narrow houses made of gray stone and damp timber that lean against each other like love-starved kids.

Though it looks nothing like any campus I've ever seen, the dorms and faculty housing are supposed to start on this circle. I find the address Rainier de Morel indicated in his letter, a three-story townhouse with a large four-leaf clover stamped over the entrance. I tap in the security code, climb up a set of creaky stairs, and unlock the door marked with a brass 3.

The room beyond is cramped and squat. Who the hell lives here usually? Elves? The walls and floor are weathered wood, and so is the bed frame, claw-footed nightstand, three-drawer dresser, and armoire covered by a speckled mirror. A window made of square panes looks out onto the shiny road peeking from beneath the dense fog. No ensuite bathroom, no dusty art on the walls, no knick-knacks on the dresser. I chuck my bag on the bare mattress.

Pop music leaks from the room next to mine, the sort Bastian adores, the sort that makes my stomach turn. I can't stand boppy love songs. Just like I can't stand having neighbors. Especially carefree students. The whole set-up feels way too much like a foster house. At least I have a door and a lock, more than I had back in my formative years.

After checking the contents of the dresser and armoire—both empty—I decide not to ring in the New Year alone in this elf hole. I button up my coat and shut the door, the brass 3 swinging from side to side as I lock up and pocket the key. I forgo the winding road for a set of stairs sprinkled with salt that lead me back to Second Kelc'h. Snow starts to drift down. Like this town isn't wintery enough already.

I buy a cup of mulled wine and a ham and cheese *galette* from an eatery called *Merlin's Baguette*, then pound the cobbles toward the square. At some point, I find myself discussing the cost of a decent drink with a bunch of inebriated sophomores. We buy several bottles of wine from a *tabac* ranging from dirt cheap to mildly expensive to test our theories before coming to the conclusion that, after several drinks, anything's decent.

But even with all the distraction and the booze, I can't get the gall of Rainier de Morel off my mind. I swallow a mouthful of Pinot Noir every time I think of him. And with every mouthful, I get more and more pissed off.

The villagers begin to sing a melancholic song in Breton. It feels like they're burying the past year instead of celebrating the coming one.

I leave the square and stagger down the windy road, the half-drunk bottle and brimming anger my only companions.

I want to do *something*. Something petty to make me feel better. So, when I stumble over the cemetery grounds and find myself outside a mausoleum with DE MOREL etched into the stone, I grin from ear to ear. I recall Bastian saying, *"Loot his home. Would that make you happy?"*

It's not his home but will do just fine.

My vision blurs before clearing and sharpening. *And yes, Bastian, it would make me very happy.*

I'm about to make the acquaintance of the legendary Viviene, a few dusty great-grandparents, and a pervy second cousin, because every family's got one of those. Or at least, all the families I lived with had some touchy-feely relative. Not that anyone's ever managed to slide their hands down my pants, but some tried. One ended up with smashed knuckles; the other with a missing phalanx. Booze dulls the memory of their ugly faces.

The granite structure sparkles intermittently behind the mist, a miniature version of the pantheon, complete with a portico of four columns. I step between the columns and practically kiss an iron bar. Damn fog.

Behind the metal gate, I make out the statue of a woman, carved so that her stone tunic and hair are perpetually blowing in the wind. She stands atop a weather-beaten tomb inscribed with the name VIVIENE that's so worn it's practically illegible.

Putain de merde. I shake the bars, but they don't even rattle. This can't be the only way in. There's got to be a door worthy of the tools I carry around. I stumble back into the snow and round the structure. Sure as shit, there's a side entrance that might as well display the words BREAK IN HERE in neon tubing.

I take my rake pick and tension wrench from the inside pocket of my coat and jimmy the padlock. The rusty hinges scream as I push open the iron door. The reek of mildew, soil, and rotting meat reminds me a lot of my third foster home. Such fond fucking memories.

With my phone light, I take inventory. Eight coffins lie on

recessed shelves carved into walls covered with spiderwebs and moss. A stone sarcophagus with an engraved four-leaf clover on the lid sits in the middle of the crypt like a beacon.

I gulp another mouthful of Pinot Noir, then drop the bottle onto the packed-dirt floor. It tips and spills, tingeing the foul, musty air of vinegar.

I start with the coffins set out like hors d'oeuvres, just ready for the picking. One good kick and the decaying wood on the first coffin snaps. A skeleton glares at me from inside, ancient pennies where its eyes should be.

The other seven are just as easy to open. I pocket a pearl brooch, two necklaces made of precious stones, several gold rings, and sapphire buttons. There's really no reason for me to put any effort into opening the sarcophagus.

The rule when looting is *in and out*. My second foster father, Hector, taught me that. He learned the hard way, spending time behind bars for taking an extra forty-three seconds to open a drawer he should've left shut.

This is different, though. This is personal. So I'm leaving no stone unturned.

I'm here to do damage.

Using a thighbone from coffin number three as a crowbar, I begin prying the heavy stone lid, my breath coming out in white puffs. The marker on the sarcophagus reads *Amandine de Morel*— Rainier's Sister? Cousin? Mother?—and dates her death as February 29th, seventeen years ago. I'm drunk enough to find that both funny and kind of heartbreaking. Imagine the anniversary of your death only being marked every four years.

It makes me wonder when my parents died exactly. And how? And if maybe they're buried somewhere in this eerie, frozen cemetery.

I'm not really sure I want to know.

The stone cover inches to the side as I coax it with my nifty bone. When there's finally enough space for me to grip the edge, I shove the damn thing with all my might. It slides over, revealing a shiny mahogany coffin inside. The lid pops off like a rotten tooth, and like a rotten tooth, the stench is eye-watering.

My first reaction, after wanting to heave up all the wine, is disappointment. All that artifice for a decaying corpse with no jeweled crown or tiara. She doesn't even have worthless pennies over her lids like the others, and her palms aren't sandwiched in prayer around a family heirloom.

She only has one hand resting over her heart. Her left arm is tucked underneath the rotting silk of her skirt. With one gloved finger, I push the material aside.

Holy. Fucking. Hell.

Jackpot.

A gold ring with an enormous scarlet gem adorns the retracting flesh of her bony finger. The oval stone looks like something out of a museum. Something housed behind bulletproof glass and protected by a hi-tech security system.

I whoop in celebration, hiccupping from my wine-fest, then take my phone from where it's propped on a ledge and beam the flashlight directly onto the ring. The red stone's so translucent it seems to pulse and swirl. I like beautiful things. But this . . . this goes beyond beautiful. It's exquisite.

I pick it up. It's larger than expected, heavier. Amandine de Morel must've had some seriously big hands. There are words engraved inside the band, written in a language I'm unfamiliar with. Still, I sound them out for the fun of it: "*Erenez e v'am.*"

In my head, I'm already compiling a list of potential buyers for this beauty.

Tugging off my leather glove with my teeth, I slide the ring onto my middle finger. The gem, which covers my finger to the knuckle, is oddly warm. I raise my hand and flip off the entire crypt. But what I'm really doing is giving the finger to Rainier de Morel himself.

"Screw you, De Morel, you *enfoiré!*" My voice reverberates off the dank walls.

In my drunkenness, it feels like the whole damn crypt shakes and tilts. I grab on to the stone casing and wait for the tremors to pass.

I pull at the ring to stash it inside my pockets with the rest of my loot, but the damn thing won't budge. Which is really messed up, because it was loose going on.

I yank at it. With each tug, the skin of my middle finger twists and stretches as if the band's been superglued to my flesh.

"*Bordel de merde!*" I curse.

For the next fifteen minutes I try everything I can think of to remove the damn ring short of sawing off my finger. I try slathering it with the lip balm I keep in my coat pocket. I try wedging it against the inner corner of the sarcophagus and wrenching it off. I try to pry it off with my teeth. I poke it with my dorm key. Nothing. As a last attempt, the heretic that I am tries praying.

Suffice it to say, it doesn't do shit.

Panic grips my lungs like iron fists as I stumble out of the crypt. The snow has stopped falling, but the temperature has dropped. It takes me a minute, but I'm finally able to stretch my leather glove over the ring. Just barely.

The lump makes me rage harder against that *salaud* Rainier de Morel. His name runs on a loop inside my head.

I keep my eyes down, putting one foot in front of the other, not paying attention to anything but my own drunken fury. That's when I collide with something soft and skid on the freezing ground. I fall, and the momentum upends the contents of my pockets.

"*Putain de merde!* Watch where you're going!" I spit out, grabbing at my fallen loot.

"Why don't *you* watch where *you're* going?" demands a feminine voice. Deep but melodious enough not to be confused with a man's.

Thin, pale fingers reach down and swipe the brooch. I snatch it back. I know I'm acting like an overgrown toddler, but I really don't give a flying fuck. Not tonight.

"I wasn't going to *steal* it; I was just trying to help." She shuffles backward on black combat boots peeking out from underneath a long black skirt.

I lift my eyes and crane my neck to keep going. The scratchy black skirt hides her legs, and a puffy silver coat, although cinched at the waist, hides her chest. But I catch sight of her face—very straight nose, slightly pointy chin, full red lips, and eyes that seem translucent in spite of the shadows cast by the brim of a ridiculous witch's hat.

The white puff of my breath blurs her face. I hold back my next exhale, long enough for her delicate features to sharpen.

Fuck, she's . . . angelic.

Any other time, any other place, I'd turn on the charm, but tonight, I'm on a mission. And that mission is revenge. I need to focus.

"Help? Did I ask you for help? I don't think so." I gather all my baubles, shoot to my feet, then brush myself off and stalk away.

She calls after me, an insult, I think, but the wind snatches her words before they reach me.

Rainier de Morel, Rainier de Morel, Rainier de Morel.

I input the address from his letter into my phone and follow the glowing map to an adjacent colossal stone manor. And I don't mean outsized compared to the dollhouses dotting the cobbled hill; I mean properly colossal with sprawling grounds and a tall wrought-iron gate.

A pretentious gold sign is nailed to the open gates: *Manoir de Morel.*

I pull my gloves tighter over my hands and start up the path that wends toward the sound of laughter and music.

4

CADENCE

A thief.

That's what the strange guy I just ran into must be. What man carries around a brooch? Who even wears brooches nowadays? Unless he bought it as a present for his grandmother, but shouldn't it have been wrapped up if that were the case? Also, it wasn't the only thing that spilled out from his pockets. Maybe I should report him. But it's New Year's Eve, and I'm feeling generous.

I'm also feeling really cold.

The dusting of snow has frozen over Brume. The slate roofs, bare oak branches, and holiday decorations look covered in vanilla icing and faceted crystals.

As I walk up the stairs toward Second Kelc'h, I clamp my tingling fingers into fists inside my puffer jacket's pockets. Alma said she was having "just one drink" at the Tavern, but that must've turned into two because she isn't at our meeting spot.

I shouldn't be surprised she hasn't arrived yet. She's *always* late. I scan the crowd in the square, searching for her coppery mane. When I talked to her on the phone earlier, her voice was so squealy I told her I'd meet her in town instead of letting her make her own way down the treacherously steep stone stairs alone. I didn't want her spraining an ankle, what with her penchant for sky-high heels

—a penchant shaped by her acute dissatisfaction with her five-foot-three frame.

I look at my watch for the fourth time in the space of two minutes. The hands seem particularly sluggish. Maybe they, too, are partially frozen.

I puff warm air into my hands, wishing I'd worn real gloves instead of the lacy fingerless ones I found in the attic. At least I'd donned a long wool dress buttoned up to my neck. Alma tried to dissuade me from wearing it for the party when we uncovered it last week in the dusty trunks filled with Maman's clothes, but the garment screamed witchy. Besides, even though it's silly, knowing that Maman wore it makes it sort of special.

The pointy black hat trimmed in burgundy faux-mink is the only thing new about my outfit. I saw it in *Au Bon Sort*'s shop window the other day and couldn't resist buying it for tonight. Gaëlle said she'd only gotten the one in, so I wouldn't have a twin at the party.

Gaëlle's family, like mine, is one of the founding families of Brume. She's twice my age, but something like a sister. Ever since her husband ran out on her a month before she gave birth to twins, I've helped out by babysitting or manning the shop whenever her stepson can't.

"Hey, sexy witch!" My friend's high-pitched voice makes me jump a little.

Her natural curls bounce and glint copper underneath the fairy lights strung up around the chained street sign for Second Kelc'h. She's wearing a shrunken version of my pointy hat, askew. It's fastened to a clip and has a little veil with a rhinestone spider. Her dress is also a shrunken version of mine, hitting mid-thigh and mid-boob. And just as I predicted, her knee-high boots have platform heels that almost make her reach my five-nine stature. I'm very obviously not the sexy witch in Brume tonight.

I stick my hands back into my pockets. "How are you not freezing?"

"I have tights."

"Fishnets don't qualify as tights."

As she walks toward me, her legs glimmer.

"Are there sparkles on them?" My words form a milky cloud.

"Yuh-huh. Hot-glued them myself." She spins, and her dress flounces, flashing me—and a small group of college guys sucking on cigarettes in front of the tavern—the color of her underwear: hot pink. The girl has *no* shame. She hooks her arm through mine. "Thanks for coming to get me. You're the bestest, Cadence."

"You sounded a little tipsy." She smells *a lot* tipsy, though, like she's wearing equal parts Cabotine and Dom Pérignon.

She giggles. "It's New Year's Eve! Of course I'm tipsy. The question is, why aren't you?"

"Because we're going to a party at my house, and Papa would ground me until my fortieth birthday if I was drunk."

"There's a big difference between tipsy and drunk. Besides, you need to live a little. You know, I thought maybe you'd actually started partying because I felt the ground shake earlier. But then I checked for flying pigs. And zilch . . ."

I knock my shoulder into hers. "Haha." I felt the ground shake earlier, too. The orchestra Papa hired for the party had been testing out the sound equipment, so I chalked it up to that.

Alma continues, "That should be your New Year's resolution: to finally let loose and act seventeen instead of seventy!"

"I don't act seventy."

She makes a noise in the back of her throat.

"You know what? I feel this is the year you're going to get together with that groomstick of yours." She cinches her fingers around my puffer jacket sleeve, her heels clacking against the cobbles.

"Groomstick?"

Her eyes glitter as though she hot-glued some sparkles on her irises, too. "Broom-groom? You don't like my witchy humor?"

I crack a smile. "How much champagne *did* you ingest?"

She just grins and then gossips about her housemates while we make our way through the twisty, glittery street, down the stairs, and toward the open gates of my house.

The old stones of the path leading to my front door vibrate with new-age classical music. Every year, we throw Brume's New Year's Eve party. It's been a tradition for generations. The town visitors dress up like witches and wizards to celebrate Brume's history, and we do the same. Only indoors with *hors d'oeuvres* and central heating.

A man stationed by the entrance pulls the heavy lacquered wooden door open, and we step into the foyer. Alma lets out a low whistle of appreciation. Papa hired a team of professionals from Paris to decorate this year. The house is festooned with garlands of lights hidden in silver tulle, and fancy clockfaces hang like snowflakes from the white-painted timbered ceilings. Tall arrangements of pine needles, white lilies, and red roses adorn every surface of the massive foyer and the rooms spilling beyond.

As Alma hands her short faux-fur jacket to the coat attendant, she grimaces and gestures with her chin to the reception room. "Don't look now, but Charlotte's dangling off your groomstick."

I peer into the crowded room, my gaze zeroing in on Adrien's dark-blond, gelled-up hair. He's chatting with the Chair of the Science department and his husband, and sure enough, black-haired, green-eyed Charlotte is hooked to Adrien's arm like a Christmas ornament.

I press my lips tight and heap my puffer jacket over Alma's before she winds her arm back through mine and tugs me through the throng of twittering witches and warlocks nibbling *canapés*.

"What does he see in her? Besides every strain of venereal disease in Brume?" Her voice carries over the din of harp, violin, and piano, and raises the bushy eyebrows of a silver-haired warlock. It takes me a few seconds to realize the warlock is none other than Adrien's father.

He looks me up and down in a way that makes me clutch the scratchy woolen barrier of my dress. "You're wearing Amandine's dress." The fact that he knows this adds to his general creepiness. "Your resemblance to her tonight is simply astounding."

I don't think he'd ever try anything, but his fascination with Maman, and now with me, makes every warning bell in my head clang when we're in the same space.

In spite of the fog of alcohol, Alma must sense my discomfort, because she steps in front of me. "And your resemblance to an old necromancer is simply mind-blowing. Where *did* you get that black velvet vest, Monsieur Keene?"

The corners of his eyes crinkle with a smirk. "Always so delight-
ful, little Alma."

She shoots him a smile that's more teeth than lip before hauling
me away. "Dinner with him last week was painful enough. Why
must he be everywhere?"

"Maybe because he's the mayor?"

She scrunches up her nose, making the small bump at the top
stick out. "I know Adrien isn't like him, but imagine if you two end
up married, and Geoffrey becomes your father-in-law."

"*Married?* I just want to kiss the guy, not marry him."

Alma lets go of me to seize two glasses of champagne from a
passing tray. She pushes one into my hands, then clinks hers to
mine so hard I worry for the etched crystal. "To this year being the
year you crawl out of your little shell."

I take a small sip, the bubbles bursting deliciously against my
lips. "I like my little shell."

"I know. God, I know." She hiccups-snorts. And then she just
hiccups. "You like it way too much." She downs the rest of her glass.
"Ah, the man of the hour!"

My father wheels himself to us. "*Bonsoir,* Alma *chérie.*"

While she plops a big kiss on his forehead, he eyes my glass.

"It's my first drink, Papa."

"I didn't say anything."

"What smells so divine? Oh. Ooh. Mini quiches." Alma all but
tackles the waiter passing around leek and egg tartlets.

Papa readjusts his simple black wizard robe until it lays flat on
his lap. "I suppose it's not Alma's first."

I smile down at him; he smiles back. I may have only one
parent, but what a parent he is.

"Make sure she sleeps over. I don't want her traipsing around
campus inebriated."

I realize Papa's staring at my dress, and his blue eyes, a few
shades darker than my own, slicken, resembling the lake on a frosty
morning. "Is that—Is that Amandine's?"

Biting my lip, I palm the black wool. Maybe I shouldn't have
worn Maman's dress. It's obviously paining him. "*Oui. Pardon.*"

"Don't be sorry. You wear it so well, *ma chérie.*"

I didn't even consider what it would do to him to see me wearing it.

"Rainier, I need two minutes of your time." Sylvie, Brume's one and only physician, lays her silk-gloved hand on the back of Papa's wheelchair. She's dressed in a purple tutu with a matching satin bodice so unlike her usual garb of tweed that I might not have recognized her had it not been for her waist-long gray hair. "I'll have him back to you in no time, Cadence."

Alma traipses back toward me, brandishing a paper napkin with a couple of fried shrimp. "Grabbed some for you."

I pop a shrimp into my mouth as we weave around the boisterous crowd. It seems like *all* of Brume has congregated inside my home. The crazy thing is that all of Brume could probably fit inside our giant manor.

"So, who's your victim tonight, Alma?"

"*Victim.*" She snorts. "You mean, the lucky man upon whom I'll bestow a kiss? Haven't decided yet. What about you?"

It's tradition in Brume to lock lips with someone for good luck at the stroke of midnight. That's how I got my first kiss. I was fourteen, and Romain, Gaëlle's then twelve-year-old stepson, rose onto his tiptoes to smack his mouth against mine.

Raucous laughter rises from one corner of the room. *Speak of the devil* . . . Romain, now fifteen, is chatting with some other kids his age, his wheat-blond hair shimmering as brightly as the crystallized clockface dangling over his head.

Alma must've followed my line of sight, because she says, "He's sort of cute now that he's nearly grown-up."

"You are *such* a cougar."

"Says the girl who uses his lips as a good luck charm *every* year."

I redden. "Only because he always volunteers, and I don't have the heart to turn him down."

As though he hears us discussing him, Romain's brown gaze surfs through the sea of pointy witch hats toward us. The second his eyes alight upon us, he flashes a dimply grin and saunters over. He's so tall now that I'd need to get on my tiptoes to reach his mouth, but he's still a kid with his rounded jaw and splash of acne. A good kid. Although I had bigger dreams for my first kiss, all in all, it wasn't so bad.

Alma tracks her gaze up his lanky body. "Dude, did you grow another foot since Thanksgiving?"

His grin strengthens. "Nice mini-hat, Alma."

"And this is why I like this guy." She latches on to his arm. She's touchy-feely and gets in people's spaces. It used to drive me insane until I understood that her need to touch others is visceral. "Any other guy would've commented on my tits or ass, but nope. Not this one."

Romain's dimples deepen so fast I expect them to leave a permanent imprint.

Alma cranes her neck. "What are you doing at the stroke of midnight, Romain?"

He glances at me, fuzzy jaw pinkening against the lacy white collar of the chemise he's paired with a black cape. He looks more vampire than warlock. Then again, warlocks don't exist, and if they did, they might be into capes and froufrou shirts.

"Or rather, *whom are you doing*?" Alma adds seductively.

I shake my head and laugh. To think Papa worries for *her* safety. We should be worrying for the poor boys of Brume.

"I, uh . . ." He rubs the back of his presently brick-colored neck. "Cadence?"

Alma winks at me. "She has a groomstick all lined up."

Romain raises a blond eyebrow. "Groomstick?"

"Don't ask." I shake my head some more. "Seriously, though, you don't need to take pity on me *every* year."

"It's tradition, not pity."

I sigh. He really is sweet. If only Adrien could be as sweet. Of its own accord, my gaze stretches back to him. He's no longer chatting with the science professor; he's now making the rounds, grin in place. Everyone loves the young, brilliant, handsome professor of history, especially since he's lost his mother. Every girl and her mother want to coddle him.

He catches me staring and smiles. My heart catapults against my ribcage. Which is all kinds of silly since he smiles at me often. He smiles at everyone often. Affability is as much part of his nature as flirtatiousness is part of Alma's.

"If it doesn't work out, come find me, okay?" Romain says, and I blush when I realize he's trailed my eyes' trajectory.

I flash him a grateful look, but then my gratitude turns to astonishment when I spot a head full of wild black curls over Alma's shoulder. The boy I bumped into near the cemetery is here, in my house, studying the oil painting of Viviene trapping Merlin in a cave.

When he strokes a gloved finger along the ornate, gilt frame, I stick my half-drunk glass of champagne in Alma's hands, tell her and Romain I'll be right back, then weave through the crowd.

"I don't think your pockets are large enough."

The boy pivots to face me, his brow going from furrowed to smooth. "Whatever are you insinuating, Bellatrix Lestrange?"

Bellatrix Lestrange? His Harry Potter allusion temporarily makes me forget what I rushed over to say. *Right . . . the painting.*

"I'm insinuating that you're clearly not here for the party." I nod toward his attire—slim gray jeans, black turtleneck, leather gloves.

"Why? Because I left my magic wand at home?"

At home, or at the bar? He smells like a distillery. "What's with the gloves?"

He stares down at his hands as though he's forgotten all about them. Something protrudes from his middle-finger, straining the leather. I'm suspecting it's a big ring. Unless it's a giant wart. Or boil. Or an identical twin he devoured in utero.

"My fingers are very sensitive to the cold."

I cross my arms. "Uh-huh."

"Besides, you're also wearing gloves. So are half the people in this room." He looks over my shoulder at the pointy assortment of hats, brooms, and wands. "What's with the crazy-fest anyway?"

"It's a Brumian tradition."

"People take their lore very seriously around here."

"*Very.*" I drag out the word menacingly. Or at least, I'm going for menacing. Maybe I just sound haughty. "So, what are you really doing here?"

He stares down at me, tipping his head a little to see under the brim of my hat. I hadn't noticed how tall he was back in the cemetery. Then again, he was on his hands and knees for most of the two minutes we spent in each other's company.

"I'm a new student."

I raise an eyebrow. "Really?"

"Yes, really." His breath flutters the hat's burgundy fur and some of the loose brown tendrils of hair framing my face. "Not very trusting, huh?"

"*Should* I trust you?"

"Probably not. I'm a man of *extremely* loose morals."

Even though I don't mean to smile, a corner of my lip twitches. I iron out my expression immediately. "If anything disappears, I'll know it's you."

He snorts, and his eyes squeeze and curve like tiny black arches. I've heard of people smiling with their eyes, but this is the first time I've actually seen it.

"Except, you don't know who I am."

"But I know what you look like," I answer back sweetly.

The camber of the boy's eyes increases.

"Cadence! There you are." Alma's voice bounces against my eardrums, and then her hands wrap around my arm. "Who's your new friend?"

"He's not . . . *my friend*," I grind out the last part. "He's a new student. *Apparently.*"

She hums, or maybe she purrs. "And what's your name, new student?"

"Slate." He daintily picks up her hand and brings it to his mouth. "Slate Ardoin." He doesn't touch his lips to her knuckles, but his mouth comes close.

Slick. This guy is *so* slick.

For a second, I feel a little miffed that he didn't greet me this way until I notice Alma's bare pinky. "Give her back her ring."

Alma's gaze widens when she realizes Slate's filched the pearl jewel, a homeschool graduation gift from her parents.

"How did you do that?" Instead of sounding peeved, she sounds amazed.

"Sleight of hand." He opens his fingers with a flourish. Atop the black leather rests Alma's white pearl.

She plucks it from his palm and slides it back onto her pinky. "Is that how you got your name?"

His good humor collapses. "No." He closes his fingers slowly, the smooth leather whisper-hissing. "But it would make a hell of a better story." Whatever annoyance gusted over him is gone, and although he isn't back to being Mister Smiley-Eyes, he's also no longer Mister Moody.

"So . . ." Alma leans in. "It's tradition to kiss someone at the stroke of midnight."

"It is, huh?" Slate asks, distracted by something behind me.

I turn to find Adrien chatting with Papa.

When I spin back around, Slate's attention is back on Alma.

"For good luck," she says.

A nerve ticks in his jaw, beneath the black stubble, and then his eyes bow with a smile that matches the one on his lips. "I'm starting to like this town and its fanciful traditions."

Slick. Slick. Slick.

Alma snakes her arm around my waist. "Cadence, here, has no one to kiss."

My heart skitters to a stop. "What?" She did not just toss me under the cauldron!

"It'll get Adrien's attention," she murmurs inside my ear. "Trust me. I know what I'm doing."

As though the air isn't thick enough with my embarrassment, the music stops, and the countdown begins.

Alma lets me go so suddenly I almost topple over. "I promised to show Romain how a real woman kisses."

She winks at me as everyone begins to shout: "Seventeen, sixteen." I'm going to kill her.

Fifteen.

Maybe put a real spider on her puny hat.

Fourteen.

She hates spiders.

Thirteen.

Or soap on her toothbrush.

Twelve.

"So, who's this Adrien?"

I murder my best friend in my thoughts. "No one."

Eleven.

All of his face is smiley. "Ex-boyfriend?"

Ten.

I look over my shoulder and see Charlotte skipping to Adrien's side, and then I spot our town's good doctor in her purple tutu-like frock prancing toward Papa in spite of her bad hip.

Nine.

Oh my God. Please tell me she's not going to kiss him. Papa's gone a bit pale. He probably doesn't want Sylvie, who's two decades his senior, anywhere near his mouth.

Eight.

I turn back around, and my gaze bangs into Slate, who's staring at me like he's a cat and I'm a new ball of yarn.

Four.

Where did seven, six, and five go? And when did his hand land on my hip?

Three.

He leans over.

Two.

Lower still.

When the crowd yells *one*, his mouth whispers across my cheek toward my earlobe. I feel the heat of his lips against the shell of my ear.

"If I relied on kisses for luck, I would never have made it off the streets alive."

I'm so surprised by his confession, and the fact that he didn't use the pretense of a tradition to kiss me, that I gape up at him.

He picks up my limp hand, bows his head, and brushes his mouth over my lace-cloaked knuckles. "Word of advice . . . make your own luck. It'll last you longer." And with that, he's gone, slinking like a shadow through the embracing crowd.

When I shake off my daze, I remember the thin diamond bracelet with the emerald quatrefoil charm I clasped over my glove tonight. I'm already imagining it gone, which is probably the reason for how startled I feel when the white diamonds and green stones blink wildly back at me.

5

SLATE

My lips are warm where they touched Cadence's ear, and the fruity scent of her shampoo lingers in my nose. I could've kissed her. Hell, I think I would've enjoyed it. Immensely. She's quick and shrewd, and her lips are like ripe cherries, but there's an innocence in those blue eyes that made me hold off. I'm normally surrounded by girls with hard edges and harder hearts. Girls who thrive off of power games and greed. This one is different. A naiveté emanates from her. A kind of goodness.

I glance back. She's still standing by the far wall surrounded by all of De Morel's dead relatives immortalized in their precious frames. Her curly-headed friend has returned to her side, chugging champagne like it's laced with rainbows. Side by side, they resemble before-and-after shots of Christmas morning—Cadence all wrapped up head to toe, and Curly-head completely exposed, ready to play with.

Cadence absently runs a hand over the wool hugging her waist. *Yeah.* I have a feeling there's something amazing under that wrapper. Before leaving this dumpy, gray town, I might try to find out.

My cell phone vibrates in my coat pocket, and I turn away from the girls, ducking back into the foyer frosted with so many damn silver garlands I'm almost blinded. *LITTLE BRO* flashes on my screen.

I lift the phone to my ear, stepping closer to the wall to peer at a graphite drawing. "Everything all right?"

"Yeah. Just checking up on you. You didn't text me when you got in."

"Sorry, *Maman*." The way the women are sketched reminds me of Gauguin. I check for a signature. Sure enough, at the edge of the aged vellum, Paul's sketched his name.

Bingo.

Bastian sighs. "Are you drunk? Your voice is a whole octave lower than usual."

"Nah. I'm almost sober." But my tongue chooses that moment to stick to the roof of my mouth, and it comes out, "Um ummalst soba."

"Shit, Slate. Don't do anything stupid. You always do stupid stuff when you drink too much."

"No, I don't." I turn away from the drawing and slip my gloved hand under my armpit despite the fact that Bastian can't see a damn thing.

"So, what's it like there?" Bastian's chewing on something—it better not be my madeleines.

"Like a damn Harry Potter convention. They worship magic here, man." I grab a salmon mousse thing from a passing waiter and pop it into my mouth. "The town looks like it just stepped out of the Middle Ages—all stone and cobbles and shit. And it's cold as a witch's tit. Fucking glacial." Little Miss Cadence steps into my line of sight again. "But the view isn't bad."

"And the De Morel dude? You find him yet?"

"Yep. Just need to get him alone."

After Bastian makes me promise to call him, we hang up. Only eighteen, and he's already such a mommy.

I peer into the now-dancing crowd for Rainier de Morel, aka "the one in the wheelchair," as Coat-check Girl graciously informed me. I could've guessed without the tip, though. *Pretentious entitled asshole* might as well be tattooed on his smug forehead.

He's parked beside the bay window, an aging purple fairy fawning all over him.

Leaving behind the Gauguin, for now, I round a couple who are grinding to an instrumental rendition of the Monster Mash. Or maybe that's the song I've cued up in my head to fit this strange-ass crowd, and the orchestra's playing something else entirely. When I step in front of Rainier, the old fairy squawks and removes her paws from the arms of his wheelchair. He looks up, relief etched across his blue eyes and barely-lined face, until he sees who just saved him from getting mauled by a woman too old to be wearing a tutu. His smile falters for a second, then slides back into place.

"Monsieur de Morel." I keep my voice even despite the fact that I want to punch the taunting cheer from his face. "Do you know who I am?"

He studies me a moment before nodding. "I believe I do." Without taking his eyes off me, he says, "Sylvie, will you excuse us, please?"

She frowns but recedes into the crowd like a smudge of grape juice.

"You must be Rémy Roland." He holds out his hand, waiting for me to shake it.

I cross my arms and ignore the gesture. "Actually, it's Slate Ardoin."

"Ah. Slate." His eyes spark in amusement. "Well, regardless of what you call yourself, you're a Roland."

"How the *fuck*," I growl, "do you know who I am when I never knew?" My emphasis on the word *fuck* gets partygoers glancing our way in spite of my low tone.

One of his eyes twitches. "Let's talk somewhere private, shall we?"

"Oh, yes," I say, my voice mocking, "let's."

He spins his chair around and leads me through the monstrous living room—or maybe it's an actual ballroom . . . wouldn't put it past this man to have a ballroom in his house. With me hot on his wheels, he maneuvers his chair into the foyer, past the split staircase, past the coat-check ladies, and into a glass elevator adorned with the same intertwined *M* and small *d* as his wax seal. Inside, he reaches over to press 1, and then we're gliding upward at the speed of a dozing slug.

Just like downstairs, the first floor looks like a florist shop puked up Christmas decorations. Bastian would love it. Although, *dieu sait pourquoi*, the kid actually has a preference for light-up plastic reindeer and waving Santas.

I follow Rainier into what must be his study. I can't get over how incongruous this house is. From the outside, the manor resembles a medieval castle; from the inside, it looks like some modern catalogue spread. The brushed cement walls are lined with sleek wooden shelves holding up row upon row of books illuminated by recessed lighting. No rug covers the veined marble floor that's polished to a reflective shine. Rainier's desk is specially made to be at his height. It's immaculate, the only items on the pristine kidney-shaped glass are a framed photo I can't see the front of, a pricey Baccarat paperweight, and crystal ashtray in the shape of a four-leaf clover. What is it with this town and shamrocks?

Rainier parks behind the desk, then tents his fingers together. He's got two distinguished streaks of gray at his temples that shine silver in the dimmed glow of the spotlights entrenched in the smooth, white ceiling. "I'm so pleased you've come to study with us."

"Cut the bullshit, De Morel. How the hell do you know who I am, and how did you find me?"

He taps his index fingers to his lips. "I'm not sure how much research you've done on your family tree since my letter, but since you're here, let me enlighten you. The Roland name goes all the way back to the early centuries when the wilds of Brume went by the name *Brocéliande*. You might have heard about the forest in Arthurian tales. Merlin and Viviene—"

"I don't give two shits about Merlin."

"Of course you don't." He says it like it's a major disappointment and exhales before continuing. "Anyway, your parents were a part of the ancient Roland bloodline. They were respected in this town. I knew them well. But when they died, you . . . disappeared."

"Disappeared?"

"Yes. We couldn't find you."

"Toddlers are pocket-sized, but come on . . ." I wait half a beat for him to clarify. When he doesn't, I glare harder. "Are you saying I *wandered away* and into the system? That I *toddled* my way to social services?"

"No, not at all." He shakes his head. "Your parents lost their lives in a fire. You were there as well. To be completely honest, I thought you'd perished along with them."

I rub the patch of puckered skin that resembles dripping wax along the inside of my left arm. I can't remember ever not having it. Did I get it here? In Brume? My childhood was so violent that it never occurred to me that I got it by accident. I always thought it was one of my foster parents who'd tried to use me as kindling.

"Doesn't Brume have this thing called forensics? Didn't they look for my bones? Or teeth? Or whatever the hell it is those people look for . . ."

"I'll admit, the fire and aftermath were quite a mess." He looks to the side. A tell that he's lying, but about what? The fire?

"Okay, then how did I get to Paris?" I spent my first ten years in the capital before being kicked farther south.

"This village has a long history, Monsieur Roland—"

"Ardoin."

He lets out a long breath. "Monsieur *Ardoin*, this village has a troubled past. Feuds between families. Secrets of betrayal and death. Someone probably thought you'd be safer away from it and kidnapped you." He finally looks back at me. "I only found out that you were alive a few years ago." Then he adds as if it's a good thing: "Since then, I've had my people track you. You seemed safe, so I didn't intervene."

"A few *years* ago." I can't help but laugh. "I don't know what safe means to you, but at *no* point was I safe. I had foster parents break my bones, other kids try to kill me. I scrounged like a rat most of my life."

He lifts an eyebrow. "But here you are, alive and well. *Safe.*"

"No thanks to you."

"I wouldn't be so sure," he says slowly. "Didn't you ever wonder about Vincent?"

Vincent was my fourth foster father. The one who planted that steak knife in the fleshy part of my hand the night I told him not to involve Bastian in his drug runs. The old man used to rough me up, but the knife was something else. A week after the incident, the day I'd planned on running away with Bastian, Vincent didn't come home. Just up and vanished.

I narrow my eyes. "*You* made him disappear?" He doesn't answer me, which I suppose is answer enough. "Why didn't you ever help in any other way? Why didn't you reach out? Send a check? Something? *Anything?*"

Fuck, I sound desperate.

I am not a desperate person.

He shrugs. "It really wasn't my place to get involved."

The rage suddenly coursing through me is like liquid fire inside my veins. I ball my fists so my nails gouge my palms through the leather. "More like, it wasn't *convenient* for you to get involved."

"So young and yet already so jaded."

I'm devoured by the savage urge to throw him out the floor-to-ceiling window, chair and all, but he's the only one who can answer my questions. Questions that have been burning my gut long enough to give me an ulcer.

"So why did I grow up with the name Ardoin? Why did no one tell me about my parents? Why did social services act like I was a stray?"

"Because whoever hid you found it prudent to keep your existence a secret." He runs a hand over the glass desk. "Your parents were very influential in Brume, and with great influence comes great enemies."

I want to make a joke. Something about him copping lines from *Spiderman*, but a needle of ice pierces my chest. "Are you saying my parents were murdered?"

An emotion crosses Rainier's face, making his jaw tick and his eyes darken. "*Non.* They perished in a fire."

"But—"

"A fire. No foul play was involved. It's as simple as that, Monsieur Ardoin."

None of this is simple.

He moves toward the low row of metal filing cabinets that runs the length of the wall across from the bookshelves. Over it stretches a yellowed scroll of parchment encased in plexiglass. Drawings of triangles, black bugs, quartered human bodies, and strange plants are interspersed with cramped lines of script, burn marks, and ink smudges.

A drawer clanks shut, pulling me from my observation. And then Rainier is parking himself back behind his desk and slapping a file on it. My name—well, the name *Roland, Rémy*—graces a label glued on the tab.

"Enough of this. Let's get down to the matter at hand—your studies. I've taken the liberty of enrolling you in a variety of classes to find out your strengths and shortcomings."

"About your little university . . . *j'en ai rien à branler*, De Morel. I came here for answers. And if you won't give them to me, I'm leaving Brume."

His pupils seem to pulse with annoyance. "I summoned you for a reason."

I let out a bitter laugh. "You *summoned* me?"

"As one of the founding family members, you're to be a part of the Quatrefoil Council meeting in two weeks."

"Quatre-whatta Council?"

"Quatre*foil*." He gestures to the ashtray. "Surely you've noticed the shape is an integral part of Brumian history. It's the symbol for the magic birthed here centuries ago."

I snort.

"Whether you believe in magic or not, Monsieur Ardoin, under-stand that there is a Council, a very ancient and very real one, and *it* believes magic exists. Now that you are over eighteen, it is your duty *and* your birthright to claim your seat at the table."

And Bastian thinks *I'm* drunk? What's wrong with these people? But then I remember the ring that won't come off.

I thumb it through the leather. "You can't exclude me for twenty years and then suddenly expect me to contribute to your little Quattro-fucking Council."

"Quatrefoil."

"Whatever."

"And you're right. I can't expect you to contribute or to stick around." He looks at me like I'm a cockroach. "But perhaps I can appeal to one of your baser senses, like greed. How about I promise that if you stay, I'll make it worth your while?"

That pisses me off to no end. I cross my arms over my chest so I don't punch him right in the throat. "I don't need your money, since I have so much of my own."

A conceited smile curves his lips. "Ah. Are you referring to that trust fund I mentioned in my letter?"

My biceps feel like stone.

He *tsks*. "You see, not only am I the trustee, but also the account is in the university bank. In order to access it, you need my permission. In order to get my permission, you need to attend the Council meeting. Since I pride myself on upholding traditions, that's my single condition. After the meeting, I'll grant you full and sole custody of your inheritance. So, now let's go over the subjects I enrolled you in."

There's a knock on the door, three short bursts followed by a nasal voice. "Monsieur de Morel? I'm terribly sorry to bother you, but some of your guests were worried. Is everything all right?"

"All's well, Jaqueline. I'll be down in a minute." He turns back to me. "Seems we're out of time. You can check your classes online. And we have a world-class library on campus. If you're grappling with questions about the Council or your heritage, look through the archives. Do you have any more questions for me?" He cruises toward the door.

I've never been conned. But here I am getting conned. By a middle-aged paraplegic who believes in fucking magic no less. I feel like my brain's about to explode. I run my hands down my face, my leather gloves catching on my skin, the band of the ring bumping against my cheekbone.

I'm tempted to remove the glove, shove the gem in De Morel's face, and ask him why his family heirloom is stuck to my finger. Would he even know? He's not a mortician. It's probably some weird substance from the corpse that's doing it. Some body fluid that turns gummy like glue after death.

Now I want to vomit.

After swallowing back the rising bile, I burrow my hand inside my pocket, my fingers bumping against the brooch. Nah, I can't show De Morel the ring. Not even to gloat about looting his family's mausoleum. No doubt he'd call the police. Bastian would be gutted if I went back to jail. Especially since this time, I wouldn't go to juvie.

Besides, if the damn thing's valuable, then I certainly don't want to give it back.

No. I'll return to that tiny cave of a dorm room and lube it up with soap. And if that fails, I'll buy some damn bolt cutters. But I'm keeping the stone.

The Baccarat paperweight on Rainier's desk glints hard, and I'm itching to swipe it, but my pockets are already bulging.

On the landing, I tell Rainier, "I'll take the stairs."

He nods, his keen eyes scraping over my face as though trying to spot a resemblance to my parents. I don't like his stare. I don't like *him*. I jet down the grand staircase, ring-free hand on the wrought-iron railing wrapped in prickly silver garlands. In the ballroom, the party's still in full swing, witches and warlocks and odd magical creatures swaying to the music, their chatter and laughter rising like helium.

I've officially lost my buzz, and with it, any will to be here.

Even though I now have to stay for two whole weeks.

Unless I can pawn the stone in Marseille.

Rainier didn't say anything about sticking around. All he said was that I had to sit on the Council when the time comes.

Silver lining.

I'm out of here until then.

6

CADENCE

I didn't drink last night, not much anyway, and yet I feel like crap this morning. Doesn't help that the fog lifting off the lake is so thick it reaches Fifth Kelc'h and billows over the temple library's stained-glass cupola. Why am I hanging out in the stacks, sorting through books on January first at eleven o'clock in the morning with folk rock music blasting from my AirPods? Because Alma was sleeping, and I was bored.

And annoyed.

Did I really think Charlotte's nonattendance at Christmas dinner meant she and Adrien had broken up? Well, they didn't. They even left together last night. I shove the image away in time with the book I'm shelving—*Anna Karenina*. I probably damage the cover, but it's not a first edition. Just another depressing Tolstoy love story.

I hate love stories, because they make me think there's someone out there for me, someone I'm destined to meet and live with happily-ever-after. I mean, I share a house with a living, breathing example of someone who was robbed of his happily-ever-after.

Thinking about my father's loss replaces my sullenness with gloom. I grapple to feel crabby again, because I don't want the sorrow. Not on top of feeling tired.

Why did Alma have to snore so loudly? And why did she have to sit up in bed at four o'clock in the morning, swipe the tissue box from the nightstand, and toss Kleenexes around, chanting *Happy New Year*? She freaked me out so much that it took me a solid hour to fall back asleep while she just dropped against the mattress and rolled over like she hadn't just sleep-shrieked. Not that my slumber was relaxing after that. I dreamed of that boy with the smiley eyes and unkempt black hair. I dreamed he was trying to steal my witch hat, and I was really not okay with it.

So. Weird.

I shiver as a gust of cold air permeates the thick fibers of the cream wool turtleneck I've paired with skinny jeans. Maybe my sweater screams librarian, but my stonewashed jeans don't. *Take that, Alma. When you finally pry your lazy ass out of bed, read my text, and climb up to Fifth to meet me so we can go to lunch, you'll see I put some effort into my outfit.*

Another burst of air snakes toward me. Central heating is spotty in the temple, but that more to do with the space being so high-ceilinged and the Brumian temperatures being so frigid, than with the belt of heaters running along the circular walls.

As I slot a book in a curved shelving unit, a pat on the shoulder makes my heart spin in time with my body. Adrien's mouth moves, but my music is so loud I don't hear a thing.

I pop out my earbuds, then stash them inside my back pocket. "Hey. Sorry. What were you saying?" My mind, which has felt sluggish since my lids cracked open at seven-thirty, is whirring now.

"Do you hear that?" His hazel eyes are luminous in the pale light trickling from the multi-colored cupola.

If by that, he means my hammering heart, then yes, I hear it. It's the only sound presently registering against my eardrums, but suddenly I hear a second one, a slow, rhythmic ticking, and the blood, which had risen to my cheeks at the sight of my unrequited crush, drains right out.

"Is that the—the . . .?" I sidestep him and rush toward the curved plexiglass guardrail that keeps students from stepping on the astronomical clock.

The giant, golden quatrefoil, which spans the entire clockface, shimmers as brightly as the hands adorning the two dials. Neither move, but then the *dihuner* doesn't tell time; it tells astronomical information. Until now, though, it told nothing. It just sat there, looking pretty with its blue ombré lunar dial and clear-topaz encrusted celestial one. Now, it emits a steady tick . . . tick . . . tick.

"*Mon dieu*, it works," I whisper in awe. "Adrien, it works!"

He's already standing beside me, gaze on the recessed enameled face, fingers loosely gripping the thick edge of the guardrail.

The hand tipped with a crescent moon has gone from its regular place on the darkest part of the lunar dial to the whitest one.

"It's reading the phases of the moon!" I laugh, but then I sober up, because, "How?"

There's a strain around his mouth. Around his eyes, too. "Maybe the earthquake last night jumpstarted it."

"Earthquake?"

"You didn't feel the ground shake?"

"I thought it was the orchestra." I breathe. Just breathe. "After all these years . . . I need to call Papa. He'll want to see it." I pat my pockets, but my phone's on the book trolley. Never mind, I'll call him later. Especially since he might still be sleeping. As my eyes wander over the shorter, star-tipped hand, I ask, "You had a good time last night?"

Adrien angles his body toward mine. "I did. You and your father really outdid yourselves."

"I take zero credit. It was all Papa."

He smiles, and the intensity of it melts my organs. And I mean, all of them. I turn into a gooey mess held together by cream wool and tight denim.

I nervously twirl the end of my ponytail around one finger. "So. What brings you to my hood on January 1st?"

More perfectly aligned white teeth appear between his curved lips. "Believe it or not, I came to take pictures of the clock. My alma matter wants me to give a speech to the freshmen about my thesis on Brumian history, and I thought illustrating it with some pictures would liven it up. Little do they know they're about to get never-before-seen audio footage." His hazel eyes are still on me, but they seem glazed over somehow. "I should contact Thierry. Let him know. Although I think he might still be visiting family in Dijon."

Thierry's the Master *Horloger* whose specialty is medieval, mechanical objects. He's the only one the university trusts to put a finger on the gears of this relic.

As Adrien taps out a message on his phone, hinges groan and then the massive wooden door bangs shut, injecting icy wind into the library.

I swivel my neck, certain it must be Alma this time, but the person coming down the aisle is tall and wears black leather gloves currently cupped around his mouth.

The boy I dreamed about is here.

The cocky thief who told me to make my own luck.

His eyes seem to grow round, which is a feat for eyes shaped like his. "Almost didn't recognize you without your witch hat," he says once he's reached us. His tone is so falsely cheery my teeth grind a little harder. "Hi." He holds out his gloved hand to Adrien. "Slate Ardoin. Brume's newest student recruit."

"Pleasure to make your acquaintance, Slate. I'm Adrien Mercier. I teach history."

Slate's bowed black eyes take in Adrien as though he were a dial lock on a safe. "I don't hate history."

"Then I hope you'll join my class."

Slate disengages his hand from Adrien's. "Are you in Professor Mercier's class, Bellatrix?"

Bellatrix? Does he think my name is Bellatrix?

"Her name is Cadence." Adrien's tone is sharp enough to crack ice. "And yes she's in my class. Speaking of . . . I need to be in Cambridge tomorrow, so I was wondering if you could fill in for me."

"Me?"

He nods. "You could teach a class about Brumian lore. After all, no one knows our town's mystical history better than you."

"I suppose I could do that." His compliment makes my ego shine as brightly as the brooch that fell out of Slate's pocket last night.

Slate's eyebrows writhe minutely. "I didn't know you were a history buff, *Cadence.*"

I cross my arms. "Why would you know anything about me, *Slate?*"

Adrien clears his throat. "I'm going to head downstairs to check on the clock's gears, see if I can pinpoint what's changed." He smiles as he backs away, but it flickers like a faulty bulb as he takes in Slate again.

Slate who's taller and broader. Then again, thugs need to keep in shape to run from the law.

I'm not being fair. Maybe Slate had the brooch in his pocket because it's some good-luck charm or something. But what about all the other glittery baubles that tumbled out? No, he's most definitely a crook.

Slate watches Adrien wrench open the trapdoor before locking his gaze on the clock again, probably scheming how to steal it. Good thing it's huge and embedded into the ground. Still, I wouldn't put it past him to try and wrench one of the hands off or pry out a coin-sized topaz.

"Don't even think about it," I hiss.

His gaze settles unhurriedly back on mine. "For someone so lovely, your stare is fearsome. Ever thought of joining the police force?"

I roll my *fearsome* eyes. "What is it you want?"

Almost a full minute goes by before he says, "I've been seeing this four-leaf clover motif all over Brume, and I was wondering if a librarian could help me find some Brumian history books on the subject."

I frown, not because I'm surprised—the Quatrefoil is a big tourist attraction—but because he didn't strike me as someone who'd venture into a library to look up my town's history.

His fingers curl at his sides. "Can you direct me toward a librarian?"

"You're looking at an honorary one."

"You?"

"Yeah."

"Huh."

"What is *huh* supposed to mean?"

"You don't strike me as a librarian."

"You don't strike me as a student."

His lips quirk. "What do I strike you as?"

"A criminal."

"And criminals aren't allowed to be educated?"

Did he just admit to being a criminal? "You're not contesting my assessment?"

He shrugs.

I take a small step back.

"Relax. It's not like I'm an axe murderer. Criminals come in all forms." He simpers at my expression. "So? The shamrock aisle?"

Once I get over the shock of his confession, I cross my arms. "This library is for students and faculty only. I'll need proof that you're attending the university before I can direct you toward any book."

His knuckles tighten, his large ring or wart . . . or maybe it's some sort of egg-shaped swelling from punching someone . . . straining the leather.

"Such a stickler for the rules, Cadence." He sighs, then digs something out of the inside breast pocket of his tailored coat. "Will this do?" He unfolds a piece of paper and dangles it in front of me.

I make out the logo of the school—a gothic U speared through a B, then quickly scan the sheet. It's a letter of acceptance signed by the dean, aka Papa. Sure enough, it's addressed to Slate Ardoin.

He folds it back up and slides it into his pocket. "Is my proof satisfactory?"

I nod, making a mental note to ask Papa about this boy later, about why he arrived mid school year. "By shamrock, you mean the Quatrefoil?"

"Yeah. *That*."

"We don't have an aisle for it, but we do have some books. However, they're kept in the archives, which is a cold room—"

"Good thing I'm wearing a coat and gloves."

"—with extremely restricted access."

"I'm imagining you have access to it."

"I do."

"I have a pair of sapphire earrings that would complement your eyes."

"Are you trying to bribe me with stolen goods?"

"Who said anything about them being stolen?"

"Do you usually carry around women's jewelry in your coat?"

He drags his hand through his tousled black curls. "What you saw last night . . . I was getting pieces repaired. That's what I do. I'm a middleman. I pick up jewelry from customers, bring them to professionals, then drop the fixed pieces back with their rightful owners."

I squeeze one of my eyes shut a little.

The nerve at his temple pulses. He's definitely lying.

He clears his throat. "You really *should* be a cop. Not a librarian. Then again, if you were a cop, I suspect the crime rate would escalate in these parts."

My arms loosen, and my hands land on my hipbones. "That's not nice."

"Not nice?"

I puff my chest a little. "I'd make a terrific cop."

"I'm sure you would." He smiles with his eyes *and* with his mouth. "I was implying crime would escalate, because men would be begging for you to cuff them."

Oh. Heat fills my face so suddenly that I want to peel off my wool turtleneck. But then I remember that he's slick, and so his compliment—if that's what that was—is simply a veiled attempt at getting what he wants. Plus, I'm not wearing anything underneath the chunky knit.

I level a glacial stare. "Give me a real reason to let you look through the archives, and maybe I'll consider your request."

The charming mask slips off his face, and I see the hardened boy who told me to make my own luck.

"Fine." He digs through his pocket again, pulls out another folded paper, then drops it in my hands.

It's a birth certificate. Which is weird. Who the heck carries around their birth certificate?

He points to the line bearing the name. *Rémy Roland.*

I frown. "I thought your name was Slate?"

"It is. I only just found out about the unfortunate other one."

I wrench my neck back. "But I thought . . . I thought the Roland bloodline died out."

"Is everything okay?" Adrien's making his way back toward us, his strides slow but long, as though he's trying to reach me quickly but without spooking Slate.

"It lives on." Slate's harsh tone reveals a nest of anger.

"What lives on?" Adrien asks.

"Slate . . . he's . . . Rémy." I lower my gaze back to the birth certificate. I'm not sure whether I could tell a fake from a real, but for
some reason, I don't think Slate's lying about his lineage or the fact
that he's just found out.

I hand the paper over to Adrien, whose forehead grooves, then
smooths. "Rainier mentioned he'd found you." Something flickers
in his expression as he returns the paper to Slate, who slots it back
into the breast pocket of his coat. "And so he has."

Slate's mouth moves and then Adrien's, but I've checked out,
hurt Papa confided in Adrien but not in me.

Adrien touches the back of my hand, jerking me out of my
bubble. "Everything okay?"

"Yeah. Peachy."

He frowns.

Before he can comment on my mood, I spin around and all but
bark at Slate, "Follow me."

The guy has the nerve to answer, "To the ends of the earth."

As our footsteps echo on the tiles, I toss him a blistering look.
"Quit the charm. It won't work on me, Rémy."

"Slate. And is that a challenge?"

"No."

"I like challenges."

"It's *not* a challenge," I mutter as I lead him toward the glass
trapdoor and the subterranean floor beneath.

The gears of the clock take up almost all the space, but around
it, Papa's built a glassed-in archival room to preserve Brume's oldest
and most fragile books. Not all are about the town. There are some
first editions Baudelaire, Hugo, and Rousseau. National treasures.

As I unlock the door with a swipe of my thumb on a digital
keypad, I look behind me. Slate's eyes are wide with wonder.

He goes to touch one of the enormous cogs when I stop him
with a sharp, "Don't."

Surprisingly, he doesn't.

7

SLATE

I follow Cadence's gently swinging ass into a modern archival room decked out in glass. The view is stunning, and I'm not talking about the clock gears or rough stone walls; I'm talking about the view of blue denim that hugs this girl in all the right places.

It almost makes me forget I want out of this goddamn village in which I'm stuck.

And when I say "stuck," I mean, *stuck*.

After the De Morel party, I bought a ticket for the earliest train out of here. In blizzard-like conditions, I trudged back to the station. The thirty-minute walk almost froze my balls off. If hell existed, this would be it, this life-sized, snow-globe of a town with its swirling flakes and icy winds.

Never had I been so ecstatic to see a train.

That's when the next-level crazy shit went down.

I crossed the platform and raised my foot to climb into the orange bullet when I hit a wall.

Literally.

Only it was an invisible wall. And I seemed to be the only one who couldn't get past it. I watched a couple of other people get onto the train with no problem. I thought maybe there'd been some toxic chemical in one of those salmon things from the party. Something that would cause me to hallucinate. So I took a deep breath and tried again.

And again, I hit a fucking wall.

I moved farther down the platform, tried another entrance. Same damn deal. I looked like one of those sad mimes pretending he was in a box, my palms out, pushing but going nowhere. All I needed was to paint my face white and stencil a black teardrop on my cheek. Hell, at some point—that point being my breaking point —someone tossed a two-euro coin my way.

I swore and shouted, which made a ticket inspector step off the train and inch toward me as though I were some rabies-infected dog. When I said I wanted to get on the train, he sniffed the air, trying to breathalyze me with his nose, then gave a little shake of his head.

Yeah, I smelled like wine, but I was stone-cold sober.

I took a step forward.

Bam!

"*Fait chier*," I growled. Then, "Push me!"

"Look, Monsieur, I really can't—"

"*Putain de bordel de merde!* PUSH ME ONTO THIS TRAIN!"

A handful of people eyed me like I was missing my straitjacket. The ticket inspector wouldn't touch me, but a freckle-faced kid shoved me toward the door, only to have me bounce off the invisible wall. Everyone scattered like I was contagious.

The train whirred to indicate the doors were closing. In a last desperate attempt to break through, I banged my fist against the invisible force that trapped me in this quaint shithole. The doors shut, and then the train shot away like a missile.

I wasn't on it.

I got a cheap bottle of Beaujolais to numb my brain, then went back to my gnome headquarters, aka my dorm. Found the *Toilettes Hommes*, which looked like they'd come straight out of a retro horror movie—mildewed white tiles, yellowed plastic curtains, hair-speckled soap on a stick. There was one toilet stall and two urinals set so close to the row of white porcelain sinks I could have probably taken a leak and brushed my teeth at the same time. At least the showers were semi-private. I stood under the hot water, lubed up my fingers, gagging as I picked out the wet hair that came off the soap, and went to work on the goddamn ring.

I yanked and pulled, twisted and rubbed. The last time I'd worked up so much friction in the shower I'd gotten myself off. This? Well, this was a fucking nightmare. The ring didn't even budge.

After dressing and going back to my room, I tried again.

And again.

And *again*.

No dice.

"You had a good night last night?" Cadence asks, pulling me out of my head.

I bet she senses it was craptastic—which is saying a lot—and is needling me to test my mood.

"Just awesome." The ring bumps the wall, shooting pain into my swollen finger. I gnash my molars and curse under my breath.

". . . no longer use gloves for paper, only photographs," Cadence is saying as we walk through the archival room arcing around the mechanism of the astronomical antiquity.

The glass walls are thick, and yet the slow, steady ticks of the turning crown wheel penetrate them.

I cock an eyebrow, having no idea what she just said. "What?"

"You can shed the gloves."

I shrug, playing off the glove-thing like it's a personality quirk.

The glass room is cold but warmer than outside. They must have had it specially outfitted not too long ago. Everything that isn't glass is white metal, from the floor to the ceiling to the three long curved tables to the shelves.

Cadence tucks her hands into the sleeves of her turtleneck. "So, what is it you'd like to see?"

For starters, what's underneath that bulky sweater. I clear my throat. "Two things, actually. The history of the Clover Council—"

"Quatrefoil Council." Her mouth pinches as though she's pissed I muddled the name.

"—and whatever you've got on a magical ring with a red stone."

A faint frown touches her brow. "That's very specific."

"I'm a very unambiguous man."

"You're the exact opposite of unambiguous."

"Not when it comes to what I want." I take a step toward her, going for my well-oiled intimidation technique.

From the quickening pulse in her neck, I suspect it's working. Her gorgeous red mouth pops open but nothing comes out. Instead, she backs away and takes a special pair of gloves from a drawer, then turns to a row of shelves near the middle of the crescent-shaped room. And, yeah, I cop a look at her ass again. Especially when she stretches to reach a high shelf and her turtleneck rides up.

She eases out a tome of leather and vellum, which she deposits carefully on the nearest table. A gold-leaf quatrefoil brightens the pebbled green hide.

"This is *Istor Breou. The History of Magic*, specifically the one in Brume." She looks pointedly at my hands. "If you want to page through it, no leather gloves. Leather sticks to paper, which could ruin it."

I fuse the tip of my middle finger between my teeth, then slowly ease the glove off my left hand.

When I make no move to take off the other, she sighs and opens the book. "The language is a mix of old French and Breton."

The words scrawled over the page are tiny and jittery, as though written by a broken hand.

"Do you speak Breton?" I ask.

"A little."

I don't ask her to translate anything, too busy taking in the accompanying illustration—an illumination of the clover resting behind a tangle of trees, ferns, and fog. Various moon phases dot the top of the page, from full to crescent to new. I scan the text, catching some French words: *Berceau. Magie. Pouvoir.*

Cradle. Magic. Power.

I try to decipher the Breton beneath the image but can't. "What does the caption say?"

Cadence tucks back a brown strand that's escaped her ponytail and reads, "*The source of all magic can be traced to a golden Quatrefoil found in the forest of Brocéliande. For millennia, people flocked to Brocéliande to live near the source of magic.*" She glances at me. "Local lore says that over time, more and more people settled in the forest, thus turning it into a town: Brume. Named, of course, for the ever-present cloud of mist that covers it."

How depressing. "No wonder Brumians worship something golden and shiny."

Cadence rolls her eyes but smiles, and that tiny crack in her serious countenance reassures me that she's not some magic-crazed zealot, even though I might be turning into one after last night.

She carefully flips the page to one with illustrations of fantastical beasts wreaking havoc, half-submerged people cupping flames, and what looks like a rave in a windy field.

"*Back at the beginning, magic was not good or evil, it simply was,*" Cadence continues to read. "*It existed in the elements—Air, Water, Earth, and Fire. It bore creatures formed of these elements, creatures to be both revered and feared. It flowed through the veins of humans, blessing them with the ability to connect with one of the elements.*"

I reach out and turn the page. Despite the controlled air temperature, the paper feels warm under my fingertips. The drawings turn more menacing. A sea of people spewing blood. A pile of corpses covered with boils and black spots. I drag my finger under some of the French words: *Peste. Le mal.*

Pestilence. Evil.

"So, it wasn't all rainbows and unicorns?" I end up saying, but it comes out like a question.

"Modern researchers talk about the Plague being caused by fleas and rats. But according to Brumian legend, it was dark magic that created the very first wave of Black Death."

"Must've been one twisted wizard to do that."

"Warlock. Wizards deal in good magic." She shrugs. "If you believe in that, of course."

"Do *you*?"

A tiny groove appears between her eyebrows. "I'm not sure. Yes and no." She tips her head from side to side. "Part of me wants to believe it's real, but the logical and disillusioned part of me has trouble accepting it's true."

I frown. *Disillusioned?* She doesn't strike me as a disillusioned person—a little uptight, sure, but not cynical.

Whatever's on her mind blots out the light in her eyes, dimming their blueness. Yet somehow, perhaps because she doesn't seem

OF WICKED BLOOD | 57

quite as naïve and coddled as I expected, it heightens her attractiveness.

"The Black Death killed 60% of the population in Europe." Then she spews out more facts that glance off my skull. I'm too busy absorbing the sweet scent of her hair and the red tint of her lips that's so deep I wonder if she's wearing lipstick. They don't look glossed-up.

A renewed light enters her eyes as she continues schooling me in history. I really should be paying attention but physically can't because most of the blood in my body has gone south.

"Slate?" She turns those Mediterranean-at-midday eyes of hers on me.

"Yeah?"

"Are you listening?"

I shouldn't smile, but I do. Not because of all the sad, dead medieval saps, but because history turns her on. Then I stop smiling, remembering the way she was looking at that dickhead professor earlier, like he was a god.

I snap my gaze down to the illustration she's pointing to in the giant book—two women and two men in wizard robes holding a gold thing in the shape of a quatrefoil. They're standing on a circle that reminds me a little of the clock upstairs, the colors under their feet gradually deepening from white into a midnight blue. One woman points to the center of the golden shape, her finger resting on the bright-red dot at the heart of the clover the same way Cadence's finger rests on the page.

"The magical committee," she says. "Or Quatrefoil Council. In 1350, when Brume was literally dying, they appointed the most powerful families of Brume to be *diwallers*, or guardians of the Quatrefoil. The Council was furious with how people used magic to cause destruction rather than growth, so they removed it from the world by fracturing its source."

"They broke the giant shamrock . . ."

"Quatrefoil." She turns the page.

The next drawing shows the thing in pieces, the red dot snapped off the rounded wings.

My heart rate kicks up. Holy hell. Could that be the red stone I'm sporting on my sprained finger?

She turns the page again. An illustration of those same four men and women covers most of the paper, but this time they each hold a leaf of the Quatrefoil in front of them, engulfed in an element. Cadence doesn't seem to notice that my breathing has quickened. She continues to explain, half-reading the text on the page, half-recounting it like it's a love poem she's memorized.

"The *diwallers'* intent was to hide the leaves until they felt humanity was once again worthy of magic, so they each took ownership of an element, then cast spells to protect their piece and keep it in Brume."

Spells to keep the pieces in Brume . . . I feel the swell of the stone on my finger. Did the ring erect the invisible wall on the train platform?

Cadence's breath flutters the wafer-thin pages. "Legend has it, the *diwallers'* descendants could bring magic back."

"That's some crazy-ass history." I attempt to keep my voice smooth, but dread ices my vocal cords, making my speech sound choppy. "What's the red thing?"

"Oh. Right. That's the Bloodstone. It holds the blood of each family of *diwallers* and the power of *all* the elements. The Bloodstone is the most important piece of all. Without it, the leaves can't bind together." She lifts her chin, a smug smile on her lips. Like she just aced an exam.

My saliva thickens. I swallow, and it goes down like tar. "So, it stands to reason the Bloodstone's cursed like the other pieces?"

She nods before gazing back down and flipping through a few more pages. "But it doesn't specify how. Guess that's the surprise for the poor soul who finds it."

I can't even appreciate how flushed her cheekbones are, or how wet her lips look. I'm way too busy reeling over the whole Bloodstone-curse bit. I clear my throat. If the stone on my finger is the stone we're talking about, I'm officially *foutu.*

"Sometimes I fantasize the tales in this book aren't just legends. Imagine how amazing it would be if this really *was* Brume's history? If the founding families really were guardians and magic bearers? If—"

"If items like the Bloodstone were actually cursed and the wizards at the New Year's party weren't just a bunch of LARPers?"

"Larpers?"

"Live-action-role-players."

A smile—a genuine one—brightens her face. It's so magnificent it momentarily makes me glad I'm in a library on New Year's Day in bumblefuck Brume.

Until I remember *why*.

"If all of it were true, Slate, it would mean that we could restore magic."

We're silent a moment; she, contemplating a lone archival box at the top of a shelving unit, daydreaming of possibilities; me, living a nightmare with few options. I need to find out if I'm wearing the Bloodstone or just some knock-off.

I have little doubt about the answer, but I ask anyway. "That Bloodstone's got to be worth a lot. Where's it kept? A museum? A safety deposit box? Dracula's coffin?"

Cadence's gaze narrows. "Why? Looking to steal it?"

Been there. Done that.

"You don't care about Brumian history at all, do you, Slate?" She slams the book shut and shakes her head. "You're just after something valuable. You're not some middleman in the jewelry business; you're a main man in the thieving industry." She's breathing so hard the thick turtleneck is vibrating. "I thought you wanted to know more about your origins, but"—she gestures to the room a little spastically—"all of this was just a ploy to find out about the stone, wasn't it? Are you even a Roland, Slate?"

This girl is such a paradox—soft like cotton candy one moment and then hard as a lollipop the next. Between her volatile attitude, my severe lack of sleep, and my throbbing finger, I can't help it . . . I laugh. Harder than I've laughed in a long time. I'm still chuckling after she's rammed the book back onto its shelf, stashed the gloves, and stalked toward the door, hands splayed on her hips, glower fearsome.

I finally stop and inhale a long breath. "Whew."

"I'm happy you got such a kick out of my history lesson."

Even though I'm liking her feistiness, her comment sobers me. "I wasn't laughing at you, Cadence."

"I don't care."

She does.

"Good." As I stride by her, I add, "You should never care what people think of you."

We don't say a word to each other after we leave the icebox, but her storming out ahead of me isn't a total loss—I get a better view of her ass on the way up than I did on the way down. The temperature warms with each step. When we're out of the hatch, the air's downright tropical.

Cadence huffs, grabbing a few books off a cart and concentrating way too hard on locating their proper places.

I lean against one massive bookshelf and watch her stuff *Les Liaisons Dangereuses* between two thin books. "Thank you for your help."

She snorts.

"I mean it. And I may be back with more questions."

Her gaze cuts over to me. "Why don't you save them for Professor Mercier's history class?"

"You mean your boyfriend's class?"

"My boyfriend? No. Adrien's not—" Pink dots her cheeks as she fingers the glossy spines in front of her. "The professor isn't my boyfriend. He's an old friend."

I cross my arms over my chest. Ridiculous as it is, her blind worship of the dude grates me. "Why was he here then?"

"How is that any of your business?"

"Doesn't he have a clock at home?"

Her eyes narrow. "I'm sure he does. He came to take pictures of the *dihuner* to supplement his thesis. Now if you're done with your cross-examination, I have work to do."

Cold air snakes around us, and then a girly voice calls out, "Cadence?"

"Over here, Alma!" She shoves past me and rounds the bookshelf.

Pulling my glove back on, I trail her out of the maze.

Cadence's curly-headed friend from last night lets out a squeal and rubs the little pearl on her pinky finger. "Slate! Do you have any more tricks? Can you make something else disappear?"

"Your virginity."

That gets a booming laugh from Alma and a look of absolute repulsion from Cadence. You'd think I was a leper.

"Too late for that." Alma's smile is as wide as the Strait of Gibraltar. "We're going to go grab something to eat if—"

"Slate was just leaving."

I can take a hint.

I bid them goodbye, glancing up at the cupola dripping colored light on the giant, gunmetal-gray clock face decorated with none other than a golden outline of the quatrefoil—of *fucking* course. I stride down the aisle, the ochre-and-white floor tiles brown with slippery slush, then shoulder the heavy wooden door open. When it clangs shut behind me, the icy level of hell that is Brume hits me anew. The mist sinks into the wool of my peacoat. The cold freezes my nostril hairs and eyeballs. The only part of me that's warm is the hand with the ring.

I crunch across the campus lawn, past a giant building that looks a little like a fancy art museum what with its limestone façade and ginormous picture windows. As I follow the windy road that laces around the village, I go over what I learned in the library.

I'd been hoping for a set of step-by-step instructions on how to get the damn thing off so I could hock it for a pretty penny, screwing De Morel over at the same time. But now, I have no choice but to pay the man a second visit, because I finally believe in magic.

CADENCE

L*a Taverne de Quartefeuille* is busy, which isn't surprising considering nothing else is open in town.

When I walk in with Alma, it seems like all of Brume is wedged between the roughcast stone walls of the bistro that doles out the best fare in all of Brittany. Nolwenn, the owner, stops on her way to a table to greet me with a kiss perfumed by puffs of savory steam curling out of the ceramic casserole dish she's carrying. The buckwheat and meat stew makes my stomach growl.

"I just cleared a table upstairs, *ma chérie*." She nods to the crooked wooden staircase at the end of the bar, her puffy, peroxided hair not even shifting thanks to her passion for hairspray.

As we pass behind the jampacked row of red leather stools, I catch sight of black curls and gloves. *Ugh.* Why does Slate have to be everywhere? I speed-walk past him, towing Alma along before she can invite him upstairs or into her bed.

His little joke about absconding with her virginity has run on a loop inside my brain since we left the library. I've never met a man as crude and slick as Slate. To think that, when he showed me his birth certificate back in the library, his eyes teeming with hurt, I felt sympathy for him. The grief, or whatever I saw in his expression, was probably all an act.

I hate that I fell for it.

The wall along the stairs is covered in framed black-and-white pictures of Nolwenn and her white-haired, white-bearded husband, Juda, their arms around various celebrities who traveled through Brume on magical pilgrimages. Romain, their grandson, is also in a few, as are Gaëlle and Matthias. Matthias is Nolwenn and Juda's son, but since he abandoned Gaëlle with three kids, he's not talked about much. Or at least, not here.

"I still can't believe it just up and started ticking," Alma says, the stairs creaking like old bones under her platform boots. At least she traded in her skimpy black dress for a low-cut emerald V-neck sweater and black leggings.

"I know." I tried calling Papa when we left the temple, but I got a text message that he was in physical therapy and that he'd phone me as soon as he was done.

I scan the low-timbered second story for the free table Nolwenn mentioned. It's all the way across the room, beneath the window swathed in lacy white curtains. The square panes are steamed from the arctic chill outside and cozy heat billowing inside.

As I ford through the room, I wave hello to a few people and lean over to kiss Gaëlle's toasty cheek. A smudge of magenta lipstick adorns her light-brown skin, courtesy of Nolwenn.

"The hat looked amazing on you last night, sweetie," she says with a smile.

"It's officially my favorite hat."

"I told her she should wear it every day. I think it would vastly improve her style." Alma winks at me, then turns her dazzling smile on Romain.

He goes crimson and tries to drown his blush by gulping down his entire glass of water.

"It's not like anyone would judge you. I mean, we live in Brume," Alma adds.

I roll my eyes. "No offense, but I think I'll save it for special occasions."

Gaëlle chuckles. "None taken."

After wishing a few more people a *bon appétit*, I shrug out of my jacket and hang it on the back of my chair. My knuckles ache, and I stretch them out as I check the chalkboard on which Juda writes the daily offerings. I'm not sure why I do this since I almost always get the same thing: a paper-thin buckwheat *galette* filled with ham, spinach, cheese, and a fried egg followed by a crêpe drizzled in Juda's homemade *salidou.*

"Know what you want, Alma?"

"The usual. And coffee. *A lot* of coffee," she says as Nolwenn bustles up the stairs with four pitchers of cider.

Once she's deposited them on the long table crowded by college kids accounting for most of the noise in the tavern, she weaves through the hodgepodge of tables toward us. Even though she gets up at the crack of dawn and only goes to sleep once the last customer leaves, that woman bursts with energy.

She jots down our order, whispering conspiratorially, "I'll get yours in before theirs." She nods to the big table.

After she vanishes back downstairs, Alma leans over. "So, now will you tell me why you were hanging out with the hottie newbie?"

"He had questions about Brumian history." I unfold my red gingham napkin and place it on my lap. "And he's not hot."

"Um. Yeah he is. You're just too blinded by—"

I kick her shin under the table before she can utter Adrien's name when Gaëlle is sitting two tables away.

"Ouch." She leans over and rubs her leg. "I wouldn't have said his name out loud."

Better safe than embarrassed.

Her long, copper curls rush around her face. "You're awfully grumpy today."

"Might be because someone sleep-screeched Happy New Year at four o'clock in the morning and tossed tissues on me."

Alma breaks into a grin. "I was wondering why there were so many Kleenexes on the bed."

As we wait for our food, I study the four-leaf shape stamped on the floor tiles. "Do you think the Quatrefoil really existed?"

Alma's been in the archives. She's perused the books, so she knows all about the *diwallers* who supposedly confiscated the magic and locked it away for safekeeping.

"Remember all those treasure hunts we went on when we were kids?" she asks.

"Yeah."

"Do you remember all the treasure we found?"

"We didn't find any."

"Exactly."

"So you think it's all lore to attract tourists?"

I sense Gaëlle looking over at us, but when I raise my gaze to hers, I find she's staring at her stepson, so maybe I imagined her attention.

"I don't know if it was invented to better tourism, but it's a real good story. I wish it were true. If *I* had magic, the first thing I'd do would be to cast away the fog."

"Yes, because that would greatly improve the world."

"It would greatly improve ours." She wrinkles her nose at the fog pressing against the window. The denseness of the gray mass gives the impression the tavern's suspended on a cloud. "Can we go back to talking about the new guy?"

I sigh. "I'd rather not."

"Is he a good kisser?"

"What exactly do you think we were doing in the library?"

"I meant last night, at the party."

"Oh. He didn't kiss me."

She gasps. "Is that why you're pissed at him?"

"Of course not."

"I can't believe he didn't kiss you. The way he was staring at you last night . . . Babe, trust me, I'm a real-live pheromone-detector, and that boy—"

"*Al-ma,*" I hiss, decomposing her name in two very distinct syllables to drive in the fact that I don't want to discuss him or last night or this morning.

"Fine," she grouses. "I'll shut up."

We talk about the clock and its repositioned hand, and then about the lesson I'll be teaching. I run ideas past her, and since she's as good a listener as she is a talker, I feel like I have the entire hour fleshed out by the time our food arrives.

On her way out, Gaëlle stops by our table to ask if I can watch the twins sometime next week. She promised to take Romain into Rennes to buy him a new wardrobe. "Just doesn't stop growing." Her full lips curve with pride.

Romain might not be her biological son, but she loves him like he is. She levers her wavy, dark hair out from underneath her yellow scarf.

"We need to get going. Samson and Arthur are being watched by my neighbor's teenage daughter. I trust her to keep them alive but that's about it."

"My brothers probably have their own social media accounts by now," Romain says.

I laugh while Gaëlle shakes her head.

Once they're gone, I have a chat with Alma about not leading Romain on. I wait for her to promise she won't toy with his young heart before heading downstairs to the bathroom. When I notice Slate's no longer sitting at the bar, I breathe a little easier. That is, until the door of the bathroom opens, and I come nose-to-Adam's-apple with him.

He smells like winter nights by the fire—a mix of cider, coffee, and cloves. I wish he smelled like damp old socks.

"Looking for me?" He's tugging on his gloves, his coat already on.

"Looking to avoid you," I mutter as I step aside to let him pass down the cramped hallway that leads to the kitchen's swinging door.

"Trust me, if I could get out of this place, I'd be gone."

I raise an eyebrow. "I'd be more than happy to direct you to the train station."

Even though the hallway's dim, I catch his eyes flicking to one of his hands. The one with the lump. "Oh, I know how to get there."

"Then what are you waiting for?"

The kitchen door flaps open, and Nolwenn emerges clutching three plates. "Your crêpe's in the pan, Cadence." She slants Slate a look as he backs up to let her pass.

Ribbons of rosemary steam linger in her wake, clouding the dark outline of his body.

Once they clear, he presses away from the wall. "See you later."

"Hope not."

He glances over his shoulder at me, black eyes curving with amusement. He thinks I'm joking but I'm being deathly serious. I really hope he'll leave, and I don't mean the restaurant.

I mean Brume.

Even though he may have had roots in this town, he doesn't

belong here. He belongs to a big city where disregard for people and its customs is tolerated, even encouraged.

AFTER LUNCH, Alma heads back to the dorms and I head home via the cemetery. Every first of the month, I go to our family crypt to talk to Maman. I don't believe in spirits or ghosts or magic of any sort, so I'm aware that when I go "talk to her" I'm actually talking to myself, but I find solace in this little tradition. It allows me to vent about school and boys and growing up, and put some order inside my heart and mind.

A fresh layer of snow cocoons the frozen ground like a duvet cover drawn snugly over the graves. I pass the Mercier family mausoleum and decide to stop by. The hinges are oiled, so the door whispers open. Geoffrey Keene might be a creeper, but he keeps the Mercier mausoleum in pristine condition.

I pad over to Camille's raised coffin. The etchings are still so recent they cause a shiver to slink down my spine. Although Papa was both a mother and father to me, Camille was the one I ran to when I had my first period. The one who bought me my first bra and took me to the gynecologist.

"I hope it's warmer where you are." I split open a packet of sugar and pour it atop her carved name and dates of life. It's an old Brumian tradition—instead of flowers, we celebrate the dead with sugar to sweeten the afterlife. "Your son's getting famous. I don't know if he told you." I suspect that, unlike me, he doesn't hang out in cemeteries. "He was invited to speak about his thesis at Cambridge. What an honor, huh? You'd be very proud of him. Oh, and he's dating some girl you probably wouldn't approve of . . ." I let my voice trail off before I add something vicious.

Outside, the wind presses against the small, marble-slabbed building, howls.

"Some new guy arrived last night. He's awful." I push some flyaways off my icy cheeks. "He claims he's Eugenia and Oscar Roland's son. Which is crazy because he was supposed to have died in the fire, too."

Something awful strikes me . . . something I remember from the one and only time I stopped by the Roland mausoleum: beneath Oscar and Eugenia's names is Slate's. Well, Rémy's. If they really are one and the same, then I hope he hasn't walked through the cemetery and spotted the inscription.

I push the macabre contemplation away and refocus on Camille. "I was reading *Istor Breou* again this morning, and it made me wish magic were real. Is it, Camille? Are there any truths in that book?"

Because if there is . . . *oh, the spells I'd cast.* I'd bring Adrien's mother and mine back, give a pixie-haired girlfriend some warts, and make an infuriating thief vanish.

And this is why Humans were stripped of magic: we aren't worthy.

"I miss you, Camille." I run my fingertips over the quatrefoil and *Loving Mother and Honorable Citizen of Brume* engravings, tucking in the sugar crystals. "Why didn't you tell us you were sad? Why did you resort to arsenic? Arsenic!"

Anger and grief cloud my vision. I scrape at my eyes and then, ruing the poison peddler, stalk back outside. A sprinkling of sun darts through the cloud cover and gilds the snow and old headstones, yet brings me no pleasure.

I pass by Viviene without so much as a glance in her direction, then round our mausoleum. The narrow door is agape. Is Papa here? Who else has the key to our crypt? The undertaker? Unlike the Merciers, ours is always kept locked. Papa says grief should be private.

"Hello?" I call out.

Except for the wind jostling the bare branches of the linden trees, there is no sound.

Could the earthquake have cracked the lock and blown open the door? I inch closer and squint into the darkness, then press my fingertips into the cold iron door. The hinges screech.

My heart freefalls into my boots, then vaults into my throat as the room comes into focus, and I see Maman . . . or what's left of her. Stumbling backward, I fling my hand up to my mouth and bite down on my knuckles.

I try to rip the image of ochre silk and gray flesh from my eyes, but it's seared into my retinas. Bile rises so fast that I just have time to clutch my shaky knees and lean over before vomit blazes up my throat.

Who'd do this? Who'd desecrate someone's grave? And why?

A long while later, I pick up a handful of clean snow and scrub my mouth, then kick some over the mess I've made. And then I stare back toward the open doorway, wishing I were brave enough to tuck Maman back in her stone bed, but I'm not brave and probably not strong enough to lift the lid.

As I shut the door, my fingers shaking as hard as my heart, I catch a glint of something on the dusty floor. Is that—is that a bottle of wine? Did someone use our crypt to hang out and get drunk?

Anger blasts back inside of me, and I wheel around. And then I'm running home because I need to tell Papa.

He'll fix this.

My father can fix anything.

9

SLATE

Not even twenty-four hours have passed since I trampled the treads left behind by heeled boots and shiny loafers in the crusty snow, yet it feels like centuries. Like I've aged enough to have traveled through another ice-age and landed in the new dark ages.

Manoir de Morel looks just as dramatic and pretentious in daylight. Last night, thousands of sparkling holiday lights outlined the building. Today, filtered rays from the setting sun polish the old gray stones, making them glow a reddish-umber. The place looks like it's lit by hellfire, and here I am, the asinine soul walking directly into it.

I reach the massive blue door adorned by a pattern of metal grommets forming a quatrefoil—that symbol is starting to feel as ominous as blood smeared on doors to prevent the wrath of God. Ever since I set foot in this damn town, nothing has gone according to plan. From my teeny room to my conversation with Rainier de Morel to the fucking ring. Hell, even my flirtation with Cadence hasn't been ideal. If we were in Marseille, we'd already have shared a five-course dinner, a bottle of fancy champagne, and most probably, body fluids. Instead I got freakish stories of warlocks and honed death stares.

The bell dings, echoing inside the manor.

A heavy-set middle-aged woman in navy scrubs opens the door. Her lipstick is knock-out red, and her dark hair is cut into one of those severe bobs that only movie stars and dominatrix wear. I'm pretty sure she's not a movie star.

"Can I help you?" The disdain in her voice is evident.

Sure, my hair's mussed and the bags under my eyes are as pronounced as the protuberance on my finger, but my clothes cost way more than the little diamond comet dangling in the crook of her flabby neck. "I'm here to see Rainier de Morel."

She narrows her brown eyes at me, intensifying the crow's feet bracketing them. "Is he expecting you?"

"Jacqueline?" Rainier's voice calls from somewhere behind her. "Who is it?"

"Slate Ardoin," I say.

Jacqueline repeats it even though Rainier is many things, but not hard of hearing.

A satisfied chuckle. And then, "Let him in."

She frowns and calls over her shoulder, "But your exercises—"

"We'll finish them later. Let him in."

She purses her lips and ticks her head to the side.

We travel in the opposite direction of the grand room, through an open set of double doors, and into a humongous living room with black marble floors. Carbon-gray walls are sandwiched between white baseboards and crown moldings. There's a peach granite fireplace wide enough to roast a horse on a spit, and angular furniture in various shades of eggshell. Everything's shiny and spotless.

Guess no one snacks on madeleines in here . . .

Rainier sits in his wheelchair near the bay window, a stretchy green physical therapy band in his hands. Jacqueline relieves him of it before hustling out of the room, forgoing an offer of coffee or *apéritif*.

I round a glass coffee table as big as my bed back in Marseille and sink into the soft leather sectional. And keep sinking until the couch all but gulps me up. I shift, but it doesn't help. It's like a weird chapter in *Alice in Wonderland*—I'm feeling smaller and smaller with each movement I make.

This couch isn't made for relaxing; it's made for intimidating.

Damn. De Morel is good.

Now, Rainier rolls himself a little closer. Despite whatever exercise he was just doing, he's perfectly put together—from the ironed crease of his khakis to the smooth fibers of his gray cashmere sweater to each gelled hair on his head.

He lifts the corners of his mouth up into what I suspect is supposed to resemble a smile, except there's zero warmth to it. "How are you getting on here in Brume?"

"So well I can't bring myself to leave. Insane, huh?"

He narrows his navy eyes. "And to what do I owe the pleasure of this visit?" He makes the word pleasure sound like a dirty smudge.

I recognize this for what it is: a typical dick-swinging contest, with Rainier and I taking our places, readying our stance.

I swing first.

Pulling the glove off my right hand, I reveal the scarlet stone on my middle finger by flipping him off with a flourish. I'm waiting to feel a rush, but I'm way too pissed off and agitated for any other sentiment. This ring has sapped me of even the most basic pleasures.

Rainier's skin goes from snooty aristocratic alabaster to zombie gray to stomach-flu green, and his fingers grip the armrests of his wheelchair. "How did you get that?"

"Let's just say I visited the family. Your family. It was supposed to be a short visit. The fuck 'em and leave 'em kind. Just long enough to swipe a few things and bruise your ego. But, well"—I raise my hand higher, middle finger still extended—"this little baby took a liking to me. And now it won't let go."

Rainier is still for a moment, not moving, not breathing, just staring me straight in the eye with a lethal glare. Then he rolls right up to me, his left wheel squeaking against the leather couch, his right wheel banging against the glass table. When he's close enough that I can see the pores on his nose and the sweat beading around his lips, he shouts, "You *bloody idiot!*" Spittle lands on my chin and cheeks. "You goddamn witless *fool!*"

And then he's maneuvering his chair like an angry drunk. Tries to go backward but bangs into the coffee table. Then the couch.

Then both. The sleek, black bag hanging from his armrest gets half unsnapped, and the strap catches in the wheel. Rainier's skin tone veers to an unflattering eggplant as he swears, using expressions that I imagine are Breton because I've never heard them.

Astonishingly, I get no joy from watching him wriggle like a worm in weeks-old bread. With Herculean effort, I push myself up from the soft leather sinkhole and make my way around the couch to yank on his chair and roll it back until he's no longer stuck between furniture.

He doesn't say anything, just snaps his bag in place, then pulls out a brown leather case. I'm silent as his trembling fingers go to work sliding out a Churchill, cutting it, and lighting it with a fancy torch lighter.

Once he's puffed a few times, he rolls the cigar between his finger and thumb and bellows, "Jacqueline!"

Is he going to ask his physical therapist—or naughty nurse—to forcibly remove me? Not sure how that would work considering I outweigh her in both muscle mass and shrewdness. Unless she carries a hunting rifle . . . I wouldn't put it past the people living so close to a magical forest to know their way around firearms.

She comes running so fast, her hair chops the air around her jaw like an axe. "What is it, Monsieur de Morel?"

"I won't have time to exercise any more today. I'll see you tomorrow."

"Are you certain? I don't mind waiting."

"I'm certain." Even though he's speaking to her, his glacial eyes are on me.

He takes a long drag of his cigar before puffing out donuts of smoke. Keys jangle, rubber squeaks on marble, and then the click of a door followed by a heavy bang. Minutes tick by in silence as thick as the pearl-gray cashmere throw draped over the back of the couch.

"You've ruined everything, Monsieur Roland." Before I can answer, he puts a hand up. "I know. *Ardoin.*"

This time I sit on the arm of the couch. I don't sink down. So my face is level with his when I say, "Besides a rank crypt, what the hell did I ruin?"

"Careful." Rainier raises his cigar-free hand and brings his thumb and pinky within a millimeter of each other. "I'm this close to snapping."

I snort. "Planning on running me over with that fancy wheelchair?"

The front door opens again, then slams shut, and I imagine Jacqueline forgot something, but the voice that accompanies the ruckus is not the old woman's.

"Papa!" The scream is high-pitched and breathy. "Oh, Papa!" Cadence runs into the room, tripping over the corner of the beige rug, before launching herself into De Morel's arms. Her body trembles beneath her silver puffer.

Papa?

No.

Fucking.

Way.

How did I not catch that?

Her face is sallow, her eyes as scarlet as her lips, and wet tracks shine on her cheeks.

An odd and violent rage flares inside my gut. I'll fucking wreck whoever put her in this state. As fast as the thought fires across my brain, it snuffs out. What the hell's wrong with me? She's De Morel's spawn. She neither deserves my pity nor my protection.

I owe the De Morels *nothing.*

"What is it, *ma* Cadence?" Rainier asks.

She peels her hands off from around his neck, then stands and paces between the marble and rug. "I went to see Maman today and —" Cadence's voice splinters, and she presses the heels of her hands into her eyes. "The door was open. And there was wine. And I—I saw . . . I saw her. My God, Papa." She presses her knuckles against her mouth. "I saw her," she whispers.

Rainier's stare turns as sharp as the steak knife Vincent planted into my hand.

A gasp falls from Cadence's mouth in time with her hand, which knocks against her thigh. "Slate? What are you doing here?"

I don't answer.

Her breathing hitches suddenly, and she blurts out, "*You* did it."

"*It?* You're going to have to give me a little more to go on, Mademoiselle de Morel"—I grit out her hateful surname—"because I've done *many* things."

"Last night, you were coming from the cemetery when I bumped into you." It's not a question, so I don't bother answering. "You're the one who opened Maman's grave?" Her voice is barely above a whisper now.

I become rigid, as though someone dumped a bucket of concrete over me.

The corpse in the sarcophagus was Cadence's mother. The corpse I left in plain view.

Oh, fuck.

A tremor passes through Cadence as though she's seeing her mother's rotten body again, and fresh tears drip down her cheeks.

My stiff jaw hardens some more as the sweet taste of my vengeance turns unpalatably bitter.

To me, graves are just boxes full of bones. Not *people*. And certainly not people that meant anything to anyone. Last night when I was looting that crypt, the only thing on my mind was my fury at Rainier de Morel. Not once did I stop to consider how my actions would impact anyone else. Apart from Bastian, I don't give a damn about anyone. Not even myself. Not really. But I think *what if Bastian died?* And what if someone defiled *his* grave?

I'd fucking rip their throat out, that's what.

I've felt a lot of things in my life—anger, despair, jealousy, pride. The one emotion I've always seemed to lack is shame. It's the reason I've been able to rise so high in my line of work. You can't succeed at being bad if you're concerned about being good. You just can't. You have to put your conscience on hold.

But now . . .

Now, a searing pain radiates through my chest, my temples throb, and my ears ring, because *I'm* the one responsible for Cadence's tears.

"What have you got to say for yourself, Monsieur Roland?" Rainier taps a finger on the armrest of his wheelchair, managing to lend that minuscule gesture a massive amount of violence.

My throat works but not to produce any sound, just to swallow the vile taste of what I've done.

I feel like dog shit smooshed under someone's shoe. Like a wad of chewed-up gum stuck to a subway bench. Like the garbage social services always told me I was.

Cadence's eyes are a stormy blue. "The brooch and all that other stuff in your pockets . . . You stole them from my family's mausoleum, didn't you?" She's breathing like she just ran a marathon, her shoulders heaving. Her slender fingers have curled into her palms, and her small fists bump into her jeans. I don't know why she's not pummeling me with them yet. I don't know why she's not gouging my cheeks with her nails and spitting into my face.

She sinks onto the sofa opposite where I sit, making it clear she doesn't want to be anywhere near me. "I hate you."

Not as much as I fucking hate myself right now.

"I want to hurt you," she says.

There's no point in me saying I'm sorry. The situation is way beyond apologies. In fact, saying sorry might just infuriate her further.

So, I do what I do best—I act like a prick. "Get in line, Cadence, because your *maman* beat you to it." I raise my hand, not just my middle finger this time.

"Where did you—Is that—" Cadence's mouth drops open. "Is that . . . what I think it is?" There's a note of reverence in Cadence's voice.

"The Bloodstone? We were just about to cover that with your old man." My eyes glide back to Rainier, focusing on the features blurred by a cloud of cigar smoke.

I'm not sure what snaps Cadence out of her daze, but all her breathy reverence vanishes when she shouts, "You . . . you . . . *crook!* Take that off right now. It's part of Brumian history. It doesn't belong to you!"

"No can do, sweetheart. Your maman got me good."

"My mother? What does the ring have to do with Maman?" Her teeth are so clenched her question is growled. "And what do you mean you *can't* take it off?"

"He means"—Rainier's voice is calm, chillingly so—"that no matter what he does, the ring won't budge. Isn't that right, Monsieur Roland?"

"It's a little stuck. Don't happen to have some quality bolt cutters lying around, do you?"

He sighs in a drawn out, dramatic way. "Alas, my stupid, stupid boy. Bolt cutters won't help. Not even on your finger. The stone's fused to *you*, to your blood, not to your skin."

"What kind of bullshit is that?"

"The cursed kind. The kind you get when you mess with dark magic." His lips curve around his cigar as though he's done with anger and has moved on to derision. "You reap what you sow in Brume. Welcome."

I shiver from the chill of his greeting.

Cadence looks at her father like she's seeing him for the first time. "The Bloodstone's real?"

Every line on Rainier's face softens as he nods.

"And it was in Maman's grave?"

He exhales more smoke. "I've been planning to sit you down for some time now. To explain your family's history. To tell you about the Quatrefoil Council and your role now that you're of age—"

"Me? The Quatrefoil Council?"

"You're a De Morel. Like your mother." Cadence doesn't seem surprised by Rainier's statement, but it makes me pause. Rainier took his wife's surname? Not unheard of, just unusual. Unless he isn't her biological father but some uncle she calls Papa?

Little seems to make sense right now.

Cadence shakes her head like she's trying to clear it. "So, the Council exists? And the *diwallers*? And magic—"

"Magic exists. Well, existed. Since 1350, it's been contained inside the separate leaves of the Quatrefoil."

A new light burns beneath Cadence's mottled skin. "Magic is real?" she breathes.

A whole world of emotions and unsaid words pass between them as they look at each other. It's like they've forgotten I'm here. Like they've forgotten a stone filled with blood has bonded to my veins.

As I watch her gaze at Rainier, something dawns on me: Cadence may lust after that Adrien professor dude, but she doesn't worship him. The man she worships is her father.

I attempt to get up in silence, but the leather under my ass groans as I shift. Both Cadence and Rainier's gazes snap over to me, then to the red stone glinting garishly on my finger. "So, I'm stuck looking like a pimp for the rest of my life?"

Cadence grunts; Rainier takes a long puff of his cigar.

"Yes. You're stuck like that for life." Smoke makes his face appear wavy. "But the good news is it won't be that long."

"That long until what?"

His smile suddenly seems genuine, as though he's getting off on torturing me with scraps of information that my muddled brain is trying to keep straight and piece together. "Why . . . until you die, of course."

I take a step toward Rainier. "Are you threatening me?"

Cadence bounds off the sofa and sticks herself between us before slamming both her palms into my chest. If I weren't so distracted by the whole insanity of the conversation, I'd be impressed by how fiercely protective she is. Since I'm fuming, I grip her wrists as gently as Slately possible and push them off. I don't advance, just glare at Rainier over the top of Cadence's head.

"I wasn't threatening you, Monsieur Roland; I was simply stating facts." He sucks on his cigar, taking his sweet time explaining what's in store for me. "The Bloodstone is cursed to keep magic contained. Ironically, the only way to free yourself is by restoring that magic."

I'm aware it's my own fault the ring's stuck to my finger, yet my urge to poke his eyes is mighty strong. "Stop with the goddamn riddles!"

Cadence's breath whispers over my clenched jaw. "You need to reunite the pieces."

The odor of her shampoo fills my nostrils. *Putain*, she smells good. Does she wash her hair with jam? And why the hell am I sniffing her right now?

I take a step back and throw my hands up, careful not to hit Cadence. "Okay, then. That's what I'll do."

Rainier laughs, a deep, soulless laugh. A Disney villain laugh. "This is not a game of Connect Four, Monsieur Roland. This is a battle against potent magic. First, you must locate the pieces, pieces that are hidden by magic. And then you must fight for them. And believe me, you'll lose. The curses put in place to keep them hidden are formidable. And the stone's curse is the strongest of all."

"You don't know that," I say.

"Ah, but I do." He clears his throat and looks directly at the back of his daughter's head. "I know because it's the Bloodstone that killed my wife, Amandine."

10

CADENCE

Magic robbed me of my mother?

"Why the fuck did you tell me to come to this fucking town!" Slate's voice slaps the tension-filled air, bashing right through my thoughts.

I step to the side so I can keep an eye on both men. I don't want to have my back turned to Slate. I don't trust him.

Papa's face turns the color of raw beets. "I didn't tell you to pilfer my family's crypt!"

Both men's chests heave equally hard whereas mine is quiet. I'm still processing. That my mother died because of magic. That magic is real. That it's stored inside four hidden leaves and a ring that's presently choking the thief's finger.

"Why didn't you ever tell me?" I whisper.

"What?" I don't think Papa means to snap at me, but that's how the word comes out.

"About magic? That it existed?" I stare at the bronze bonsai in the middle of our coffee table, at the grooved bark, delicate branches, and raindrop-sized leaves. "That it stole Maman from us?"

"Telling you was putting you at risk. Until Rémy came home—"

"My name's Slate. Not Rémy. And this isn't my home."

"Until *Slate* came back to Brume, we had no way of bringing magic back, so I didn't see the point in getting your hopes up for nothing."

Slate backs up until his calves hit the couch and then sinks down but doesn't lean back, his spine as rigid as a fire poker. "Until I came back?"

The large red stone catches the dying sunlight outside, beaming it onto Papa's chest. The red dot looks like a bloody hole against the pale cashmere.

Papa sighs. "It's complicated." His navy eyes rove over Slate's face, then off, settling on the long bay window and the lake beyond, which gleams gold and sapphire-gray under a thin layer of mist.

Slate thrusts a hand through his mussed black curls. "Try me. I'm good at complicated."

"Let's hope you are," Papa says. "With Amandine and the others, we tried to assemble the Quatrefoil. And we failed."

"The others?" I venture.

Papa's gaze climbs up to me. "The other founding families. The other guardians."

"We're . . . we're *diwallers*?" I don't think I've ever experienced so many extreme and mixed emotions in the space of such a short while.

"I was hoping we'd have more time . . ." he adds quietly.

"More time?" Slate's clutching his knees, the knuckles of both hands pale, the tendons so taut they look about to snap the ring off his purple middle finger.

My heart almost goes out to him, but he did this to himself. Actions have consequences. It's about time he learns this.

"The moment the ring binds to a descendant, the pieces appear. If they're not found and assembled before the new moon, they all vanish again."

"Okay." Slate's still breathing laboriously. "So, that gives us how long?"

"Full moon's tomorrow." Which reminds me. As I shrug out of my puffer jacket and toss it on the back of the couch, I gush, "Papa, I tried calling you earlier, because the clock—"

"Started ticking." He sighs.

"Did Adrien tell you?"

"No."

"Then how do you—"

"Rémy, here, woke the magic."

"For fuck's sake, it's *Slate*," he growls.

"And now you only have two weeks to assemble the Quatrefoil," Papa says quietly.

Slate's grip slackens. "Good thing finding things that don't want to be found is my forte." Beneath the confident inflection, I sense agitation.

"Except you won't be able to retrieve them on your own," Papa says. "All four *diwallers* will have to play in order to win."

Goose bumps rise everywhere on my body. "All four? I'm going to have to"—I gulp—"*help* Slate?"

"Yes."

"Who are the other two?" Slate asks.

Papa stares out the window. "Adrien Mercier and Gaëlle Bisset."

Of course . . . the descendants from the founding families. What exactly was I expecting? That these other guardians would be strangers?

"Oh, goodie," I think I hear Slate say. He might've just emitted a caveman grunt. Wouldn't put it past him to make sounds of an animalistic nature.

"What happens if we can't get the pieces in fifteen days' time, Papa? Do they go back into hiding?"

Papa shuts his eyes, and his nostrils pulse. "Unless Slate has fathered a child, it's game over after this new moon. And not just for a while, but forever. He's the last Roland."

Both Slate and I frown.

"If the ring doesn't come off before the new moon, it kills the carrier."

Slate doesn't make a sound. He seems to have stopped breathing.

"My original plan was to bring Rémy—I mean, Slate—home, fill him in on our shared history, fill *you* in"—Papa's lids reel up, and he stares at me—"then call a meeting with the others. One of the *diwallers* was going to put on the ring . . . I wish it could've been me, so that if we failed, if anything happened—" His voice catches, and his eyes begin to shine like the lake. "But no thread of dormant magic runs in my blood. All I can do is teach the four of you all the lessons we learned from past mistakes."

Another chill scatters over my skin. I must pale because Papa wheels himself closer and clasps my limp hand as though to remind me that he's here. That everything will be okay.

"Thank goodness you can't put it on," I say, closing my fingers around his. "I'd rather have a parent than magic."

"You're almost eighteen—"

"So what?"

He glares at his useless legs. "*Ma* Cadence, you think I enjoy being in a wheelchair?"

I know it's hard. I know he's often in pain and resents relying on others for everything, but I just can't—I just . . .

"Papa, I'll *always* need you." Tears pop out from underneath my lids and leak down my cheeks.

His thumb comes up, and he swipes them away.

Why am I weeping over this? It's not like losing him is an actual possibility. I mean, I'll lose him eventually. No one lives forever, but at least it won't be a ring that removes him from my life. Not like my mother.

God, a ring . . .

I lost her because of a cursed jewel. It still seems so . . . so—

"Not that this little moment isn't heartwarming, but I have fifteen days left to live, so if you could both focus on me for a second and explain what the fuck I'm looking for, it'd be real appreciated."

I narrow my watery gaze on Slate. He's so hateful that I don't even feel bad that he might die. *Okay* . . . I feel a teeny bit bad.

"Slate's right. We need to get to work." Papa fishes his cellphone from the wheelchair pocket and scrolls through his contacts.

When I see the name he selects, I bite my lip. "Adrien said he was flying to London today."

"Then he'll have to fly straight back," Papa says.

My heart pumps so much blood that it sounds like the lake is rushing through my skull. Still, I manage to catch bits of what Papa is saying, and it doesn't sound like he's leaving a message.

After he hangs up, he scrolls through his list again until his thumb stills on Gaëlle's number. "Adrien's on his way."

His way back or his way here? I suppose they're one and the same. Relief pokes through the haze of dread. I don't know whether Slate is smart or a team player, but I know Adrien is both.

Slate's head is bowed in contemplation of the Bloodstone, probably ruing its power and *his* stupidity.

Once Papa hangs up, he says, "They're both on their way. Cadence, can you go down to the cellar and grab a bottle of wine?"

"Make that two," Slate says.

I dip my chin into my neck and glower at him. "Planning on sharing one with Maman again?"

Slate's dark eyes go pitch-black. He doesn't say a word. I'm almost surprised he doesn't have a clever comeback since he has clever comebacks for *everything*.

"Cadence, *chérie*." Papa prods my ribs and nods to the door. "And grab five glasses."

"Five?"

"Yes. Five."

Not that he's ever prohibited me from drinking, but he's also never encouraged me to do so. I suppose he thinks I'm going to need a little buzz, but is that to stomach what he's just confessed or to endure all that he's about to?

I cross the room in a few short strides. I don't bother closing the doors since no one else is home. Jacqueline is long gone—I passed her on my way in—and our housekeeper only comes in the morning. I head into the kitchen, a state-of-the-art space filled with Corian and stainless steel, then through a door that leads to the basement which contains a giant jacuzzi and a walk-in wine cellar. I enter the dank room, free a dusty magnum from its cradle, then shut the door and traipse back upstairs. After I've pulled out the cork, I hook five long-stemmed glasses through my fingers and grip the bottle's neck as though it were Slate's.

A ring killed my mother.

The same ring Slate is wearing.

Slate will die if we—Adrien, Gaëlle, Slate, and I—fail to find four magical leaves.

If we succeed, Slate lives, and magic . . . magic will reappear.

Maybe I should've grabbed vodka from the freezer instead of wine, because this is all just so crazy.

When I burst back into the living room, Papa and Slate hush up.

"Don't stop chatting on my account," I say, wondering why they're wearing matching guilty looks.

Both watch me set my loot down on the coffee table, the soft clink of glass on glass rivaling the whir of the convector heaters, which have been working full-time since the blush of autumn swept over Brume.

"Papa, if I'm part of this, I want to know *everything*."

As I start to pour, he says, "I was just explaining to Slate how Amandine"—he pauses—"how your mother . . ." Again he stops talking.

"How my mother what?"

"What the end will be like for him in case we aren't successful," he says in a single breath.

My blood turns to sleet in my veins, transforming my arms into unyielding branches like the ones Alma and I stick into the snow-women we build every year on the university quad.

The wine almost overflows from the first glass. Would have if Slate hadn't risen from the couch and lifted the bottle from my hands.

"Bet you're thinking I should've puckered up and planted one on you last night," he says.

I don't know if he's trying to alleviate my mood or his own. Unless he's just trying to get under my skin and embarrass me in front of my father.

My cheeks flame. "Trust me, that's not even remotely close to what's going through my mind at the moment."

Slate's eyes curve with a touch of humor. "De Morel, I think that if the ring doesn't murder me, your daughter might."

Papa's expression clears of some somberness.

I plant my hands on my hips. "How can you be making jokes right now? Your life's hanging by a thread!"

Slate's expression turns so serious it makes him look years older. How old is he again? I try to remember the date on the birth certificate he showed me mere hours ago. "That's precisely *why* I'm making jokes. I don't do sobbing and lamenting. Like I said last night, a person makes their own luck."

"Or their own misfortune," I mutter.

He *tsk*s. "Such a pessimist, Mademoiselle de Morel."

The doorbell shrills.

I move my seething gaze off Slate and onto the foyer. Since the front door isn't going to open itself, I stride toward it. I'm so angry slash annoyed slash perplexed by this entire situation that when I fling the door open, the butterflies that usually take off at the sight of Adrien don't even flap their wings.

His head jerks back as though I've punched him. He must think I'm glowering at him.

I attempt to smooth out my expression, because Adrien doesn't deserve my contempt. Only Slate deserves it. "I thought you'd be halfway across the Channel."

"My flight was tomorrow morning."

Was. Not *is*. I suppose he's not planning on going.

I nod and am about to close the door when I spot another figure coming up our driveway. Gaëlle's eyes find mine in the spreading dusk. "Did you know—"

"Shh," Adrien says, and I understand he must be warning me not to speak about the Quatrefoil beyond the walls of this house.

He shuts the door behind Gaëlle, then offers to help her with her coat. That he can still be gallant at a time like this stuns me, but Adrien is like Papa, a gentleman to the very core. I precede the new arrivals into the living room. Slate's now standing beside the mammoth peach fireplace, nursing a glass of wine and poking a fire he must've just kindled.

Adrien pauses in the doorway. "I'd almost forgotten about you."

Slate smiles, but there's acid in that smile. "Hi, Prof."

Adrien's gaze drops to the hand Slate's wrapped around his glass, the one with the enormous red Bloodstone, then zips over to Papa. "Already? Rainier, this is ridiculous! We were supposed to wait until after the new moon."

He knew?

Gaëlle unwinds her yellow scarf, then drapes it beside my jacket. "I thought we were waiting until Spring."

She knew?

"Winter's the worst time," she adds. "The ground's frozen solid. The lake in places, too. What if we have to dig? Or swim?"

"Swim?" And here I thought I'd reached the pinnacle of shock, but nope . . . I sense there are miles of steep and mysterious terrain ahead of me before I can get to the top and look down over all this new knowledge and make sense of it.

"I haven't gotten to explaining the finer details of the Quatrefoil to Cadence and Slate yet. And, yes, we *were* going to wait. However, my hand has been forced." Papa skewers Slate with a look. "Both of you, grab a glass and get comfortable." He taps his cigar against the ashtray on the coffee table. The ashes collapse off in one big chunk before crumbling into small heaps.

Gaëlle pushes up the sleeves of her sweater and steals a glass from the middle of the table. "So glad I'm not breastfeeding anymore, because I need a drink. Or ten," she says to no one in particular, or maybe she's voicing this so we don't judge her.

Right now, the only person I'm judging is Slate.

Slate, who's slotting the brass poker into the accessory stand. He straightens but doesn't return to the couch, just steps toward the steel-gray wall and leans against it. Adrien drops down beside Gaëlle and takes the glass she's poured him.

I take the seat closest to Papa's wheelchair. It almost seems like we're picking camps, but technically we're all in this together.

All of us supernaturally screwed.

11

SLATE

I lean my head back against the wall and close my eyes while the little group before me gets settled, babbling on about the wine and the weather.

Meanwhile, I'm dying.

Fifteen days . . .

I don't have a last will and testament or anything like that, so I need to make a few calls. To my bank. To my other bank. To my other, other bank. To my lawyer. If something should happen to me, I want to make sure Bastian gets everything I own—my money, my apartment, my Aston Martin, and Spike, of course. That prickly soul needs to be taken care of.

De Morel told me what to expect should this all go to shit. He said the magic works like a poison in the blood. It would take a whole day and, during that time, I'd be in such excruciating pain that I'd probably try to peel off my own skin. His wife tried scrubbing her arms with a goddamn cheese grater before he took it away.

I shudder.

The only way around this pitiful end is to get the Quatrefoil pieces and put them together.

So that's what I'll do. It's not like I have a fucking choice.

And like I told Cadence, you've got to make your own luck in this life.

The mood in the room changes. Voices less relaxed. Higher pitched. Angry. I open my eyes and see they're all glaring at me. Oh, *goody*. De Morel must've explained the finer details of how the ring got on my finger.

The professor Cadence has the hots for has been giving Rainier shit about the lack of time. Now he shakes his head at me like I've been a bad puppy, annoyed but not panicked like the others. He gives his chin a firm rub with nails shaped into perfect crescents. His skin has that uncracked porcelain sheen to it, like he's been massaged in lotion his entire life. I bet growing up, he found chocolates on his pillow instead of rat droppings and his shoes never pinched his toes.

After he lowers his hand, he shoots Cadence a reassuring smile. One that says, *Don't worry, I've got this*. I bet she really believes Monsieur tweed-pants-and-matching-vest can save the day.

I drain my wine glass, and push off the wall for a refill. Gaëlle, who's been drinking her wine like it's water, extends her glass, and I fill it up, too.

She scoots back into the couch, nursing her drink as though it were a newborn's head. "So, now that the Bloodstone's out of hiding, the pieces are too, right, Rainier?"

"Yes and no. They show up one after the other. But the first should show itself soon."

Cadence tilts her head to the side. "Or we could save ourselves the trouble and let Slate die. An amoral guy like him must have a kid or two somewhere."

Cute. "Or we could use the next fifteen days to make a baby instead of hunting down those pieces, Cadence." At least, I'd die happy.

Her cheeks burn pink, and she crosses her arms over her chest. The usual satisfaction I get from seeing her blush doesn't hit me. Probably because I'm still feeling like shit about her mother's grave. Jesus. I've got to get it together. I'm too far off my game. I blame the ring.

"There'll be no procreation. Especially not with my daughter." Rainier pins me with an impressively unpleasant glare.

Mercier, too, for that matter. I wonder why *he* cares.

"If we're going to have any chance at succeeding, everyone here needs to understand the mechanics of the Quatrefoil. Slate?" I turn my attention back toward Rainier. "Consider this an accelerated lesson in unofficial Brumian history."

"Unofficial and undisclosed," Mercier adds. "In other words, *secret*."

"Thanks for clearing that up, Prof. Big words confuse me." What a dickhead.

"Adrien?" Rainier tips his head. "Will you explain it to him?"

Adrien plants his elbows on his thighs and links his hands together before rehashing what I learned at the library with Cadence. I sip my wine in silence, allowing him to feel important as he drones on about the Black Death, the mishandling of magic, and the Council's decision to have the *diwallers* break apart the source of all magic to punish the undeserving and undisciplined masses.

"What they did sounds simple: four leaves and a Bloodstone key. But because records are sparse, it took the last generation a lot of trial and error to grasp the actual complexities of assembling the Quatrefoil."

Gaëlle swirls her wine, then drinks it in one swallow. "And deaths. It caused so many deaths."

Cadence's expression ripples with shock. "*Deaths*? It wasn't just Maman?"

"*Non, chérie.*" Rainier gives her a pained smile. "It's not just the ring that kills. In my generation, four people lost their lives."

"Out of how many?" I figure it's all about averages.

"Eight."

"*Half* the group died?" I laugh. "Pretty shitty odds."

"And I lost the use of my legs." Rainier's voice is razor-sharp.

Cadence drops her glass, which spills over the rug like blood, splattering her jeans and the cream couch on its way down. "You said it was a car accident!"

The liquid beads over the leather, striping it purple.

Gaëlle extricates herself from the sofa cushion. "I'll go grab some salt. It'll soak up the stain."

I don't think Cadence or Rainier care about the stain at the moment.

As Gaëlle leaves, Rainier takes his daughter's hands and

cocoons them between his. "*Ma* Cadence, I was trying to protect you—"

"By lying?" Her eyes shimmer with disappointment. "What else have you lied to me about, Papa?"

"*Chérie* . . ."

Cadence pulls her hands free, then swipes the glass from the rug and plops it on the coffee table so hard I'm surprised neither cracks. Hands shaking, she takes the bottle from the center of the table and starts pouring but misses her glass more than once.

Adrien, ever the fucking gentleman, scoots off the couch and gently peels her fingers off the large, dark-green bottle, before accomplishing the job she was botching. With a wink, he grabs a tissue from his vest pocket and cleans up the base and stem.

"I forgot to tell you, Rainier, but the clock started ticking," Adrien says as he returns to his seat. "Could that be one of our pieces?"

"No. The clock's like an hourglass. It'll mark the number of moon phases you have left."

"What about the star dial?" Mercier asks.

"The hand on that one didn't move last time. I suspect it'll start working once the Quatrefoil is assembled."

"What is this about the clock?" Gaëlle blusters back in, armed with a wet dishcloth and a canister of *sel de Guérande*—of course this is the only type of salt these people would own.

Rainier fills her in as she blots Cadence's jeans, then energetically scrubs the sofa before sprinkling the salt flakes over the rug.

"Thank you," Cadence murmurs, her skin the same shade as her thick turtleneck. She's in shock, and if her white knuckles are any indication, she's also pretty ticked off. She should be. Lies are hard to stomach, even if they're dispensed to protect.

"So, let me get this straight, De Morel. I'm not the only one who risks dying if we go after these pieces?"

He nods. "The pieces can only be earned through challenges."

"Then I'm going at this alone. Just give me the instruction booklet, and I'm good. No one else needs to be involved."

Adrien scoffs. "This isn't a game, Roland. There is no instruction booklet. Besides, the rest of us have no choice in participating."

"Really, *Mercier*?" I bite down hard on his family name. Dick thinks he can call me Roland. "Why?"

"Because each one of you has a specific piece to find and win. We learned this the hard way." Rainier stares at his emaciated thighs. "I was with Amandine when she faced her challenge of retrieving the Earth piece. She succeeded but then she handed it to me for safekeeping." His crow's feet deepen. "I was lucky it was only my legs I lost."

Gaëlle runs a hand through her snarled, dark curls. "Also, last time, they didn't know that the pieces could only be touched by the descendants of that specific element or it activated the curse contained within the piece." She nibbles on her lower lip. "That's how I lost my father. He didn't realize that our piece was Air." Her ruddy-brown eyes set on the gray mist billowing over the inky lake. "Not Water."

Rainier sighs. "It was only after your parents died, Monsieur Roland, that we managed to put the Quatrefoil puzzle together."

I don't even bother correcting him with my name anymore but do question his declaration. "You said my parents died in a fire."

"Their element was Water." He contemplates the flames devouring the logs behind me. "They touched Camille Mercier's leaf: Fire."

I absentmindedly rub the scar under my shirt sleeve.

Rainier takes a drag from his Churchill, which is nothing but a glowing stub now. "After Pierre—Gaëlle's father—and your parents died, we finally understood how it worked."

Magic killed my parents . . . might very well kill me. It probably shouldn't be restored. But at the same time, I really don't feel like dying.

"So, we each have a specific leaf to find and collect?" I pour more wine into my glass, even though I'm tempted to grab the bottle and chug it.

Rainier nods. "Yours is Water. Adrien's, Fire. Gaëlle's, Air." He reaches out toward his daughter, who hesitates but ends up yielding to him, wrapping her slender fingers around his. "And Cadence's is Earth."

Gaëlle drains her glass, but it does nothing to loosen the stiffness of her shoulders. "Each of us will have to face a challenge brought forth by our element. We can help each other, but we cannot, under any circumstances, fight another person's battle or touch their piece."

"Sort of like a treasure hunt," Cadence says, "but with cursed artifacts."

"Which is why it's incredibly dangerous, *ma chérie*."

"And not just for Slate," Adrien adds.

I'm glad for the reminder. I *had* almost forgotten about my dire predicament.

I take a swig of wine. "You just might get your wish after all, Mademoiselle de Morel."

She makes a face before dropping her gaze to her knees, to the patch of wet denim. "I don't actually want you to die, you moron."

Gaëlle slides her glass onto the table and cradles her face in her hands. Her voice is muffled when she says, "I need to ask Nolwenn and Juda to take care of the twins. Not just over the next two weeks, but . . . but I need to make plans, in case." She sighs and drags her hands down the sides of her face which seems gray in comparison to the rich shade of her fingers.

"It'll be okay, Gaëlle. We know so much more than before." Rainier's reassurance makes the thirty-something woman shoot him a grateful smile.

"How do we know where to look?" Cadence's voice is as wispy as the dark smoke rising up the chimney. "What if they're scattered all over the world?"

Rainier smiles. "The pieces have been magicked to remain within the confines of Brume, and they'll be located within their element. In the next day or so, someone will claim to have seen a whirlpool in the lake or will report a sinkhole. There might be a windstorm in only one part of town, or a house that catches fire without reason. These natural happenings will lead us to the pieces." He juts his chin toward my hand. "Not to mention, we have a live artifact detector."

I hold up my swollen finger. This time I get a tiny rush at flipping him off in front of everyone else. Maybe I'm not as off my game as I thought. "You mean, this old thing?"

"You're such a jerk," Cadence mutters under her breath.

My gaze slides to hers. I don't say it out loud, but I'm thinking,

Really? Even more of a jerk than that asshole who let me rot in the system my whole life? I'm guessing, that in all the excitement, Rainier's failed to inform her of his hand in my *upbringing.*

Rainier continues, "The stone reacts when it nears a piece of the Quatrefoil. Slate will feel a burning in his blood, cramping in his limbs."

"How . . . *nifty.*" I examine the bottle. It's empty. I could really use a refill.

"We have to keep our eyes on the prize. We're going to bring magic back. It'll be . . . *extraordinary.*" Rainier's voice has the high timbre of a fanatic. Easy to get all creamed up when you get to sit back and twiddle your thumbs.

My gaze sticks to his legs, then to Cadence, and I realize that was uncalled for.

Mercier sighs. "Guess I should cancel my plane ticket and inform the head of the history department at Cambridge I won't be visiting."

"I'm sorry," Cadence says, before turning to me like she expects me to apologize.

Hell, no.

Gaëlle stands and begins to wind her ridiculously long scarf around her neck. "I've got to get back. If I see or hear anything, I'll let you know." After three loops, the yellow yarn still hangs to her knees.

Adrien stands, too. "I'll walk you home. Goodnight, Rainier. Cadence." He sends her a smile that stains her cadaverously-pale cheeks pink.

While Gaëlle winds another coil of scarf around her neck, I pick up my coat that's slipped off the back of the couch and puddled on the floor like tar. I spear my arms through but don't bother with the gloves. Cadence accompanies us to the foyer, or rather walks Adrien and Gaëlle to the door while I trail behind my new squad.

What a team we make—a preppy professor, a woman with a yarn fetish, and a girl way too pure of heart for all this bullshit. The ultimate underdogs.

To think my life is in their hands.

My ever-practical mind reels to my cell of a dorm room. I need sheets and towels. Although I have my pride, I doubt the village has a twenty-four-seven *Carrefour*, and since my pimp jewel prevents me from leaving this godforsaken town, I ask Cadence if I can borrow linens.

When she scrunches her forehead, I say, "You'll get them back in two weeks. Either I'll be dead or I'll be gone."

Shaking her head, she sighs. "Just follow me."

12

CADENCE

"**F**or someone so convinced about making their own luck, you're awfully pessimistic," I tell Slate as I lead him through the kitchen.

"Just being realistic."

"We have fifteen days ahead of us."

"Two weeks to find four magical leaves that might curse me to death before we even reunite them. Realistically speaking, I'd have better odds jumping off a plane with a faulty parachute and surviving than accomplishing this mission with the three of you."

"Just because we aren't deceitful thieves doesn't mean we're useless."

He gives me the side-eye.

"You're not going to die in fifteen days, Slate." Hopefully, though, he is going to leave.

His head keeps swiveling from side to side as he takes in my house, probably mapping it out for a future heist. His gaze lingers on the light fixture over the dining room table, a sculptural piece made of bronze maple leaves interspersed with glass ones.

"Maman cast the bronze leaves. She was a sculptor. She also made that little tree on the living room table."

Slate glides his attention back to me. "She had a lot of talent."

I nod.

"Did you inherit it?"

"Ha. No. I'm a paint-by-number sort of girl." As I stare at her work of art, I can't help but ask the dreaded question, the one I'm sure Papa would never answer. At least, not truthfully. "Did she suffer a lot in the end?"

Slate is quiet for so long I start to suspect the worst. "No. The Bloodstone leaked such a high dose of poison into her veins, she went quickly."

My heart squeezes. "I can't even imagine how hard that whole period must've been for my father. It must kill him to see the ring out of hiding."

Slate's lips contort as though he's biting back words.

I sigh. "Just say what you're thinking."

"He was going to dig it out himself, so it must not be *that* difficult."

"Why do you think the worst of him?"

He stares down at me hard, as though he's seeing my father instead of me. "Why don't you ask him?"

I splay a hand on my waist, crimping the thick fabric. "I'm asking you."

"I'd rather you hear it from him."

Why is Slate suddenly being so tight-lipped?

"So. Towels? Sheets? 6-in-1 soap?"

Sensing I'd have an easier time shucking an oyster with my nails than getting Slate to open up about Papa, I whirl around and start toward the stairs that lead to our basement laundry room. "6-in-1?"

"You know, the manly sort—for hair, body, face, teeth, eyes, ears."

I snort. "You're a very strange boy, Slate."

Again, he's quiet. I check over my shoulder to make sure he didn't take it the wrong way. Since when do I care how he takes it, though? He desecrated my mother's grave. I shouldn't care at all about how he takes *anything*. I miss a step and stumble. I fling my hands out to catch myself, but Slate is quicker. He cinches my bicep and steadies me.

My breathing quickens. "Thank you."

I notice it was the hand with the ring that caught me. His finger is so bloated and purple, I'm surprised he can still bend it.

"Did the ring do that?"

A tiny groove appears between his black eyebrows. "Give me fast reflexes? No. I learned those to stay alive."

Stay alive? Where did Slate live that he needed to develop survival skills? And how did he end up out of Brume? I decide to file this question for later. Or for Papa. Since he found Slate, he must know where Roland's heir has been all these years.

"I meant, the bruise on your finger."

"Oh." He makes a fist that must hurt, because his smooth forehead crimps beneath the mess of corkscrew curls. "Trying to get it off did that."

"Must be weird. Not being able to remove it."

"You have no idea."

I turn and stare at my feet so I don't trip again. Next to the laundry room, there's a medicine cabinet where we store a pharmacy's worth of ointments, bandages, and pills. Although Papa hasn't had an infection in some years, we're ready for one. We're ready for anything. I slide my finger down the line of pill packets until I find a painkiller that isn't sold over the counter. I pick it up and hand it to Slate.

"Take one in the morning and one at night. It'll help with the pain."

He studies the packet, then my face, as though surprised I'm worried about how he could be feeling. I push a strand of hair behind my ear as I crouch in front of the shelf of toiletries and select a few bottles from my father's stash before closing the medicine cabinet and walking over to our teal-tiled laundry room. I grab an empty plastic basket off a shelf, toss the bottles inside, then open a cupboard and snatch two fluffy white towels.

"Do you need a duvet and a pillow?" I ask, sorting through the neat piles of sheets and pillowcases for ones not intended for Dad's medicalized bed.

"Yeah. If you got any extras."

I push up on tiptoe to reach the top shelf, but my fingers don't even skim its underside. I turn to look for the stepstool when the tip of my nose bumps into Slate's chin. I whirl back toward the shelf, heartrate picking up speed. He extends his arm and plucks a folded duvet off the shelf with ease. My pulse strikes my neck faster when he doesn't step back. He still needs a pillow after all, so there's no reason for him to move.

As he lowers the feathery comforter, his gaze drops to mine. "Can I take this one?"

I slide my palms against my jeans to rid them of the sudden moisture. Without even looking at what he's clutching, I nod. And then I swallow because his eyes are still on mine, and he's standing so close that the fragrance of dark berries and cloves wafting off his skin overtakes the scent of talc and detergent surrounding us.

"I'm sorry about your mother's grave, Cadence."

I inhale sharply, his apology sweeping over my mind like a hand through steam. Suddenly, instead of his dark eyes and dark hair, I see her.

And I shudder.

Slate backs up and drops the duvet inside the laundry basket propped on the ironing board.

"A pillow. You forgot a pillow." My lucidity surprises me. Then again, I'd rather concentrate on a real bed than on Maman's death bed.

He nods. I back away this time so our bodies don't collide. He reaches for a pillow and chucks it on top of his load.

"Slate, why did you"—my throat clenches—"vandalize my family's crypt?"

Keeping his gaze fastened to the narrow hallway, he heaves the basket up. "I was angry with your dad."

"For bringing you back to Brume?"

He slides me a look before he utters a dry, "No," and steps out of the teal-tiled room.

I close the cupboard and turn off the lights. He's already halfway up the stairs.

"Slate, what did he do to you?"

He pauses on the landing, his broad frame scraping the kitchen doorway. His back is to me, shoulder blades pinching together underneath his tailored coat. "I'd rather he tells you, Cadence. But if he doesn't, come find me." He glances over his shoulder. "I'll probably be nursing my oblivion-bound soul at the tavern. Unless something else is open?"

"Probably not tonight."

He nods. "Are you going back out?"

"I don't plan to." I sense he wants company, but mine?

As we emerge into the foyer, his boots' thick soles squelch against the white marble, and the Bloodstone catches the light from the heavy crystal chandelier, scattering scarlet tinsels over the glass protecting Gauguin's sketch, a sketch my father bought my mother for their first anniversary.

I'm still studying it when the front door bangs shut behind Slate, making the frame vibrate.

I cross my arms and clutch my elbows. "Papa?"

"In the living room."

I go to him.

He's sitting beside the window, watching the misty lake glazed in moonlight. "It froze over once."

I approach him and look out.

"Your maman insisted we buy ice-skates even though neither of us had ever skated before. I spent more time sprawled on my backside than I did upright. Amandine was a natural, though. She managed pirouettes after an hour." His eyes shimmer, and I think he's seeing her, vibrant and full of life. Alive. And it makes me think of her tomb, but not in anger. Slate's apology abated some of that. So did the whole idea of magic. I need to call the custodian and ask him to put the lid back over her grave. I don't want Papa to see the dried husk of silk and bones she's become. "She was so graceful."

"I wish I remembered her."

"I wish you did too."

A tear curves down his cheek, and that tear terrifies me because I've never seen my father cry. He's my rock. Rocks don't weep.

"Papa, why does Slate hate us so much?"

He rubs his fingers across his cheek before looking up at me. "He doesn't hate *us*. He just hates me."

"Why?"

Darkness blunts the shimmer in his gaze. "He thinks I left him in foster care because I didn't care."

"Foster care?" I don't know much about the system but imagine children don't always end up in happy homes. "He didn't grow up with any relatives?"

"He has none."

Right. His bloodline ends with him. For some reason, the fact that Slate was an orphan hadn't clicked when Papa mentioned it was game over if Slate perished.

"Why didn't you take him in after his parents died?"

"I only found out he was alive a few years ago."

"How come?"

"Someone smuggled him out of Brume. Most likely because they thought he'd be safer away from this place."

I chew on my bottom lip. "Why does Slate blame *you* then?"

"Because when I found out where he ended up, I didn't go get him. I left him in the system. I thought it better for him to grow up before he was brought back to Brume. I wanted you kids to be ready once we set the Quatrefoil gathering in motion."

A web of fear spreads through me, sticky and cold. "And you told him all of this?"

"I did."

I try to put myself in Slate's shoes. Would I be bitter?

Papa sighs. "I probably should've done background checks on the families he lived with. Had him placed with better people."

"Why didn't you?"

Papa looks at the flames licking the blackened logs, filling the living room with the crackling scent of winter. "Because I'm not perfect."

I think he must be seeing the fire that devoured Slate's parents, because his expression is troubled.

He returns his gaze to me. "I might have failed him, but I won't fail you, Cadence. I'll be there every step of the way."

I have no doubt he will. "I don't want you to get hurt again though."

He gives me a sad smile. "I'll be careful."

Could one be careful around magic? It seemed so unpredictable. A Bloodstone that poisons the wearer? Metal leaves that can hide themselves and curse people?

"You think magic could heal your legs?" I'm grasping to feel something other than dread.

"Yes." Papa's certainty shoos off my fear.

Fantasy and reality are about to collide, and however terrified, a part of me, the one that spent her childhood dreaming Brume's books of lore held some truth, reels with excitement.

I wonder how the others are feeling. The others being Gaëlle and Adrien, because I can't imagine Slate will feel anything other than anxiety until the ring comes off his finger.

13

SLATE

If I didn't know any better, I might say Brume was a charming place with its twinkling holiday decorations and cast-iron street lights.

A magical place.

Ha. That makes me chuckle.

"Happy Fucking New Year," I shout to no one in particular as I reach Second Kelc'h.

One guy yells, "*Ta gueule!*" the charming French way of saying *shut the hell up*, but a couple others hoot and wish me a Happy Fucking New Year right back.

I hitch the plastic laundry basket up under my armpit and hang on with one hand while I scrabble in my coat pocket for my phone with the other. Pain lances from my middle finger all the way up to my elbow as I grip the basket.

When I finally have the phone in my palm, I tap Bastian's contact info with my thumb and wait for him to answer.

"What's wrong?" he asks.

"Why the hell do you assume something's wrong?"

"Because you're calling me, and it hasn't even been twenty-four hours since we talked."

What the actual fuck? "You *told* me to call."

"Yeah. And you're doing what I asked. Hence, something's wrong."

Bastian knows me like no one else does. "Just wanted to check up on Spike."

Unlike last night, the town square isn't cluttered with witches and wizards. There are people, but the drunken crowds are gone. The villagers must be playing it safe since tomorrow's a workday.

"Spike's living it up. Yesterday, they had a sale on cute little succulents, so I got some. Should've seen him ring in the new year with all these juicy babes. I think he just might be falling for the Mexican Snowball. She's got it going on, if you know what I mean." Bastian can't keep the grin out of his voice.

This is why I want him to have everything when I die. "You're such a dweeb."

As I enter the code to my new front door, glowering at the quatrefoil stamped above it, I let him know I probably won't be back in Marseille before his classes start.

He nearly weeps with joy. "Aw, man, Slate. I'm so glad you're going to study there. You'll see, you've got the brains for it. You can start a new life. A *legit* life. No more dangerous coups. No more wondering if you'll live to be twenty-one."

Yeah.

Right.

"Anyway, Bastian. Stay safe, and don't do anything I would do."

A snort comes from his end right before I hang up and toss the phone in the laundry basket, where it slides between the layers of fluffy linens that smell sweet and powdery like the girl who gave them to me. I inhale, and it eases some of the tension along my spine.

I climb up the rickety stairs, unlock door number three, and shoulder it open, which sends the brass number rocking. The odor of dusty wood and mildew hits me full force, as does one of the beams crossing the elf-high ceilings.

"*Bordel de merde!*" I rub my throbbing forehead and swear at the beam as though it came at me on purpose.

Just what I need . . . a good concussion. Because my day hasn't been shitty enough.

When the black spots in front of my vision clear, I drop the basket, shrug out of my coat, and make up the small mattress with military precision, then scrub my hands over my face and take a deep breath. I haven't slept in two days, but before I crash I've got a few things to do. First, I call Philippe, my . . . *uh* . . . lawyer and financial advisor. I tell him my last wishes. He's a bit perplexed and possibly high, but I'm a good client, so he gets right on it. Next, I slip back into my coat and gloves, wrap my scarf around my neck, and grab last night's loot.

A sour bubble of guilt expands in my stomach as I descend the steps to First Kelc'h and crunch along the frozen snow toward the De Morel crypt, using the flashlight on my phone to guide my steps. An owl hoots somewhere, and black wings flap so close to my head I duck. My blood pressure soars, thumping like the wings on the bat? Crow? Vampire?

"Creepy-ass town," I grumble as I reach the crypt.

Everything's exactly like I left it: the open iron door, the smashed wooden coffins, the bones strewn about like toothpicks, the sarcophagus lid discarded like a forgotten sock, the bottle resting in a pool of wine that resembles dark blood.

What a fucking mess I made.

My boots thud over the packed dirt as I inch over to the sarcophagus. I imagine Cadence coming in here. Imagine her looking down on her mother and seeing nothing but rotting fabric and skin and bones. My lungs squeeze tight.

"I'm sorry. Your daughter should've never seen you like this," I tell Amandine.

She leers at me with her toothy grin and hollow eyes, seemingly pleased I might die because I stole her ring.

I upend my pockets and dump it all back inside the coffin. I don't want any of this tainted shit, priceless or not. Brume lures you in like a tasty lollipop, and it's only when you see the blood dripping onto your shoes that you realize you're licking your own heart speared onto a stick.

I shut that eerie thought down and grab the lid of the sarcophagus. At first, I can barely get it to move. When I do, the damn thing slips, and the edge slams down on my foot. My boots are steel-toed, but it still hurts like a motherfucker.

I howl and hop around the crypt. "*Fuck*. Fuckity fucking fuck!"

Amandine's grin seems to get wider.

I grip the stone lip of the sarcophagus and wriggle my toes, testing if anything broke besides my sanity. The digits move, which I take as a good sign.

I get back to trying to seal her shut, wiping the sweat off my brow and grunting like a pig. Finally, the lid slides back into place.

I toss bones back into the other coffins and piece together lids like I'm working a jigsaw puzzle. When everything's sort of fixed, I pick up the wine bottle and limp out into the fresh night air, banging the heavy door shut behind me.

My actions don't make me feel better, but they do make me feel slightly less monstrous.

A thin skin of ice has formed over the snow. My feet punch holes into it, each step sounding like the crunch of breakfast cereal. I focus on the sound, hoping to numb my mind of any real thought. Or should I say, any thought that this is actually real. It's such a nightmare, almost worse than when I lived with Vincent. Except this time, no one's waking me up with an earful of insults and a sharp crack across the cheek. I almost miss the guy, and he was a pitiful human being.

I instinctively bring the wine bottle to my mouth for a swig when I feel cool, grainy dirt against my lips. Damn it. I forgot the bottle was the one from the crypt. I spit, then wipe my mouth on my sleeve and crunch across more snow, passing headstones and spindly trees. When I find myself back on a winding cobblestone road, I chuck the bottle into a trash bin, the thick glass clanking against the iron can, then head to the tavern. I take a new route down a narrow alley bent like a crooked arm where the stone walls have crumbled in places and the wooden shutters are gray. Yet even this neglected corner of Brume, with its scraggly evergreen boughs nailed above doors like overplucked eyebrows, holds more quaintness than the places I grew up in with their misspelled graffiti and soundtracks of gang fights and police sirens.

As I skirt the historical well in the town square, the small hairs on the back of my neck rise the same way they used to when I walked around my old neighborhoods.

Three girls clutching copper goblets and taking drags off cigarettes stand beside the entrance of the tavern, pointing to a couple sitting on a bench groping each other.

"Get a room!" one of the girls shouts to the couple, while her two friends break into giggles.

None of them look my way, yet the sensation of being watched strengthens. My gaze sweeps higher, to the second and top floors of the buildings. No eyes shine back at me from a shadowy window. No figure is crouched on the rooftops. Nothing seems off. Nothing that should get my spidey-sense tingling. Shaking off the sensation, I take another step, and it's like someone injected my veins with liquid fire.

I stumble, catching myself on the edge of the well. My breaths come in hard, raspy pants, as though the fire is spreading and has begun to char my lungs. I cling to the cold stone as mind-shredding pain cramps my muscles and wraps around my joints. It's enough to make me grit my teeth and let out an involuntary snarl.

My insides feel like they're melting, like the time I got a stomach flu and spent two days sprawled on my cool bathroom floor, wishing I were facing a gang armed with deadly knives instead of a torturous virus. I heave, but nothing comes out.

Maybe I drank too much wine. Or maybe—more likely— Cadence poisoned my wine.

My muscles seize, and icy sweat lines my brow. I grunt and groan, and the well echoes and amplifies the animal sounds.

Wait . . .

I stumble away from the well, hobbling to the far side of the square. Even though my toe is still throbbing, my joints and stomach aren't. I rip the glove off my hand with my teeth and stare at the fugly ring. Then, swallowing a breath of frigid air, I approach the well again. The girls standing outside the tavern are watching me now. I salute them, which makes one smile and the other two whisper.

The burning in my veins starts up again. Then the cramping in my muscles and a general creepiness, like a spider's egg sac has just hatched on my spine and the creatures are skittering all over my vertebrae. The closer I get to the well, the stronger the sensation. The ring flares, the stone glinting like a giant drop of luminous blood under the garlands of holiday lights trussing up the square.

Putain. De Morel was right when he said the ring was an artifact detector. If the thing came with a battery and sound effects, right now it would be going *beep... beep... beep... beep beep beep beep.*

A piece of the Quatrefoil is in or near the old well.

I study the shiny cobbled rim, the pointed, slate-shingled canopy shading it, the rusted chain wrapped with ribbon, and the hanging bucket filled with poinsettias—probably fake ones, unless someone took the time to stick a real bouquet in it. Wouldn't put that past these weird-ass townsfolk. Either way, I'm guessing no one uses this well to get their water anymore.

I need to get closer, but the girls are still watching me. And the pain . . . The mere memory of it makes me grit my teeth. *Fuck it.* I need to know if one of the leaves is in there. I lunge toward the well, bones burning beneath my skin, blood blazing. I clutch the damp ledge and shine my phone's flashlight down into it, feeling like I'm about to retch again.

There's a grate at the top—probably to stop drunks or stupid kids from falling in. Below, the empty cylinder stretches far and deep. I'm guessing it leads straight into hell.

With shaky fingers, I dig a coin from my pocket and toss it in. It plinks wetly, breaking water.

Does this mean it's my piece? Unless it's Cadence's . . .

If it is *mine* to get, and if I could get it tonight, we'd be ahead of the game. I eye the rusty chain. Would it hold my weight?

I reach out, close my trembling fingers over the icy metal, and tug to test the chain's sturdiness. It groans like something's coming loose, and ochre flakes chip off. Yeah. Not happening. If I'm going to do this, I need to do it right. That means decent equipment. That means not hurling myself into a black pit on too much wine and too little sleep.

On that note . . .

I could use more wine to help me sleep.

I release the chain, then back away, rubbing my palm over my jeans.

My breathing quiets the farther I get, and the fire in my veins subsides.

Maybe I will live to my next birthday after all.

I stride across the square to the tavern with a little more bounce in my step that has nothing to do with the fading pain.

"What did you wish for?" one of the girls standing by the entrance of the tavern asks.

"Wish?"

She juts her chin toward the well, her eyes running down my body.

Right . . . the coin. "To get the fuck out of Brume."

Her smile wanes. Obviously, she wanted me to hit on her, which is alarming on several levels, the first being that I was acting like a madman barely a minute ago, and the second, that I probably smell like the inside of a liquor casket . . . or plain old casket, for that matter.

"Cheers." I step past them and push open the heavy oak door.

The noise inside is loud enough to wake a dead man, but the cheery music and stifling heat are welcomed. I squeeze onto a squeaky red barstool, between two older men nursing drinks. The bartender's the same wiry middle-aged guy with crooked teeth and stick-straight hair as earlier. As he fills a glass with tap beer, he holds up a finger to indicate he'll be with me in a minute.

The lady with the puffed-up whitish hair who shot me a warning look when I was talking to Cadence earlier bustles in behind the bar. She sets down an empty tray near the sink and looks to the rack where wine glasses hang upside down like sleeping bats.

"Nolwenn," the bartender says, "can you take over for five? Gotta hit the head."

She motions with her hand to shoo him off, then turns her attention to those of us on the stools. Within seconds she sees there's no drink in front of me. "What can I get you, young man?"

"I'll take a . . ." I scan the shelves behind her.

"I've got the best *chouchen* in town. Brewed right on the premises."

I have no clue what the hell that is, but if it's brewed, then there's alcohol.

"Hit me." I rub my hands together trying to get rid of the lingering pins and needles.

As she pops the cork off a clear bottle, her gaze falls to my finger, lingers there.

Huh. Either she recognizes the Bloodstone or she's appalled by my choice in accessories.

She blinks and clears her throat. "That's quite a gem you've got there."

When I sense one of my neighbors copping a glance, I cross my arms, burying the stone under my elbow. "Family heirloom. Passed down from generation to generation. No accounting for taste, though."

She quirks up an eyebrow as she pours yellow liquid into my glass. "You from around here?"

I shake my head. "Marseille. Night and day these two places."

Her hand dips, *chouchen* spilling over the side of the glass. She wipes it up with a wet cloth. "And what's your name, Marseille?"

"Slate. Slate Ardoin." I purposely keep my Brumian identity under wraps.

"Nice to meet you. I'm Nolwenn." She holds out a red-knuckled hand.

Is she being friendly, or does she want another look at the ring?

Keeping my eyes on her face, I shake her hand, which is more calloused than mine, and notice her attention drift to the stone.

"You really like this ring, huh?" I look for a reaction, but the bartender comes back then, and Nolwenn untangles her fingers from mine. Before she leaves, I ask, "That well out there . . . how deep is it?"

She glances over her shoulder at me. "About thirty meters. Why?" She tilts her head to side. "You studying aquifers at the university?"

I'm not even sure what that is, but I go with it. "Yeah."

Her eyebrows gather. "You look a lot like someone I used to know."

"I get that all the time. I have a very unoriginal face."

She shakes her head, and her hair doesn't even shift. "Enjoy the mead, Marseille."

I might be imagining it, but as she leaves, her frown deepens. It strikes me that she must've known my parents. I wonder if she has stories. She looks like the type to have stories. Busybody running the town's watering hole.

Maybe I should ask her. Maybe—

"Marseille, huh? I don't think I've ever met a person with so many different identities."

I smile even though I don't look over my shoulder at the person who's just spoken. Don't have to. I know that scent, and I'd recognize that sultry voice anywhere.

"Thought you weren't coming back out, Mademoiselle de Morel."

14

CADENCE

"I couldn't sleep. *Surprisingly*, I have too much on my mind."

Slate spins around on his stool, smiling smugly. "Would a curly-haired Adonis be to blame?"

"Could you be more arrogant?" Technically, he's right, though. He *is* on my mind, but not because of his mussed hair or chiseled face, neither of which are *that* attractive. "What happened to your forehead?"

He touches the yellowing bruise. "A ceiling beam. I'm taller than your average elf."

Okay . . . "I'm going to go sit at a table."

"Is that an invitation?"

I unzip my puffer coat, the heat of his gaze combined with the heat of the hissing radiators making my body uncomfortably warm. I almost wish I'd changed out of my turtleneck. "Did it sound like an invitation?"

One of his black eyebrows juts up, vanishing behind a springy curl. "Guess not." He turns back toward the bar.

I stand frozen in place for a second. Here I was, certain he'd leap off his stool and trail me to a table. I'm usually good at reading people, but Slate's confusing. Even though I was joking about his multiple identities, I realize I might've not been so far off the mark after all.

I swallow my pride and say, "If you get bored drinking alone, come find me," then head over to an unoccupied table in the corner.

I should've stayed at home. Why did I think coming out to the tavern was a good idea?

"*Bonsoir, chérie.*" Nolwenn drops by my table as I'm sitting. "Is Alma coming?"

"No. It's just me. We missed you at the party last night."

"Wish we could've made it, but we closed up so late. Or rather, so early. Did Sylvie behave, or was that old bat all over Rainier?"

I smile because Sylvie is Nolwenn's age. "She was, but I don't think Papa's interested."

She smirks. "So, what can I get you?"

"The cheese plate and chamomile tea with honey."

"Good choices. Found Juda asleep over the stove earlier, so I sent him upstairs to rest and I'm not quite the cook he is."

"I hope he didn't burn himself."

She flaps her hand. "The old man's sturdy as a witch's cauldron."

I sit up a little straighter, itching to ask if she believes in magic but bite my tongue. She's not a descendent, just one's in-law. After she leaves, I pull up a search page on my phone about Brume and the Quatrefoil. If I'm going to be sitting here alone, might as well make the most of it. I'm scanning the webpage when the chair across from me scrapes against the brick-red tiles.

"I got bored drinking alone." Slate sets down his goblet of . . .

I sniff the air but have trouble smelling anything over his spicy fragrance. "What are you drinking?"

"*Chouchen.*" He drops his coat on the back of his chair.

"Huh."

"What does *huh*, mean?"

"That stuff will make you go cross-eyed."

"Hmm. Doesn't sound like such a bad fate right about now."

As he scoots his chair in, I hear a cringy voice say, "He's definitely not from around here." Adrien's girlfriend is sitting across the narrow dining room from us with two of her friends.

They're all seniors at the university, all pretty, all annoying, and all looking in Slate's direction. Charlotte catches my eye and shoots me a smile that really isn't one. She doesn't like me, even though

I'm not sure why. It's not like I'm much of a threat to her relationship with Adrien.

"Friends of yours?" Slate's angled his chair out, arm draped around the back rungs, gaze on the trio.

"Nope."

"Isn't the girl with the short hair your favorite professor's—"

"*Shh* . . . And he's not my favorite anything," I grumble as one of the girls flips her blonde hair over her shoulder, eating up Slate with her large, brown eyes.

He tips his goblet to her, then to his lips, and takes a lengthy swallow of Nolwenn's mead, his Adam's apple gliding up and down.

The blonde, whose name I can never remember—by choice—winks at him.

"If you'd rather go sit with them"—I shrug—"go right ahead."

"If I wanted to go sit with them, I'd do it." The wood creaks as Slate shifts in his chair. After a quiet beat, his voice rises over the cheery holiday tune, "So, I think I found a piece."

My gaze snaps to his face. "What?"

He stretches his fingers as though they were cramping. "Damn ring lit up like Rudolph's nose when I was close to the well. Not to mention, I got to experience all the pleasant symptoms your papa warned me about."

I blink. "You're kidding?"

"Sadly not."

"I thought they would take a while to reveal themselves."

"Apparently this one was in a hurry to be found."

"Let's go get it." I push my chair back and start to stand, but Slate claps his palm over my wrist to keep me in place, the red stone gleaming like an unblemished ruby.

"Slow down there, princess. First off, I'm in no state to leap down a thirty-meter pit filled with Satan knows what. And secondly, I want to check with Rainier if it's yours or mine."

"You think it could be mine?"

He removes his hand from my arm. "Wells are technically inside the earth."

"It's in the well?" My pulse skips and strums. "Let me call Papa."

"There are a lot of people around, Cadence." Slate's dark eyes don't stray off mine. "Ask him when you get home."

"But—"

"Take it from someone who treasure-hunts for a living—"

"Treasure-hunts?" I cock up an eyebrow. "*Really?*"

A smile leaps into his dark eyes. "A job well done is eighty percent preparation, twenty percent execution. Without careful planning, you set yourself up for failure."

I lean my forearms on the table. "Never thought I'd be taking advice from a crook."

His shoulder muscles bunch as he matches my posture, his forearms flopping heavily on the table. "Never thought I'd be sitting in a tavern in the middle of bumblefuck-nowhere across from a fifteen year-old librarian."

I jerk back. "Fifteen? I'm not fifteen!"

"Sorry. Sixteen."

"I'm *seventeen*." But he knows that. He heard Papa mention I was almost eighteen earlier.

Both corners of Slate's mouth curve up.

"You're such an ass," I mutter.

He chuckles.

Nolwenn arrives with my plate of cheese, a basket of sliced baguette, and a thick ceramic mug of tea. Both Slate and I lean back to make room on the table.

Slate's pushed the sleeves of his sweater up, and I see Nolwenn's eyes snag on a scar there. It's puckered and shiny, like a burn.

"Glad to see you're making friends, Marseille." Nolwenn's voice is softer than usual.

His eyes meet mine. "Yeah. Me, too."

"Cadence is like a granddaughter to me, so you be good to her."

"Yes, ma'am." He pinches a piece of goat cheese from my plate and sticks the white glob inside his mouth as Nolwenn leaves to tend to her other customers.

When he filches a second piece, I drag the plate closer to me. "Hey . . ."

"I might die in a few days."

"That's low."

"But true."

"Fine. Eat my dinner."

He smiles, and I think he says something, but I'm too distracted by the person who just walked into the tavern. Adrien unfastens his coat and looks around, his attention snagging on Charlotte, who's waving him over like one of those lucky Japanese cat figurines.

"What do you see in that guy?" Slate asks.

Cheeks flaming, I shush him. He's worse than Alma, and Alma is *not* subtle.

Adrien glances our way. *Dear God, please let him not have heard Slate.*

"He's just a close family friend," I mumble.

Slate splits a piece of baguette, squashes some goat cheese inside, adds a dried fig, then tosses his makeshift sandwich into his mouth. "Uh-huh," he says around a mouthful, before upending his goblet of *chouchen* and wiping his lips on the back of his hand.

As I mix some honey into my tea, I wrinkle my nose. "Where did you grow up? A pigsty?"

"A pigsty would've been one hell of an upgrade."

My spoon freezes as I realize how insensitive that was.

He snatches a piece of hard cheese, then scoots his chair back. "Anyway, I haven't slept in a few days, so I'm gonna go hit the sack."

I tilt my head up, guilt swarming me. "Slate . . . I didn't mean . . . that wasn't very nice of me." I bite my bottom lip.

"Don't sweat it, princess." Saluting me, he grabs his coat and heads toward the bar where he taps the varnished wood.

He's not seriously going to grab another drink? Hasn't he had enough?

My sight of him becomes obstructed by a pair of pressed trousers. I trail the legs up to an unbuttoned vest worn over a dress shirt and catch the tail end of Adrien's sentence.

" . . . just wanted to check on you after the *talk*."

"Oh. Um. I'm okay. Shocked but okay."

"Glad to hear it."

I crane my neck to see beyond him. Slate's no longer at the bar.

Adrien looks over his shoulder. "Did Roland just up and leave you?"

"He was tired."

"Still, that's not very chivalrous of him. Especially after everything he set in motion . . ." Adrien dips his freshly shaven chin into his neck.

I sigh. "I'm sure he regrets it more than anyone else. By the way"
—I lean forward and whisper—"apparently he located one of the
pieces. He's not sure if it's mine or his."

Adrien's hazel eyes widen. "And he went to retrieve it?"

"Not yet. Since we don't know whose it is . . ."

He sits in the chair Slate vacated. "Is it in water or on land?"

Out of the corner of my eye, I catch Charlotte frowning . . . or
rather scowling, and even though it shouldn't procure me any pleasure, it sort of does. She might not understand this now, but Adrien
and I have more in common than the two of them ever will.

"It's in the well." I relish being the sole recipient of his attention.

His pupils dilate as he absorbs the information. "If there's water
in the well, it's his. If the well's dry, I'd imagine it's yours. I'd check
with Rainier, though." He's silent for a beat. "I can't believe we're
really doing this."

"I know." Excitement and dread are going head-to-head
inside me.

We're going to bring magic back. Magic . . .

He reaches over and covers my hand with his, and my heart
migrates right into my fingers.

Adrien Mercier is holding my hand.

In public.

"Cadence, I know this must all be very thrilling to you, but you
need to remember that this isn't a game."

I pull my hand away. "Maman's dead, so I'm very much aware
that this isn't a game."

"Hey. Don't get mad."

"I'm not mad."

"You are."

"I'm not. And don't talk down to me. I may be younger than you,
Adrien, but I'm not a child."

"I know you're not a child. Would I let a kid teach my class?"

I press my lips tight.

His expression softens. "I'm just worried. Genuinely worried."

That unstaples my mouth.

"I care about you, Cadence. I care what happens to you. You're
the closest thing to a sister I have."

Sister? My heart freefalls right into my boots. Silly . . . so silly, but

I don't want Adrien to see me like that. I bob my head, because what else am I supposed to do? Tell him he's like family, too? He's not.

I pick pieces of cheese off my plate, stuffing them way too quickly into my cheeks. I must look like a hamster. Whatever. It's not like Adrien sees me as a woman anyway. As far as I'm concerned, rodent is a step above sister.

"Do you want to join us?" He tips his head toward Charlotte's table.

I'd rather jump in the well and get cursed by a magical leaf.

"I need to get home, but thanks," I add courteously, because that's how Papa raised me.

As Nolwenn passes by the table, I touch her sleeve. "Nolwenn, can I get the check?"

She smiles down at me. "It's already been taken care of." When I frown, she adds, "That boy . . . Marseille. He covered it. Left some extra in case you wanted something more to eat and drink. Do you want anything else? A crêpe, maybe? I'm good at those."

Slate paid for my meal? How . . . unexpected.

"Nothing else, thank you." I drain my tea and get up.

Adrien watches me zip up my coat. "You no longer have to replace me tomorrow, by the way."

The zipper whispers shut as I tug it all the way up, bumping the underside of my chin.

"Still need to go to class if I want to graduate someday," I say before arrowing toward the door. When I burst onto the cold street, my rapid breaths coalesce into a thick white cloud.

I study the well, then stride over to it and peer into the darkness beyond the grate. I can't tell what the bottom looks like, so I shine my phone, but the beam gets lost in the endless stretch of velvety black. I forage for a coin inside my pocket, find a heavy two-euro one. Hoping it doesn't activate any curses, I drop it in, then hold my breath as it tumbles.

And tumbles.

I'm still holding my breath when the coin connects with something and generates a distinctive splash.

Water.

I jump back, because if there's water, then it's Slate's piece. And if it's Slate's piece, then the leaf might not be too happy to be disturbed by someone who isn't meant to go after it.

Something sloshes. The blood in my veins?

I hear it again, and this time, I know it's not my blood, because it's accompanied by successive slaps, like waves against rocks. The water's either rising or something's moving around down below.

I stumble backward, then whirl around, slipping and going down so hard I think my kneecap cracks. I shove back up onto my feet, and even though my leg is screaming, I run like I've *never* run before. And I don't stop until I reach our front door even though I topple over twice more on the way.

When I get home, my palms are bleeding. I lock our door, smearing blood over the frame and metal deadbolt. "Papa!"

What have I done what have I done what have I done?

A door snicks open.

"Cadence?" my father yells, the rubber tires of his wheelchair squealing on the first floor landing. "What is it?"

My entire body shakes as I take the stairs two at a time.

"*Ma chérie*, what is it?"

Gulping down air, I tell him everything that's happened. It takes me several attempts to get all the words out, and God only knows how he understands any of my crazed rambling above my heavy panting.

He latches onto my palms, his complexion white as toothpaste. "Did you touch it?"

I shake my head, my ponytail flogging my cheeks, strands sticking to my skin that's coated in a mixture of sweat and tears.

I've never been so scared in my entire life. "Is it . . . is it . . . is it coming for me?"

"*Non, mon amour*. You're safe. I promise you're safe." He tugs on my arm until I fall into his lap. And then he hugs me and kisses my forehead. "*Ma Cadence*. Shh. You're safe."

I scrub my eyes with my sleeve. "What was it?"

He sighs. "The Quatrefoil only knows." But I sense, from the way the muscles in his arms have hardened, that he has some theories and that none of them are going to be comforting.

"Is it a monster?"

He pushes hair off my damp face. "I'm sure it's nothing more than the leaf trying to scare you away."

Is he telling me the truth? Do I even want to know the truth before sleeping? I swallow, my throat aching as violently as my knees. "Can I sleep in your room tonight, Papa?"

"*Bien sûr, ma chérie.*" He glances toward the front door, which looks like the entrance to a crime scene.

"You promise it's not coming for me?"

"I promise. It's not how the pieces work. They only protect themselves. They don't chase you."

I breathe in deeply, but it mustn't be deep enough because my lungs are still tight after my hot shower, and my pulse still gallops when I dive under Papa's bed covers and drag them all the way to my nose.

15

SLATE

I reach across the bed for Cadence, wanting to feel the heat of her soft skin underneath my fingertips. It's only when my hand brushes against empty spun-cotton sheets and flops over the edge of the puny mattress that I wake up and realize she's not here. That she never was.

I inhale deeply. Her smell is everywhere . . . on the sheets, on the goose-down pillow. Powdery and fresh, with a hint of something floral and fruity. It takes over my entire freaking mind. *Shit.* Now I need a cold shower.

Grabbing a towel and the soap, I shuffle out of my bedroom and down the weakly lit hallway that's lined with three more numbered doors to the one that bears the sign TOILETTES HOMMES.

As the old plumbing creaks to life, I step under the stinging spray and pop the top off the soap Cadence gave me. A flash of her half-open mouth flares behind my lids. Damn sheets. Sniffing them all night must've locked Rainier's daughter inside my brain the same way the Bloodstone sealed her mother's ring to my finger. I stare at the stone, which is the same shade as Cadence's lips, and grumble insults at it under my breath.

Because I can't get her mouth out of my stupid head, I spin the hot water knob off until icy needles batter my chest, then grit my teeth to avoid squealing like a baby as my skin brightens and burns. Sluggishly, my mind finally clears. Only then do I spin the hot water knob back as far as it will go. It takes forever to heat up. I scrub my skin hard with the soap, the thick white lather streaming down my legs and around my feet. I notice that one of my toes is purple, the same shade as my finger. Brume isn't good to my extremities.

When I step out of the old enamel stall, I almost regret not air-drying, because the towel I've wrapped around my waist smells like Cadence. Not that air-drying would have been an option considering I'm no longer alone.

A guy's brushing his teeth, while another one's standing at the urinals. I miss my gargantuan bathroom back in Marseille, possibly more than I miss my brother and cactus, not necessarily in that order.

The guys and I nod to each other in that stiff way one uses when half-naked and among strangers.

The redhead spits toothpaste into the sink. "You're new to the university?"

Will I ever attend classes? Who the hell knows. I look at my reflection and see the lump on my forehead, feel the throbbing in my toe and finger. Right now, I just need to survive until the middle of the month.

And to think I haven't gotten to the perilous bit yet.

I shrug as I finger-comb my black mop. "Guess so."

"Cool." The guy bobs his head and wipes his face with a hand towel.

"You should take Mademoiselle Claire's class," the blond at the urinal says.

"What does she teach?" I ask.

"Astronomy." Carrot-top grins. "But that's not the reason Liron takes her class."

"We all got our vices, Paul. At least, mine's legal." Liron's voice resonates against the grimy tiles.

"But you got to admit, my vice has the best ass in Brume. And lips. God, her lips." I can tell he's picturing them on his body. Dude needs to get laid.

Liron zips himself up. "Your *vice* is also related to the dean, Paul."

I freeze with my fingers shoved halfway through my hair. "Are you talking about Cadence de Morel?"

Carrot-top's ears go red. "Um . . . yeah?"

Rage barrels through me, and before I can even think, I shove Paul against the scummy wall.

"Hey!" Liron shouts. "What the hell's wrong with you?"

I check myself and peel my hands off Paul's flushed skin. "Cadence is a human being. Not a piece of ass with great lips. Show her some goddamn respect," I say, before limping out of the bathroom and toward door number three. Sure, I'm a giant hypocrite, but Cadence doesn't deserve to be talked about like Grade A meat.

There's an envelope taped to my door. The last envelope I received sent me to Brume. Logic tells me this can't be worse, but my stomach still tilts. I slide a finger under the flap, pull out the paper, and scoff. A welcome and reminder to confirm my class schedule online. *Yeah. Whatever.* I ball up the paper and chuck it into the wastebasket on the other side of the bed. Three points.

I don't know if I'm going to need a scuba suit or a miner's helmet for the well, but considering I own neither, I dress in black jeans, a white button-down, and my scuffed boots. My plan for the morning is to head back to the square to get a better look at what I might be facing, and then stop by De Morel's manor to squeeze every last ounce of knowledge from the old man's brain and confirm if it is, in fact, my piece.

I punch my arms through the sleeves of my coat. In the dim light, the Bloodstone looks black as a bullet wound. I'm still studying the ring when I open my door and feel a fist knock against my pec.

I look at the owner of the fist and can't help smiling.

Cadence jumps and trips. I reach out and catch her arm. Her puffy sleeve is cool under my touch and dispenses a whiff of her scent. I groan without meaning to.

Get it together, Slate.

Her brows fly up under her pearl-gray beanie, and the furry pompom on top flutters. "Your finger!" She sounds almost panicked as she gazes to the hand still cinched around her bicep.

I release her. "What?"

"You groaned."

"I'm pretty sure I made no such sound."

Her eyebrows dip. "It was either you or the hinges on your door."

"Definitely the hinges." I stretch out my digits. "The finger's feeling loads better." *Not.* But there's no way I'm letting Cadence believe that moan came from me.

A door slams shut down the hallway, then a key jingles.

Cadence and I both turn. When I catch a glint of copper, my shoulder blades tighten. Cadence shoots the boy a smile.

His steps falter. "Ca-cadence, good morning."

"Hi, Paul."

He looks from me to her and back again, freckles melting into his blush. He's a dick, but at least, he's a perceptive one, because he power-walks by us, muttering, "Don't want to be late for class."

He glances back once; I glower. He almost stumbles down the stairs, steadying himself on the weathered banister.

When we're alone again, I check my Rolex for the time—7:30 a.m. "What brings you to my door at the crack of dawn, Mademoiselle de Morel?"

She drags her front teeth over her perky bottom lip, and *putain,* I need another shower.

"Last night, I threw a coin into the well, and it hit water." She frees her lip, and it glistens. I must be sporting one hell of a blank stare, because she adds, "Which means it's your piece."

I clear my throat. "Right. I assumed as much."

"Anyway, after I tossed my coin"—color leaches from her skin— "there was splashing."

I lean against my doorframe and cross my arms. "That's usually what happens when something solid meets something liquid."

She regains a little color and shakes her head. "There was *a lot* of splashing. Like there was something down there."

My vertebrae bolt together until my spine feels more steel rod than flexible bone.

"And then this morning, on my way over, I passed by the square, and it's . . ." She swallows.

I push off the doorframe, my pulse going from zero to a hundred. "Don't leave me hanging. It's what?"

"Just . . . come." She heads down the rickety stairs and opens the front door.

What the hell am I in for? "If there's a monster eel out there—"

One corner of her absurdly fascinating mouth curls up. "Here I thought you were brave."

The challenge in her voice combined with her half-smile injects something into my veins. I wouldn't go so far as to call it courage, but something strong enough to make me lock my door and pound down the stairs.

I grab the edge of the front door and draw it wider. "Smart mouth."

She levels me with a smile that cordons the blood off from my head and limbs.

Her mouth moves, and it takes my starved brain a moment to make sense of her words. "Did you manage to sleep? You look . . . dazed."

I grip the collar of my coat, tightening it so no cold air seeps in. "I slept quite well actually. Had some real pleasant dreams."

"That's good."

The sky's black as pitch. Even so, people are up and about, rushing off to their workplace or heading to the university buildings for early classes. No one looks particularly spritely. My guess is half of them are still recovering from New Year's Eve.

"And you?"

She shakes her head no.

I'm imagining it was our imminent game of *capture-the-cursed-leaves-before-Slate-croaks* that kept her up. "What's the deal with school starting back up so early here? Back in Marseille, classes are out until the middle of the month."

"Brume runs on a slightly different calendar than the rest of French schools. A lunar one. We start classes on the full moon."

"For all the werewolf students?" I stage-whisper.

She lets out a cute snort. "Werewolves aren't real."

"Are you sure?"

She slows her pace a little, her gaze running over the ice crystallizing the wooden shutters of the stone houses. "There's no mention of lycanthropy in the history books."

"And in books, we trust."

Instead of calling me up on my derision, Cadence becomes pensive.

"So, why do classes start on the full moon?"

Even though her mind seems a mile away—in the library meat-locker to be precise—she says, "Full moons are conducive to learning. It supposedly makes everything clearer, more powerful. Even spells."

"Is that in the university handbook?"

"Just part of the local lore." Her eyes lose focus for a second, and I imagine she's thinking how everything she once considered lore is now up for reinterpretation.

"So then, why do we need to get the pieces together by the *new* moon?"

"Because the new moon is for new beginnings."

Or crap endings.

The sinuous street turns upon itself, and we suddenly find ourselves at the edge of the town square, which is lit up like an airport runway. Besides the strings of twinkling lights and glowing window panes, there's a large spotlight focused on the well. Four tall guys in shiny helmets and navy coats with *Sapeurs Pompiers* emblazoned across the back are fencing off the area with yellow tape and shooing away curious bystanders.

It takes me a moment to understand why they're here . . . the square has transformed into a skating rink. An inch-thick layer of ice coats the cobbles.

"The water overflowed." Cadence points to the frozen cascade rimming the side of the well.

"Whoa." I wonder if the water is frozen only on top. Maybe I'll need to ice-fish for my piece. And how the hell am I going to get into the well with the fire department blocking the damn thing?

The low chatter of rubberneckers is the only sound in the square. Then, all of a sudden, a high-pitched keening fills the air. Like an animal in pain.

An angry animal in pain.

A giant, angry animal in pain.

Cadence and I both slap our hands against our ears, but the curious lurkers don't even flinch. Did no one else hear what sounded like an orca being slaughtered while calving?

When one of the firemen lumbers toward the well, Cadence presses a fist to her mouth, eyes flaring with terror. "He'll get cursed. Or killed."

"He's just looking." My voice is calm, but Cadence's worry makes my gut twist.

She shakes her head, staring wildly around the square. "We've got to do something. Where are Adrien and Gaëlle? I called them over twenty minutes ago. Adrien will know what to do."

At the mention of Adrien's name, I clench my hands into fists. I don't check Cadence's eyes for hearts and stars, but I bet they're in there, popping right out of her pupils. She thinks her beloved professor is some sort of superman. Super Douche is more like it, or Professor Prickhead.

Professor Prickhead. The right side of my mouth tilts. I like that.

The keening intensifies as the firefighter reaches the well. I'm guessing he's heard it.

Cadence bounces on the balls of her feet. When she says, "Oh, hell," and takes a step onto the ice, I shoot my arm out to block her.

"Don't," I say.

"Slate, he's going to . . ."

I don't hear the end of her sentence over the rushing in my ears. I back up several feet to get a running start, then dive under the yellow tape, skidding across the square on my belly like a seal, whooping and hollering the whole time.

It's not my finest moment, but it distracts the firefighter, who turns away from the well and swears, then swears some more as other idiots follow my lead and pull their own little skating stunts. There is no better distraction than mass stupidity and no better crowd for it than college students.

Now the square is like a spoof of *Disney on Ice*. One dude barrels into the firefighter clomping toward me, bowling him over. Two other firefighters are busy trying to push back a guy who's spinning like a top and another who stands and falls, stands and falls.

Stomach numb with cold, I do the breast-stroke until I reach the base of the well—can't fall when you're already down. The frozen waterfall is a suspicious shade of urine that makes my nostrils flare. It smells cold and tinny, but ice cloaks smells. Even noxious ones. Hoping the rusty grate tinted the water, and it's not sewer overflow, I grip one of the yellowish bulbous layers and pull myself up. The lug-soles of my boots slip like they're buttered, and I land face down once again, whacking my forehead, right on my goose egg.

Putain de merde. I hate Brume.

More than I hated it last night, but probably not as much as I'm going to hate this fucking town when I go ice-pick-crazy on the enchanted well. It doesn't help that every single atom in my body stings and burns, and a creepy tingling sensation slithers up my spine. I grit my teeth and do my best to ignore the pain.

At least the animal cries have stopped.

Silver linings.

Glancing back toward Cadence, I find Professor Prickhead and Gaëlle bracketing her. They're deep in discussion, but all three have their eyes on me and my pathetic progress.

I tow my sore body upright and manage to stay vertical this time. Before I can slip again, I reach over and grab one of the wooden posts holding up the pointed gazebo-roof thing. The spot-light the fire department has set up is bright as shit and nearly blinds me as I shift position to look down into the well at the amber water.

Behind me, it's all laughter and shouting, the idiot college students still keeping the firefighters busy. But here at the well, it's eerily quiet and still.

I lean further over the opening, the frozen cascade and glacial stones pressing into my ribs, and squint to see past the grate. A bubble forms under the ice and pops. Then suddenly, instead of my reflection, I see a woman's face. A familiar face. Her eyes are closed, her lashes so long they caress her cheekbones. Her skin has a pearly shine to it, and her cherry lips look as moist and luscious as the fruit. A cloud of caramel-brown hair floats around her.

The pain in my limbs melts away, and I feel woozy and warm, like I've just swallowed a glass of cognac. Or three.

I twist my hand around the post, the spotlight catching on the Bloodstone. A ruby-red beam streaks over the well water.

The woman's eyes open to reveal pale-blue irises. She blinks, and then her lashes hit her browbone, the blue now surrounded in white. Pale fingers slide through the grate and grip it. Her mouth opens in a terrible scream.

Cadence.

Fucking hell, it's Cadence! She's trapped. And she's drowning.

But wait . . .

That's impossible.

I whip my head to where Cadence stood only moments ago.

She's no longer there.

I frantically search the crowd for her long hair. Her silver jacket. Her fuzzy pompom. But she's fucking nowhere.

Oh, Jesus, no. No, no, no.

The warm feeling in my veins is replaced by a cold blade of fear and adrenaline.

This must be my test. Magic locked her inside to motivate me to dive in. I'll get her out. I'll rip this damn well apart stone by stone if I have to.

I punch at the ice with my right hand. Again and again. I smash through the frozen crust over the grate, the ring acting like a fucking hammer. The first layer becomes white dust. I brush it away. Find Cadence thrashing, knuckles white, lips parted around my name.

I shatter more ice until I reach the grate. The frozen metal is brittle and three of the rusty bars snap. I tug on them, bending them backward like the fingers on the last guy who tried to screw me over back in Marseille. There's enough room to shove my arm through, but not my body, or hers.

Cadence's pale fingers twine through mine but then slip.

16

CADENCE

I gasp and almost fall, and not because of the ice. Thankfully, Adrien's solid hold on the table we're carting out of the tavern to stick atop the well doesn't falter.

Slate's just smacked Gaëlle, sending her flying backward, her yellow scarf streaming like a ribbon in the dawn-tinted air. She lands on the ice, missing one of the wooden beams that holds the pointed roof by a centimeter, maybe less.

"*Merde*," Adrien mutters as Slate, whose coat sleeve is drenched, reaches into the well again.

When Adrien drops his end of the table, I almost go down, but my soles grip the ice.

"Slide the table, Cadence!" He takes off, half-skating half-flailing toward the well. When he reaches it, he hisses Slate's name, but that doesn't even break his concentration. Adrien reels his arm back and lets his fist fly into the inside of Slate's elbow, forcing it to bend.

Slate's entire body jerks, including his gaze, which gleams ferociously in the firefighters' bright beam. He snatches his hand out of the well and pulls his arm back so fast it blurs. His fist comes flying at Adrien's jaw.

Shoving the table on the ice as though it's a hockey puck, I scream Slate's name.

He freezes and looks over at me. His eyes go wide, and he blinks. At me, then at the well, then back at me.

"Keep talking to him, Cadence," Adrien yells.

"Want to grab breakfast with me at the tavern?" I shout, slowly sliding the table closer. Almost there.

Sloshing followed by a heartbreaking cry for help make both Slate and me turn to the well. Gaëlle, who's back on her feet, pushes in front of Slate, and her face blanches. And then she's reaching into the well, but Adrien seizes her wrist right before it can vanish over the stone lip.

"Look away, Gaëlle," he hisses.

She shuts her eyes and winces when the cry for help echoes against the peaked wooden roof sheltering the well. The voice is deep and familiar. So familiar it raises goose bumps over my arms.

My hands slip off the legs of the table. "Papa?"

Fingertips topped with buffed, blunt nails poke out from the well.

Oh my God.

Papa is in the well! I slip and slide toward it.

"It's not real, Cadence." Adrien's heated whisper makes me skid to a stop. "And don't look into the well." He turns to the others. "All of you, look away!"

I snap my gaze to the frosted ground. Adrien pushes the table forward, then flips it right-side-up so that its legs straddle the round opening. Tapping begins and then scratching. Adrien flattens his palms against the tabletop to keep it in place.

One of the firefighters shoos a student off the ice and lumbers toward us. "Monsieur Mercier, you really think a *bouchon en bois* will prevent the well from overflowing?"

"Yes, I believe a wooden cork will do the job." Adrien's brow glistens with sweat. "For the time being, at least."

"I realize you're trying to help but—"

Adrien shifts to lean his right forearm on the table and fishes his phone from his pocket with his left. "Actually, it's my father and Rainier de Morel who gave me instructions to cover the well. If you'd like to speak to either one of them directly, I'll give them a call."

"No need." The fireman zips his lips shut.

"Would you have anything heavy to put on top?" Adrien asks.

Whatever's in there scratches again and yelps a muffled *help*.

I expect the fireman to rip the table off, but instead, he says, "I'll go find something to weigh it down." His cleated boots grip the slippery ground as he trudges toward his squad.

Adrien must notice my surprise because he whispers, "The piece only calls to the four of us."

I stare at his face and notice it's streaked with blood, but I'm too perplexed by what he's just said to comment on it. "The piece?"

"Yes. It's the piece that's trying to lure you in by sounding and looking like someone you'd do anything to save."

Slate's rough breathing becomes suspended.

"That's why I heard Papa," I murmur.

Adrien nods.

"And me, Romain." Gaëlle rubs her cheek, still red from Slate's slap.

Slate doesn't volunteer who he saw. Not that it matters. His hands are locked into tight fists at his sides. His knuckles are cracked, and blood streams off his fingers and into the ice, staining it crimson.

I gasp. "You're bleeding!" I grab onto his hand, but he tears it away and backs up, letting out a snarl that sounds a lot like the one we heard earlier. His black curls are matted with perspiration and cling to his slick forehead, and his chest is rising and falling quickly again.

"He's probably still in shock, Cadence. Especially since he touched *it*," Adrien adds in a whisper.

Juda emerges from the tavern and tromps over to us, his white hair flapping in the cool breeze, his skin flushed red from the weight of the giant soup pot cradled in his arms. "Heard you needed something heavy. If you fill this old thing with water, not even gale force wind will be able to shift it."

Adrien asks a fireman to fetch a hose from his electric utility vehicle. The man hooks one end to a fire hydrant on the edge of the square and drags the nozzle all the way toward the well.

Once the pot overflows, Adrien turns to the tavern's bearded owner. "Get back inside. You're going to get sick, Juda."

Juda casts a long look at the well before catching sight of his

OF WICKED BLOOD | 133

daughter-in-law. He sucks in a breath. "What happened to your cheek?"

Gaëlle shakes her head. "It's nothing. Just slipped and bumped it on the post."

He purses his lips but walks back toward Nolwenn, who's standing by the entrance, bundled in a thick down jacket that reaches her slippered feet.

Profound worry bleeds into her maze of wrinkles. "Come inside, all of you. I'll steep some tea and put on a pot of coffee."

"In a second, Nolwenn." Adrien's dark-blond hair isn't as neat as usual, which lends him a slightly rugged edge. A heroic one.

In fact, he *is* a hero. He's just saved Slate, Gaëlle, *and* me from the dark magic of the Quatrefoil.

He turns to the fireman. "Can you make sure no one removes this?"

"*Bien sûr.* We'll take shifts."

Adrien pats the man's arm. "You're a good man, Francis. *Merci.*"

"Just doing my job, Monsieur Mercier."

Adrien rubs his hands together, probably to drag warmth back into them, then tilts his head toward the tavern door. "We're done here. Come on."

Gaëlle loops her slender arm through mine, and we begin to trek across the rink. When I hear Adrien call out to Slate, I glance over my shoulder. He's as rigid as my mother's bronze bonsai, but his eyes aren't glassy, which reassures me that he's alert and not lost in some nightmare.

"*Allez-y.* We'll catch up," Adrien says. When I don't move, even though Gaëlle's tugging on my arm, he adds, "I promise I won't leave him out here alone." A gentle smile buffets the apprehension crinkling his eyes and grooving his forehead.

Inhaling a long, icy breath that scorches my lungs, I turn around and pad cautiously across the ice. Gaëlle slips more than once in her shearling boots, and I hold her up. This morning is a preview of the support we're all going to have to give each other.

17

SLATE

Every breath was a blade slicing through my lungs. I couldn't hear a thing over my pounding pulse, couldn't see a thing either. My vision wobbled. The square, the crowd, the well—they all went in and out of focus like a bunch of strobe lights. But then I saw Cadence, her face a horrified shade of white, and everything stopped.

Cadence.

The real Cadence.

Not the twisted magical one that duped me as though I was some naïve kid.

With my eyes, I trail her treacherous hike into the tavern, arm in arm with Gaëlle. Gaëlle, who's cradling a hand over her reddened cheek.

Shame burns me like hot oil.

I hit Gaëlle. I've *never* hit a woman. Ever.

I didn't even realize what I was doing. I was trying to reach Cadence's writhing fingers when I felt a yank on my shoulder and reacted on instinct. It was only after I hit Adrien, and after Cadence —the real Cadence—called out my name that I saw Gaëlle's face and made the connection.

I'm a goddamned idiot. On all accounts.

Now, Adrien's coming toward me, each step careful and slow on the ice, hands out and head tilted in a nonthreatening manner like I'm a rabid dog who needs calming. "Hey, Roland. You okay?"

I skate toward the other side of the square, trailing scarlet droplets. My knuckles look like they've been through a meat grinder. But the ring's unscathed.

I reach the edge of the provisional rink and step into a narrow street. I have no idea where I'm going. I don't care.

I just need to walk and get my head together. Is that even a possibility anymore?

18

CADENCE

I draw open the heavy velvet curtain protecting the tavern from the bone-cold chill of winter. The restaurant smells like early mornings—dark coffee, bergamot tea, sweet citrus, and browning bread.

The moment the curtain falls back in place, Nolwenn's there, gasping and wrapping her arms around Gaëlle. "Your face!"

Gaëlle grimaces. "It's nothing, Nolwenn."

Nolwenn frowns like she doesn't believe her daughter-in-law. "You two go sit. I'll press some oranges. Then we can talk." She tips her head toward the oval table by the window. A coffeepot, two baskets filled with pastries and toast, and a saucer of home-churned salted butter are laid out beside a stack of plates, gingham napkins, and scratched cutlery.

"Does she know about . . . the hunt?" I whisper to Gaëlle.

Her eyeballs move from left to right, and she raises a finger to her lips. I'm guessing that's a no.

"Tell me about Slate," she says, probably to change the subject.

I unzip my jacket and pull off my hat. "Not sure what to tell you. I only just met him."

"I heard he was in foster care, but does he have friends? Did he come to Brume alone?"

I stuff my hat into the arm of my coat and drape it over the back of one of the chairs. "He's not exactly the most open person." Not that I've asked him about his life before Brume. I wasn't feeling particularly friendly because of the whole crypt-desecration episode. "But I'm pretty sure he came alone."

"So, no friends? No girlfriend?"

"I—" Does Slate have a girlfriend? He's such a flirt that I don't think so, but what do I know? He didn't kiss me on New Year's. What if it was because he didn't want to cheat on someone instead of his make-your-own-luck excuse? "He must have *some* friends back home. Why do you ask?"

"Just to get a better sense of the person we're working with. He seems like such a . . . *wild* boy."

"Didn't Papa tell you about him?"

"Your papa told me not to worry about anything. That he had everything handled. And between Romain, the twins, and the shop, when someone tells me not to concern myself with something, I don't." She rubs her cheek again, and I notice there's still blood on it, but it mustn't be hers because she has no cuts.

"There's some blood on your temple."

She wrinkles her nose and grabs a napkin, spits on it, then scours her skin. "Is it gone?"

I nod but notice a yellowish-green mark has bloomed along her cheekbone. "You're going to have one heck of a bruise."

"Doesn't surprise me. He hit me with the Bloodstone. That thing's harder than a diamond."

Can Nolwenn hear us? Probably not over the whir of the juicer.

Gaëlle unloops her yellow scarf. "I still can't believe we're actually doing this."

"You're telling me? I didn't even know *this* was real."

Her lips press into a repentant smile. "I advised Rainier to tell you years ago." She pours herself a mug of coffee and fishes a *pain au chocolat* from the basket.

"I wish he had." I take a thick croissant and plop it onto a plate, my stomach making as much noise as the thing in the well.

I look through the window toward it, expecting to see Adrien and Slate still standing out there, but find only a lone fireman beside the massive pot. Even the bystanders have dispersed, probably heading back to bed or classes.

"What did you mean by *wild boy*?"

"Slate doesn't strike me as someone who trusts easily, and for this to work, we're going to have to rely on each other implicitly."

"It'll probably take him time. I've known you and Adrien since I was born; we're all strangers to him."

"We don't *have* time," she hisses.

A chill envelops me, almost as violent as the one that rocketed up my spine last night after I tossed a coin inside the well, and I knock my knee into the table leg. The contact reawakens the plum-colored bruise.

The velvet curtain hedging the entrance shifts, and I think it's them. Hope it's them. But it's not.

"Oh . . . my . . . God . . . it's insane out there." Alma pulls off her coat and mittens and trots over to us in thigh-high heeled boots that she's paired with black leggings and a thick sweater with a slanted hem.

Her outfit makes mine look so stiff and bland. Not that my sense of fashion is of great importance at the moment.

She drops into the chair beside mine, pushing her strawberry-blonde curls back and filling a mug with coffee. "You think some underground pipe burst or is it because of global warming?"

"Global warming?" Gaëlle asks.

"You know"—Alma flaps a small packet of sugar, then tears the top, and pours it into her coffee—"ice caps melting and all?"

"It's a pipe," I lie.

Alma shakes her head. "*Incroyable.*"

"How come you're up so early?"

"Class is in ninety minutes, and I thought you'd want to practice your lesson."

My . . .? *Oh, right.* I squeeze her hand for being so thoughtful. "Adrien ended up staying, so he'll be teaching it." Where was he anyway? "Didn't you see him out there?"

"Nope. Just a couple of hot firemen." She looks past my shoulder and out the window. "I mean, did you see the size of that one?" She tips her head to the uniformed man guarding the well. "He's a little old for me but perfect for you, Gaëlle." Alma waggles her eyebrows.

Gaëlle coughs, as though her bite of *pain au chocolat* went down the wrong pipe. "I have enough men in my life."

I don't really know what happened with her ex-husband—is he even her ex? All I know is that he's not a good man. I mean, who up and leaves a woman with his son from a previous marriage and twins on the way? Someone with *zero* morals.

"But they're all under the age of fifteen," Alma points out.

Gaëlle's still clearing her airway, eyes so round I almost spring out of my chair. Instead, I grab a glass and fill it with water for her.

She downs it in one long swallow. "Imagine . . . death-by-pastry-flake." She shoots us a watery smile. "The ultimate embarrassment for my boys."

"You could put a spell on the next man," one-track-minded Alma suggests.

"What?" Gaëlle wheezes.

"Mix up some eye of newt with a dragonfly heart and a tube of superglue to bind your next lover to you." Alma winks to show she's teasing, but knowing my friend's passion for all that is mystical, I sense she's only half-joking. "If only potions were real."

"Maybe they are." Nolwenn sets down a carafe brimming with orange juice and a platter of creamy scrambled eggs she must've just fetched from the kitchen, because a ribbon of steam twirls off the top. "Maybe Gaëlle's a real witch."

Alma smiles. But I don't, because Nolwenn's tone isn't playful. It's solemn, like she actually believes this could be true.

I sit up a little straighter. "Do *you* believe in magic, Nolwenn?"

As she pulls out a chair to join us, she arches an overplucked eyebrow. "Doesn't everyone in Brume?"

Gaëlle scoots out her chair as though the table were digging into her abdomen. "I'm no witch, Alma, but I believe in the power of the mind over our circumstances. Have you ever heard of *la poudre de Perlimpinpin*?"

Alma pops an eyebrow up. "The miraculous cure for all ailments that was nothing more than dirt or oil or something?"

Gaëlle nods slowly. "That's right."

Nolwenn waves a hand. "I contest. What you sell is *not* snake oil. You use real ingredients in your potions and poultices. Sure, they don't miraculously melt pounds or give eternal youth, but I've used your butterbur migraine aid, and it works. I no longer have to spend an entire day in a dark room with a belt tied around my skull."

Gaëlle's complexion brightens from the compliment.

"So, maybe you are a bit of a witch"—Nolwenn pours some milk into her coffee and stirs—"just like your ancestors."

For a moment, the only sound in the tavern is her spoon clinking against porcelain.

She blows on the top, sending the sweet, charred steam into her daughter-in-law's face. "Just like Cadence's maternal ancestors. And Adrien's." She sets her brown gaze on mine. "And Marseille's."

The knot in my stomach, which had begun to loosen, tightens anew.

Alma frowns. "Marseille?"

"The handsome boy with the black hair."

"You mean, Slate?" Alma asks.

"Is that his name?" Nolwenn asks, sipping her coffee. "I couldn't remember."

But I think that's a lie. Nolwenn seems to know an awful lot. Does her knowledge of Brume bloodlines stem from serving alcohol that loosens tongues or from having witnessed the previous generation's hunt?

My gaze releases hers to trace the quatrefoil motif beneath my feet. Brume lore is everywhere. In every cobble and tile. In every stone and plank. In the earth and in the trees.

"Some even believe that the symbol on my floor is based on a real artifact that, if found, could restore magic to Brume. To the entire world."

I whip my gaze back up to hers.

"Wouldn't that be *so* cool?" Alma chirps, sloshing orange juice into her glass.

I force myself not to look over at Gaëlle when I ask, "Do you believe the Quatrefoil exists, Nolwenn?"

A long swallow of coffee makes the older woman's throat contract. "Yes. But I think it's the source of all evil and should be left alone."

Panic flashes across Gaëlle's features. Is she worried Nolwenn might try to stop us?

In a tone too serious to be a joke, her mother-in-law adds, "Remember what happened to Pandora when she opened her box."

Curses escaped and damned the world.

The heavy velvet curtain shifts again, inviting in the icy morning and dragging away Nolwenn's unsettling gaze.

She sighs and rises. "Work beckons." She puts a hand on Gaëlle's shoulder. "The boys are all set for the day?"

"Twins are at daycare, and Romain's spending some extra time in the arms of Morpheus. I swear, that boy's been sleeping thirteen-hour nights *every* night."

"He's growing. Juda had to bang pots to get Matthias out of bed when he was an adolescent."

The mention of Matthias has Gaëlle tugging on a long spiraling lock. "I should . . . should go." She pushes her chair back brusquely and starts winding up her scarf. "Fill in Rainier. About the well."

Alma frowns as both Nolwenn and Gaëlle depart. "Well, that was . . . *weird*."

Understatement of the year. Then again, the year's two days' old.

"Oh my God!" She slaps her palm over her mouth.

"What?"

"She's having an affair with your dad!" Her exclamation is thankfully muffled by her palm.

"What?" We were discussing magic and curses, and this is what came to her? "No."

Alma nods, lowering her hand and wrapping her fingers around her juice glass. "She *so* is. Seriously, she's *always* coming over to your house. And did you see her face when Sylvie kissed your papa on New Year's?"

"Nothing romantic is going on between them," I say, defensively now. I don't want Alma spreading rumors of an affair.

"Maybe that's why her husband left. Maybe the twins are your half-brothers."

"Alma, stop!" I scrape my chair back so hard the wooden feet clack across the tiles.

She shuts up. But then, because her lips are incapable of staying closed, she adds, "Why are you getting so annoyed? You love Gaëlle."

"I'm annoyed because it isn't true."

"Are you sure? She didn't even glance at that fireman . . ."

"I can't do this right now. Have this nonsensical conversation when there are so many real and *important* matters to worry about." I get up and pluck my coat off the chair. "I'll call you later." I ram my arms through the sleeves, but one gets stuck. I wrench my hat out, then jam it on my head, stick my coat on, and stalk out of the tavern.

I glare at the well, anger simmering beneath my skin. I'm so angry I want to knock over the giant soup pot. My father is not having an affair with a woman over a decade younger than him, and the twins aren't my siblings. He wouldn't do such a thing. Matthias was his friend.

I stomp down the stairs to First Kelc'h. My feet carry me to the cemetery, to Maman before I remember I haven't called the groundskeeper yet. I almost turn around, especially when I notice the door of our crypt is closed. I inch closer and push the door open a crack. I blink, press it wider. The stone lid's been placed back on top of the sarcophagus, the other coffins all have lids, and the bottle of wine no longer litters the floor. Papa must've contacted the custodian himself.

I'm so grateful because I couldn't have stomached another glimpse of my mother. Plus, that he took care of this shows he thought of her. That he hasn't replaced her with another woman. That he still loves her.

I shake my head, trying to wring Alma's words out of my mind, but they cling like the fog obscuring my view of the manor. I'm tempted to stomp over and check that all Gaëlle and Papa are doing is talking, but that would mean I'm harboring doubts.

Besides, I have way more pressing matters to worry about.

Like saving Slate.

Where is he anyway?

19

SLATE

A drien's like a giant burr. He stopped trying to talk to me a while ago but hasn't stopped trailing me.

"Don't you have a class to teach, Prof?"

"Not for another hour and a half."

We go another fifteen minutes without talking. I don't even know where I am on the hill. All I know is that I'm still in Brume, and I know this because I have a ring that won't let me escape this freezing hole that's turned me into the shittiest version of myself.

I arrive in front of a set of vertiginous stairs. Unlike the staggered sets of stairs between each *kelc'h*, this particular set goes on for eternity. It leads directly down to the lake. The sun's just coming up, so there's enough light for me to make out the smoking waterline through a break in the cracked ramparts below.

Gripping the icy metal rail, I start the descent, each step reverberating through my body like cymbals in a brass band. My boot slips on a patch of ice, and I almost go down.

"Roland!" Professor Prickhead jogs two steps below me and readies his hands to catch me like I'm an octogenarian with a bad hip. "Careful, there."

I can't even imagine what I must look like for him to do that.

My head aches. My toe smarts. My fingers throb. My knuckles sting. And my elbow . . . I clench my jaw.

What really hurts, though, is my pride.

"Just leave me alone," I grumble.

"Can't. I promised the others I would stick with you."

"I don't need a babysitter, all right?"

"Look, we need to discuss what happened back there. And I can't let you go off on your own half-cocked—"

"Thanks for the concern, Prof, but I'm not going off *half-cocked*. I was on my way to the lake." A lie. I had no damn clue this led downward, although maybe water calls to my blood, what with it being my element and all. I can't fucking believe I have an element. "I need to think and seeing the water helps."

"Okay. Okay. If you really want to see the lake, I've got a better idea." He points to a painted wooden door set into the stone wall back at the top of the stairs.

I would go down the trillion steps just to spite Adrien. I *want* to go down them to spite him. But there's a real possibility that, in my current state, I'll keel over and split my head open. Wherever that door leads seems like a safer option.

"Fine," I mutter, trudging back up the three steps I've already taken.

The door opens onto a garden terrace. Instead of flowers and shrubs, scraggly sticks poke out of windblown mounds of snow. A dirty path of footprints leads to three green benches that face out over the edge of the ramparts and onto the fog-cloaked lake.

Though it's a water view, it's nothing like the one from my apartment. There, everything is drenched in color, from the cerulean of the sea to the ochre wash of the buildings to the glowing halo of the sun. Here, it's all in grayscale—a placid steel pool, ashen sky, cottony smog, leaden fortifications. Even so, staring down at what I can see of the liquid expanse makes me feel more at home than I've felt since stepping foot in this fucked-up town.

Adrien tugs at his wool overcoat and settles on the first bench. I stay standing, knees locked and arms crossed.

He pats the lacquered wood. "Have a seat, Roland."

"I'm good." I'm not; I'm just not sure my joints can fold. My body feels stiff and achy, the tinman in need of an oiling. And by that, I mean I need a drink. And yes, I know it's eight in the morning, but my life sucks that hard.

Adrien lifts an eyebrow. "You don't look too hot."

I snort.

"Which is normal." He brushes his fingers over the tweed leg of his pants. "You saw someone you care about—a lot—in the well. You thought they were drowning."

Someone I care about a lot? An insane laugh bubbles out of me, and I bite down on it, shoving it back. I care about Bastian. About my cactus and my bank account. How the hell did Cadence de Morel scale the ladder of my stunted emotional hierarchy? The memory of her panicked face under the ice makes my whole body seize up like I've been tased.

"I'd be a mess too if I'd given in to my urge to look down."

But he didn't, because he's not weak like me.

"Who *did* you see?" Adrien asks.

I narrow my eyes. Like I'd tell him. "Does it matter?"

"No. I guess not." He cuts his gaze to the water. Despite the wind lifting his hair into a rooster comb, he manages to still seem elegant. Poised. Serene.

Is that why Cadence likes him so much? Because he's so composed and grounded?

He looks back at me. "What was it like? Did you feel like you weren't yourself? Like you were acting out of character?"

"It was fucking terrifying. I really believed she—" I swallow thickly, cutting myself off before I slip and admit who *she* was. "I felt like I was . . . drunk. Like the world was tipping, and everything but the person in the well was out of focus. I suppose that was the magic." I squeeze the wet sleeve of my pea coat, frigid water still dripping out. My hand and wrist don't feel cold, but I sense that's a side-effect of the ring that's still radiating heat. "How did you know what was happening back at the well? That I was seeing . . . someone in there?"

"Because that's what happened last time. Well, not a person; a thing. A coveted thing. It was in the lake, not the well, but Gaëlle's father and my mother both saw something they really wanted bob atop the lake." Adrien's mouth twists. "It was Gaëlle's father, Pierre, who went into the water, hooked onto a rope to reel him in. Pierre understood he was facing dark magic, fought it, and got the piece, but because that piece wasn't his to get, he died. Drowned on dry land. Apparently, it was gruesome. My father still gets agitated when he remembers. And that's saying something considering he couldn't even see what they'd seen."

Sounds like Adrien's life isn't a hundred percent perfect, and that makes him somewhat more likeable, like he might not deserve his new nickname even though it's quite catchy.

Every inch of me hurts. Even my nose hairs are sore. "I wish it was a thing this time, too." I shift my weight to lean against the low wall of the terrace and wince as my elbow bumps the stone. The elbow Adrien slammed his fist into.

Yeah. He's staying Professor Prickhead.

"Does this mean the challenges will be similar?"

"Maybe. Maybe not. But at least, now we know it's a possibility. And we can prepare." Adrien rubs his jaw, swollen and blue from my punch.

I clear my throat and motion to the bruise that's forming. "Sorry about that."

"Hurts a heck of a lot. I'm actually surprised you didn't dislocate my jaw."

"I was off my game. Believe me, if I hadn't been distracted, you'd be in the hospital right now, crying like a baby."

He smiles. "Guess I should thank the *groac'h* you saw in there."

"Grow-whatta?"

"*Groac'h.* Shapeshifting water sprite."

A sprite? I touched a fucking fairy? "Better thank her before I get my hands on a harpoon gun." My tone is lighter, like my mood, like the sky.

Adrien breathes out a short chuckle. We both stare out at the misty water for a moment.

Then he says, "I remember your parents. I remember you."

I twist my neck back fast enough to get whiplash. "You do?"

"Yeah. I have this one memory of Eugenia carrying you in this kangaroo pouch thing, and your big, bald head was sticking out. I remember thinking it looked like an ostrich egg." He gives me a mocking smile. Like it's hilarious for him to remember me bald and tiny and helpless.

"Fuck you, Mercier." *Super Douche. Professor Prickhead.*

His smile widens. "We were all at some party. I don't know for what. I don't even remember where it was. The only reason I remember you in that carrier is because your mother was wearing it when she gave me a gift: an illustrated book on the history of Brume. I loved that book. I think that's what whet my appetite for my studies."

A needle of pain pierces my chest. I hate to be petty, but it galls me that Professor here got something meaningful from my parents when all I got was a crappy stay in foster care.

"You look like Eugenia. She had the same curly hair."

As a Bloodstone-sized lump forms in my throat, Adrien's phone dings. He pulls it out, the color draining from his face as he reads the message.

"What?" I step forward. "What is it?"

He runs a hand through his hair, before standing. "Gaëlle just talked to Rainier. We have until sunup tomorrow morning to get the piece."

Snow and gravel crunch under his spiffy boots as he makes his way to the door.

I haven't moved. "I thought we had until the new moon to gather the pieces."

He opens the little door. "As a whole, we do. But apparently, once the *diwaller* touches his or her leaf, it only remains visible for twenty-four hours. Then it disappears."

I still don't move.

"But we know how to get this one. It'll be fine, Roland."

When I still don't step away from the rampart, he drags the door wider. "I know you don't trust me, but I never make promises I can't keep."

"You're not the one diving into the well."

"I'll be the one standing beside it, holding the rope tied to your waist to haul you back up." He shoots me a smile that seems genuine. "You're not alone, Slate."

I think it's the first time he's used my name. It feels like an olive branch for some reason and unbolts my limbs.

As we step back into the whorl of stone streets, I say, "What if the fairy grow-ass-shit—

"*Groac'h.*"

"Yeah. What if this *groac'h* saws off the rope?"

"I'll jump in."

I doubt he'd sacrifice himself for me, but the sentiment is heart-warming. I rethink his nickname a second time. "Is the library open at this time?"

"If it's not, Cadence has the keys."

"I don't have her number."

"Oh. I can text her. Tell her to meet us."

As we head toward the temple at the top of the hill, it starts to snow.

If the water fairy doesn't kill me, this fucking weather will.

20

CADENCE

I can't shake the chill in my bones, maybe because it's composed of so many layers—the thing in the well that made me think Papa was drowning, Nolwenn's allusion to Pandora, Alma's insinuation about an affair. Not having slept doesn't help. Even though I'm dying for a thermos of scorching coffee, I don't dare bring any liquids into the archival room for fear of spillage. Especially now. We can't afford to ruin any documents.

I'm only on the tenth page of *Istor Breou*—I'm not as fluent in Breton as Adrien, plus I'm jotting down everything and anything that sounds remotely linked to dark magic—when the glass door beeps open. It's Adrien, and he isn't alone. He kept his promise, which shouldn't surprise me. The man's never broken one before.

They approach the laminated white table over which I've spread out my research—*Istor Breou* and other books I got from the library mentioning fantastical aquatic monsters. I'm hoping there could be some applicable truths inside works of fantasy fiction.

Adrien examines the mess of papers and open books. "Find anything interesting?"

"The giant Pacific octopus has three hearts, nine brains, and blue blood."

Slate, who stands behind Adrien with his hands stuffed in the pockets of his coat, snorts.

Adrien blinks. "Why are you researching octopi?"

"I'm researching all aquatic monsters. Especially shapeshifting ones." I look at Slate again, at his mussed black hair dusted with melting snowflakes, at his thick lashes that shield guarded eyes. "I saw Papa, but I know that was personal to me. Was it my father you saw in there, Slate?"

He stares at the cover of a Greek myth anthology. "No. But I also didn't see a nine-brained octopus."

My lips quirk, which is a feat considering how stressed I feel.

Adrien steps past me and lifts one of the books. "Good. You got Homer out."

"I was looking for a siren's weaknesses. I didn't know if we could use methods written in works of fiction—"

"Maybe some of these aren't fictional accounts," Adrien says. "After all, the world *did* have magic."

Adrien's comment stuns me into silence. After a beat, I say, "I keep forgetting that part."

"I don't blame you." He skims a page, then flips to the next one. "Magic was stripped from humans in 1350, so we should probably focus on works written before that time."

That pretty much excludes everything but *Istor Breou*, *The Odyssey*, and a couple translations of Asian myths.

Adrien lifts my notepad. "Does *Istor Breou* mention a *groac'h*? Or something that lures men in by taking the shape of a person they love?"

"I think love is a strong word," Slate interjects.

I wonder why he feels the need to make the distinction. "You seemed pretty desperate to fish out the person you saw."

He rubs his jaw. "Why does my benevolence surprise you, Mademoiselle de Morel? I might not have three hearts like your giant squid, but I do have *one*."

There he goes again, heaping derision over something that clearly scared him back in the town square. "Octopus, not squid."

"Bickering's not going to help us get the piece," Adrien says.

"We're not *bickering*," I mutter, disliking how Adrien manages to make me feel like a rambunctious three-year-old.

"Gaëlle found out from Rainier that I have twenty-four hours"—

Slate peers down at his bulky gold wristwatch—"more like twenty-three now, to recover the piece."

Bile swishes in my stomach at the mention of Gaëlle and Papa in the same sentence. "What happens after that? Do you turn into a pumpkin?"

Slate's lopsided grin makes an appearance. "If turning into a pumpkin is a euphemism for dying, then yes, I turn into a pumpkin."

I suck in too much air and wheeze. "You're kidding?"

"Last of my bloodline, remember."

"Any more rules I should be aware of?"

"Why don't you phone up your papa to find out?" There's an edge of something in Slate's tone—disgruntlement, hatred . . . a mix of both.

"Maybe if we blindfolded you," Adrien muses.

"I'm not going in that well blind," Slate says. "Did I mention I hate dark, tight spaces?"

"Maybe earphones will help." Adrien suggests. "I have some that sync with my phone so you can listen to music while swimming."

"I'll take those." Slate walks to the other side of the table and plucks a book up.

I'm not too worried about how forcibly he flips through its pages, because it's a glossy travel guide mentioning famous land-marks in Brittany.

He stops thumbing through the pages and reads the section mentioning the *Puits Fleuri*. "It says there's close to a meter deep of coins down there."

"I really don't think now's the time to devise a scheme to steal money, Slate."

He spears me with a look I wouldn't even wish on Adrien's girlfriend. "I was only pointing it out, *Cadence*, because unless the goddamn leaf is the size of a plate, I'm going to have to rake through all those coins to find it."

Oh.

He drops his gaze back to the guidebook. "Your concern about my finances is touching, though."

Adrien glances at us and, although he doesn't say anything, I sense his thoughts from the slant of his light-brown eyebrows.

Harsh.

He thinks I was harsh.

"According to Rainier, the leaf will be about the size of your palm, Slate."

I bite my lip.

Silence sets in after that, disrupted only by the sluggish ticking of the clock, scratching pen tips, and whirring air-conditioner.

Adrien pushes back his chair. "I need to get to class, but I'll meet you back here after lunch. If you two are still at it. You're staying here with Slate, right?"

I nod.

He slides one hand over his hair to flatten his windblown locks. "Can you believe that, by tomorrow, we'll have the first leaf?"

Slate's jaw tightens. Although he doesn't say anything, the hard edges of his face speak volumes. He's not his usual confident, happy-go-lucky self. He's nervous.

I am, too.

One of Adrien's eyes keeps twitching, a sure sign that he's not as confident as he's pretending to be. But is he anxious because Slate might die or because magic might be gone forever?

Once Adrien closes the door, I study Slate's sharp profile—his straight nose that dips a little at the tip, his scruffy jaw, his wild black curls. I can't imagine him gone, which is weird, because yesterday I desired nothing more.

Before I can look away, Slate turns and catches me staring. I wait for him to say something lewd or teasing, but he's silent and grim, which makes my heart pinch. A current passes between us, charged with words and emotions that seem outrageously strong considering we're both still such strangers to each other.

Empathy.

That's what it is.

I'm feeling empathetic, because he doesn't deserve to die so young. Yes, the old adage says we must pay for our mistakes, but the cost of stealing a ring shouldn't be his life.

"Bronze daggers can apparently paralyze sirens." It's the only thing I've read that feels useful.

"Any idea where I can purchase one of those?" He's still looking at me, and I'm still looking at him.

"Maybe Gaëlle carries one in her shop . . ."

Saying her name makes my stomach contort. But no longer in irritation. Doesn't my father deserve a second chance at happiness? Plus Alma was right . . . I do love Gaëlle.

I sigh long and loud.

So long and so loud that Slate asks, "Don't think it'll work?"

"What?"

"The bronze dagger."

"Oh. No. I do."

He frowns.

Even though I don't especially want to talk about it, I think that airing my problem—which really isn't one—will take Slate's mind off his—which truly is one. "My best friend insinuated that Gaëlle and Papa might be seeing each other, and it bothers me."

"Because Gaëlle's married?"

I shake my head. "Her husband left her last spring, when she was pregnant with twins."

"Bastard."

I chew on my bottom lip. "What if he left because she cheated on him with my father?"

"Huh. Who knew Brume was so full of amorous intrigue?"

I find myself smiling. "You make it sound like we're living on the set of a Spanish soap opera."

He smiles, not with his lips . . . with his eyes. They curve and shine. "I wish. Then my greatest challenge would be figuring out how to get the girl instead of the malevolent leaf."

My humor disintegrates, and the weight of reality settles back atop my shoulders like the heavy soup pot over the well.

"Oh, Slate . . ."

"Remember what I told you the first day we met? That a person makes their own luck. Well, I still believe it. Besides a bronze dagger and a playlist, what else would you suggest I bring to face a shapeshifting water sprite?"

"A mask and a flashlight."

"Hmm. Good thinking, Mademoiselle de Morel."

"An insulated dive suit and some fins. Oh, and an air tank. Or at least an air hose . . ." I scribble all these items down, a grocery list of sorts. "Have you ever scuba-dived?"

"Nope, but since water's my element, I'm probably part amphibian." He stretches his fingers, as though checking if they've suddenly become webbed. "Adrien suggested tying me with rope in case I decide not to get out."

"That's wise."

"He seems like a wise man."

"He is. We're lucky to have him on the team."

Slate's Adam's apple jostles in his throat as though he didn't appreciate me calling us a team. Trust really isn't his forte.

We both go back to reading after that, and the quiet that expands between us is surprisingly pleasant.

In between a passage about an orchard that bloomed in the winter and saved Brume from famine and a blacksmith whose forge produced swords able to turn enemies into allies, I ask, "Do you have a girlfriend?"

Slate looks up, and I blush. I'm not even sure why.

"Or close friends?"

"Why? You want their phone numbers in case I don't make it out of the well?"

A chill spreads over my heated cheeks, as though someone tampered with the fan's speed in the vent overhead. "That wasn't why I was asking."

"Then why were you asking?"

I set my elbows on the table, twirling the pen between my fingers. "I saw Papa in there. If the well were my mission, then I'd want constant reminders that it's not my father. Instead of playing music on those earphones, maybe hearing the voice of the person you're seeing could help your focus. That's why I was asking about girlfriends or friends. Maybe they could talk you through it."

His eyes darken as fast as the Brumian sky in winter. "No." His tone is final, brooking no argument.

No to girlfriends and friends? Or no about involving anyone else?

"How about *I* talk you through it, then?"

His lips purse as though I've just suggested slathering him in stinky Maroilles cheese to make the siren, or whatever's in the well, flee.

"I seem to have a talent for annoying you, which might help keep your brain sharp."

"Fine."

I'm so surprised he relented that the pen tumbles out of my fingers and rolls off the table. As I bend to scoop it up, I say, "Great."

But is it all that great that he finds me so annoying?

21

SLATE

I nstructions come at me like bullets:

"Don't hold your breath, *or you'll die.*"

"Control your anxiety, so you don't burn through the air supply, *or you'll die.*"

"Don't ascend faster than the bubbles, *or you'll die.*"

"Remember what you're seeing is a siren's ruse, *or you'll die.*"

"Get the piece before morning, *or you'll die.*"

My gaze flits from Rainier to Gaëlle to Cadence to Adrien and back to Rainier again. I don't know what kind of leadership seminar they all attended, but their motivational speech stinks. I'm giving them and their Brumian *Come Out a Winner* tutorial a zero out of five.

"All right! I've got the gist: one wrong move, and *I die.*"

The four of them blink at me, their faces drawn and pale. I spent the whole afternoon and evening with the motley Quatrefoil crew, preparing for this moment. We raided Gaëlle's stock for any items that might kill a supernatural creature. I now own a bronze dagger, a silver hunting knife, and an iron pick, all strapped to my thigh. We hit the hardware store and bought rope and a headlamp. Adrien offered up his set of ultra-waterproof earphones. And then they threw me into three hours of intensive scuba-diving lessons with an angry, scar-faced ex-commander of the French Foreign Legion who made Vincent seem like a creampuff.

Now that it's after midnight and the square is quiet, I'm as ready as I'll ever be to get that damn piece.

In other words, I'm so fucking not ready.

I pound my feet on the cobbles to keep my circulation going. The ice is melting, and brown slush clings to my diving boots. We left the fins in the shop. Not even the short model would fit in the well. The floodlights are gone, as are the firefighters. Rainier told the brigade and other Brumian busybodies that I was a professional oil rig welder and that I was going to fix their beloved *Puits Fleuri*, but it might overflow again, so everyone was advised to clear the square and keep away until morning, or until Rainier gave the all-clear. De Morel's command had them all skittering away faster than I can pick a pocket. I swear, the man is like royalty, esteemed and kowtowed to, more important than the mayor.

Most of the windows in the buildings surrounding the square are dark. The only frosty panes of glass glowing are on the third floor of the tavern. A curtain twitches, and I spot Nolwenn's bulbous hair and shining eyes.

I'm about to tell Rainier we have spectators when he barks, "Roland!" He pats the pale wood box on his lap, the inside of which is lined with leaden sheeting. "When you come out, first thing you do, is put the leaf in here. No one else must touch it."

"*Or they'll die*," I add in an ominous voice.

That doesn't get a single laugh.

Adrien steps forward and clips the rope to the weight belt around my wetsuit. "If your BCD doesn't work like it should, and you can't ascend on your own, just give this a yank. I'll reel you in."

I test the buoyancy again, compressing the red button. My jacket fills up. I look for the little ball dangling at my back and yank it to free the air. Sergeant Suffering's warning not to ascend too fast shrills in my mind, but getting the Bends is at the very bottom of my list of worries.

Cadence holds up Adrien's phone. "I'll talk you through it. We don't know how deep the connection will work, but I won't stop talking."

Gaëlle huddles further into her yellow scarf, the whites of her eyes glittering. She clears her throat. "Good luck, Slate. And break a leg."

I stomp my feet again, and my bruised toe throbs. With my recent lucky streak, I might actually break a leg. Or two.

This is the worst fix I've ever been in. And that includes the time when Tiny Tim found out I stole his lucky rabbit-foot keyring with the key to his storage unit.

I look into the well.

Before I put on this ridiculous seal suit, Adrien and I got the firefighters to help us lug the huge pot, remove the table, and snap off the grate. I'd been expecting to see Cadence or Bastian or even poor old Spike under the surface of the water, but there was nothing except an icy pool of darkness.

Most of the ice has inexplicably melted, and the water line's receded. It's now a good two meters below the lip of the well. I sit on the edge, small air tank strapped to my back.

I switch on the headlamp and adjust the diving mask that smells like chemical lemon. I shove the regulator between my lips, its edges scraping my gums, and suck in, hearing the *ka-shoook* of the nitrogen-enriched oxygen filling my hose.

Putain. My heart is going a mile a minute.

"I'll ease you down," Adrien says, unspooling the rope.

There is no fucking way I am going to let him lower me into the eerie tunnel of gloom without keeping some sort of grip on the thing. I tilt forward to put one hand on either side of the interior of the well. Even through the diving gloves, the chill in the stone bites my fingers.

I slide my ass off the ledge, and for a split-second, I'm in freefall. Then I feel a jerk as the belt tightens around my middle, and I'm dangling a foot above the slick surface of the water. My headlamp shines on the dips and dents in the stones, but its reach isn't long enough to fill the encroaching blackness.

Despite the arctic cold, sweat beads underneath my neoprene diving hood, and a crushing pain squeezes my chest. Bile rises in my throat, and I force it back down. There's no way in hell I'm allowing a panic attack to set in. I'd rather die trying than die hyperventilating.

Suddenly, Cadence's voice is in my ears. "Adrien's giving the rope slack. Once you're in the water, adjust your buoyancy. You're doing great, Slate."

Oh, yeah. Abso-fucking-lutely. I haven't shit myself yet. That's a win.

I twist my neck, catching a sliver of Cadence's moonlit face. The backdrop of twinkly lights makes her look like a goddess in a sky of stars, if goddesses wore slouchy knit caps with fuzzy pompoms.

Lower and lower I go, first my feet enter the frigid water, then my legs, then my chest. When my head dips under, I instinctively start to hold my breath. Sergeant Suffering's booming voice reels through my brain, *"Breathe, you pussy, breathe!"*

I suck on my regulator as I whirl on the rope like a leg of lamb on a spit. Around me, layer upon layer of stones stretch down into the mucky channel.

The in and out of air from the tank echoes behind Cadence's steady voice. "So I was hesitating between a classic tale and a personal one." She pauses. "Since I'm betting you want to hear the personal one . . ."

Damn right.

" . . . I'm going with the classic tale."

Tease.

"Have you ever heard of *The Little Mermaid*? I thought it fit the moment superbly." I hear a smile in her voice, and it momentarily makes the entrenching obscurity less forbidding. "Far out in the ocean, where the water is as blue as the prettiest cornflower, and as clear as—" Her words cut off. "—very, very deep. So deep indeed that—"

Fizzing silence. *Come on. Bluetooth, don't leave me hanging.*

"There dwell the Sea King and his subj—"

My heart jolts at the sound of her voice, then jolts again when the depth interrupts the broadcast. I long to hear Cadence's story crackle back against my eardrums but don't even get graced with static.

Pressure builds in my ears, and I pinch my nose to release it. I keep going down, scanning the darkness for movement. Fear pounds so hard it's probably creating a current.

I look up and the beam of my headlight hits something. Something that moves around the length of taut rope anchoring me to the surface. My BCD seems to grow tighter, as though I've inflated it to maximum capacity even though I haven't pressed the red button.

I catch another flutter of movement and realize it's just the slow, steady stream of bubbles I'm exhaling.

Can't believe I almost pissed myself over some bubbles.

Come on . . . show yourself. Let's be done with this.

My feet bump against something hard. I jerk my head down. I'm at the bottom of the well, standing atop a shiny carpet of coins. I scan the water above me, but nothing circles the tight rope. I don't know whether to be relieved or scared shitless. Is the Quatrefoil piece even still here, or was Rainier wrong?

Maybe we had less than twenty-four hours to retrieve it.

My already racing heart kicks up a few notches.

I wait and wait. Time trickles by slower than my exhaled bubbles.

Instead of being a sitting duck, might as well be a crouching one. I lower in slow motion onto my knees and sweep my gloved hands through the thousands of Euro coins and older Francs. The metal's tarnished on most, the round faces tinged black and green. If the leaf is in here, it should be easy enough to locate, since it'll be shinier and bigger than any of these coins.

A shrill cry pierces the steady *ka-shoook* of my breathing, in time with the splash of a body dropping into water. I jerk to my feet and crank my neck, bumping the back of my head against the yoke valve. Skull smarting, I squint into the length of liquid black, spot a dark shape floundering in the dim circle of light.

My muscles harden, my joints tighten, my palms tingle, and my heartbeat bounces between my ribs and air tank.

Fuck.

Fuck fuck fuck.

"I fell in! Help, oh God, I fell in!" Cadence's voice erupts inside my ears. "Help!"

Cadence?

Cadence is in the well?

How the hell did she fall in?

Grab the rope, I think. It's got to be easy enough for her to reach.

"My boots. My coat! They're so heavy, Slate." My name combined with her yelps wrenches my heart. *Merde.* I press the button on the BCD and push off the mound of coins, rocketing upward. In the back of my mind, I hear Sergeant Suffering calling me an idiot and lots more Breton swear words.

I've got to help her. I've got to—

Wait. No. Her voice doesn't carry this deep. Dark magic. That's what this is. It's trying to distract me from getting the piece. No freaking way will it fool me this time.

I propel my body toward the curved wall and grip the rough edges of a stone, halting my brusque ascent, then rifle blindly for the little plastic ball fluttering at the back of my jacket. My feet and legs rise, buoying me up. I dig my fingertips into the scraggly space between the rocks, slashing my other hand through the water like a clock pendulum in search of the dump valve. The second my palm closes around it, I tug hard, releasing the air in one fell swoop.

My feet and legs arch back down. The line tied around my waist dangles in the dark pit like a child's skipping rope. I sink and sink. The stress is starting to take a toll on me. A headache blooms at my temples and stretches over my forehead. I'm hot in the dive suit. My mouth is dry.

The darkness of the well suddenly seems darker. I look up and see Cadence floating downward. She's in her fur-lined boots and fluffy silver jacket. Tendrils of her hair float around her face like kelp, her pompom flutters at the top of her knit hat.

Every molecule inside me is urging me to take her into my arms and speed back up to the surface.

It's not her. It's not her. It's not her. I repeat the mantra over and over in my head, grinding my teeth over the rubber mouthpiece.

She sinks deeper, and her back bumps my shoulder, driving the soles of my feet against the pile of chucked human wishes. Her eyes are closed, and she's pale as death, the outline of her lips tinged blue. I'm waiting for her to spring at me. For her to try to choke me or rip off my mask or anything a monster would do.

I press myself against the side of the well as she lands on the mound of coins. One lone bubble escapes from her nostril.

I step forward. She doesn't move.

What if it really is Cadence?

It can't be.

The others were with her. They wouldn't have let her dive in.

Unless the dark magic somehow propelled her inside.

Fuck.

I pass my hand over my neoprene hood, trying to make up my mind.

What if it's really her?

Fuck fuck fuck.

I can't just let her die.

Fumbling about with the tubes and gauges, I find the extra regulator hooked onto my jacket and shove it between her lips. She's still unresponsive.

Panic twists my gut and squeezes my lungs. *Come on, Cadence. Don't die. Please don't die.*

I slide one arm under her knees and the other under her neck, and then, hugging her to me, I pump a little air into my BCD and scissor-kick to the top. As we inch higher, she leans closer, her head lolling against my chest, and lays her hand on the back of my neck.

I close my eyes for a second, relieved she's still alive. My ears pop, and then static bursts into my ears, and Cadence's voice hits me loud and clear and strong. "She looked once more at the prince, hurled herself over the bulwarks into the sea, and felt her body dissolve into foam."

My eyes snap open and Cadence—the one in my arms—removes the regulator from her lips and asks, "Did you like my story?"

Her story? Was I not hearing her through the earphones?

"You're my hero, you know?"

Her words hit me square in the heart. No one's ever called me their hero.

"I told you I saw my father in the well, but it was you, Slate. You're who I saw."

I blink at her. Never has Cadence looked this beautiful. Like a siren . . .

Wait.

Sirens aren't good.

"Won't you kiss me?" Cadence says.

Bubbles don't stream out from her mouth. Because she isn't human.

I'm cradling a monster.

I yank my arms down and away, but she doesn't fall into the

dark pit. She just hovers there in front of me, one hand locked on the back of my neck. Her throat's so thin and breakable. I look for the flutter of a pulse, but her skin doesn't vibrate.

She isn't real.

"You let me go," she murmurs. "Look at me."

I shut my eyes and reach for the dagger strapped to my thigh.

Something sharp slashes the skin on the nape of my neck through the thick neoprene. I snap my eyes open and bounce away from her before she claws through a vital organ. Cold seeps into my skin, followed by warmth. The water between my mask and her face turns red.

That's when I'm jerked upward. What the hell?

The rope . . . *Adrien, no!* I didn't give the signal. If he pulls me up now, it's over. I twist around and grip the taut cord, giving it a good yank. Instead of stopping, he reels me in even faster.

Shit.

The siren stares up at me, annoyance marring her borrowed face. She looks so much like real-Cadence again. Real-Cadence who's now screeching into my earphones, "Slate? Can you hear me? Oh, God, Adrien, get him up. Get him back up . . ." In the background, I hear Rainier's voice growl something. He's probably telling Adrien not to listen to his daughter. "We can't leave him in there, Papa!" Cadence's cry lends me the strength for what I'm about to do.

I raise the dagger and saw through the rope, back and forth, back and forth. The siren's eyes light up, and her sternness dissolves into a look of pure bliss. She thinks I'm choosing her.

The rope snaps. The frayed end rises in the water.

Yelling pounds against my eardrums. Yelling and crying. Cadence cares about me, and fuck if I don't feel like I'm flying rather than sinking.

As my body drifts lower, the noise from above crackles, then buzzes, before vanishing completely.

The water fairy's ruby lips arch up and up, and her pale eyes blaze into mine, pupils wide and full of desire. "You came back for me, Slate."

I slide my fingers through the tendrils of hair waving around her porcelain face and anchor them to the back of her skull with my gloved hand. The ring burns hot and radiates into my veins, filling my body with exquisite warmth.

Cadence parts her lips, and every cell in my body buoys as though my air tank's hooked to my veins. She eases the regulator from my mouth and tilts her head in invitation.

I tighten the fingers that span her skull and tug her head closer. And closer.

Just before our lips connect, I thrust the dagger into her side, just beneath the ribs.

Her scream nearly rips my eardrums.

The water churns and the walls of the well shudder as if an earthquake has hit Brume. Fake-Cadence's blue irises morph to blazing orange, and her pupils stretch to vertical slits. The creature lunges at me and screeches, revealing a mouth full of yellow, curved, needle-like teeth.

I don't expect its strength, and it must sense it because it takes advantage of my lapse of attention, cutting clean through the straps of my BCD with its sharpened nails. The jacket flaps open like stubby wings. The creature bellows out another scream before coming at me again, sending me farther and farther down the well. Sealing my lips to conserve my supply of air, I yank the dagger out and jab it in again. The thing's jaw gapes, then clenches, then gapes again, like a piranha in a ski cap.

It writhes, breaking my grip on the dagger.

I shoot my hand back down to my thigh for my second weapon. My fingers close around the iron pick just as the siren shoves me into the mound of coins. My hand skitters off my weapon and bangs against the coins, which rise and float around us like glimmering snowflakes. My lungs squeeze as the creature flings itself down on me. I wring my body from side to side, expending precious energy and air, but what choice do I have? I refuse to be slurped down like fish food.

I punch it, the ring making the inhuman thing's face snap to the side, and it wails like a banshee, its orange eyes flaring with rage. As it lunges at me, I reach for the iron pick again. The siren's teeth graze my jaw, setting my whole face aflame. I gasp, releasing my meek supply of oxygen. Icy water floods my throat. With one last burst of adrenaline, I snatch the pick and yank it out of the holster, then plunge it over and over into the monster's neck, chest, waist.

Its mouth pops in a soundless scream, or maybe I can't hear it anymore. My vision dots, then darkens.

I blink, my lids sluggish.

A black, viscous cloud seeps into the water.

Air. I need air. I wave my arms like a starfish until I feel something long and rubbery . . . a hose. I pray it's the one connected to my octopus and not to my depth gauge.

Lungs on fire, I swing the hose in front of my face. I think I see something round and black attached to it. I bring it to my mouth and almost faint with relief when my teeth close around rubber and not hard plastic. I suck but swallow water, and my chest spasms.

Choking, I scrabble to remember how to get air. *The purge!* My fingers graze the button in the middle of the regulator.

The well turns gray then black. Did my headlamp go off?

I press the purge button to clear my mouthpiece of water.

Air . . . *glorious* air streaks into my lungs.

I breathe in long and deep, lying on the mound of coins like a crack addict sprawled on a dirty couch.

The black shadow sharpens, and I realize it's the creature liquifying. Dark, gloppy bits curl and bloat like oil in a lava lamp.

Something shines amidst the dirty sludge.

Something gold and smooth, big as my palm.

I reach up and rake through the gunk in slow motion.

When I was a kid, I'd climb onto rooftops to hide from the terrible humans populating my world and stare up at the night sky to wish on its stars. I quickly understood that stars didn't listen, so I stopped whispering to them.

Tonight, as I lay at the bottom of the black well, and my gloved hand closes over the falling disk of gold, I feel like that kid again, the one who looked for light in the darkness, who believed that if he reached high enough, he could pluck the stars from the very sky.

22

CADENCE

My lids are bloated, and my eyes sting. Slate is dead. Gone.

I saw his blood redden the water.

I saw the frayed end of rope Adrien fished out.

I saw the bubbles stop popping and foaming, and the surface slicken like oil.

"We can't . . . just leave him . . ." I hiccup around a sob.

I stare at Adrien, who's as white as the linens I lent Slate last night. Gaëlle and Papa, too, are uncharacteristically pale.

"I'll send someone in there tomorrow." Papa swallows. "Around noon to be safe."

I sniffle, the arctic chill singeing my nostrils as hot tears flood down my cheeks, and glare at the rope as though it has personally wronged me. Anger replaces my grief. I want to wring the neck of the siren, even if it curses me into an early grave. I'm mad enough to believe that I could kill it before it could kill me.

"Um, guys." Gaëlle's breathy voice slashes through my thoughts. "Did I just—did you . . . Did you see that?"

"That?" I swing around and grip the edge of the well. A firm arm snakes around my waist and levers me away. "Let go, Adrien! I'm not going to jump in."

His eyebrows jolt up, vanishing behind a stiff blond, wayward lock. He releases me but doesn't step back, just to the side. I sense he doesn't trust me not to jump in.

I focus on the well again, and sure enough, a jumble of bubbles ripple and foam.

"Cadence, don't get your hopes up." Adrien's voice is quiet and gentle.

My heart rattles so hard inside my chest I imagine Adrien must hear its frenzied thumping.

"It could be the thing in the well."

"Or it could be him." It has to be him.

"His BCD could've inflated and is lifting him—"

"Will you stop it, Adrien?" I growl.

Even though I don't look away from the water, I sense his posture stiffening.

Something shines in the black well. *Slate's lamp!* It must be his lamp!

The shine grows and grows along with my hope. I lean forward, the stone edge of the well digging into my abdomen. I suddenly wish I hadn't let Papa take the phone away from me. I want to talk to Slate. I want him to hear my voice. To know that he's awaited. That we didn't abandon him.

I start to shiver with anticipation and have to grit my teeth to prevent them from clacking. The bubbles get larger and fiercer, bursting in time with my pulse.

Come on. Come on. Come on.

His hooded head pierces the rippling surface.

I hold my breath. Wait for him to move. When he tilts his head back, and his eyes, open and bright with life, land on mine, my heart comes untethered and floats up in turn.

"You're alive!" I'm not sure whether to cry or smile, so I do both. I ugly-cry and grin so wide my cheeks quiver and ache. "You're alive. You did it," I whisper as a great big sob rattles my chest.

Slate spits out his regulator. "I'm not sure whether to be offended or surprised you doubted I would, Mademoiselle de Morel." His eyes curve and glitter softly.

You conceited ass, I think, and would say it out loud if my throat actually worked, but I'm crying, and it's really hard to talk around tears.

His arm rises from the water. "De Morel, you got the box ready?"

"It's"—Papa clears his throat, as though he, too, has become emotional—"it's ready, Roland."

Slate bobs at the surface, his BCD floating around him like a buoy. "I might be a remarkable mermaid slayer, but I have yet to develop Spiderman's skill for scaling up walls, so a rope would be greatly appreciated."

"Show us the piece," Adrien says, and I want to smack him for not tossing the rope in to help Slate climb out.

He must be freezing. And wounded, if the blood that darkened the surface came from him and not the thing.

Slate raises his arm. Although he doesn't open his fingers, I spot the shimmering edge of something golden, and my heart wallops my ribs again, this time in excitement.

A piece of history rests in his glove.

I stare and stare, refusing to blink.

"I'd toss it up to you, Prof, but I wouldn't want to curse you." Slate smiles, and that smile sets my pulse on fire even though it's not directed at me.

The rope drops into the well with a heavy splash. Slate wraps it a few times around the hand not clutching the Quatrefoil leaf. Gaëlle stands behind Adrien, holding part of the rope. I race behind her and grab a length as well.

Adrien leans back, then Gaëlle, and then me, and the rope tautens. I squeeze the wet, ice-cold fibers, and back up as though I'm carrying Slate alone. I doubt I'm helping much. I'm pretty sure Adrien's doing most of the work.

Slate's head appears over the rim of the well, and then his broad shoulders, and the rest of his long body. He tumbles over, pitching onto the cobbles like a drunk. I release the rope and stride around the two others to reach him, but Adrien bats his arm out.

"Don't touch him until he puts the piece in the box," he says.

I suck in a startled breath.

Slate heaves himself up, and even though his body looks whole and unharmed, I catch a tremor in his limbs. The aluminum bottle hooked into his BCD drags the flapping jacket down his arms. Both fall onto the cobbles with a deafening clang.

Papa wheels in closer to Slate, birch box propped open on his lap.

Slate takes one step, then another, then extends his arm slowly, as though his elbow isn't quite cooperating. He shakes so hard that I wonder if it's from the rush of adrenaline or from the freezing temperature of the water. His lips are purple, and the oval of skin peeking from his hood is as white as Nolwenn's meringues, except at the bottom right where the skin is marbled and dark like his lips. A fresh bruise? Slowly, he positions his hand over the box, so close his knuckles graze the propped lid. Several seconds later, metal clangs against the leaden lining.

Papa shuts the box. For a long moment, we stare at it as though expecting the piece to leap out or start rattling, but all is still.

"*Bravo,* Roland." Papa's congratulatory words cloud in front of him, remaining suspended before dispersing.

I exhale a puff of frozen air, and then I'm circling the well toward them. Slate must see me coming from the corner of his eyes, because he turns. His shape blurs as new tears rise. I lunge toward him and hook my arms around his neck before muffling my sob against his spongy wetsuit. He stiffens, but I don't care. I want him to feel how relieved I am that he's alive. How proud I am that he defeated the monster and won the challenge.

Hesitantly, his arms curl around my back and press me into him, and then his chin perches on the top of my head. "*The Little Mermaid,* huh?"

I laugh, but since I'm midsob, it comes out sounding like a honk from a lunatic goose.

"I think I'm officially creeped out for life by sirens and wells." His voice rumbles softly in the cold air. "Not that I was much of a fan of either before."

His body isn't shaking anymore, but he must be freezing. I release his neck, my fingers coming back slick with blood. I gape at them, then at him. From up close, his jaw is swollen and dotted in tiny holes trickling blood.

"I could've used some nail clippers down there. She had one hell of a set of claws. *Yeesh.*" He shudders. "That iron pick was a good call, Adrien."

Nail clippers? She sliced the back of his neck with her nails? Did she also plant them inside his jaw?

My mind snags on something else. Something silly—the pronoun Slate just used. *She* . . . My heart tumbles like a tossed coin.

Something clanks against the floor—his weight belt—and I stare at it, because it's easier than letting him see how conflicted I feel.

"Cadence?" Slate speaks my name slowly, as though confused by my mood swing.

"Turn around. I want to see what *she* did to your neck." I hate how testy I sound.

A frown gusts over Slate's face, but he indulges me. As he pivots, he peels his hood off, then drops it to the floor. It slaps the stone like a dead fish. The skin on the back of his neck is puckered and leaking blood.

Gaëlle whispers, "Oh, *mon Dieu*."

"That's going to need stitches, Roland," Adrien says.

"I'll call Sylvie." Papa's already wheeling himself in the direction of our house. "Let's all get to the house."

I stare at Slate's neck, at his sharp Adam's apple now.

It bobs. "Cadence? Are you okay?"

I swallow and scrub my cheeks with my numb hands. "I wasn't in a well with a monster, so yes, I'm fine." Even to my ears, I don't sound fine. I sound mad.

I turn sharply and start toward Papa's wheelchair, grabbing onto the handles and jerking him faster across the square. The wheel-chair motor whirrs, and the jostling leaf clinks and clanks.

Papa tilts his head. "What's going on with you, *ma chérie?*"

"Just emotional."

"I can see that. But why?"

"Because this is all so insane."

It's the truth.

A piece of it.

The other piece of truth I'm not sharing with my father is that I'm jealous. Which is all types of crazy, because I don't know Slate.

I don't even like him.

I shouldn't care that he saw a girl down there.

23

SLATE

his is getting ridiculous.

I'm not sure there's more than an inch of skin on me that's not bruised or beaten or bloody. I clench my teeth as I peel off the wetsuit, trying not to cry like a fucking baby in De Morel's guest bathroom. Along with the dirty well water, my blood dribbles onto the floor, creating rust-colored tributaries on the white marble slabs. Finally, the whole suit plops to the ground in a wet heap.

There are eight entire inches of skin that have managed to remain intact. The best eight.

Putain. What a relief.

The bathtub is a clawed-foot porcelain recipient of monstrous proportions. I slide into the steaming soup of aloe infused bubbles —Cadence's call—unable to stop a moan from escaping my lips as the water licks my battered body. The heat all at once hurts and soothes as it thaws out my numbed flesh.

Now that sensation is coming back, the gash on my jaw where that bitch bit me burns like a mother. And I don't even want to think about the back of my neck. It's in fucking ribbons.

I close my eyes but see the siren, so I pry them open and stare at the moonlit lake beyond the foggy window.

Not nearly long enough later, two knocks sound on the door of the Jack and Jill bathroom. You'd think that considering their wealth, the De Morels could afford private en suites for all their bedrooms.

"Slate?" It's Cadence. "The doctor's here."

"I just got in the bath."

"Yeah. Well, just get out."

After her effusive hug, which might've rated in the top three moments in Slate Ardoin's pitiful life, she started acting strange. I assumed it was my blood that freaked her out, although, what do I know? Maybe it was seeing me rise back out of that well like a phoenix rising from its ashes.

Sighing, I get up, sloshing more water onto the tiles. There are four fuzzy ivory towels hanging on the rack. I pull one off and press it to my face and chest. Already its soft off-white fibers are turning a bloody brown. By the time I've dried my whole body off, the towel looks like it was used to wipe down a crime scene.

Rainier insisted I stay the night here, and I didn't even attempt to turn down his invite. The room is all puffy white pillows and velour throws and crystal light fixtures. Luxury that reminds me of Marseille, of the life I made for myself there, of the life I'll be going back to as soon as the others face off with their pieces.

The clothes I changed out of to put on the dive suit are folded on a fat, cushioned chair in the corner of the room. They smell clean. The pure, elegant odor of *savon de Marseille*. I shake out my shirt, which has been ironed.

Well, look at that.

That's what it's like for the rich—having little house elves spiffing things up.

I frown as I put on the shirt. I'm rich now, too. Especially after selling that Renoir. Guess it's time for me to get a house elf. Spike sure as hell isn't going to iron my shirts. Although Bastian might.

Once I'm fully dressed and have run my fingers through my hair, I open the door. Cadence is leaning against the wall in the corridor, dragging her fingernails over the embossed stripes of the wallpaper.

She's changed into stretchy black leggings and a heavy gray hoodie with *Université de Brume* embroidered in navy thread across the front. Her hair's pulled into a high ponytail, and her face is scrubbed clean. How could I have mistaken the siren for her?

Cadence is a thousand times more beautiful than that creature in the well.

"Hey." Her scent revs up my heart.

She crosses her arms over her chest. "I'm supposed to remind you not to tell the doctor the truth about your injuries."

I tilt my head to one side and immediately regret it. A sharp pain scissors across my neck, and I groan. "I doubt he'd believe me, anyway."

Color rises in her cheeks. "*She* is from Brume. So, she just might."

Ouch.

Cadence leads me down the hallway, past oil paintings of landscapes and ancient battles, to Rainier's glass elevator. We get inside, and she punches the button for the ground floor so hard I wince. Especially since she's gazing murderously up at me.

What did I do now? Did my assumption that the doctor was a man peeve her? I mean, yeah, it was small-minded but not an egregious affront to the female sex.

"Are you okay?"

"Great."

And that's the last word she says to me as the glass box slides down two floors. Cadence strides out first, streaking across the grand foyer like a comet, obviously in a hurry to get away from me. I trail behind, hands shoved in my pockets.

I recognize the doc, a woman in her sixties with a rope of gray hair and large brown eyes—the purple fairy at the party. My *Blair Witch Project* crew surround her, probably still here because they don't trust me to keep quiet.

I take a seat on the sectional and peel off my shirt, the collar of which is already stained red. Should've kept a towel around my neck. Hopefully, De Morel's little elf works overtime. Then again, if it's a French elf, probably not.

"*Mon Dieu!*" If the doc's eyebrows shot up any higher, they'd take off.

As she opens her satchel, I look around the room. Adrien is sitting across from me, elbows propped on his thighs, fingers clasped together and supporting his chin. Gaëlle is perched on the arm of the couch next to Rainier's wheelchair. Cadence is leaning against the wall beside the picture window, arms still crossed. Her cheek keeps dimpling, and since she doesn't have dimples, I assume she's biting the inside of her mouth.

"That stray dog really did a number on you." Doc turns my face, eyes going from my jaw to my neck. "You're lucky Adrien was walking around and found you."

So that's the story? I got attacked by a stray and Adrien, forever the hero, saved me? Damn. Why couldn't I have just saved myself?

"Yeah. Thank the good lord his girlfriend kicked him out of bed in the middle of the night. Prof, remind me to thank . . . What's her name again?"

It's a really low blow, and I daresay I'm not too proud of it, but Cadence is still seething, angry with me, and I don't know . . . it makes me spiteful toward the man she worships.

The muscles in Adrien's jaw twitch. "Charlotte."

The doctor pats an alcohol-soaked square of gauze against the teeth marks on my jaw. "I don't believe I've ever seen a wound quite like this. What sort of dog was it?" She's now putting some kind of ointment on my skin, and it stings.

"It was—" Adrien starts, but I talk over him.

"A German Shepherd-pug mix." I'm going to make this story mine.

The doctor's entire face scrunches up. "That's an . . . odd mix."

"Ugly, too. Tiny legs, wrinkly head, beady black eyes, super shaggy."

"Are you kids sure it wasn't a rat?"

"That's what I thought, but Adrien insisted it was a dog. Insisted on the mutt's breed too. Canine mixes are his hobby."

Adrien pinches the bridge of his nose.

"Is that so, Adrien?" The doctor discards the reddened gauze. "I love dogs too. I've been meaning to get one but wanted help picking the right breed. Maybe you can suggest one? If you have time, that is. I know teaching keeps you busy."

He breathes in, then out and offers the doc a smile. "As soon as I get Slate acclimated to Brume—he just started at the University— I'll make the time to come see you and discuss breeds." Damn, the guy is suave.

"A heart of gold, just like your maman." The doc's eyes gloss over with tears, which she whisks away with a couple lash battings.

There's a melancholic lull in the atmosphere. *Well, crap . . .* I'm guessing his mother either left or died.

"The dog that attacked this boy is going to need to be found." Doc thankfully puts an end to Mercier's pity party. "And we need to issue a warning to the college students."

"Prof, you called Paw Patrol, right?"

Adrien stabs me with an irritated look. At least he doesn't look weepy anymore. "Animal Control. And yes."

The doctor asks me a shitload of questions: How did the stray act? Did I provoke it? Was it foaming at the mouth? I fake my way through the answers while she numbs my skin. I grit my teeth as the needle goes in and then break out in little beads of sweat when she sticks me with another anesthetic shot. Wasn't one enough?

As she stitches up the back of my neck, she says, "I'll be putting you on antibiotics. Any allergies?"

Through clenched teeth, even though I'm not in pain, I answer, "Not that I'm aware of."

"And you'll need a tetanus booster."

"Does it come in pill form? I really hate shots."

"No." I hear the snip of scissors and then the plasticky peel of a big-ass Band-Aid. She lifts the hair curling at the nape of my neck and presses the plaster to the numbed skin. "I'll leave you some antibiotic cream and some extra bandages. Change them once a day. As for the shots, I'd like to give you one for rabies, too."

I can handle two shots. I handled a crazy-ass mermaid, I remind myself.

"In total, you'll need five doses of the rabies vaccine over the next twenty-eight days."

"You've got to be kidding me!"

Adrien smiles, getting a kick out of my needle-phobia. *Son of a bitch.* I glare at him, but that just intensifies his grin.

Two shots, fine. But *six*? No way. Not when there wasn't even a fucking dog to begin with. Unless magical mermaids have rabies. Maybe if I don't get the shots, I'll sprout scales. I rub my arms, which tingle. I check for scales . . . just in case. When I find none, I heave out a sigh and relax my shoulders.

I look over at Cadence, and our eyes meet, but the contact is brief. She dips her chin into her neck and concentrates on her hoodie's ties, wrapping them around her finger, unwrapping them, wrapping them again. She's not radiating anger anymore, but she's also not radiating empathy or warmth.

As I put on my shirt and do up a few buttons, Doc gives me a prescription for antibiotics and instructions to visit her office in three days for a follow-up rabies shot.

She clicks her satchel closed, then puts on a khaki parka fit for Antarctica. "Rainier, will you see me out?"

Nodding, Rainier motors himself out of the living room. I return my gaze to Cadence, hoping to catch her eye, but she's observing Gaëlle, who's twisted around, watching the doctor and Rainier exit. A moment later, the front door snicks shut and then the wheelchair's rubber tires squeak back into the room.

Rainier parks himself in the doorway and removes the birch box from the wheelchair's pocket. Part of me wants to open the lead-lined box to look at the piece I retrieved from the mermaid's guts, but it's too risky. Besides, I can still see it in my mind, its rounded triangular shape, its smooth golden sheen. I can still feel it in my hand, lighter than I expected and warm like the ring.

I curl my fingers, the thick gold band strangling my still bruised digit.

Rainier tips his head toward the first floor. "Slate, come upstairs to my office. We need to put it away in the safe."

I frown. "And you need my help with that?"

"I can't exactly handle the piece myself."

I feel my eyebrows rise. "We're taking it out of the box?"

"Best way to ensure no one steals it."

Cadence's red lips pop open. "Who do you think might steal it, Papa?"

Rainier exchanges a weighted look with Gaëlle.

Cadence eyes them. "What are you two not telling us?"

"A lot of people in this town believe the Quatrefoil is real," Rainier says.

"I know that, Papa. Nolwenn mentioned she believed in magic, but you're not worried *she* might take it, are you?"

"She was watching us tonight," I toss in. I'd racked it up to being a busybody, but combined with her scrutiny of my ring, it's starting to feel like something else. "She was also very intrigued by my ring." I rub my palms over my legs.

"Nolwenn believes in the magic of the Quatrefoil and the Bloodstone"—Rainier drums his fingers against the box—"but she also believes in the curses, so she won't take the risk of stealing a leaf."

"Why are you putting it in the safe, then?" Cadence asks.

"Mainly, so we don't misplace it."

My fingers cramp around my knees. "Misplace it? Yeah. Please avoid *misplacing* it, De Morel."

Adrien stands. "I should go. I've got classes to prepare. And then attend," he adds with a tired smile. "If there are any disturbances" —he looks at Gaëlle and Rainier, at me, and finally at Cadence— "my cell phone is on."

"You're seriously worried about prepping your classes?" I say, not just because it's my life on the line, but because it's *everyone*'s life on the line.

"You may not care about school, Slate, but four hundred students depend on Adrien." Of course Cadence misinterprets what I'm saying. She really has it in for me tonight.

Women are confusing, but Cadence de Morel takes that to a whole new level. I'm starting to question whether she actually hugged me or if I imagined the entire thing.

Small trenches appear on Rainier's forehead. At least, I'm not the only one confused by her mercurial attitude.

"Slate?" He taps the box.

My cue to leave. I get up and follow him to the glass elevator.

As we trek across the marble foyer, he asks, "How do you feel?"

"Like I was attacked by a bull shark, and it won."

His lips, that have been tight all night, curve a little. I didn't even know the old man was capable of smiling. It's a sight. Makes him look almost approachable.

He rolls himself inside the lift, and I follow him in. As the glass box rises, I catch a glimpse of Adrien and Cadence walking out of the living room. He has one arm slung around her shoulders, and although her arms are crossed and her shoulders hunched, annoyance makes me fist my fingers.

Gaëlle's trailing after them, wrapping her yellow scarf around her neck.

"I wish I could've prepared her better for all of this." I'm guessing Rainier means his daughter and not his girlfriend.

Wait? Is she his girlfriend or was that just Cadence's speculation?

Rainier sighs. "Adrien said I should've been honest with her sooner, but I wanted to spare her as long as I could."

Because this is the slowest elevator built by mankind, I can still see them. Adrien winds his second arm around her back and pulls her into his chest just as the glass box jerks to a stop. I almost face-plant against the window that's fogged up from my heavy breathing.

"You don't have any designs on my daughter, do you?"

"Why?" I turn around slowly. "Have you promised her hand to Mercier?"

All traces of Rainier's smile vanish. "You didn't answer my question, Roland."

"The minute this ring's off my finger, I'll be on a train out of here."

"Without my daughter." I'm not sure if it's a question or a warning, but his eyes have become a truly frightful shade of blue.

"Well, I'm not planning on kidnapping her."

He narrows his eyes; I narrow mine.

"Don't know about you, but I'm beat, so point the way to the safe."

We head into his office, the site of our first confrontation. De Morel wheels himself to one of the filing units. He touches something on the side of the unit, and the entire front of it swings open and reveals a heavy safe.

"Are they all decoys?" I gesture to the other four units surrounding the one he just opened.

"No. Just this one."

He punches the keypad, not even trying to hide it from my line of sight. I'm guessing there's nothing in that safe worth stealing. Still, I memorize the numbers—three, two, six, one, eight, four.

The door clangs open. "Here." Rainier pops the lid on the birch box.

For a second, we both stare at the leaf, at the smooth gold shape of it. Everything that happened in the well flashes behind my eyes —fake-Cadence who looked so real, the wisps of blood and cloud of black gore, the stinging cold, the bitter darkness. I grit my teeth and snap out of it. No way am I getting PTSD because of magic. Not happening.

My fingers close roughly over the disc, and the ring ignites. "Where do you want it?"

"Top shelf. Behind the stacks of bills."

I all but chuck the leaf inside, wiping my hands on my jeans to get rid of the clinging heat. I'm so agitated I don't even try to swipe some bills, which honestly, would be damn easy. They're just sitting there for the taking. Pfff. Probably on purpose. Probably some kind of test.

"How will we know it's mine once all four are in there?"

"There are four shelves, Roland." Rainier points to the safe. "Besides, it won't matter anymore. As soon as the Quatrefoil comes together, the leaves won't be cursing anyone. They'll be funneling magic back inside the four of you . . . and the world."

Not entirely reassured, I back up so that he can close the safe. "When am I getting my inheritance again, De Morel?"

His hand slips as he's pushing the safe shut, and it slams with a loud thud. The timeworn scroll on the wall shudders from the impact.

"After the new moon, I'll sign it over to you."

"Might not serve me much by then."

Rainier concentrates on closing the fake filing cabinet.

"Look, it's not like I need it right now, but if the others aren't successful"—I palm the back of my neck but wince when my fingers hit my huge-ass Band-Aid. I tow my hand back down—"I want all of it to go to someone . . . a friend."

Rainier angles his wheelchair toward me. "I'll draw up the papers tomorrow."

I have to admit I'm a little surprised he's being so agreeable about this. Maybe I've somehow proved my worth.

"Good night, Roland."

I nod and head for the door.

"And Cadence is off limits. Don't make me regret allowing you to spend the night."

I look over my shoulder and salute him, my index and middle fingers bumping into the lump on my forehead. "You got it, old man."

He shoots me a glare on par with the water fairy's once she realized I wasn't under her charm. As I take the stairs toward my borrowed bedroom on the second floor, I yawn long and hard. Even if I was going to seduce Cadence, I wouldn't pick tonight. I'm way too beat, broken, and bruised.

I push my bedroom door open, then kick it closed, my fingers working the buttons on my shirt. On my way to the bathroom, I fling the soiled white material over the back of the armchair, then start on my jeans. I open the bathroom door, and a shriek rids me of several decibels of hearing.

Shit. I forgot this was a shared space.

24

CADENCE

"**G**et out!" I yell at Slate, who's just standing there, eyes planted on the towel I whipped off the chrome rack and wedged around my body at record speed.

Thankfully, I was still wearing a bra and my underwear when he barged into the bathroom, and thankfully, neither were particularly revealing.

According to Alma, I should be wearing thongs and pushups at all times—the key to being sexy is feeling sexy. Even though I own some nice lingerie, I don't see the point of wearing it, since no one can actually see them underneath my layers of wintry clothing.

"Don't the doors lock?" He asks this as though it's somehow my fault.

"I don't usually have to share my bathroom."

The shower's running, and steam curls over the edge of the glass door.

"Can you leave?"

"I can." He doesn't, though. He leans against the doorframe and crosses his arms.

I'm momentarily distracted by the sight of so much skin and muscle. I saw his chest earlier when he was getting stitched up, and its definition had made my stomach dip. I'd known Slate was well-built but hadn't realized just *how* well-built until tonight. I also hadn't realized how many scars he had—fresh and old ones.

So many old ones.

This really isn't the moment to ogle a guy. Especially one who cares about another girl. I fling my gaze to the long oval mirror over my marble sink top. In the foggy glass, I catch the corners of Slate's lips tipping up, accentuating the camber of his eyes.

"Mademoiselle de Morel, were you just checking me out?"

My cheeks redden. "No."

"I don't mind being objectified."

Oh. My. God. I glower now, and not through the mirror this time.

His smile grows as he says, "If looks could kill . . ."

He'd be dead.

The same thought must occur to him because he shudders, losing both his smile and his proud bearing.

My arms loosen a little around the towel. Not enough for it to fall off, but enough for it to stop compressing all of my organs.

He starts to turn but stops. "Can I ask you something?"

Warily, I acquiesce.

"Were you mad at me earlier, or did I misinterpret your silent treatment?"

My cheeks prickle, and I don't have to look in the mirror to know they're pinkening. Again. Maybe they never stopped. I lower my gaze to the floor, to the mess of soiled towels balled up in one corner, and then farther, to the blackened toe of his left foot. I noticed it earlier, but now feels like the appropriate time to bring it up.

"What did the *groac'h* do to your foot?"

"That wasn't her. That was all me." I feel his gaze on my face. "I dropped something heavy on it."

"Is it broken?"

"My toe or the—"

"Your toe."

"Might be. Most of me feels broken." He gestures to his body.

I see bruises but also flexing muscles, pebbling skin, and corded tendons. "Brume hasn't been kind to you, huh?" My voice sounds so husky I pray he blames it on the emotional rollercoaster I've been riding since the piece showed up.

"It's been . . . challenging, but not all bad."

"What part *wasn't* bad?"

For a long time, he's quiet. So quiet I raise my gaze back to his.

"The cheese and *chouchen* last night were nice." He tilts his head to the side, and a black corkscrew slides across his forehead. "So, am I delusional, or were you angry with me?"

Over the water needling the marble, I let out a long sigh. "I wasn't angry with you."

He frowns, clearly dubious.

I want to pin my earlier bout of jealousy on something else, *someone* else, but curiosity is a cruel, crafty thing. "You mentioned you saw a girl in the well. Who was she?"

His black eyebrows almost collide over his nose, and his stance changes: his shoulders roll back, and his arms tense, the tendons straining. He looks like the terracotta statue my mother made of a Greek god when she was studying at the university. Even though I've asked Papa for it, asked him to display it in our outsized foyer, he refuses to remove it from where it sits in the college's art department.

"Why do you ask?" His words are quiet but tense.

"I guess I'm trying to get to know you, and since this person is obviously important to you, it made me curious." And *wildly* jealous.

Logically, I leave that part out.

His eyes take on the same shade as the bottomless pit he miraculously climbed out of alive. "She's someone I don't know very well but whom I inexplicably feel strongly about."

"Does she live in Marseille?"

"No."

"Did you meet her in one of your foster homes?"

"No."

For someone so glib, he's not giving me much to go on. "You should tell her that you like her. Maybe she feels the same." He narrows his eyes, and I shrug. "What do you have to lose?"

For a moment, he doesn't move. Just watches me. "I'll think about it."

I tighten the towel.

Finally, he nods to the glassed-in shower stall. "Better get in before you run out of hot water. Nothing worse than freezing water." He unbinds his arms from their firm knot. "Knock three times when you're done, okay?"

The hard click of the door shutting resonates around me. I don't think he'll come back in, but I walk over and twist the lock. As I toss the towel and my undergarments off, my heart pounds as hard as the running water.

I'm attracted to Adrien. Not to Slate.

Adrien, who's gentle and compassionate.

Who still cajoles me as though I were a little girl.

Unlike Slate, who seems to see me as a woman.

His comment about me being a teen librarian comes back to me, and I loofah my skin until it's as red as my flushed face.

No one sees me as a grown-up.

Maybe tomorrow I'll heed Alma's mantra and wear sexy underwear. Before going to bed, I text her an apology and knock three times on Slate's side of the bathroom.

SLATE

The three knocks come. By the time I peel myself off the bed, the bathroom is empty and Cadence's side of the Jack and Jill is closed. I'm both relieved and a little disappointed. Mostly relieved, though. I don't want to lie to her. If she asks me one more time about the girl in the well, I might just cave. Which would surely be a bad idea. On par with sticking the De Morel heirloom on my finger.

I inhale the sweet, crisp steam that smells of Cadence. I was dead tired a second ago, and now all of me is awake. Damn soap.

After brushing my teeth with a gifted toothbrush, I flick off the lights and stare at the door opposite mine, tempted to knock. Or just to barge in and ask her point-blank why she cares so much whom I pictured in the well.

Wait. Could she be jealous?

I remember the googly eyes she made at Adrien back at the tavern and their hug earlier. *Nah.* I'm totally delusional. There's no way Cadence is jealous. She's hung up on Professor Prickhead.

If I'm totally honest with myself, Adrien isn't *all* bad.

But I don't like him on principle. On several principles.

Back in the bedroom, I slide under the duvet. It's thick but lightweight, so it doesn't rest uncomfortably on my sores and scratches. My head sinks into the pillow and within seconds I'm out like a dead man.

When I wake up, the sky outside the windows is steely gray. The clock on the nightstand reads 8:00. *Shit.* Did I only get four hours of sleep? I yank the duvet over my face, but it's too late. I'm up. My body is so stiff it creaks. Pain in my jaw radiates up through my ear to the top of my skull. There's blood on the pillow. The industrial-sized Band-Aid is soaked through, despite the zipper of stiches underneath.

On the bright side, my toe's feeling better.

I knock on the bathroom door.

When there's no answer, I let myself in and wash up. The room still smells faintly of Cadence and her girly soap. My temperature goes up as I remember the glimpse I got of her last night. The pale, smooth surface of her stomach. The soft curve of her hips. The black cotton of her bra, straining to hold in her breasts.

Putain. I've got to get myself together.

I look like Frankenstein's monster with all the stitches and cuts and lumps. I change my bandages, put on yesterday's clothes, and head downstairs for something to eat. When I get to the kitchen, I see the magical house elves have been at it again; a large platter of fresh *croissants, pains au chocolat,* and buttered *tartines* coated in chunky strawberry jam sits on the island, along with a butcher board laden with cheeses and paper-thin cold-cuts. So this is what life is like for the De Morels . . .

I'm gullet-deep in a *pain au chocolat* when Cadence breezes in.

At the sight of me, she jolts like she's just been electrocuted, and then her mouth twists into something that's more grimace than smile. "You're up."

I swallow the pastry, lick the melted chocolate off my teeth, and give her my most disarming grin. "Good morning to you, too."

A blush rises in her cheeks, and she hurries over to the coffee machine on the stainless-steel counter. "Espresso?"

"Hell, yeah," I say.

She fiddles with the machine, keeping her gaze pinned to the little cup under the spout. "Papa's in physical therapy with Jacqueline right now."

Like I give two shits where her dad is at the moment. "Sleep well?"

"Not as well as you. Papa said you'd be tired, but I didn't realize he meant out-for-over-twenty-four-hours tired." Without making eye contact, she slides the cup in front of me on the island, then retraces her steps to make herself one, brow crinkled as though facing a puzzle instead of a one-buttoned machine.

"Wait. What?"

"You missed all of yesterday. It was a red-letter day, too. The sun broke through the fog for a full five hours."

"Holy hell." I didn't even know it was possible to sleep that long.

"Sylvie—the doctor—said it was perfectly fine, so long as you showed signs of life today." She slides her bottom lip between her teeth. I sense she's nervous, but why? Because I slept so long she thought I was dead? Not likely. Because I saw her in her underwear last night . . . or, well, the night before? Possibly.

A thought suddenly occurs to me and makes my chest seize up.

What if she knows I saw *her* in the well? What if she thinks I'm some twisted deviate that gets obsessed over a girl he barely knows?

I mean, shit, I've only known her for *three days*. Or four, actually, though I'm not sure yesterday counts.

I've fallen for objects I wanted but never for a person before. Unlike Bastian. Shit, the girls he's blubbered over. The nights he tossed and turned because he was trying to interpret a look or a conversation or a text from a girl. Now, I'm the one analyzing every facial twitch and mood swing, every spoken word and fleeting look.

Something's appallingly wrong with me.

I need to get back to normal, aka arrogant, crafty, and apathetic. And I need things to get back to normal with Cadence, too.

"What's up, Mademoiselle de Morel?"

She finally looks away from her cup. "Up?"

"You're usually chattier."

Her pupils tighten against their exquisite blue backgrounds.

"Did seeing me without my shirt get you so hot and bothered that being in my company now flusters you?"

The black pins expand, usurping the blue. "Get over yourself, Slate." She sucks down her espresso in one quick shot.

"Ah. But can *you* get over me?"

Irritation brightens her cheeks. "You're such a jerk."

There we go. Welcome back, Slate. Welcome back, Cadence.

I take a mouthful of the hot liquid and let its bitter flavor coat my tongue. "Ah, but such a handsome one. Makes me harder to hate."

"Oh my God." She rolls her eyes so hard I don't think they'll ever level back. "You're just trying to get a rise out of me, aren't you?"

"Perhaps. Or perhaps I'm really this conceited." I put the cup back down and call a truce with a softer tone of voice. "Which piece should we go hunting down today?"

She sighs. "It has to show itself."

I hold up my hand with the ring. "Not necessarily. I've got a detector, remember?"

She bites her bottom lip again, and again I'm transfixed by her white teeth denting the full red flesh. "I've got a couple classes today."

"With all this magic shit happening, you're really going to class?"

"If I drop everything, then that shows I've lost faith that we'll succeed, which means the dark magic wins." She lifts her chin to display confidence, yet her eyes glitter with fear.

"We've got the first piece, Cadence. There's no reason we won't get the others."

She nods. Before I can think better of it, I reach out and take her hand. Her fingers are warm and soft. So soft. My mind blanks and then whirs back to life, her touch waking me quicker than caffeine.

Her fingers jerk out of mine, and then with a trembling hand, she snatches a croissant before striding back toward the foyer. "I'll go grab my stuff."

Operation *getting things back to normal with Cadence* is a fail. The hand-holding probably did it.

I eat another two pastries and scoop up some ham. As I wash it all down with a glass of pulpy orange juice, Cadence trundles back in, silver jacket zipped up to her chin and slouchy hat wedged over her ears.

My heart holds still, and goose bumps rise. And not the good sort. The bad sort. The sort that use to pebble my skin when I'd hear Vincent pound down the creaky corridor toward my bedroom.

Cadence's red lips part just like the siren's, but no sound comes out. They part wider. This time, I catch my name, loud as a zinging bullet, followed by, "Are you okay?"

I stand up slowly, my joints stiff and my skin slick with the memory of the chilled well water. I tunnel my fingers through my hair, hoping my hand isn't shaking. I need to kick this PTSD before it sets in any deeper. I focus on the end of my mission, on the cloud of black gore and the shine of the leaf.

The cursed piece wasn't successful; I was.

I was.

Curling my fingers, I amble toward Cadence. "I'll get my coat."

I don't remember where I put it but assume the house elf stashed it in the foyer closet. I pull open the door and *bingo*. I tug it off the hanger and slide into it. Once I've buttoned it up, I stick my hands inside my gloves, my ringed finger feeling a lot less swollen.

As we make our way up the circles toward campus, I ask Cadence if I got it right, if her father did take her mother's last name. I find it odd but that's because society has brainwashed me to think a certain way. Why not take your wife's last name? I think of my own last name. Or rather my two last names. Who am I? An Ardoin or a Roland? Both. Neither.

When we reach Fourth Kelc'h, we hit an expanse of snow-covered lawn tattooed with dirty footprints going every which way. Students scurry from one ivy-choked gray limestone building to another, books and binders in their arms or in heavy bags slung over their shoulders.

Cadence grins and turns into a tour guide. "So, this is where the campus buildings start." She points out some faculty housing, a couple of amphitheaters, the cafeteria, a massive gym. All are outfitted with modern gadgets, but the stone walls and slate-tiled roofs are in tune with the ancient feel of the whole town.

Up on Fifth, the fog fades into vaporous webs. Far below, I spy the silver mirror of the lake on one side and the green slope of pines on the other.

Cadence gestures to the four buildings spaced evenly around the temple-turned-library. "Centuries ago, these were the founding families' homes."

I lift an eyebrow at the massive size of the structures. "Guess magic was profitable."

She points to a long building with an even longer glassed-in promenade. "The Bisset Esplanade, center of physics and biology." A square, limestone chateau is next. "The Mercier Humanities Center, the seat of history and social sciences." Then a circular stone and glass edifice. "The Roland Amphitheater"—her eyes flick my way, then back to the building—"for business and engineering."

I swallow but say nothing.

"And this," she says proudly, "is the De Morel Beaux-Arts Edifice." She leads me past an arch carved with the words ARZOÙ-KAER, which I imagine mean art.

"Snazzy," I mutter, taking in the royal spread.

"What's your class schedule, by the way? I could show you where you need to go."

"I didn't come to attend school, princess."

She frowns. "Then why did you come?"

"For my inheritance. 'Parently, my biological parents left me a trust, and put your daddy in charge of it."

Her eyebrows pinch together.

"Rainier's taking his sweet time signing it over. I think he's using it as a motivator." I rub my hands together, feeling the Bloodstone under my glove. "He forgets I literally can't leave this place before the Quatrefoil is united."

Cadence blinks up at me. "So you won't stay and study after?"

"Not planning on it."

"Oh." Her mouth puckers as though she's truly disappointed.

Probably no one's ever turned down studying in her family's grand old school. "But who knows. If I survive, I might reconsider."

Her disappointment veers to another emotion, one that makes me want to kick myself for reminding her of our perilous hunt. "Can you tell me more about this building?"

In increments, her fear subsides, and the light in her eyes returns. And then her mouth moves a mile a minute as she leads me through the palatial art department, telling me about the symbolism for the tiny human faces, flower stalks, and mythological creatures etched into the pillars that hold up the impossibly high domed ceiling adorned with plump cherubs surfing on clouds. We walk past corridors dotted with wooden doors running off in two directions, and a double, wide stone staircase twisting upward to the heavens . . . or more likely, to the next level.

The main hall's lined with centuries' worth of art: massive paintings in gilt frames, a strip of vellum with characters that range from hieroglyphs to biblical font to typewriter letters, glossy marble busts of men with curled hair, polished statues of everything from the human form to the abstract, suits of armors complete with massive broadswords and shields. There are cases full of masquerade masks, six-faced clocks, gaudy costume jewelry, old playbills and posters, and even . . .

I raise an eyebrow. "Magic wands?"

She smiles at the mess of sticks in the glass case. "No. According to lore, magic of the elements—the magic of Brume—doesn't require a wand. These are said to be pieces of kindling that never lit when ten Brumian women were supposed to be burned at the stake for witchcraft."

I take a closer look and, sure enough, the sticks look charred at the ends. "So these sticks are hundreds of years old?"

She nods, face aglow. "And the craziest part about this witch hunt is that it took place four centuries *after* the *diwallers* supposedly destroyed magic. Yet the fire wouldn't burn."

I smile. That's right. It's *history* that gets her hot and bothered, not the sight of my bare chest. "I take it the women survived?"

She shakes her head, smile dimming. "No. They ended up being hanged."

The fact that I even slightly believe the tale shows how much this town has derailed my life. "Bastard witch hunters."

Her cell dings, and she checks it. "I need to get to the Bisset building." Then she looks up at me, pulling her bottom lip back into her mouth as though debating something. "But I want to show you something before I leave."

She leads me farther down the hall, to a glassed-in gazebo-like alcove, where, on a pedestal, stands a terracotta statue of a scowling giant wearing nothing but a one-shouldered toga and an ancient-looking helmet, the kind with a crest of plumes. He's holding a round shield and a sword as long as my body. Despite being made of clay, he looks about to leap out and smash skulls.

It's fucking creepy. And pretty damn cool.

Cadence gestures to it with pride. "Maman made this. Her war god."

"Ares," I murmur. I wasn't a good student, but some things did stick, like mythology. We had to memorize gods along with their symbols, lineage, the whole shebang. Ares was one of the unpopular ones, because he represented brutality and ruin. Which is probably why I remember him best.

Cadence lifts an eyebrow. "Mythology enthusiast?"

"God of War enthusiast." I can't get over how realistic the statue is. "This is really amazing."

The doors all along the corridor start to open, and students pour out. Suddenly, we're in the middle of a crowd. Several people ogle me as they walk past.

I get it. I'm new here, and *here* is small. But still, it's grating. One guy, who's like forty, is just standing in the middle of the hallway, gawking at me. Everything about him is faded and pale. From his pasty skin to his dull, dust-colored hair to his colorless lips. He's like one of those frumpy professor types, his clothes all askew, his tie almost completely undone, his shirt untucked, and his cardigan badly buttoned.

Dude looks like shit, yet he's eyeing *me* like I'm the turd here.

I'm about to go up to him and ask what his problem is, but all of a sudden, pain wrenches my muscles and fire streaks through my veins.

What the hell?

My shoulder muscles spasm and bunch, and it hits me that I forgot to take the pain pills this morning. And yesterday, since I was passed out. Or maybe it's the shot the doc administered. When's my next one supposed to be again?

As I rack my brain, Cadence says, "I really have to go, but I'll see you later?" She sounds hopeful, and it makes my pain take a giant leap back.

Before she can get very far, two girls, who look familiar, approach us.

The one with the super short hair says, "Hey, Cadence, I've been meaning to ask ..."

A fresh wave of pain slams into me. I can see the girl's mouth move but can't hear anything. It's like I'm underwater again. As I force myself to take even breaths, I focus on a freckle on the second girl's chin. The hallway blurs, but not that brown dot. I feel like if I can just keep that in my central vision, I won't faint in fucking agony.

A hand touches my forearm—Chin-freckle's—and I stiffen. I want to fling her off, but a bolt of electricity makes me cramp up. I breathe hard, as though oxygen could somehow lessen the effect of my battle wounds. I even shut my eyes.

And then *poof!*

The pain's gone. I lick the sweat off my top lip and crack open my lids. Even though I don't miss it, I wonder where it went. Did my breathing just defeat it?

"Great. I'll email you the rest of the deets," Pixie-hair says, then spears her arm through Chin-freckle's.

They turn in perfect synchronicity, their narrow hips swaying.

Suddenly, Pixie-hair flips back around. "Oh. And, Cadence, you're welcome to bring your boyfriend."

Cadence's hands fumble off her crossbody bag's strap, and her cheeks burn as pink as the terracotta statue at her back. "He's not my boyfriend," she mumbles.

Chin-freckle leans over to whisper something in her friend's ear. The girl with the short hair smiles and bobs her head. And then Chin-freckle winks at me.

"Bye, Slate." She wiggles her fingers before turning back around.

What the hell just happened? I'm about to ask Cadence who they were when she grunts.

"Birthday party. Adrien will hate it."

I rub the back of my neck, but my fingers collide with my Band-Aid, and I wince. Which reminds me of the agony I was in a minute ago. Could another piece be nearby? But if it is, how come it's gone? Shouldn't it still be killing me?

"Adrien's birthday's coming up?" I ask, so as not to worry Cadence in case it *is* another piece. As soon as she leaves I'll walk around the hall and see if my ring lights up.

"Yeah. Next week. If you hadn't been so busy checking out Jasmine, you might've caught on."

I frown. Jasmine?

Cadence backs up. Stops. Her lips part as though she's about to say something, but then she shakes her head and strides away, abandoning me with the oversized warlord.

"Women," I tell him, shaking my head before pulling off my glove and walking up and down the hallway he guards.

The red oval glints from the sunshine pouring through the gazebo but doesn't light up, and my body doesn't feel like it's being quartered again. Pain killers. That's what I need before my next flareup. And a shirt that doesn't have blood smears on the collar. No one can see them with my coat on, but without it, I'll be Brume's grand attraction now that it's no longer the well.

26

CADENCE

I sit through two classes. Nothing sinks into my brain, which is too busy dissecting what happened in the hallway earlier. I write Jasmine's name and drag my pen through it, slicing neatly through the paper. If I were a witch, I bet this would hex Charlotte's bestie somehow.

Who fondles random men's arms?

Also, Charlotte thought Slate was *my* boyfriend, so Jasmine must've assumed the same.

Who touches another girl's boyfriend?

Also ... *again* ... and this is really the most perturbing part, why do I care?

The bell rings, and the pen I've been wringing the ink out of falls from my fingers. I bend over, pick it up, and fling it inside my bag where it rolls between my laptop and astronomy notebook.

Slate isn't your boyfriend, Cadence, I remind myself because myself somehow thinks she has a right to be jealous. *Slate's not even your friend. He's just your fellow Quatrefoil gatherer. A pompous stranger who looted your family crypt. There's no reason in the galaxy—certainly, not his great abs or fearsome scars—why you should be attracted to him. Plus, he's the guy who broke your New Year's tradition because he didn't want to kiss you.*

You don't like him.

Not one bit.

This isn't my first inner monologue, but it's definitely my lengthiest, which should probably worry me, but considering the events happening around Brume, I decide talking to myself is not all that concerning. What *is* concerning is that I'm more worried Slate might like Jasmine than I am about surviving the Quatrefoil.

Even though I'm not especially hungry, I have two hours to kill before my afternoon classes, and Alma's still in hers, so I decide to head down the hill to Gaëlle's shop for her magical soup and scones —they aren't spelled or anything . . . at least, not yet. Plus, I need answers as to whether she is seeing Papa. I didn't ask him yesterday, and this morning, he was already with Jacqueline by the time I woke up, and it didn't feel right bringing it up in front of his physical therapist. I could, of course, wait until I get home, but for some reason, I feel more comfortable discussing this with Gaëlle than with Papa. I'm still not sure how I might react if Alma's hunch turns out to be true, and I don't want to hurt my father by responding badly to the news.

Au Bon Sort is bursting with students by the time I arrive. All of the small round tables fitted between the aisles of witchy wares are occupied, and the line to the glass case displaying today's lunch offerings snakes around twice. I spot the top of Romain's blond head bobbing over the hungry crowd, and then I spot Gaëlle coming out from the small kitchen in the back, a pen stuck through the hair she's twisted and piled on top of her head. Between her undereye circles and the questionable stain on the shoulder of her gray T-shirt, I take it this isn't the right time to confront her.

I'm about to leave when I take pity on mother and stepson and carve a path through the crowd toward them. "I have an hour. Need some help?"

She looks up from scooping *crème fraiche* onto bowls of cider-braised apples. "Oh, yes, please!"

Waving hello to Romain, who grins at me as he rings up a customer, I circle the glass case and head to the back kitchen where I drop my bag and coat, and wash my hands. Before going back out, I tie a red *Au Bon Sort* apron over my white blouse. I stare at my reflection in the narrow mirror glued to the door. I didn't fasten the buttons of my shirt all the way to the collar, but close. So much for dressing a little sexier.

I finger the buttons, hesitating to undo one or two. In the end, I leave them be. Walking around looking like a naughty school girl just isn't me. Besides, I don't want to hook a guy with a lace bra—yes, I wore one, even though, frankly it's so itchy I'm dying to take it off—I want to hook a guy with my personality.

Pushing my hair behind my ears, I walk back out and help get the lunch orders bagged or plated. Thirty minutes later, it quiets down. And then another fifteen minutes after that, and *Au Bon Sort* all but empties out. Only a few people remain, munching on the *Magie Noire* cookies Gaëlle bakes daily, or sipping one of the home-made caffeinated brews, or browsing the narrow aisles of witchy-inspired products that run the gamut from costumes and spell books to board games and scented candles to jars filled with dried herbs and ointments with supposed magical properties.

"You're a lifesaver, Cadence." Gaëlle grabs the last Dark Magic cookie with a piece of waxed paper and hands it over.

"It was nothing." I take the treat from her and bite into it, moaning.

Her lips arch with pride.

Licking a glob of gooey chocolate off the corner of my mouth, I say, "I remember you promising to teach me how to make these."

"I haven't forgotten. It's just that between the twins, Romain, the shop, and—" She stops herself from mentioning the Quatrefoil out loud. Unless it was Papa she was about to mention.

"Gaëlle, do you have a minute to talk? Not about the . . . leafy thing."

Her eyebrows jut down low. "Um. Sure."

After asking Romain to check if anyone needs refills or sweet treats, she grabs a bottle of hand-squeezed orange and ginger juice from the refrigerated glass case and gestures to a table at the very back of the shop, against a shelf bursting with tins of tisanes that can supposedly mend anything from a broken heart to a broken bone.

"Is everything all right, sweetie?" she asks as we take our seats, the old wooden rungs of the chairs creaking.

This place has been in her family forever, which leads me to wonder if it was an actual magic shop back in the day.

Peeling the parchment paper off my cookie, I say, "I'm going to ask you something, and I want you to be completely honest with me."

She unscrews the top off her bottle and brings it up to her mouth. "Okay . . ."

"Are you and Papa dating?"

She gags midswallow and then pounds her chest, coughing. "Oh, Cadence. No. No, no, no. Your papa and I, we're just friends." Her brown skin deepens in color, though, and I don't know if it's because of my question or the juice or any feelings she might be harboring for her "friend." She must sense I'm not convinced, because she reaches across the table and wraps her fingers around mine. "I love your papa, but not romantically. Besides, like I said, I have enough men in my life." She adds this with a smile. "And trust me when I say this, no man wants a woman attached at the hip to eight-month-old twins who haven't figured out that nights are meant for sleeping."

I nod.

"Whatever made you think he and I"—she coughs again— "were together?"

"It's just something Alma said."

Gaëlle's deep brown eyes grow wide. "Oh, gosh, I hope not too many people believe this."

"I don't think so. At least, I haven't heard any rumors."

She screws the lid back on her bottle, then twists it back off. "Your papa has helped me through a lot of things, emotionally and financially, which has brought us closer, but I promise you that nothing untoward has happened."

"I trust you, Gaëlle." And then I reach over, because she's still toying with the cap of her bottle, and I feel guilty to have made her feel uncomfortable. "And if anything did, I wouldn't be mad. I guess I would just want to be the first to know."

I realize that, as I'm speaking these words, I actually mean them. I'd be happy for my father to connect with someone again. Especially since I sense his handicap has a lot to do with him being on his own. Even though he's never burdened anyone with his condition and is supremely independent, dating someone in a wheelchair cannot be easy.

I pull my hand back to break off a chunk of cookie. As I chew on it, my gaze slides to the shop window where a little girl has her face squashed against the glass, attention riveted to the store mascot: a tarantula named Tracy. The thing freaks Alma out so much that I need to physically drag her into *Au Bon Sort* to get her inside the shop.

Last spring, when we'd stopped by for iced coffees on one of the rare days not filled with cold rain and mist, we'd found Romain kneeling beside the shelf laden with Ouija boards. When we asked him what he was doing, he said he was looking for Tracy. Alma shrieked so loudly it caused a wave of panic. First, a shopper sniffing a candle dropped it, and glass sprayed everywhere. Then, Gaëlle, who'd been carrying over a platter of drinks, jumped, which knocked the cups over. They splashed her pregnant belly before teetering off the platter and breaking like the candle holder. And then two little girls, who'd come to shop for costumes, clawed at their mother's legs, bawling.

When Romain had risen back up, face as red as the apron tied around his waist, mumbling "April Fool's" and pointing to Tracy, lounging about in her tank, Gaëlle, usually an extremely placid person, had turned so livid I was a little afraid she'd go into premature labor. I caught Romain's eye over his stepmom's shaking shoulders and had grinned. Feeling bad for him, I'd gone to grab the duster to help clean up. Had Tracy really been on the loose, I would've probably pulled an Alma and skipped out of the store, minus the banshee-screaming part.

I frown as I catch sight of a man standing outside the shop, right behind the little girl ogling Tracy's tank. At first, I think he might be a homeless drifter loaded on too much *chouchen*, but then my breath hitches because I recognize him. "Gaëlle!"

"What?" The cap of her bottle jerks out of her hand, hits the sugar dispenser, and rolls off the table.

"Matthias! He's outside!"

Her face turns ashen.

I don't wave hello to Gaëlle's ex-husband. Instead, I glance toward Romain, who's wiping down the glass case. I worry how he'll react if he catches sight of his father.

A cold stream of liquid drips onto my lap, and I jerk away from the table.

Gaëlle's spilled her drink and is so shell-shocked that I don't think she notices. I grab a handful of napkins from the dispenser beside the sugar and blot my jeans as she slowly, slowly turns in her chair.

Matthias looks miserable and pasty, his tie loose, his cardigan buttoned all wrong. Gaëlle goes as still as my mother's statues. I think she might've even stopped breathing. A second later, she stands, walks over to the door of the shop and twists the deadbolt. And then she flips the OPEN/CLOSED sign, croaks something to Romain, which makes him look up but not out, so it's probably not about his estranged dad showing up out of the blue. The boy nods, then unties his apron and, folding it carefully, heads toward the staircase that leads to their private apartment atop the shop.

Like a ghost, Gaëlle floats toward the three remaining customers and tells them she has an emergency and must close up early. Her spooked look makes them gather their things quickly and without protest. Once lined up at the door, Gaëlle unlocks it to let them pass through. None look toward Matthias; they all walk right past him.

As she locks the door again, a shudder goes through her, making her bun shake so hard the pen escapes. Curly strands fall down her rigid back.

I toss the wet napkins on the table, then walk over to her. "Do you want me to go talk to him?"

"No!" The word snaps out of her mouth.

The mother of the little girl ogling Tracy must notice Matthias, because she holds out her hand to beckon her daughter away. The little girl pouts but obediently backs up. Straight into Gaëlle's ex. Scratch that. Straight *through* Gaëlle's ex.

Oh.

Crap.

Gaëlle slaps her palm against her mouth, stifling another gasp. "C-call Rainier. C-c-c-call him."

I race into the kitchen where I left my bag. My phone feels lubed up because it takes me three attempts to wrestle it out of the front pocket. Speed-dialing Papa, I run back into the shop. I'm half expecting Matthias to have drifted right through the glass, but he's still standing outside. His mouth curves into a terrifying smile, terrifying because he's missing so many teeth and blood is trickling out of his mouth. And what's wrong with his head? It's a little concave around his left temple, as though he was hit by a crowbar, and it remolded his skull.

Forget the *groac'h.*

This man—this *ghost*—might be the most terrifying thing I've ever seen.

I hear a deep voice seep out of my phone and remember I've dialed my father. "Papa," I whisper. The ghost breaks eye contact with his wife and turns his pale eyes on me. "Papa," I murmur again.

My poor father yells, "What's going on? Where are you?" and I'm in such shock that I can't blubber anything but another few *Papas* out.

Gaëlle takes the phone from me. There's so much blood rushing through my ears that I can't hear what she says. She races to the back of the store, grabs a jar of something, knocking over another. The loud shatter of glass penetrates my eardrums and makes me jump. She sprints back toward me, all but tossing my phone on a nearby table, then unscrews the pot and pours whatever's inside in a straight line down *Au Bon Sort*'s façade, peppering the tangle of string lights, plastic vine leaves, and length of black tulle that frames the large square window, heaping some over Tracy's tank and the quatrefoil made of twisted branches propped next to it, and finally onto the doormat.

"Dried garlic and black pepper." Her breath rattles.

She sprinkles some of the mixture onto me, and then onto herself. A flake must get into my right eye, because it starts watering.

"It'll keep unwanted spirits away," she adds.

I swallow because I don't know what to say. No, that's not true. I know what to say, I just don't know where to start. Again, not true. I know exactly where to start.

"Your husband's a ghost?"

She's regained some color, but her eyes are glassy as though she, too, got some of the spice blend inside.

"I thought . . . I thought . . ." I thought he'd boarded a train and headed out of Brume. I definitely didn't think he was buried six feet under. "If he's a ghost, then that means . . . that means . . ." Besides the fact that ghosts are freaking real! "He's dead?"

The gray specter outside pivots a little, and the contours of his flesh curl as though he's made of smoke. How could I have mistaken him for a real man?

On a breath, she gushes, "He's my piece!"

I blink.

"My element is Air. He's my piece."

My heart misses a lot of beats but then settles. The ghost must be the projection of Gaëlle's worst fear, not her husband risen from the dead.

I've almost recovered from my freak-out when I remember the girl. "Gaëlle, the child made contact with him!"

"I know."

The chocolate cookie feels like it's spoiling inside my stomach. "Does that mean she's cursed now?"

Gaëlle sweeps her lashes over her eyes, up and down, up and down. A tear snakes out. Then another. "Maybe she'll be okay."

Papa is in a wheelchair because he touched a piece. I don't see how she'll be okay. I'm half-expecting to hear screaming ring through the street, but the piece will probably take its sweet time cursing her.

"What if other people touch him? What if—"

"I know, Cadence!" Her voice is so full of nerves it feels as though it shakes the hardwood floor beneath my shearling-lined boots.

I glance toward the stairs wondering if Romain will come back down, worried by the yelling, but I don't hear any footfalls.

She clutches the half-empty pot against her heaving chest. "I need . . . to go . . . out there." She swallows. "I need to . . . draw a circle . . . around him."

I hike up an eyebrow. "To keep him corralled in? Are you sure garlic and pepper will work?"

"No. But I d-don't know what else t-t-to do."

Something begins to vibrate on a nearby table. My phone. When I see Papa's name flash across the screen, I answer immediately. "*Oui,* Papa?"

"Cadence, are you still with Gaëlle?" If I thought Gaëlle sounded nervy, my father sounds downright strung out.

"*Oui.*"

"Put me on speakerphone."

It takes me two attempts, but I manage to punch my screen in the right place.

"Gaëlle, you need to go to the Rolands' house."

Gaëlle's hand crawls up her chest, then settles on her neck, and she clutches it so hard I worry she'll strangle herself. "I can't, Rainier. I can't."

"You can. I'm on my way there now, and so are Adrien and Slate."

"I c-can't." She's shaking, tears streaming down her cheeks.

"You can," Papa says with such calm that it sloughs off a little of my own fear. "We'll all be there with you."

"What if he tries to t-touch you?" she croaks.

"He can't touch us."

My skin coats in goose bumps. "Can't he?"

"The pieces can't touch you, *ma chérie*," Papa explains steadily.

The cookie feels like it's swimming back up my throat. "But a little girl walked right through him."

Papa makes a strangled noise. "Because she didn't see him. Only *diwallers* can see him." Papa sighs. "*Ma* Cadence, *you* can touch it, but *it* can't touch you. Not unless it's your piece."

"What about you? You can't see it. What if you roll right into him?"

"Once I get out there, I won't move to avoid any risk of contact."

"What about the little girl? Will she be okay?"

Papa doesn't answer.

I swallow back the wad of cookie and bile. The *groac'h* in the well was crazy, but at least she was contained. Nothing encloses this ghost. Unless the spice blend can truly keep him in place . . .

"And the Rolands' house?" I watch the ghost study his ex-wife. "Why are we meeting there?"

There's a beat of silence before Papa says, "Because that's where Matthias is buried."

The phone slides out of my fingers and falls onto the blackened doormat.

Papa's voice rises from the floor. "Adrien thinks Gaëlle needs to lead the ghost back to its bones to defeat it."

This isn't just some projection of Gaëlle's worst fear. This is . . . this is . . .

Her husband isn't gone. He's *dead*.

And Papa knew.

Gaëlle knew.

How?

How do they know he's dead?

How do they know where he's buried?

My questions must register on my face, because Gaëlle whispers, "It was an accident. Oh my God, I don't want to do this." Her voice breaks. "I don't want to face him again."

27

SLATE

I stare down at the text ordering me to meet the Quatrefoil crew. There's a quick explanation about the ghost of Gaëlle's ex-husband being the Air piece, along with the instructions to go to his resting place. But what gets me are the words *at the Roland family home.*

Why the hell is Gaëlle's ex buried at my family's home?

And also, what the actual fuck: I have a family home? Another thing the Great and Terrible Rainier de Morel failed to mention. Okay. Maybe, just maybe, I could give the guy the benefit of the doubt. Maybe the house was sold right after my parents' deaths and a new family's living there. Maybe Gaëlle's ex was part of that new family. Maybe when De Morel says *the Roland family home* he really means the *old* Roland family home.

After no luck detecting a piece in the Beaux-Arts building or in town—I walked around Brume holding my middle finger out as an antenna, which didn't make me any new friends . . . I got lots of *tsk*s and shocked looks from people misinterpreting the gesture—I headed back to the dorms to grab a clean shirt, fresh bandages, and a double dose of painkillers.

The address is not in the center of town but on the edge of First Kelc'h, near the forest. It takes a good twenty minutes to walk there from the university dorms.

At the end of a long path, a stone house with a steeply pitched

206 | WILDENSTEIN & HAYOZ

roof and red shutters materializes through the mist. It's nowhere near as large and pretentious as the *Manoir de Morel*, bigger than a cottage but no castle. Something straight out of a fairytale with its jumbled ivy crawling up the walls and lace curtains peeking from behind nine-paned windows. All that's missing are the seven dwarves.

It's charming, that's what it is. Not my style at all. I like clean, modern lines, bay windows, and city-life right outside my door, so I don't know why seeing the damn place makes my chest hurt and my throat feel raw. Like this pile of gray stones is some piece of me that I lost and have now found. Complete and utter bullshit. I was too young when my parents died to have a connection to this place.

Bastian would love it, though. It's perfect for a romantic like him. Yeah, he'd go full hog with a wife and 2.5 kids, a *bichon frisé*, and rows of tulips planted on either side of the front door. Even Spike might like it. It faces south, so if I put him in the front window, he'd get to sun his prickly ass all day.

If the mist ever clears up, that is.

There's really something wrong with me. There's no way I'd move to Dismalville. Why am I even entertaining the thought?

A miniature version of the house sits at the end of the drive. Voices drift from beyond it, so I go around and find my crew standing—for the most part—in a loose circle amidst a wide expanse of unsullied snow. A mass of evergreens stretches far and wide, corralling the backyard like a fortified wall.

Rainier eyes me from atop his souped-up snowmobile. "Slate's here." He doesn't utter the word *finally*, but it's there. On his mind.

Asshat.

"Let the games begin," I bellow with great solemnity as I stroll over to the huge X of sticks laid out between my crew.

"It's not a game." Adrien's firmly aligned lips barely shift around his answer.

No shit, Prof.

Cadence's eyebrows knit together, her hands cupped over her mouth like she's either holding in a scream or trying to warm them up. Although Gaëlle's back is to me, I notice she's shaking, the frizzy ends of her long curls wobbling against the back of her coat. A length of rope is coiled at her feet.

I crunch through the snow to stand between Cadence and Adrien.

Cadence lowers her hands from her mouth, which looks redder than usual. Maybe it's in contrast to how white her skin is at the present moment.

"Hey." She doesn't look at me as she greets me. She's wholly focused on pulling something out of her coat pocket—a saltshaker filled with soot-colored grains. "I brought you this. We're hoping it'll trap the ghost."

When she hands it over, our fingers bump, and a zing goes up my arm. She yanks her hand back, then stuffs it into her pocket and shifts away from me, adding a good three feet of distance between us.

"I've heard of seasoning stuff to trap in the juices but wasn't aware it also worked on ghosts," I say to lighten up the grim mood of the assembled folks.

Especially Cadence's.

When she showed me her mother's statue this morning, I thought everything was good between us once again. That she either wasn't so worried about me being an infatuated deviant or that she actually hadn't figured that bit out after all. But then she got all weird about Jocelyn or Julia or Jeannine, and now she's blatantly ignoring me.

I don't know what's up. As per usual.

I shoot my gaze toward Gaëlle. "If the ghost's your ex, why are we *chez moi*? Why not in the cemetery?"

"We were just establishing that," Adrien mutters between clenched teeth.

"No, we weren't. We were establishing a plan." Rainier stares pointedly at the giant X. "Why his bones are here isn't important to getting the piece—"

"It is if you want *my* help getting it. I worked with Matthias. He was a friend. What everyone said happened always felt wrong. He wasn't the type to have up and left his family like that." Adrien pins Gaëlle with a furious glare. "Why is he buried here? What did you two do to him?"

"It was an accident . . ." Gaëlle's voice is a near whisper.

Whoa. Did Gaëlle kill a man? I feel my eyebrows shoot up to the top of my forehead. I glance over at Cadence, but she's steadfastly studying the snow at her feet.

"What did you do to him?" Adrien repeats, zero empathy in his voice.

Rainier barks, "Matthias was cursed," as though this explains why Gaëlle offed her baby-daddy.

Adrien's fury morphs into bafflement. "What? How?"

"He accidentally touched your mother's piece of the Quatrefoil back when we were hunting it down." Rainier grips the armrest of his pimped-up snowmobile so tightly his knuckles strain his leather gloves. "That's the reason your mother took her life, Adrien. Didn't you read her parting note? She couldn't live with the guilt."

Adrien's mother committed suicide? Forget Dismalville; this town makes purgatory sound like a fun destination.

"Cursed, how?" Adrien mutters.

"He lost his mind. Hurt his own mother. Hurt Gaëlle. Even tried to hurt his own children."

"He came at my belly with a knife. Said the twins were monsters. Said that he was told to kill them." Gaëlle's voice is as slight and light as the flurries of snow dancing around the unmarked grave.

Cadence gasps. "Oh, Gaëlle . . ."

"Neither Nolwenn nor Juda know that he's dead, and we'd like keep it this way." Rainier stares around the circle. "They're old. They do not need to have their hearts broken. It was hard enough for them to see their son when he wasn't himself."

Cadence's lips part again, or maybe they never quite closed.

I turn to Rainier. "And you chose to bury him on my land *why*?"

"Because it's private property." Rainier's gaze slides to the thick mist rolling toward the dark evergreens. "Not to mention, uninhabited and out of the way."

Gaëlle falls to her knees in the snow, tears dripping into her yellow scarf. "When his mind was clear, he was so kind. So caring." She touches the wooden cross she laid out as though reaching through the layers of snow and earth toward her dead husband. "When he came at me with the knife, my maternal instinct took over. I didn't think. I just swung. I was making pie, and the rolling pin was right there . . . and it . . ."

Wait. *A rolling pin?*

"It . . . it happened so fast. I didn't mean to . . ."

Be quiet! A voice stabs my eardrums.

Gaëlle scrambles to her feet, eyes wild. "But it's true, Matthias! I never meant—"

I said be quiet! A man materializes out of thin air, seemingly solid except for his wispy edges.

My bones bolt together, pain radiating from the ring. Holy shit. I've seen this dude before, in the art building. He's the unkempt scholar who looked like he was living his worst life. Now that he's right in front of me, I realize that he's not just some pasty, shabby man, he's seriously messed up. His skull's caved in at one temple, one of his cheeks looks like cottage cheese, his lip is split and oozing blood, and his glazed eyes are saucers of hatred. Maybe in the past, he was borderline decent-looking, but with bloody stumps for teeth and skin the color of week-old *foie gras*, it's hard to give a real assessment.

"He's here, Papa," Cadence whispers to Rainier.

Ah. That's right. De Morel can't see what we can. I tend to forget he's not a descendent of the *diwallers* since he speaks about them as though they were his people.

The already frigid, humid air takes a nosedive. Our breaths fog in front of us. Only Matthias doesn't have a puff of white leaking from his lips.

"Remember, Gaëlle. Remember what to do." Rainier's gaze flits around, as though trying to glimpse the ghost standing by the ramshackle shed.

You hurt me. You sent me away. Matthias moves closer to Gaëlle. His voice is no longer sharp and serrated but soft and sad. *Why, chaton? Why did you do this to me? To us?*

"I'm so sorry." Gaëlle's normally dewy-brown face has turned ashen above her yellow scarf.

Matthias stands inches from her, his bruised and broken skull tilted to the side. *You stole my child. My Romain. And the twins . . . I'll never see them grow up.*

"You tried to kill them," she croaks. "And me. You tried to kill me, Matthias."

You're rewriting history to make yourself look like the martyr.

"No," she screeches. "Liar!"

"What is he saying?" Rainier asks Cadence who stands rigid as a lamppost next to him.

She whispers the words her father can't hear.

His eyes slam into Gaëlle. "He's trying to get to you. Don't give in to the guilt. He deserved what he got."

"I . . . I . . ." Gaëlle steps back, her boots crunching over one of the sticks.

The ghost looks at Rainier, then back at his executioner. *What did you tell them? What did you tell them about me?*

"Please, Matthias . . ." She takes two more steps back and raises her palms.

Her dead husband begins to sob, long howls that sound like the mistral when it blows through Marseille.

Is it me or has the wind picked up? I pull my coat collar tighter around my neck, eyeballs stinging from the violent chill.

The ghost runs his hands down the sides of his face, his fingers dipping into his cheeks until one body part becomes barely distinguishable from the other. And then he pulls his hands through his neck, chest, and away from his body again. *Did you ever even love me?*

As though to hear Matthias, Rainier leans forward a little. Any more, and he risks keeling over into the snow, right at Matthias's feet. Considering Cadence's old man was hexed once, he better keep his ass glued to the seat.

"Of course I loved you." Gaëlle's tone is fierce.

Matthias lunges at her. *Then join me, chaton.*

"Now!" Cadence yells, and Gaëlle steps to the side.

Matthias lands on the X of sticks.

Adrien and Cadence pour the contents of their saltshakers over the snow. It takes me a half-second to remember the dispenser Cadence gave me. As they draw a circle with the spice blend, I grab my pot, unscrew the lid, and upturn it, the smell of garlic and the bite of pepper tickling my nose.

Surprise fills Matthias's empty eyes. Gaëlle grabs the rope. I'm not sure what she's going to do with it, not having been privy to their little specter powwow.

Matthias throws his head back and laughs. Before anyone can

even react, he's out of the circle. Gaëlle instinctively lifts her arms and ends up poking her hands right through Matthias's middle. He shoves her to the ground and locks his hands around her neck, just above her scarf. Unlike on his own body, his fingers don't sink through his wife's flesh.

I leap forward to tackle him, but just as I'm about to make contact, a strong set of hands grips me by the shoulder.

"Don't be an idiot." Adrien's fingers dig harder than necessary into my clavicle. "Don't touch him."

Right. Shit. I rub the back of my neck, awakening the wound beneath the giant plaster.

Gaëlle thrashes about in the snow, gasping for air, trying to truss up her husband with the rope. Unfortunately, the coarse cord goes right through his body.

Cadence throws what looks like a copper spoon full of holes at Matthias, hitting him square in the back of the head. He fizzes and pops like a broken electrical wire before disappearing. Gaëlle lets out a whimper of relief.

I shrug off Adrien's grip. "What the hell was that thing?"

"An electromagnetic shield. Sharp thinking, Cadence," Adrien says.

Pink tinges her cheeks. "It was Papa's idea."

I study the thing now sitting in the snow beside Gaëlle's leg. "An electromagnetic shield? It looks like a tea strainer."

"It *is* a tea strainer," Cadence says. "But that's not why it works. It's the material from which it's made. Copper blocks radio frequencies and electromagnetic radiation."

Pride curls Rainier's lips. Is he pleased to have outsmarted a ghost, or that his daughter's so well versed in corrosive metal and zombiesque apparitions? And what the hell do radio frequencies and electromagnetic radiation have to do with ghosts anyway?

Still on the ground, Gaëlle wipes her wet cheeks.

"It's only temporary. He'll be back. The copper disrupts the electromagnetic waves he uses to appear but won't keep him away." Adrien wears his usual know-it-all air.

My eyes go to Cadence's. For once, she doesn't seem all that flummoxed or impressed.

"Gaëlle hasn't defeated the curse yet, though, right?" I ask, which is a dumb question since no shiny leaf has sprung out of the ghost.

Adrien gestures to the sticks in the snow that formed the X. "Leading him to his bones was supposed to trap him long enough for Gaëlle to bind him."

Rainier lets out a long sigh. "I fear we have to dig him up for this to work."

Silence settles over the white clearing. Matching looks of horror bloom across my partners' faces. I, on the other hand, am not overly bothered. Won't be the first time I disturb the dead this past week. Not that it did me much good the first time around.

"The ground's frozen, Papa," says Cadence. "There's no way we can dig through it."

"Guess we'll have to un-freeze it." I remove one glove and pull my phone out. The goose egg ring emits light like a blood-soaked disco-ball.

Gaëlle sits up, rubbing her neck. There's a nasty necklace of bruises developing below her jaw. "His body . . . it's not buried deep." She glances up at us, a haunted look on her face. "I-I only dug a couple feet down."

Pulling up a link, I tap the screen of my cell. "Says here to try a charcoal fire and then boiling water to soften the dirt."

Rainier gestures to the shed at the end of the drive. "There might still be bags of charcoal in there. If they stayed dry, maybe they'll work. There'll be shovels, too." He digs around a leather pocket snapped into the seat of the snowmobile. "Here, Roland." He hands over a shiny set of keys. "I've been meaning to give these to you, but between the ring and *groac'h*, well . . . I forgot."

I scoff because De Morel doesn't strike me as someone who forgets anything. After all, it's his legs that are cursed, not his mind. "You sure you were going to mention it to me?"

He frowns so hard vertical and horizontal lines appear on his forehead. "It's not fit for living at the moment. No heat, no water, no electricity. But it's in your list of assets. The papers are all in order. Once we've taken care of the Quatrefoil, I'll get your whole inheritance together."

"Right. You said you'd do it two days ago."

"I've been busy, Slate."

"Yeah. Me, too. But, hey, I get it. The Quatrefoil comes first."

"If you want to live, it does."

"Convenient that my life's tied—"

"Slate, come on . . ." Cadence's soft voice snatches my attention off her old man. "Save this conversation for later, okay? Matthias will be back any moment."

The keys' serrated edges bite into my palm as I turn and trudge through the snow toward the shed. I sense a presence behind me. I look over my shoulder to make sure it isn't the ghost. When I see it's Cadence, the knots lining my shoulders loosen.

"Can you please give Papa a break?"

I stash my phone back into my pocket and grab my glove before I add frostbite to my list of grievances. "You've seen my dorm room."

"It's warm, clean, and has a bed."

"Pfff. He's really rolled out the red carpet. Some of the bedrooms in my old foster homes were better." Not true. I just feel like whining. And I want her to take my side.

A flash of pain crosses her pale-blue eyes. I almost feel bad, but when she raises a compassionate smile I decide I don't feel *excessively* bad. I want to ask her what happened back in the art building when she nods to my fist.

"You'll need the key."

I unwrap my fingers, grab the clunkiest one, and jam it into the lock of the wide red door. Unfortunately, the door opens outward, so I have to yank on it, then shut it several times to clear the thick layer of snow before I can worm my way inside. Cadence slips in behind me, cell phone up, flashlight beaming.

It smells like dust and mildew and gasoline. Garden tools hang from pegs all along one wall. An old lawnmower stands upright near the back window. Folded up lawn chairs covered in cobwebs lean against a wrought-iron table piled with a bucket of clothespins, a watering can, and a striped green hose. Two vintage bicycles with flattened tires and crooked spokes hang from large ceiling hooks. A dusty toddler's car seat sits in a corner beside two stacked buckets, a shovel, and an industrial-sized bag of coal. A tiny, one-eyed teddy bear is propped up in the car seat. He smiles at me, and it flicks my heart, because I imagine he was mine.

Someone once loved me enough to buy me a happy bear.

Cadence touches my forearm. I jerk because I forgot I wasn't alone. She snatches her hand back, her cheeks coloring. Or at least, they look like they're darkening. Hard to tell in the obscurity.

I shake off my daze and walk over to the buckets and shovel.

"Let me help." Cadence latches onto the icy bucket handles and the splintered wooden shaft of the shovel.

I allow her to pry them out of my fingers, sensing she's trying to make up for the dorm-room-foster-care comment. This time, when our hands brush, a grimace doesn't mar her face. I wrap my arms around the bag of charcoal and duck-step out the door but I don't bother locking it because I plan on exploring after we're done with the ghost shit. I'm about to ask Cadence if she wants to tag along on my stroll down memory lane when I think I spot Matthias, but it's just a piece of fog drifting off from the ever-present wall of mist choking this damn town.

As we carry the tools back to where Adrien's readying the area for a fire, I ask, "What exactly *is* the plan?"

"According to Papa, a corpse's bones can suck in a wandering spirit. As long as it's the spirit's bones."

Adrien takes the bag of coal from me, rips it open, and pours the black chunks onto the cleared, frozen ground.

" . . . bind him to his bones," De Morel is telling Gaëlle.

"The rope went right through him, Rainier."

De Morel frowns.

"Maybe copper wire would work," Adrien suggests. "There might be some in the house's electrical wiring. I could go check."

Cadence sets down the bucket. "Wire will kick him away. It won't bind him."

Adrien's got the fire started now. It burns orange, spewing curls of lavender smoke into the bleached air. "Then how is she supposed to bind him?"

"Maybe I don't need rope or wire. Maybe the bones will magnetize his spirit." Gaëlle sounds more hopeful than convinced.

I don't pitch in my two-cents because I know zilch about ghosts. Bastian might have some ideas—*Goosebumps* was his all-time favorite book series. If I remember correctly, some of the books had a spectral character or two. I got him the entire collection for his twelfth birthday, not new but not too yellowed and dog-eared either. I itch to call him up and ask him for advice but obviously can't or he'll be on the first train over, and I want to keep him as far away from this evil town as possible. Besides, I doubt the writer ever dealt with real ghosts, unless he visited Brume in the medieval ages. Or seventeen years ago. Shit. Will magic bring back more ghosts? They're eerie, and this is coming from someone who has cohabitated with some creepy-ass people.

Three hours go by, and Matthias is still a no-show. We've all morphed into popsicles, and the sky's turned a deep gray. But on the upside, the dirt's finally soft enough to dig into. Under the beam of the snowmobile's headlights, Adrien and I take turns, and sure as shit, I'm the one with the shovel when we reach the body. I don't even have to say anything. I just lift my eyes to the rest of the group when the edge of the metal hits that first bit of bone.

They all watch as I scrape away the dirt with a spade. Whatever kind of cloth Gaëlle buried Matthias in is decayed to a greenish black in some places and completely disintegrated in others. The body's mostly bone, except where the cloth sticks to it. Soil cradles the skull, and I observe that, like the ghost, most of its teeth have been knocked out.

Note to self: never mess with a woman making pie.

"I know you don't think the rope will hold him, but I'd get it ready anyway, Gaëlle. Lay it out underneath the bones," Rainier advises.

"Oh. No." She sways, going pastier than the ghost she's supposed to fight. "Oh, I don't think I can—"

She turns and vomits into the snow. The air's thankfully so cold it masks the stench.

"Cadence, can you give me the rope?" After she hands it over, nose crinkled, I lift the rotten cloth, the bones rattling inside, and lay the rope underneath. All Gaëlle needs to do now is tie it into a pretty bow. "All done." I dust my hands to rid them of frozen dirt and dead person.

Cadence rubs Gaëlle's back, whispering soothing words into her ear, while I dump a shovelful of fresh snow over Gaëlle's half-digested lunch.

The sky darkens some more, and the temperature plummets. I'm betting the North Pole feels tropical in comparison to Brume.

Movement beside Rainier's snowmobile catches my eye, and my heart kicks up a beat. I tighten my grip on the shovel as my blood burns and Matthias takes form.

"Don't move, Rainier. He's right next to you," I say, keeping my voice low. Hell, I don't think screaming would make Matthias flit away, but I'm still not taking the risk. I want to get this over with.

The ghost's face is inches away from Rainier, his glassy eyes boring into Cadence's daddy. Matthias clearly wasn't a fan of De Morel. Never thought I'd have anything in common with a mad professor. Then again, I never thought I'd be stuck in a town fighting off monsters because of a ring.

"Matthias," Gaëlle croaks.

The ghost turns his face toward the woman who slayed him.

"I order you to leave me alone." She's not fooling anyone with her shaky voice, least of all the dead dude standing beside Rainier.

The ghost's split lips lift into a terrifying smile. *You order me, chaton? You cut my life short. I intend to return the favor.*

He moves, the outline of his body curling and disassembling like smoke before repairing and tightening. Suddenly, he's on her again, one palm clamped over her mouth and nose; the other wrapped around the back of her skull.

She wriggles about, trapped in his hold, struggling to breathe. I will my feet to stay planted, because every single cell in my body wants to help. She's suffocating, damn it.

Finally, she wriggles enough that they both tumble into the shallow grave and crunch onto his bones. She rolls until she straddles him and his back is to the skeleton. His hands fall away from her body and his eyes pop outward as though *he* just saw a ghost.

Ha. I fight off my smile because now's not the moment. However spooked the ghost looks. *Shit.* I'm smiling. I rub my mouth until I realize I'm still wearing gloves that came in contact with bones. That quiets my mirth.

"Bind him!" Adrien shouts.

Gaëlle's crying. Her fingers slip repeatedly as she kneels and attempts to knot the rope around the sack of his remains and his rigidified spectral form. "I can't!"

"You can!" Rainier barks.

Just as she manages to loop the cord, the ghost vanishes.

Shit! I'm really not smiling anymore. Did someone lob the tea strainer on him again?

The cloth catches fire, and Gaëlle jolts back, burrowing in the corner of the grave, slapping her thighs which smoke with flames. In seconds, the flimsy burial fabric smolders out of existence, leaving behind the skeleton. The clingy bits of desiccated skin begin to weave together, and muscles reappear, rounding the corpse out until it resembles the man she buried.

She claps her palm in front of her mouth and turns green as a seasick sailor. I'm expecting her to hurl all over her deceased hubby, but instead she screams. Could be because said-deceased-hubby bucks and wiggles like a worm.

"*Putain de bordel de merde,*" I mutter, backing up a little, at the same time as Adrien yells, "He's in the bones!"

As though to demonstrate the professor is forever right, the corpse's jaw widens and lets out a blood-curdling screech, *Murderer!*

Gaëlle tries to scramble up the walls of the hole but keeps skidding on mushy snow and softened soil.

"You must finish this, Gaëlle," Rainier says. "Finish him, or he'll forever haunt you."

And incidentally, I'll croak.

Gaëlle swallows, tears and snot running down her face.

Cadence crouches at the edge of the hole and takes Gaëlle's hand. "I believe in you. We all believe in you."

Gaëlle inhales a rickety breath, then wipes her face with the ends of her scarf and turns around, her hand slipping out of Cadence's mittened one.

Murderer! the corpse says again.

"Quiet!" Gaëlle screams.

You killed me in cold blood. The jaw flaps open and shut, clicking with each word.

Eyes still glistening, she croaks, "I said, *tais-toi!*"

You're going to hell for your crime, **chaton.**

"Stop talking, and don't call me *chaton!* You lost that right the day you tried to murder our children." Gaëlle unwinds the long scarf from her neck and launches herself on the writhing corpse.

"You're not real, so shut up. Just shut up!" She starts stuffing the yellow material into his mouth. *All of it.*

Mmmmfff.

"You're . . . not . . . real," she says between labored breaths. She shoves the last of her scarf between his broken teeth and releases one long, shrill cry that's so full of pain and horror and regret that it makes my gut clench.

The corpse stops moving.

And then smoke wafts from his skin and envelops him and Gaëlle until their shapes are barely distinguishable in the thick grayness. A funnel of wind appears over the cloud and sucks up the smoke. Gaëlle crawls off her husband's corpse, her long spirals whipping around. The wind rips apart Matthias's skin, flesh, and bones, disintegrating the man until nothing remains but the moldy shroud and snake-like, curse-defeating scarf.

When the wind stops blowing, the gold leaf twinkles atop the yellow yarn.

She did it. She fucking did it.

I let out a gigantic breath, feeling suddenly warmer.

That's two pieces.

We're halfway there. And we've still got twelve days.

I might not die after all.

28

CADENCE

As Gaëlle's leaf clinks into the box Papa brought, Slate picks up her scarf with the shovel.

"Shouldn't leave evidence at a crime scene." His reasoning reminds me that he's a man accustomed to infringing the law and not some happy-go-lucky kid with a mane of wild corkscrews.

"We should set it on fire," I suggest.

"Gaëlle?" Papa slides the locked box back into one of the pockets of the snowmobile. "What would you like to do with the scarf?"

"What Cadence said. Burn it."

Slate drops it back over the grimy shroud, and Adrien flicks a match.

As I watch the flames devour the fibers, it dawns on me that Papa helped her bury Matthias, which makes him an accessory to murder. If anyone finds out . . .

I can't think like that. No one knows outside of the five of us. Gaëlle won't talk since she has more to lose than he does. Adrien won't either, since he's almost family. And Slate . . . I study his sharp profile outlined by Matthias's funeral pyre, watch him toast his hands over the flames. He hates Papa and blames him for everything bad that's happened in his life, so he might just lord this over my father. I might need leverage to keep him quiet.

Oh, God. I hate these thoughts. I try hard to beat them out of my mind as Adrien, Slate, and I bury the ashes under thick layers of soil and snow.

Slate's a part of this now. I have to trust him. There's no other choice.

"You okay?" he asks as I upturn a bucket of fresh snow.

"It's the first time I've seen someone die, so . . . not really."

"That wasn't someone, Cadence. That was a ghost."

"Have you ever seen . . . a real person . . . die?"

He nods. It's a slow nod. A careful one.

I swallow. "I know I didn't kill him, but I feel like I did. Did you ever kill anyone?"

His dark eyes take on a dangerous gleam. "No. But I've been close."

"Who?"

His stubble-coated chin dips toward his neck. "Monsters. And not the magical kind."

The bucket swings from my numb fingers. In spite of my gloves, the air got to me. All of my joints feel distended and the inside of my ears ache.

He pries the bucket from my hands. "You should get yourself home. Your lips are purple, and you have ice crystals on your lashes."

"What are you going to do?"

His attention wanders to the house. "Visit my past."

"But it's night. And there's no electricity."

He presses his lips together as though taking both factors under consideration. "I'll use my phone's flashlight." And then he backs up, takes the shovel Adrien's finished with and the second bucket, and crunches back toward the shed.

"I'm sorry about what I said to you, Gaëlle. I didn't know he tried to hurt you." Guilt crinkles the outer corners of Adrien's eyes. "I didn't know he was cursed by my mother's leaf—"

I touch his sleeve. "It's not your fault."

His red-rimmed eyes meet mine.

"It's not," I repeat.

"She's right, Adrien." I can't see Gaëlle's expression since I'm blinded by the snowmobile's headlights, but I hear her sigh. "It wasn't Camille's fault either, and it devastates me to think she lived with so much guilt. That she died because of it."

"Why did Maman blame herself?" Adrien's gaze sinks to the rectangular ochre patch next to his boots.

It wouldn't take a forensic specialist to guess foul play occurred in this deserted field. Thankfully, it's private property. Plus, it'll surely snow again soon.

"Her piece caused a fire to spark on the pier. She was with Amandine, Rémy—I mean, Slate—and his parents when it started," Papa says as Slate's darkened figure emerges from the shed. "Camille picked up little Rémy and ran him to safety while Amandine tried to corral people. Eugenia went straight for the flames. And Oscar went after her."

Even though he's steeped in night, I notice Slate flinch, and my heart tightens. I almost go to him, but what exactly am I going to do? Hug him like I did after he climbed out of the well? That had been awkward. Slate isn't my friend. If he were, I wouldn't be worried about him outing Papa to the police. Or am I just trying to distract myself from other confusing feelings?

Slate bristles. "So, my parents ran into the fire instead of staying with their son."

"They thought they could fight the piece. They thought it might stop the fire. There were *a lot* of people on that pier." Papa, too, sounds angry.

"What about me?"

"What about you, Slate?"

"Camille cared, but not my own parents . . ."

"They cared."

He snorts. "Yeah, about magic."

"They wanted to save you and Amandine and the whole of Brume."

No one says anything for a moment.

"Was it also Camille who took me away from Brume?"

"No. She just got you out of the fire; I don't know who swiped you off that pier. All I know is that Matthias was also there. He was a teenager at the time. Full of enthusiasm and feelings of invulnerability as the young usually possess. He tried to go help your parents, and in doing so, touched the piece. Camille raced back into the flames and managed to get him out alive. She'd originally thought it was a miracle—he had so few burns and no obvious side effect of the curse."

I glance at Papa's legs, his obvious side effect.

"For years, we watched him, and he seemed unscathed by the curse, but then he held his father's hand over the tavern's grill. Nolwenn got scared and sent him away. Distance doesn't completely annul the curse's influence, but it lessens its hold."

"What?" I suck in too much cold air, and it burns as it travels into my lungs. "So, if you left Brume—"

"Brume is my home, *ma chérie*."

"But if you left, could you walk again?"

He grips one of his useless thighs with a gloved hand. "With a limp."

"Oh my God, Papa. Why have we stayed here?"

"Because your mother is here, the Quatrefoil, my work, our friends. I might have an easier life someplace else, but easier doesn't mean better."

His choice to stay confined to a wheelchair when he could regain the use of his legs baffles me.

"I can see the wheels spinning in your brain, Cadence. Put the brakes on them, because we're not leaving."

"But, Papa—"

"*Non*," he says firmly, sharply.

I pinch my lips shut. I won't fight now, in front of the others, but I might later.

Papa returns his attention to Adrien. "Where was I?"

"Nolwenn made Matthias leave," Adrien supplies.

"That's right. I think he went to Sweden. There, he met someone, had Romain with that person, then returned after she . . . *left* him."

Oh, God. Does he think Matthias murdered Romain's mother?

"I hope that's what happened." He glances at Gaëlle.

Her arms are crossed, and she's staring at nothing.

"His mind seemed whole again, and Romain didn't seem scarred by an unpredictable father. He was actually a happy kid. Anyway, Gaëlle babysat him while Matthias took a teaching job at the university. There were no more strange incidents. At least none that we observed, and we were observing him. And then he and Gaëlle fell into a relationship, and the rest"—he lets out a whistling exhale—"well, you're now aware of the rest."

"Death by rolling pin," Slate mutters, though I think I'm the only one to hear.

"He wasn't fine. I should've seen it coming. He was always so obsessed with setting things on fire. He used the blowtorch on insects. Fire fascinated Romain, which made Matthias's passion for burning things thrive. That scared me." Gaëlle's cheeks glitter with new tears. "I should've known . . . I should've known his mind wasn't whole."

The frigid wind whistles through the tall, swaying evergreens, then brushes over the crusty snow and licks up the length of our bodies.

"We should all get home now. The Quatrefoil only knows when the next piece will manifest." Papa wears a tight smile, probably trying to defuse the tension.

"I'll walk back with you, Gaëlle," Adrien offers.

She nods. We arrived together on Papa's snowmobile. Cars aren't allowed in the heart of town, but the snowmobile is; Papa's snowmobile, anyway. As soon as it roared down the street, Matthias poofed out of existence.

Papa revs up the motor. "Are you ready to leave, *ma chérie?*"

I bite my lip, glancing over at Slate.

As though sensing the direction of my thoughts, Adrien says, "Slate can walk back with Gaëlle and me."

"Thanks, Prof, but I'm planning on hanging out here a while longer."

I stare between Papa and Slate a couple seconds before backing away from the snowmobile. "I'll show him around his house and then walk home with him."

Papa's mouth flattens. "No. It's dark out and—"

"I'm seventeen, Papa. And it's *Brume.* Relatively safe."

"I don't want you walking around Brume in the dark while the Quatrefoil isn't whole."

"He's right," Adrien says. "Brume's become dangerous with the Quatrefoil unearthed."

"You should listen to them, Cadence." Slate's voice rings

through the darkness. "Besides, I'm only going to stay here a half-hour tops."

I notice Adrien and Gaëlle exchanging quick words, and then she's walking toward the snowmobile and climbing on.

"I'll wait with them, Rainier," Adrien says.

Papa is slow to accept Adrien's offer. "You walk her to the front door, all right, son?"

Adrien nods. And then the snowmobile carves up the snow, creating a wake of flurries in its path. Hands stuffed in the pockets of my puffer jacket, I make my way toward Adrien and Slate. I don't think I've ever been this cold. My teeth clatter and my muscles feel like bags of frozen peas.

"Take her home, Prof."

"Hello, I'm right here. Besides, a few more minutes aren't going to make me any colder." I bring out my phone, pluck one shaking finger from my mitten and press on the flashlight app. As soon as it's on, I stick my hand back into the damp wool and trudge over to the front of the house.

I stamp my feet as I wait for Adrien and Slate to catch up. They're talking. About what, I have no clue. Their voices are too low and the wind too loud and my eardrums too anesthetized.

Slate's already pulled out his keys. He chooses the correct key right away. Then again, the third key is his mailbox key, much too tiny for a house lock. The hinges groan as the front door swings inward, stretching a cobweb so thick and white it resembles one of the tavern's lace curtains. I illuminate the foyer, shining my light on the flight of wooden steps that lead to the first floor.

I only came once before with Papa to help set up the board that allows him to wheel himself into places unsuited for wheelchair access. While he showed the house to a man in a dark suit, gold bifocals, and a briefcase, I went to explore.

"Over here is the living room and formal dining room." I direct my phone toward the right. "Opposite that is the kitchen and break-fast room."

"I didn't know you'd already come here." Adrien energetically rubs his hands together to drive heat into his fingers, which are surely as numb as mine.

"I came with Papa a few years ago. He was having the house reappraised."

"Reappraised? If it's fully paid, then there's no reason to have it reappraised." Of course, Slate jumps to a conclusion that doesn't paint Papa in the best light. "Unless he was trying to take out a loan. Or sell it."

"Maybe he was having it reinsured then. I don't remember."

Besides a thicker layer of dust and more cobwebs, everything is still exactly the same—the painted walls still sky blue, the wooden furniture still whitewashed, the floorboards pale oak. I walk ahead of him into the living room, toward the granite chimney on which sit several framed pictures. Most have been washed out by the sunlight, but the happy couple smiling at the camera are still distinguishable. Eugenia, like her son, had a wild mane of black corkscrews, but her eyes were green. Slate got his father's eyes and most of the man's features.

"Your mom used to make this apricot ice-cream from scratch in the summer," Adrien says as Slate lifts one of the pictures from the mantel.

"I forget that everyone knew them around here." A nerve jumps next to his eye. Jealousy? Sadness?

Adrien sighs. "Brume's a small place, Slate. They were both well-loved professors."

"Both?"

I raise a brow. "Hasn't Papa told you anything about them?"

"He hasn't been very forthcoming with information. Keeps promising me a tell-all after we're done assembling the Quatrefoil."

I nibble on my bottom lip, my gaze dipping to the ring tenting his glove.

"Your mother taught math and your father, astronomy," Adrien says. "Maman grew up with your father. Your mother was from the south. Spain, or maybe Portugal? My father knew them well, in case you'd like to talk to him. I'm sure he could tell you some stories."

I want to warn Slate to stay away from Geoffrey Keene but obviously can't do that in front of his own son.

"Amandine de Morel and Eugenia Roland were the most reputed beauties in Brume. My mother was always jealous." Adrien smiles. "But she loved them both too much to truly dislike them."

"Your mother had nothing to envy ours, Adrien." Yes, Eugenia was stunning, but Camille was distinguished and so very kind. "I wish they were all still here."

"But they're not." Slate replaces the frame on the chimney mantel so abruptly I check the glass for spider-cracks.

He heads to the openwork bookcase that separates the living and dining rooms. It's full of dusty tomes on galaxies and black holes. Even though the current astronomy professor is fascinating, I heard Oscar was quite the entertainer and teacher. His students called him bewitching. That was the term often associated with him. Then again, Brumians have such a fascination with magic they consider everything and everyone in this town magical. Little do they know they aren't completely off the mark. Granted, no one is magical yet. But if we succeed . . . *when* we succeed . . .

Adrien's phone chirps. I imagine it's Papa. "Hey, *bébé*."

Guess not.

Something heavy falls onto my shoulders, and I jolt, almost dropping my phone.

"Are you crazy?" I try to remove the coat Slate's placed over me, but he hangs on to the lapels. The air inside the house is cold enough to turn mercury solid, so he can't possibly be warm. "You're going to freeze."

"And you're going to knock all the enamel off your pretty teeth."

I start to pull the coat off, but he holds out his palms. "I promise I'm all right."

Before I can protest any more, he backs up into the foyer and then pivots toward the kitchen, illuminating his own way. I walk past Adrien, who's still chatting with Charlotte, cross the breakfast nook with its round table and wicker chairs, then burst into the kitchen. Slate's running his light over the sunny granite countertops and wooden cupboards painted a happy yellow.

"They really liked bright colors," he says.

"Not your style?"

A side of his mouth hooks up. "I'm more of a fifty-shades-of-gray man."

My jaw tingles with a blush that I try hard to suppress. Why can't I be like Alma, who doesn't even know what shame feels like? Besides, he was obviously talking about the color not the book. The fact that my mind went to the book is all kinds of deranged. I didn't even *read* the book.

I blame the cold and the ghost.

I look away since he hasn't, then backtrack to the foyer. "Want to see the bedrooms?"

"Thought you'd never ask, Mademoiselle de Morel."

I roll my eyes even though he can't see me doing it since I have my back to him.

Since Adrien's still on the phone, it's just Slate and me traipsing around.

"You should really put your coat back on." I peel it off my shoulders and try to hand it back, but he moves off, his gaze scouring every inch of his parent's bedroom, from the bare mattress to the carved headboard, to the wooden trunk at the base of the bed bearing the initials E.H.

He lifts the lid, and dust puffs out. Coughing, he swats the air until it clears. Inside are neat stacks of yellowed linens hemmed with fancy embroideries.

"Want to grab dinner after this?" I don't know where *that* came from. Just popped out of my mouth while I was scrutinizing a black-and-white picture of the university.

The lid of the trunk bangs shut. "Are you asking me out on a date?"

Heat flares anew through me. "Not a date. Just a friendly dinner."

He chuckles. "At the tavern?"

"Or at my house. I'm sure there's a hot meal waiting for us."

"I really need a house elf."

"House elf?" I spin around, and the beam of my phone scrapes across his throat and black button-down.

"Nothing. And yes, I'd love to go out with you, Cadence, but let's go to *La Taverne*. Not in the mood to dine by candlelight with your papa. Three's a crowd."

"It's not a date."

He smiles at me. "Uh-huh."

"You are so—"

"Alluring?"

"Don't make me regret suggesting dinner."

He slings his arm around my shoulders and pivots me back toward the hallway. "I noticed one more door on this floor."

I know where it leads. "Why don't you save it for another visit?"

He grips the knob and twists it, and since his arm is still around my shoulders, when he comes to a stop, so do I. His phone's light splashes over the navy crib with the planet mobile, the four hand-painted wooden letters sitting on a shelving unit full of colorful board books, and the purple-and-blue galaxy wallpaper that's bloated on one wall from a recent leak.

I crane my neck to look at him. Only his eyes move. The rest of him has turned solid. Even his lips, usually supple, are pressed into a firm line. I thread my fingers through the hand he's set on my shoulder and squeeze. The gesture brings him back to life. The lines on his face soften first and then the rest of his body follows.

"Is it weird that I'm jealous of this kid?" His voice is so scratchy it makes my heart churn.

I shoot him a smile, which he doesn't catch because he's staring at the R, E, M, and Y on the bookshelf. I let him look his fill and then squeeze his hand again before releasing it. "Come on. Let's go shower the ghost gunk off ourselves and get some food in our bellies."

His Adam's apple jostles as he gazes around the bedroom one last time. "Are we talking shared bathing?"

I duck out from underneath his arm. "You just never stop."

"There are two surefire ways to get a woman: wooing her and wearing her down. Since you keep objecting to being wooed, I've elected to wear you down."

I raise an eyebrow. "I have so much to say about that, but first, *when* and *how* have you tried to woo me?"

"I bought you dinner."

"You mean, after you called me a teenage librarian and left me sitting alone at a table?"

"You looked like you'd rather have been sitting with someone else." He's asking me about Adrien and my unrequited crush. A question I obviously can't answer when the man in question is standing a floor below us, tapping his powered-off phone against his thigh and staring up.

"You two ready to go?"

I nod slowly. "We'll be out in a minute."

Still drumming his phone, he jets out of the house.

I turn on Slate, my hands slipping onto my waist. "Okay . . . so let me spin that question around. Why would you hit on me when you're into someone else?"

He crosses his arms in front of his chest, creasing the black cotton. "I'm into someone else? Who am I into?"

"The girl you saw in the well. I know you keep saying you don't love her, but you obviously feel strongly about her if she's the person who appeared."

A thick curl falls into his eyes.

"Is she the type you woo or wear down?" I grit out.

Could I sound any more jealous? And why am I bringing her up again? Right. Because I don't want to be the other woman . . . the Brume fling. He said he wasn't dating anyone, but that doesn't mean he isn't involved with her in some other way.

"She's the type you wear down."

Not that I liked being the wear-down type, but now I'm jealous of sharing that status with this other girl.

"She's a lot like you, actually."

Great.

"She has these really intense blue eyes. So clear they look like glaciers, but ringed with this dark, deep ocean-blue." His lips barely move as he adds, "I'd never seen eyes like hers. Well, until the *groac'h* in the well used them to lure me."

That's not true. He's seen them on me.

His arms drop from their knot, and then he's shoving one hand through his hair. "And here I thought you'd figured it out."

"Figured what out?"

He lets out a long breath. "I saw *you* in that well, Cadence."

My breathing catches. My heart, too. All of my organ's functions become suspended as Slate's confession trickles through me. And then everything starts up at the same time, and my heart detonates, and I wheeze, and then once I'm done making strangled sounds, my jaw loosens and my lips part.

"Me?" It comes out as a squeak. "But you said it was—that she wasn't from—that . . ."

I'm flooded with memories of how strange he acted the first

time he looked into the well, and how angry he got when Adrien mentioned it resembled someone we had strong feelings for.

I smack his chest.

"Ouch. What was that for?" Slate rubs his pecs dramatically. I really didn't hit him that hard.

"That was for making me jealous."

"How is that *my* fault?"

"You lied about who you saw in there."

"Well of course, I lied. I barely know you, Cadence. If I'd admitted it, you would've freaked."

Totally. "Want to know what freaks me out even more, though?"

"Do tell, what freaks you out more than my heartfelt confession?"

"How jealous I was of the siren and then of Jasmine."

"Who's Jasmine?"

Is he serious? He looks serious. "The girl who was all over you when I was showing you around the campus."

He's still rubbing his chest. "Oh. Her. I don't even remember whether she was a blonde or brunette."

Did I hit one of his bruises? Shoot, I probably did. "Did I hurt you?"

A lopsided grin takes over. "Very much. I think I might need some medical attention, doctor."

I'm torn between the desire to strangle him and kiss him. "We should go. Adrien's waiting."

"He's fine." He finally stops rubbing his chest. "He can wait." He lays his hand on my jaw, tilts it up.

My heartbeats are so loud and close together that they're probably making all six layers of my clothing vibrate.

The tip of his nose touches the tip of mine, and his breath warms my parted lips. The only boy I've ever kissed is Romain, and those kisses were always friendly and sweet. I don't think kissing Slate will be friendly or sweet. I lick my lips in anticipation.

"Can't wait for our date." He pulls back, releases my head but finds my hand in the folds of his coat, and tows me downstairs.

Yep. I'm going to strangle him.

Probably while kissing him.

29

SLATE

Keep it in check, dude. *Keep it in check.* I'm battling with myself. I want nothing more than to taste Cadence, tangle my fingers in her hair, and kiss her until she moans. But I don't. Why?

Because I'm a gentleman.

Or a masochist.

One of the two.

Maybe both.

She knows. She knows I saw her in the well and she didn't run screaming. Already that's a miracle. And she was *jealous* on top of it? Things are finally looking up for Slate Ardoin.

Unless my confession shocked her into a lie. Or maybe, she's just as messed up as I am and is falling too hard and too fast for someone she barely knows. I want her so bad it hurts, but I know not to push. She needs to set the pace.

We step out into the permanent soup of fog, and I drop Cadence's hand to lock the door of the house.

Adrien's bouncing on the balls of his feet, probably trying to keep his blood from congealing. "Finally."

My phone vibrates: *Bastian.*

As we crunch over the snow down the drive, I answer. "Yo, little bro."

"Guess where I am?"

"Euro Disney?"

"Close but no. I'm in Brume!"

I stop walking.

"The train's just pulling into the station." He says this with the satisfaction of someone who's just cleared out Carrefour's entire stock of madeleines for his sugar-addicted brother.

For the first time in a long time, I can't even speak. A thousand thoughts crash into my head. Bastian can't be here. He could get hurt. No fucking way in hell am I letting my little brother close to dark magic.

Adrien motions for me to keep moving. Cadence lifts her eyebrows at me as if to ask what's going on. Somehow I find the wherewithal to put one foot in front of the other.

Cadence removes my jacket and hands it over. I clutch it tight but don't put it on.

"Uh . . . Slate? You still there, man?" Bastian's voice rings in my ear, or maybe it's my ear that's ringing.

"Who's watching over Spike?" I bark.

"Well . . . he's a cactus, so . . . I figured he can go a few days—"

"He's not just a cactus. He's an *Eve's Needle*, and he needs care. Turn around, Bastian. I asked you to do one fucking thing: watch Spike. Go back and do it." Fear brings out my inner asshole.

He isn't fazed, too used to my moods. "Nope. I still have two weeks until school starts. There's no way I'm going back to Marseille until I see Brainy Slate sitting in a classroom. I want proof that you're bettering your life and not heisting anyone."

"Heisting isn't even a verb."

"Actually it is. Train's stopped. I'll be getting off now. Should I wait here, or do you want to send me your dorm address?"

I sigh. "Shit. Fine. Just sit tight. I'll be there in ten." I hang up, then slide on my coat. "You guys go on. I've got to head to the train station to pick up my little brother."

Now it's Adrien's turn to stop walking. "Brother?" His voice is as tight as his brow.

"Yeah. Brother. *Foster* brother," I add, so he doesn't go thinking Bastian's fair game for the next round of this merry hunt.

"It's not a good time for visitors, Roland. With us trying to put the Quatrefoil together—"

"Don't you think I fucking know that?" I refrain from punching him and speed up. "He just showed up here. And he's not leaving without seeing me."

"It'll be fine." Cadence touches Adrien's forearm, and even though I know it's to calm him, it pisses me off. "We'll walk with you."

Adrien huffs but nods.

It dawns on me that Bastian's presence puts a wrench in the plans I had with Cadence.

"*Putain*," I turn to her. "Our date."

Adrien stumbles. If I didn't know better, I'd think he didn't like the sound of Cadence going on a date.

Even in the dimness, I spot the streaks of crimson licking up the sides of her jaw. I could've used the word dinner but deliberately didn't. I realize this makes me no better than a dog marking his territory, but I want Adrien to know.

He side-eyes me, and I swear his eyes flash with a warning: *don't screw with her.* "I didn't know you guys were . . . *dating.*"

"We're not," Cadence blurts out, and damn if that doesn't chip off a little piece of my ego. "We were just going to have a friendly dinner at the Tavern. You're more than welcome to join us."

The fuck he is.

"I'm meeting Charlotte." He slants me another look. "And if we don't step on it, I'll be late."

I think I've blown the date completely, but then Cadence turns to me. "How about I call Alma? Four's a better number than three."

My pared ego reshapes and solidifies.

"Unless you wanted time alone with your brother?" Her gaze pulls me in like undertow.

I check myself from hollering *hell, no*, not wanting to reek of desperation, a sentiment that is oh-so-new-and-unwelcome.

"If I'm alone with him, he'll sense something's up, so definitely call up your friend." Then I add, "I need to get him out of town. Maybe we can get him drunk enough to board a train back to Marseille before daybreak."

Already, we're in sight of the station. I can see the glowing white letters spelling out *GARE*, like specters in the Brumian mist.

A handful of minutes later, we're standing in front of the building.

"Your stop," Adrien announces.

I peel off. Even though I'm not expecting Cadence to follow, she does.

"Cadence, I promised Rainier I'd walk you to your front door."

She shoots Adrien a reassuring smile. "I'm fine. I'm with Slate."

"Your father said—"

I tilt my head his way. "I didn't think you were that type, Mercier."

"What type?" Adrien says sourly.

"The type to ask 'how high' when someone says 'jump.'"

Cadence narrows her eyes at me. "It's called being responsible." Under her breath, she adds, "Maybe this was a bad idea. Maybe I should go home."

Panic flares in my chest. Even though the words don't want to come out, I force them past my clenched teeth. "Sorry for jumping down your throat, Prof, but everyone always assumes I'm irresponsible, and it takes a toll."

Adrien's teeth stay clenched. I'm hoping his inner struggle comes from duty and not jealousy.

After another loaded minute, Cadence's breath puffs out like Gaëlle's dead husband's ghost. "I'll call Papa, so you're off the hook, Adrien. Thanks for walking with us, and for worrying about me."

"I'll always worry about you."

She smiles at him, and he holds her gaze for a beat too long.

"If you need anything, call me." Adrien's eyes cut to me. "And make sure she gets home all right."

"Aye aye, Prof."

She waves as he takes off. "Don't make me regret hanging out." Her whispered words knock hard into me.

"Maybe I'm jealous, too." Jealous of how she feels about him and how he feels about her. Jealous of their shared history and familiarity.

She tips her head up. "Adrien is important to me, Slate—he'll always be important to me—but you're the guy I'm going to dinner with. Not him."

But is that because he's busy with Charlotte? I bite back the question, which tastes bitter on my tongue.

As I study her heart-shaped face, I wonder if my attraction to Cadence could be another Brumian curse. I mean, I have *never* wanted anything or anyone more than this girl, and I'm a man with a lot of wants. Bastian says it's to compensate for not having had much during my childhood.

Shit! Bastian.

I turn toward the station, which is pretty big for such a puny town in the middle of bumblefuck nowhere. Like everything else here, it's made of aged gray limestone and looks like it popped off those collectible miniature Christmas villages Bastian adores. I've never understood the fascination with fake little holiday towns, too cheesy and saccharine for me. But Bastian has a thing for them. Hell, I remember his face when I surprised him on his fourteenth birthday with a midnight stroll through one of those fancy shops that had dozens of these villages set up. I'd temped there over the holidays and had managed to filch not only the key but the alarm code. He'd spent well over an hour drooling over the teeny cathedrals and ice-skating rinks and plastic gingerbread houses, eyes watery and lips wobbly. I told him to take one, that I'd worry about the consequences. Righteous as he was, he refused. So, we'd gone home empty-handed to a house that forever smelled of athlete's foot, warm beer, and camembert past its prime.

I shake the memory out of my mind as Cadence and I pass under an illuminated clock with a cheery mechanical wizard that clangs a bell every hour. I realize it's only seven, even though it feels like midnight. The smell of hot chestnuts blasts into me and makes my stomach rumble like a Rottweiller.

Cadence grins. "Hungry?"

"I could eat." I'm so relieved by the appearance of her smile that I almost miss the sound of my name.

Bastian's standing by the information office at the other end of the station, a brochure dangling from his hand. Just the sight of him makes my lips curve—black-rimmed glasses sitting crooked on his nose and navy peacoat swallowing up his scarecrow frame. *Putain*, I love this kid. But my smile turns to a deep frown. However glad I am to see him, I need to get him away ASAP.

He stuffs the brochure back into the rack, lobs his backpack over his shoulder, and meets me halfway. "Big bro!" He punches me in the shoulder, giving me a half-hug, but then his grin falters. "You got into a fight?"

I put a hand to the bite on my jaw, grateful he hasn't spotted the bandage on the nape of my neck that feels soaked again. "Good news is, I won."

"And here I thought some schooling would civilize you."

"And here I thought you knew me."

His gaze slides over my shoulder to Cadence, who's hanging back to give us some privacy.

"*Bienvenue.*" She shoots Bastian a smile that makes him go a little red.

"No wonder you haven't been calling me back," he says under his breath as he skirts me to reach her. "Hi. I'm Bastian."

"Cadence." She leans in and gives him a kiss on each cheek, the normal French greeting, nothing else, but I find myself scowling.

Bastian, an expert on all-things-Slate, cocks an eyebrow. I cross my arms and wedge my lips into a firm line. He gives the faintest of nods, which is bro-code for: *Got it. Girl's off-limits.*

"We were thinking of grabbing dinner tonight." Cadence puts a hand on my arm, a spot of sudden warmth in the freezing cold station. "Unless you want to catch up with Slate alone."

"Nope. Dinner with you and Slate sounds awesome." The beginnings of a smirk grows on his lips.

I know the reason for that smirk. I've never had dinner with a woman I didn't want to strip of intel. Five days in Brume, and I'm a new man.

The crazier bit is I kinda like this new guy.

A prickly lump forms in my throat. Who the hell am I fooling? I'm *stuck* here and trying to make the best of my containment. This whole scene is not in line with my life. This new me is not in line with my life. It's not like I'm going to stay one more second than I have to once I get the ring off my finger.

Cadence releases my arm to tug down her pompom beany. "I'm going to go home to change, then meet you two at the tavern. Eight sounds good?"

"I've been entrusted"—or rather I've entrusted myself—"with your safety, so we'll walk with you."

Cadence's lips part as though to protest.

"Bastian adores sightseeing almost as much as you love dusty old books, so it'll give him the chance to see all the hotspots in Brume."

"There are no hotspots," she says, with a little curl of lip.

"Don't I know." I want to drape my arm around her again or take her hand. I do neither. In part, because I'm not sure she wants the contact, and in part, because I have *never* walked hand-in-hand with anyone before. As always, my eyeballs freeze once we're out of the station. "Welcome to Brume, otherwise known as the Ice-Crack of Hell."

Cadence grins and shakes her head while Bastian chuckles.

"The Ice-Crack . . ." he repeats, taking in the glowing street-lights, the cobblestones, the fog snaking past like a giant serpent. "You're so dramatic."

For once, I'm not. For once, I'm terribly realistic.

As we walk into the fortified part of town at the base of the hill, Bastian peppers Cadence with questions about Brume, and she answers cheerily. It's only when he says, "So do you think there really was magic here at one time?" that she bites her bottom lip and shrugs, her cheeriness morphing to unease.

And then, because the town's handkerchief-small, we've arrived in front of the tall iron gates of *Manoir de Morel*.

"Wow." Bastian whistles approvingly at the house.

Unlike me, wealth doesn't spark jealousy in him. Not that he's poor anymore. Although he doesn't know how rich he is yet. Hopefully, he won't know for a long while, because him finding out means I'm dead, and I don't feel like dying.

"We'll pick you up at ten to," I call out as she fishes her keys.

"Slate—"

"Cadence."

"That's really unnecessary."

I want to touch her but keep my hands in my pockets and back away. "Ten to eight."

A breath eases from her lips and bleaches the air. "Fine."

Once Cadence is safely inside, Bastian all but throttles me with questions about the university. I answer as truthfully as I can, leaving out the part about not actually attending classes and cursed magical artifacts.

I lead him up the stairs to Second Kelc'h, and we skirt the square. He marvels at the Christmas village state of this place, from the slate rooftops that shine like fish scales to the gleaming cobbles dusted with fresh snow. Brume, through his eyes, is a magical place. If only he knew the extent of the magic.

We pass by a gaggle of girls who look our way. He straightens his glasses.

"So, Cadence's best friend is coming to dinner tonight."

"Yeah?"

"I think you'll like her." Scratch that. I know he'll like her. But suddenly, I don't want him to like her because liking her would make him want to stay, and I don't want him to stay. Maybe I should cancel dinner.

"So how did you and Cadence meet?"

"Remember that stuffy dean who sent me my welcome packet? She's his daughter."

"No way. Actually, *duh*. The mansion had the name on the gate."

I punch in the code for the dorm's front door. "Before you ask, we're not together."

"But clearly, you wouldn't object to it." He follows me up the flight of rickety stairs.

"The only thing that's clear is that I don't want her to be with anyone else." I twist my key in the lock and present my matchbox-sized dorm room to Bastian with a grand flourish.

A grin threatens to cleave his face in half. I don't think it has anything to do with the sight of my present accommodations. "Never thought womanizing-Slate Ardoin would want to settle."

I scoff. "No one's settling." I pull off my coat, gloves, and shirt and toss them on the bed, then kick off my grimy boots and jeans, but keep my boxers on. "I need a shower."

Bastian takes in the small bed. "This'll be just like old times."

What he means by that is, he'll curl up on the floor next to my bed, which was something he used to do when we had separate bedrooms back in our foster homes. Every time I'd find him, I'd scoop him up and lay him on my bed, then take his spot on the floorboards, and since he was always such a heavy sleeper, he didn't notice until the morning.

I think of bumming Cadence's guestroom again, but leaving Bastian alone in an evil town doesn't sit right with me. I hook my towel around my neck so that Bastian can't spot my bandage, then grab my bottle of soap and the crinkling paper bag filled with bandages, alcohol swabs, and antibacterial ointment.

"Where'd you get that ugly thing?"

My gaze flicks to the hand I have curled around the doorknob and the big red stone blinking like a snake eye. "Found it in a vintage shop."

Bastian studies it, then the acres of bruises on my body. "That vintage shop has a nice upper-cut."

I smirk.

"Have they tacked up WANTED posters with your face on them yet?"

I chuckle. "Nope." I pop the word out. "They'd have to snap a picture of me in the act, and you know me: stealth-personified."

"Slate . . ."

Sensing a sermon, I say, "I promise, I'm not in any trouble." At least, not the sort he's thinking of. I hate lying to him, but I need to keep him safe. If that means dishonesty, then so be it. "Make yourself comfortable. I'll be back soon."

30

CADENCE

W hen we reach *La Taverne*, Alma's standing out front in a pair of thigh-high boots, sheer black tights, and a tiny denim skirt that makes my slim black jeans, black V-neck cami, and duster-length cardigan look homely. At least Slate doesn't give her the long once-over he gave me when he picked me up.

During the short walk over to the town square, he's barely taken his eyes off mine. Probably because I did my hair again and applied some mascara and eyeliner.

Obviously, Alma notices. "Whoa. Is that makeup I see?"

I'm half-tempted to scrub it off.

"Dude, your eyes," she says, before turning to the boys. "Hey, Slate." She tilts her head to the side to get a glimpse of Bastian, who's presently studying the well like a kid in a candy store, neck swiveling every which way and eyes as large as gumballs.

Slate trails Alma's gaze over to Bastian, and his body locks up. I wrap my hand around his arm, stealing his attention off the arena in which he fought, and mouth: *She's gone.*

His Adam's apple jostles.

When Bastian, who's trotting up to us, notices Alma, he pauses midstep and then straightens his glasses—*twice*. She greets him with the customary *bise*. In her heels, she's only half-a-head shorter than gangly Bastian.

Gangly, *starstruck* Bastian.

"I heard you're Slate's brother." She looks between the two boys, probably seeking a resemblance. She won't find one. Not only is Bastian's complexion several shades darker, but they also share zero similar features. She must decide not to pry, because she goes with, "I want *all* the stories. The more embarrassing, the better."

"No. No stories," Slate says, opening the door for everyone.

As I sidestep him, his clean, woodsy scent drifts into me, making me inhale so deeply I think he notices, even though no smug comment comes out of his mouth. Then again, his mouth is still tensed and his gaze keeps skipping to the well. I chew on my lip, wishing there was a way to hide it from his sight.

Alma pulls open the heavy curtain, dispersing the aroma of browning butter, golden onions, and fried garlic. Lots and lots of garlic. We Bretons love our garlic. Almost as much as we love our French tunes. Over the din of voices spills a vintage song from the folksy rock band *Louise Attaque.*

Nolwenn, who's bustling by with a heavy clay pot, nods to the upstairs area. "Saved you the corner table beside the stairs."

"Thanks, Nolwenn."

She smiles, but it doesn't do much to smooth out the myriad of little lines crosshatching her face. She's worried and tired. I don't think she should be working, but the last time I mentioned her taking a break, she said that idleness is the bane of the French, and that she'll rest when her bones are laid to rest in her family's crypt. Makes me think that one day, we should move Matthias's bones off Slate's property and into that crypt.

I shake my head, dispelling thoughts of cemeteries and death. I want to celebrate life tonight.

Living.

Surviving.

I must've missed something, because Bastian and Alma are both laughing, their gazes going up to Slate, who isn't laughing but who *is* smiling.

"Giggle away, little brother," he says, walking up the stairs. "I have plenty of stories about you to share."

Bastian sobers but then looks at Slate and cracks right back up. "I may giggle like a girl, but at least I don't dress like one."

Alma tosses her head back and spills that loud, contagious laughter of hers all through the restaurant. It's the sort of laugh that makes everyone look and want to join in even when they have no clue what's funny.

"A kilt isn't a skirt," Slate grumbles. "Besides, I've got damn good legs. I looked hot in a skirt."

"We don't doubt you looked hot," Alma purrs, elbowing me before sliding onto the wooden banquette along the wall.

Slate pulls off his jacket and tosses it on the bench seat beside Bastian, then surprises me by helping me out of my silver puffer. He hands it to his brother, who sets it atop the growing pile of coats.

I take the chair across from Alma, and then Slate settles in beside me, casually slinging his arm over the back of my chair.

Nervously, I sit upright, keeping my distance from his arm. "I missed the part of why you wore a kilt."

"It was for a job."

"What sort of job requires a kilt?" Do I even want to know?

Alma pours water from the carafe already placed on our table. "Were you an escort?"

"It wasn't that sort of job."

She sets the carafe down and plops both elbows on the tabletop. "What sort of job was it?"

"A profitable one," he says cryptically.

My mind goes straight to a heist. After all, this is what Slate does.

He raises his hand to grab the attention of the temp waitress Nolwenn hired from the university. As he orders wine and an appetizer platter of cheese and cured meats, I see Alma pointing out the other diners to Bastian, feeding him names and anecdotes. Sometimes, I think Alma should be studying journalism instead of political science. She'd make a great gossip columnist.

I hear the name Liron fall from her lips and turn toward where she's looking. Her ex is sitting at a table with some of his friends, one of whom is Paul. His face floods with heat when our gazes connect. Even his ears turn a crisper shade of red than his hair. I smile and wave. His brow pleats, as though he's surprised I've acknowledged him, which is weird because I always say *hi*. As I spin back, I catch Slate glaring at him. I'm guessing the two have met and didn't hit it off. I suspect Slate doesn't hit it off with many people.

The wine comes and is poured. Alma raises her glass and toasts to new acquaintances. We all clink and drink. I start to lean back but feel Slate's arm and all but pop back forward. I drain my wine way faster than I probably should, but my day has been rough, and my nerves are fried. Slate refills my glass before upending his own and pouring himself some more.

While Alma tells Bastian the story of the tavern, Slate holds his glass up to mine and murmurs, "Two down, two to go."

I tip my glass against his even though his toast has just awakened snakes inside my stomach. What if I'm next?

"I'm scared," I murmur.

His jaw becomes squarer as he leans in and pushes a lock of hair behind my ear. "I'll be by your side the whole way through. Same way you were by mine."

I wasn't only by his side; I was also in front of him. *I* was his curse.

"How can you stand looking at me after that?" I keep my voice low, not that Bastian and Alma are paying us any mind.

My question blunts the spark in his dark eyes. "She might've worn your face, but she wasn't you, Cadence."

I slide my lower lip into my mouth. "Still."

"Believe me, she needed dental work. And lots of it." He rubs his jaw, grazing the scar that's crusted over beneath the black stubble.

I want to press my lips to his wound, replace the memory of her mouth with mine, but the appetizers arrive along with a basket of chewy baguette and sweep away my audacious contemplations. I all but throw myself on the food, before throwing myself back on the wine. I should slow down but want alcohol to quiet the snakes and zap my inhibitions. After the third glass, my head starts to feel delightfully fuzzy, and I ease back into the chair, not squirming away from his arm this time.

Alma lifts her water glass. "It's not real, though."

Bastian picks up a pickle and chomps on it. "Cadence said it might be."

"What might be?" I ask.

"The Quatrefoil," Alma says.

"Oh." I cough but still sound like I have a chunk of bread lodged in my throat when I say, "Who knows?"

Alma twirls a pale-auburn lock around her finger. "How awesome would it be if it *were* real?"

Her eyes twinkle at the prospect or from the amount of alcohol she's consumed. Or maybe it's Bastian's proximity. I can tell Alma thinks he's cute because she's patted his cheek, touched his bicep, squeezed his shoulder more than once. I don't think he minds my friend's tactile attention seeing as how his entire torso is angled toward her.

Slate clears his throat. "According to the town's history, magic can only be brought back by assembling four golden leaves."

"What if they've been assembled?" Alma whispers conspiratorially.

I stiffen. Slate's thumb brushes my spine, bumping into my bra strap before dipping back down. Stone-cold sober Cadence, who didn't spend her afternoon digging up a grave, would have pulled away, but slightly tipsy Cadence, who helped slay a monster, melts into his touch.

His smell knocks into me anew, and I drag in a deep lungful. Even though it's probably the wine, I feel like all my veins are dilating. I glance at him, find him already looking at me. The room blurs around the two of us—the soft rock song growled by Johnny Halliday becomes a faraway rumble and the faces of Alma and Bastian bleed together.

"Gold leaves," I hear someone say in the haze of my mind.

It's not Slate, because his lips are immobile. Only his jaw and Adam's apple are moving, and his thumb. God, that thumb.

"If they're real gold, I bet Slate could find them. I swear, my brother's like a human metal detector. What do you say we all hunt them down?"

Slate's finger freezes midswipe, and the world comes crashing back around us.

"No." He turns his attention on Bastian. "Magic isn't real. Your buddy Harry Porter isn't real."

"Potter," Bastian corrects. "You know damn well it's Potter."

"Yeah, sure. Him." Slate shifts in his seat, his arm falling away from the back of my chair.

"You're a serious buzzkill sometimes."

Slate rolls his shoulders back, which in his black cotton turtle-neck, look especially wide. "Just keeping it real, little bro."

"I know." Bastian shoots him a smile that smacks of affection.

"How long have you two known each other?" I ask.

"Since I was eleven, and Slate was thirteen going on forty."

Only two years apart . . . I would've guessed more.

Alma wraps a slice of Emmental around a *cornichon* and bites into it. "And you managed to stay together in the system? Is that easy to do?"

"No. But if someone can make things happen—*anything* happen—it's this guy." Bastian hooks a thumb toward Slate.

Apparently, receiving compliments makes Slate uncomfortable, because he folds his arms.

"Do you know what he did when I got into college?" Bastian continues.

"Do tell." Alma tops off everyone's water and wine.

Slate is uncharacteristically quiet, and even though his eyes are fixed on Bastian, he seems elsewhere, lost in the past.

"He relocated to Marseille to live beside me. Bought an apart-ment where I have my own room whenever I want to get out of the dorms."

It's enlightening to see Slate through Bastian's eyes for whom he clearly means the world, but it's also dangerous. Dangerous, because I have feelings for this insufferable boy, and they've gone way past the simple crush phase. Way past any feelings I've ever had for any man. Even for Adrien.

What worries me isn't that they aren't mutual. What worries me is what'll happen once the ring comes off. He may have a house here, connections to this town, but he hates everything about Brume.

"That's really sweet of you." My voice is wrought with emotion.

With a slow blink, Slate slides back into the present. "Nothing sweet about it. Just normal."

"No, it's not, Slate." Bastian pushes his plastic-rimmed glasses farther up his nose. "Then again, you're not normal."

Slate gives him a small headshake.

"I was just glad to have an excuse to leave St. Tropez. What a fucking dump that was." Slate lifts the empty wine bottle and taps on it. "We need more. I can't handle all this sentimentality."

Alma kicks my ankle under the table to get my attention. The second I look her way, she shapes a quick heart with her indexes and thumbs. The wine raised my body temperature, but her gesture makes it reach a whole new level of toasty. Thankfully, our main courses have arrived, which has the boys distracted.

"Did you book a hotel room, Bastian?" Alma suddenly asks over a bite of pan-fried monkfish.

"There's a hotel in Brume?" Slate asks.

"In Brume?" Alma titters. "Nope. In the next town over."

"I have a guest room. If you or Slate need an extra bed." My heart speeds up at the idea of Slate sleeping over again.

"Bastian and I are used to tight sleeping quarters."

I'm not sure what that means, but I don't press him either way. "The offer doesn't expire in case you change your mind."

Nodding, Slate swallows a large bite of stewed meat, then wipes his mouth on his checkered napkin. For a moment, I'm stuck looking at his lips, wondering how the night would've gone had Bastian not showed up in Brume. Not that I regret anything about this dinner. My best friend is here, and I've learned so much about Slate.

He leans toward me and puts his mouth to my ear. "Better stop looking at me like that, Mademoiselle de Morel."

My body floods with more heat, which makes me pull off my cardigan. Alma hops to her feet, announcing she's going out for a smoke, and does Bastian want to come? She's a social smoker, not that it makes her habit all that great, but at least she's not addicted. Bastian doesn't even hesitate.

Once they're gone, Slate angles his body toward me, and his legs flop open around my chair. "Bastian doesn't even smoke."

"No?" My pulse is thrumming so wildly that I'm a hundred percent sure the contours of my body are blurred.

Slate eases the fingers with which I'm strangling my fork off the skinny handle and slots them through his own, pulling them onto his hard thigh.

"This isn't the evening I had in mind," he says, all low and gravelly.

"I'm really enjoying it." How I wish my voice wasn't shaking as hard as my body.

He smiles, but not with his mouth . . . with his eyes.

I lick my lips, which makes his gaze dip there. He's no longer smiling when he looks back up at me; he's cogitating. I'm too busy undergoing a complete system meltdown to do much cogitation. Is that even a word?

I suddenly wonder why I'm waiting for him to make the first move when I'm plenty capable. Fingers tightening around his, I start to lean forward but panic and freeze four centimeters away from his mouth.

Slate's hand twines through my hair, anchoring my face near his. "I'm trouble, Cadence."

"I know."

"I don't think you do. I'm not the sort of guy you bring home to Daddy."

I shake my head, or at least, try to. "You've already been to my house and met *Papa*. Besides, I don't need his approval, Slate."

His eyes roam over mine.

Sensing his doubt, I challenge him. "But hey, if you need his approval—"

"I don't need anyone's approval, besides yours." His features harden with that self-confidence I used to find so obnoxious until I understood how hard he had to fight to earn it.

"You have mine, Slate."

He moves closer. When his mouth is a hairsbreadth from mine, he murmurs, "I think you may have bewitched me, Mademoiselle de Morel."

I smile, my heart striking my ribcage with such violence I fear I may become a pile of splintered bones and smoldering flesh.

The tips of his fingers stiffen in my hair, and then he tilts his head and fits his mouth to mine. My breath catches; my pulse, too.

This is happening.

Really happening.

The kiss is gentle at first, as though he's learning the shape of my mouth, and then his pressure firms, molding my lips to his. I raise the hand he's not clutching to his shoulder and grip him, worried I might topple right off my chair. In perfect synchronicity, our lips part and our tongues meet.

The kiss turns messy, almost violent. And I'm scared of how much I adore it. How little I care that we are making out in the town's most popular hangout.

I dig my fingers harder into his shoulder, and he groans, and I think I've hit a bruise and start to pull away, but his fingers flex on the back of my head, mashing my mouth to his. I take it he must not be in pain. Still, I touch him more lightly, and then I'm gliding my palm toward his neck. When I graze the edge of his bandage under the cotton turtleneck, he springs away from me.

I slap my palm over my mouth. "I'm so sorry. Are you okay?"

He's breathing heavily, and so am I.

"Yeah. Just a kneejerk reaction." He drags my fingers off my mouth and threads them through his. "Who knew librarians could be so wanton?"

His mouth chases mine again, catches it. The second round is slower, sweeter, made even more so by our handholding and his thumbs stroking up and down my knuckles.

A slight squeal makes me jerk away from him and flush down to the roots of my hair. Alma is tottering up the stairs, Bastian right behind her.

I hunt his bespectacled gaze for disapproval but find none.

As both take their seats, he says, "And here I came to Brume because I was worried about Slate. Should've known not to be."

"Now that you're reassured, you can go home." Slate releases one of my hands but not the other, and sits back, looking like a satisfied man while I probably resemble a tween with a face rash.

"I could." Bastian leans forward, forearms overlapping on the table. "But I think I'll stick around a while longer. Just until school starts. Spike isn't half as fun and chatty as you guys."

"Spike?" Alma asks, eyebrows popping up.

Bastian smiles. "Spike is Slate's pride and joy."

Slate shakes his head, but a corner of his mouth has flipped up. I vaguely remember him mentioning that name over the phone earlier.

"Is he a dog?" Alma asks.

"A German Shepherd-pug mix, maybe?" I wink at Slate.

Bastian frowns.

"Disregard Mademoiselle de Morel. The wine's going to her head."

I pinch his ribs, but then blanch because I probably just hit a bruise. "Sorry."

He tightens his grip on my hand, his smile reaching his eyes.

"Spike's a cactus," Bastian finally announces.

"You named a cactus?" I blurt out.

"An Eve's Needle," Slate says, as though it somehow makes his plant baptism more normal.

Again, I ask, "You named a cactus?"

"Yes. I named my cactus."

"Do you name a lot of inanimate things, Slate?" Alma asks.

Bastian snickers, but Slate doesn't.

Very seriously, he says, "Spike's very animate. As are all the other things I name."

Alma tosses her head back and laughs, which makes Bastian crack up. I find myself grinning. And not just at that moment, but throughout the rest of dinner. Even though today was one of the worst days of my life, tonight is one of the best nights.

I squeeze Slate's hand, and the ring's shape and heat remind me of how he walked into my life. Every bit of the anger and hatred I felt for him a few days ago has disappeared.

I lean toward him but not to kiss him . . . to whisper, "I hate the reason you stayed, but I can't imagine you gone."

He releases my hand to tuck another lock of hair behind my ear. "Cadence de Morel, if I survive—"

"You will." I flatten my palm against his chest, drinking in the steady pulses of his heart. "You will."

His gaze softens. I don't like it soft; I want it firm and resolute.

"Just because the last generation failed doesn't mean we will," I add quietly but not gently. "We are so much more prepared than they were."

Slate heaves a deep sigh, and then he gathers me against him and nestles his chin in the crook of my neck.

And he holds me.

Just holds me.

I slip my arms around his back, hoping not to graze any bruises.

It's crazy, but I don't want him to ever let go. I don't want him to get on a train and leave.

For now, a ring keeps him in Brume but what happens once it comes off?

Because it *will*.

It has to.

31

SLATE

I only have to insist once that Bastian take the bed. The second we're home, he kicks off his boots, drops his coat on the floor, and flops about on the mattress, snoring like a freaking Harley-Davidson. I'll have to limit his alcohol intake from now on. He only makes so much noise when he's inebriated.

The floorboards are hard and cold as rock, but knowing Bastian is comfortable relaxes me. After an eyeball joust with a scuttling roach that ends in a lug-sole full of smashed shell, I finally drift off.

And wake up to Bastian shouting my name.

My body jerks to attention and *wham!* my forehead slams into wood. I rolled partially under the bedframe during the night. I scoot out, sit up, and put my hand to my head. *Putain.* I'm going to have a lump on top of my lump.

"I hate this fucking place," I mutter.

"Slate! Did you . . .?" Bastian lurches off the bed and onto his feet with the nimbleness of someone used to being fully alert and ready to run at the merest creak of a floorboard.

Unlike in our foster homes, our door's locked, and no barely-functioning excuse for a human is looming over us, breathing fumes so potent one could get drunk off of them. "Why are you shouting in my ear at the crack of dawn?"

"There was this little girl. She was here. In the room." He swipes his glasses off the dresser and thrusts them on his face.

I've never seen him so pale. Then again, there's sunlight pouring through the grimy window, weak sunlight filtered by wisps of fog, but sunlight nonetheless. Even the squashed cockroach corpse on the bottom of my shoe doesn't seem quite as black as yesterday.

"Are you sure it wasn't a nightmare?" The kid's had his share of bad nights. For three whole years, we had to sleep with the lights on.

"No, dude. I saw her. She was right here." His finger rocks in the air as he points toward the corner of the room, the small recess between the window and the mirrored armoire. The only thing *there* is a giant spider web worthy of a Halloween decoration. I don't even want to know what size the spider could be, or if it's currently roaming my room.

I'm about to curl back up when a jolt of heat runs up my arm. The Bloodstone pulses and glows like an eerie prop in a horror flick. Is it signaling the third piece's arrival? I keep the ring out of Bastian's line of sight, already thinking up ways to get him to the train station.

Wind batters the window, then leaks around the wooden frame and whips through the room. Cold air slaps me in the face, bringing tears to my eyes. *Shit. Shit, shit, shit.*

I throw on my clothes. "Stay here. I'm gonna go—"

Before I can finish my sentence, the whole room seems to fizz and pop like an old TV. And then, out of nowhere, a little girl of like six or seven is standing on the ancient floorboards in the recess Bastian pointed out, the one beneath the spiderweb. She's wearing fuzzy pink unicorn pajamas, and her cheeks are slick with tears. She takes one look at me and Bastian and shrieks.

"You see her, right?" Bastian stumbles back into the bedframe.

And *presto whamo*, the girl disappears.

What the actual fuck?

"You saw her, right? You saw that little kid?" Bastian's eyes are round as frisbees.

I rack my brain to come up with anything, anything at all that will put him at ease, but I'm not used to pulling explanations for the supernatural out of my ass. Instead, I grab my phone and send a quick text to the Quatrefoil crew: *Come to my dorm room. NOW.*

"Slate," Bastian murmurs.

The girl's there again, wavering like a bad hologram. Panic flares across her face, sapping all the color from her cheeks. Then, *zap!* A wind kicks up, and I hear a cry behind me. I whip around. She's now on the other side of the bed, bawling.

My middle finger is toasty, the ring hot as hell, but I don't have any of the other symptoms I had with the other pieces—no wicked muscle cramps or lit kerosene in my veins.

I feel a weight on my shoulder and nearly jump out of my skin. It's just Bastian's palm. His pupils have expanded to the edges of his irises.

"Is she a ghost? Like a real one? Or am I the ghost? I thought I was alive, but"—he pats himself to verify he's solid, and his voice goes up an octave—"I'm dead, aren't I?"

"What are you babbling on about? You're not dead."

"Is *she* dead?" He lifts his chin to indicate the little girl.

"No. She's not dead, either." At least, I don't think so, but now that he mentions it . . .

"Then, what's happening?"

"Jesus, Bastian. Nothing!"

"It's not nothing!" Bastian whirls on me. "You're scared shitless, too. Something freaky is going on."

I square my shoulders. "Me, scared? I'm not scared."

"Your nostrils flare when you're panicked. And right now, experts could go spelunking in those hairy canyons."

I put a hand to my nose. *Really?*

My heartbeat hammers my eardrums as I watch it happen again —the little girl's standing in one place, then *poof,* she materializes in another, her body brightening then fading.

Her mouth turns down, and once again, she shows up elsewhere, a howl of wind in her wake. She looks nauseous and terrified. "Help me!"

Bastian—reckless empath that he is—reaches for her. She vaporizes and solidifies someplace else.

Like a goddamn ghost. Like Matthias. This feels like the Air curse all over again, but Gaëlle defeated that curse. Didn't she?

"*Putain de merde.*" I grab his outstretched arm and ram it down to his side. "Don't touch her!"

The kid disappears once more. Then a gust of freezing wind slams into me and Bastian, knocking us both backward, and the little girl materializes right between us.

Snot and tears are thick as slime on her upper lip. "Help," she whimpers.

I'm not a fan of small humans. They're loud, messy, and selfish. But a child in tears? It's a punch to my gut. I see Bastian all over again, and it brings my hackles out.

I need to stop her pain.

Ignoring my own warning, I grab the little girl's hand. I expect her to teleport away. Instead, her body skips and jumps like an old vinyl record, from solid to transparent and back again, but she stays put, her grip turning viselike, her tiny fingernails leaving crescents in my skin.

"Don't let go, *monsieur*." More tears leak down her cheeks. She flickers, and as she does so, I can see right through her.

Damn it. I swallow and feel my nostrils flare further. "I won't, kiddo. I've gotcha."

A high-pitched monotone comes from the Bloodstone, grating my ears, and the stone ignites, flaring brighter than molten lava. Still, I keep my hand around hers.

Bastian gasps. "Your ring! Why's it glowing?"

"Glowing? You got to have that eyeglass prescription of yours adjusted."

The ring splashes the girl's face, turns it crimson instead of seasick-white.

"Okay, fine. It might be glowing. A little. I can explain. But first—"

"Brumian magic is real," he whispers in awe. "All those stories about this place are real!"

I squeeze the bridge of my nose with my free hand and shut my eyes a half-second. "Yes. Yes! Which is why you need to get your ass back to Marseille."

Bastian shakes his head again, and the girl goes on and off like the WIFI in my apartment before I cornered the cable guy and persuaded him, at knifepoint, to fix it.

I crouch down to her height. "Hey, what's your name, kiddo?"

She wipes the snot from her nose with the back of her free hand. "Emilie."

"Where do you live, Emilie?"

"Brume."

"And what's the last thing you remember before you showed up here?"

Emilie doesn't shoot off to a different part of the room, and despite how translucent she gets, her hand never feels less than solid in my own. "I was brushing my teeth." Her bottom lip starts to wobble.

The doorknob rattles, then Cadence's voice. "Slate? We're here!"

"Get the door," I tell Bastian.

He sprints over and unlocks it. Adrien and Cadence barge in. Cadence's beanie is askew, and her eyes bruised with sleep. I'm pleased to observe that Professor Prickhead isn't coiffed with gel, and his hair sticks out like dry hay. I let out a breath, relieved to see both. They, on the other hand, do not look relieved. Their eyes grow round and wide as they take in little Emilie.

Adrien furrows his brows. "Why is there a little girl in your dorm room, Slate?"

What exactly does he think? That I kidnapped some rando kid and am holding her for ransom? I'm about to snap at him when my gaze lands on Cadence's.

"*Oh* . . ." Her hand covers her mouth. "Oh, no, no, no, no." Her voice is muffled, but each vowel is extremely distinct.

Her expression slackens my grip on Emilie, who promptly disappears with another swirl of wind before popping up between Adrien and Cadence. He jumps; she yelps.

Doors creak in the hallway. "We need to contain this." Adrien spins around, his fancy boots squealing, and trots out of the room. "We have a rabies-carrying bat on the loose! Please stay in your rooms!" His *take charge* mode usually annoys the shit out of me, but for once, I'm glad for it.

Emilie fades, then reappears on Cadence's other side. Cadence starts to reach out but snatches her hand back, her complexion so green I'm afraid she might puke.

The girl disappears like a puff of smoke, and then her high-pitched, shaky voice rises from the stairway, "Help!"

Shit. I'm striding toward the door when Cadence's knees buckle. I just manage to catch her, hooking an arm around her waist. I walk her to the bed and sit her down gently. And then I crouch in front of her and gather her fisted hands in mine.

"Hey, look at me. I know it's weird. Freaky, even. But we've seen weirder. Stay with me, princess."

Her blue eyes finally lock on mine.

"It's gonna be okay. Slow, steady breaths. In . . . out . . . in . . . out."

Yeah. She's not following my rhythm at all. She's never panicked this hard before. Is it because we're dealing with a child?

"Monsieur?" the little girl wails.

Bastian startles as though from a deep slumber and lunges toward the landing.

"Keep an eye on her but don't touch her," I order him.

Flashing me a look that says, *I may be playing along now, but I expect a detailed explanation later,* he files out of the room just as the professor steps back in.

I friction Cadence's hands, which feel like hardpacked snowballs. "Come on, Cadence. Deep breaths."

"Slate . . . the girl . . ." she whimpers. "The piece . . ."

Of course, Prickhead has to get in on the action. He sits on the bed beside her and rubs the spot between her shoulder blades. I didn't think I was the possessive type, but I want to rip his hand off.

"I don't think the little girl's your piece or mine, Cadence. I—"

"N-no! That's not . . ." She can barely talk between hiccupping breaths.

I pry her fists open, then spear my fingers through hers, pressing our palms together.

"N-not her . . . M-Matthias."

Adrien frowns. "I don't understand."

"A-at Gaëlle's . . . sh-shop."

Dread slicks down my spine.

Adrien's hand stills on her back. "What happened at Gaëlle's shop?"

She trembles harder than Emilie, and for half a second, I'm worried she might fizz and vanish too.

"Cadence, what happened?" he repeats, louder this time, as though she's fucking hard of hearing.

"Don't yell at her! You're stressing her out," I growl, before refocusing on her. "Shh. Just breathe. You can tell us in a minute."

Behind us, little Emilie is teleporting inside and outside my bedroom like a human pinball, Bastian pounding after her. Cadence stares unblinkingly at the ghostly girl, her breaths wheezing in and out. "At Gaëlle's shop . . . a little girl walked through Matthias. *That* little girl."

My stomach flips like the floor just dropped out, and Adrien goes whiter than the rumpled duvet underneath his ass. *Oh, fuck.* Little Emilie is cursed.

I glance down at the ring on my finger.

If I hadn't been such a selfish, entitled prick . . .

If I hadn't broken into the De Morel crypt . . .

I swallow back bile, and it burns. And here I thought Cadence's father had been exaggerating the consequences. This shit is real, and this little girl is doomed because of what I started.

"Emilie!" I stand and shout. I don't know how to help her, but I do know how to give her a bit of respite. If holding her hand keeps her in place, I'll fucking hold her hand until she's an adult. "Emilie!"

She zaps to the right of me. I let go of Cadence and lunge toward the child, managing to latch on to her wrist just as she flickers. She stays solid and wraps her skinny arms around my waist, bawling into my stomach, soaking the cotton of my shirt.

"Shut the door, Bastian," I tell him.

As the latch clicks, Adrien runs a hand through his hair but then zeroes in on the glowing ring. "The Bloodstone. It keeps her in place."

Bra-fucking-vo, Prof.

A vein throbs at his temple. "But you can't hang on to her forever."

"I'll hang on as long as I have to," I growl.

"We need to get her out of Brume," Cadence says suddenly. "Distance—"

"Except I can't leave Brume, princess. And if I let her go, she'll just keep flickering."

A beat of silence settles over the room, punctuated by Cadence's still too-brisk breathing and Emilie's thin whimpers.

"Shouldn't we call a doctor? Or the police?" Bastian's taut lips barely shift as he speaks.

"A doctor won't know how to cure her," Cadence murmurs, "and we can't involve the police."

"Then who would know?" Bastian's tone is as frantic as his gaze which ping-pongs over each of our faces.

"Papa," Cadence says meekly.

Adrien takes his phone from the pocket of his overcoat and taps on the screen. "*Merde.*" I don't think I've ever heard Prof curse. "My phone's out of battery. Cadence, do you have yours?"

She stuffs her hands inside her coat pocket, then pats her jeans. "*Non.* I must've left it at home."

"Use mine." I tip my head to the nightstand. "Bastian knows the code."

Adrien's eyes twitch toward Bastian as though wondering if he's trustworthy. Hesitantly, he tenders the phone, which Bastian unlocks, giving Adrien and the lot of us the stink-eye. I guess we deserve it.

I sigh. I swore to always protect him, but because of me, because I didn't have the heart to force him back onto a train last night, he's at risk.

As Adrien dials De Morel, Bastian's stare burns a hole in the side of my skull. "Magic is real." It's not a question. It's just a flat, emotionless assessment. But I know my little brother. I know he's feeling a whole bunch of emotions. I can see it in the sharp tick of his jaw that seems to have lost all of its boyish roundness overnight, or rather, over-Emilie.

"Which is why you need to get back on a train and—"

"Shut up, Slate. I'm not going anywhere. I'm not leaving you."

I rub a hand over my face. "Bastian, we're not dealing with fun potion-brewing. This is serious. And dangerous." I nod down to Emilie shaking in my arms to drive my point home.

"Rainier, hold on a sec. Gaëlle's calling on the other line . . . Okay. We'll be over in ten minutes. Okay." And then Adrien taps the phone, and says, "Gaëlle, we're on our way to the *manoir*. Meet us there."

Emilie's brown eyes swim with tears. "I'm so scared."

"I know," I say. "And you have every right to be. But we'll figure this thing out, okay? I'll make sure of it."

She doesn't say anything. Just squeezes my waist like it's a buoy, and she's in the middle of the ocean.

"What did Papa say?" Cadence asks.

Adrien lowers my phone even though his fingers haven't uncurled from around it.

"Well?" I could use an answer.

Emilie could use an answer.

We all could use a fucking answer.

"The leaf. Rainier thinks she may need to touch it. Again."

32

CADENCE

Slate hasn't let go of the cursed child, and she of him.

He held her hand while he put on his coat and boots. And then he scooped her into his arms and carried her over to my house, hiding her inside his coat, so she wouldn't catch cold and be spotted by the passersby.

Although, can ghosts catch a cold? Is she a ghost? My stomach dips, and all the wine I drank last night gathers at the back of my throat.

The little girl's being brave, but she's asked for her maman several times. It's breaking my heart not to look her up and phone her—she must be worried sick—but the less people know about what's brewing in our town, the safer they are. Or at least, the safer they should be . . .

I see the little girl step into Matthias all over again, and I shudder so hard my teeth knock together.

"You okay?" I hear Slate ask.

It takes me a moment to realize he's addressing me. I nod to reassure him, but the truth is, I won't be okay as long as this girl isn't cured. I pray touching the leaf will help her body stop flickering, the same way it stopped Papa's curse from spreading to the rest of his body.

I feel Slate's eyes on my cheek but don't look over, afraid he'll spot how frightened I am. I'm trying to think best-case scenarios, not because I'm a particularly fervent optimist, but because it's keeping my mind off worse-case scenarios.

When we reach my house, Gaëlle's standing outside, dark circles rimming her eyes. I'm guessing she got as much sleep as I did. Probably not for the same reasons. While I spent way too many hours replaying the feel of Slate's mouth on mine, she probably spent her night replaying the feel of her dead husband's bones against hers.

Her eyes flash to the wrapped bundle of small limbs and pink pajamas peeking from Slate's jacket, then to Bastian, and all the tendons of her neck rigidify. The door opens before I can take out my keys. Papa rolls backwards to make room for us all. The moment he notices Slate's brother, he looks at me, and I know what he's thinking because I'm thinking it too: Bastian shouldn't be here. We should've insisted he stay put in the dorms, not that Bastian would hear of it, and unfortunately, we're not endowed with the supernatural ability to wipe minds, so there was little point in arguing.

"Upstairs. My office," Papa says.

Gaëlle goes with him to the elevator while the rest of us take the stairs. Adrien hasn't said much, but the strain on his face tells me he's worried. Possibly more than I am, which is worrisome in and of itself.

When we reach the first floor landing, Slate finally sets Emilie down on her slippered feet. The poor child trembles like a leaf, and not the kind made of gold and magic she's about to touch.

Why didn't I bang on the shop's window yesterday? Why didn't I yell? I should've gone outside instead of cowered inside. Heat replaces the chill that's enveloped me since morning. I yank off my hat and peel off my jacket, then dump both on the iron handrail and barge into Papa's office before the elevator doors have even released him and Gaëlle.

Adrien touches my arm. "Cadence, it's going to be okay."

"Okay?" I shriek, and he flinches. "I saw her walking into Matthias. And I just stood inside the shop and did *nothing*." The tears that didn't come earlier well up and spill over.

Adrien gathers me in a hug, and I let my head drop in the crook of his neck, dampening the fabric of his beige jacket with my guilt and inhaling the familiar scent of his peppery aftershave.

"This isn't your fault," he says softly, then repeats it twice more.

I don't know if he's trying to convince me or himself. "I was there. Right there."

His fingers slide through my snarled hair, catching in all the knots, but it feels nice.

"I hate magic," I whisper.

The rubber wheels of Papa's chair squeak over the veined marble floor, and I pull away from Adrien. As I rub my wet cheeks, I catch Slate staring at us. I take another step away, but then wonder what the heck I'm doing. Adrien's my friend. He's been my friend for years. And all he did was hug me. There's really no reason for Slate to be looking like he wants to smother the poor guy.

The beeping of the safe's keypad carries my attention away from Slate and to Papa, who's drawing the door open. Behind colorful stacks of euros twinkle the two golden leaves. "Gaëlle, can you grab your piece?"

I can't believe we already have two.

I can't believe we're still missing two.

Her arm trembles as she darts it inside the safe. "Which shelf? Oh, *mon Dieu* I don't remember which shelf . . ." Her voice quivers as brutally as her extended arm.

"The second shelf, Gaëlle," Papa says calmly.

She picks the leaf up, pinching it between her fingertips as though it were a dead rat, lips curled in repugnance.

"You have to let go of the girl's hand, Slate," Papa says. "Bodies are conductors."

Emilie's knuckles whiten. "Y-you s-said you w-wouldn't let go, *monsieur*," she stutters, tears curving around her heart-shaped mouth. I sense Slate struggle with the promise he made her.

He crouches and grips the back of her tiny neck. "This nice lady is going to hold your hand, and then as soon as you touch her pretty gold leaf, you come right back to me, okay? And then we're going to go find your maman."

Emilie's eyebrows writhe as though it's shredding her to release him.

"I promise." He strokes away her tears with his thumb. "I'll be right here, kiddo."

A breath ratchets up her throat as her fingers loosen.

"Gaëlle, the second her hand's out of mine, she'll transport somewhere. You need to catch her."

Gaëlle blinks and then she jerks her head in a nod and steps closer to the girl. What if her fingers fall right through her, though?

"Ready?" I'm not sure whether Slate's asking Gaëlle or Emilie. Probably both. "Now!" He pulls his hand from the girl's, then straightens.

Emilie tries to throw her arms around his middle, but as she lurches for Slate, she flickers, vanishes, and then reappears behind Papa's glass desk, her sobs the only noise in the room.

"Gaëlle, come on!" Slate stuffs his hands in his coat pockets as though to keep himself from catching Emilie himself.

Gaëlle whips around, her curly black hair flogging her scarf-free neck. I thought she was missing something, but it's only just hit me what. And then of course, it reminds me of why it's missing, and I taste ash. Ash and sour grape. Emilie dematerializes and then pops up between Gaëlle and me.

Gaëlle punches the air, knocking the gold leaf against the child's sternum. "S-sorry," she whispers.

Emilie dips her chin into her neck and stares down at the shiny leaf.

Gaëlle crimps her other hand around the girl's shoulder. "You need to touch it, Emilie."

Although the girl flickers, she doesn't vanish. Emilie looks over her shoulder, her eyes going straight for Slate.

"I'm right here," he says, arms folded now, hands shoved under his armpits.

For some reason, the bump on his forehead seems like it's swelled again. I make a note of grabbing something from our medicine cabinet and an icepack after this. Nursing Slate is a pleasant distraction, but a distraction nonetheless. I refocus on Emilie, who's inching her hand closer to the leaf.

Please work. Please work.

She grabs it, and her body sharpens, stops shaking. I release a breath, relief sinking through me as fast and headily as last night's alcohol. But then her mouth pops open around a noiseless gasp and her eyes glaze over. And she crumples to the floor.

Gaëlle's the first to scream. "Rainier? Rainier! What do I do?"

Slate starts to pounce forward, but I put myself in his path, planting my two palms into his chest in case he tries to bulldoze past me. He doesn't. He freezes, his eyes going from Emilie, to me, and then back to the little girl.

"What's happening, De Morel? Why isn't she moving?" he growls, brisk heartbeats filling my palms.

I look over my shoulder at Papa who's staring down at Emilie, a tightness between his eyebrows. He rubs the vertical groove as though attempting to iron it out. "Maybe the magic is still working itself through her . . ."

"Maybe?" Slate roars.

I grip on to the gray T-shirt he must've slept in because it's wrinkled.

"Get the leaf away from her!" he thunders.

Gaëlle yanks her hand away, and the leaf arcs through the air, hits the thick plexiglass frame enclosing the ancient parchment scroll on the wall, then clinks against the buffed veined marble floor. The sound is deafening in the dreadful silence.

Although livid, Slate gently peels my fingers off his shirt and sidesteps me to reach the girl. I find myself staring at Bastian and Adrien who are standing rigidly side by side next to the wall of shelves.

"Gaëlle, get the leaf," Papa orders.

Her boots squeak.

"She doesn't have a fucking pulse, De Morel!" Slate's voice cracks like a whip, makes Bastian and Adrien flinch. I'm half expecting the strength of his fury to obliterate the glass desk.

"Maybe if I make her touch the leaf again . . . or lay it on her heart?" Gaëlle's suggestion goes unanswered.

Papa's staring down at Emilie, whose blonde hair is fanned around her pale motionless face like rays of sunshine.

"Rainier?" Gaëlle's hand shakes around the leaf.

"When I touched it, it stopped the curse from progressing instantly," Papa says.

Slate's hunched over Emilie, obscuring most of her body. "Try, Gaëlle! At least try."

"Okay. Back up. Please. I don't want—I don't want it to . . ."

Slate stands and takes a miniature step back. Gaëlle kneels beside Emilie, pulls up her unicorn pajama top, and presses the leaf against her ribcage.

I wait for Emilie's lips to flutter.

They don't.

Gaëlle picks up the girl's limp wrist and places her stubby fingers on the gleaming metal.

Nothing.

"Fuck this!" Slate growls.

Gaëlle bounces away from the little girl just as he drops to his knees and begins chest compressions.

"Come on, kiddo."

I don't know how long we wait. Perhaps it lasts all of a minute, or perhaps a half hour goes by. By the time Gaëlle deposits the leaf back inside the safe, I feel rooted to the marble. I can't even move I'm so . . . shocked . . . revolted . . . disappointed . . . despondent. All of these things and more.

I want to destroy the Quatrefoil and vanquish magic once and for all. I think of Maman, and although I don't remember her, it feels like I'm looking down at her body. It feels like I've lost her all over again.

Papa shuts the door of the safe with a clank, and still no one says anything.

Growling his anger, Slate stops the useless compressions and sits back on his heels, hands locked in fists on his thighs. He stares at the cursed child. Just stares, and then his fingers move to her forehead, and he brushes away a lock of hair before delicately lowering her puffy lids.

The silence in the room is deafening.

"Aveline needs to be told—" Adrien starts.

Papa interrupts him. "That her daughter's run away."

"She's six, Rainier. Was six." Adrien shudders. "Six-year-olds with happy home lives don't run away."

"Aveline spent years doing IVF to get pregnant with Emilie. We

266 | WILDENSTEIN & HAYOZ

tell her that her daughter's dead and we'll have more blood on our hands. Let her have hope."

"Hope?" Slate pops out. "Hope's a cruel thing, De Morel."

"Hope's better than having nothing, Rémy."

Slate's shoulders square. "Don't fucking call me Rémy."

Papa purses his lips and clutches the armrests of his wheelchair as though they were Slate's neck. He's going to hate finding out that Slate and I are—What are Slate and I? Besides two strangers who kissed in a restaurant. It's much too soon for a label.

Slate finally stands, and his eyes go straight to mine. I want to reach out, but Papa's watching, so I leave my hands hanging at my sides. Slate thrusts his fingers through his mess of curls, pushing them off the bruised lump. *Icepack.* He needs an icepack. And I need a reason to get out of this room and away from this innocent, dead child. I shiver when a ray of sun catches in her hair and makes it glitter gold.

"Adrien, phone your father and tell him to come over." I meet Papa's blue stare as he speaks. "It's time the mayor gets more involved. We need to prepare for a town-wide lockdown to make sure no one else gets hurt."

Slate snorts. "Hurt? You mean, lethally hexed?"

Adrien jerks away from the gray wall, his phone already in hand. "What about the girl, Rainier?"

"Cadence, *ma chérie*, can you grab a sheet from the linen closet?"

I nod and tail Adrien to the door when I hear Papa ask, "Now, can someone tell me who this boy is and what he's doing in my office?"

I stop and turn back toward Slate, who has his back to Papa. "This boy's my brother." His fingers flex and straighten. "He's the person I want my estate to go to in case the Bloodstone doesn't come off, De Morel."

"And you thought bringing him here to strongarm me into signing over your trust during the Quatrefoil hunt was a sound idea?"

"Papa!" How could my father think such a thing?

Slate smiles, but it's not a smile at all.

I'm sorry, I mouth, ashamed.

"There's a dead child in the room, Rainier. Maybe you can

discuss this after we . . ." Gaëlle's eyes are so red they resemble the Bloodstone. "After we bury her?"

"We can't bury her. Not unless you want to dig around the Rolands' backyard again."

A nerve ticks in Slate's jaw.

"We need to put her in the crypt or in the lake; I vote the lake." Papa stares out the bay window at the ice-capped lake hedging our property line. "Cadence, the sheet."

My skin pimples with dread as I back out of the office. I keep thinking it can't get worse, but apparently it can. I think of Emilie's mother as I take the elevator down to the laundry room, and the knot in my throat grows thick. So thick that I don't return to the office right away. I press my forehead against the cool tiles on the wall and wade through my guilt-laced sorrow until it converts to anger, then I push the laundered sheet against my mouth and scream into it. Over and over.

I almost wish my piece would show up right now, because I'm feeling exceedingly ready to defeat it.

33

SLATE

I've done some dark shit in my life. Breaking bones. Selling secrets. Lying. Cheating. Stealing. Backstabbing.

None of it even compares to this.

Not. Even. Close.

I killed a kid.

An innocent little kid.

And not only that, I lied to her. I told her it would be okay. I told her I wouldn't let go of her hand. And then I fucking did.

The look in her eyes right before she died was a hammer to my heart. The look said, "But you promised, *monsieur*."

I shouldn't have let go. I should have hung on. If only I'd told De Morel to go fuck himself and kept Emilie's fingers in mine when Gaëlle gave her the leaf. Maybe Emilie would still be alive. Maybe I'd be dead instead, and this whole shitshow would have a decent and worthy ending.

Why couldn't I have died instead? *Why?*

I bite down on my bottom lip until I taste blood. I want to smash my fist through a window. Or rip the wheels off of Rainer's chair. But Bastian's here, standing by my side, his eyes wide and distraught. I've got to keep it together for him. For Cadence. Hell, even for Gaëlle and Professor Prickhead. I can't lose my cool or make any mistakes. Not anymore.

One false move and someone else could die.

As if reading my thoughts, De Morel gives me a cruel smile. "Regretting the decision of bringing your brother here, Monsieur Roland?" His voice is serrated steel.

Bastian clears his throat. "He didn't bring me here. I came of my own accord."

Rainier's eyes flash over to Bastian. "Then may I suggest you *leave* of your own accord."

"I'm staying." It's barely more than a whisper, but I know Bastian means it. Whether I like it or not, he never gives up on me.

I wish this time he would.

Rainier's gaze slides over to Emilie's body. "It's a dangerous town, young man."

"*Non.*" Gaëlle's voice is broken but strong. She puts a hand to her bare neck, stroking the skin no longer girdled by her scarf. "It's a ruinous town."

Rainier doesn't deny it.

Cadence is back, face the color of the folded white sheet in her arms. "For your forehead." She hands me one of those old-fashioned hot-water bottles.

Right. The newest addition to my collection. The pain isn't gone, but it pales in comparison to the clenching in my gut. "Thanks."

She nods but avoids looking at me, keeping her eyes fixed to the length of cotton she unfurls. Her hands tremble, and dried tear tracks stain her cheeks.

I begin to reach for her but stop, guilt chomping through my chest. Once again, it's my fault she's in this state. First, her mother's crypt. Now . . . Emilie.

No wonder she can't look me in the eye.

I tuck the icepack under my armpit and pick up two corners of the sheet. Together, we drop it gently over Emilie's body. The edges float like angel wings before settling on the veined marble floor.

As I stare silently at the impossible smallness of the shape underneath, I lift the lined cotton bag to my forehead, wishing it would numb more than just my skin.

Footsteps and hushed chatter ring in the hallway, and then Adrien and an older version of himself enter the study. Same tweedy clothes, same haughty stance, same hazel eyes. Just the blond hair turned silver is different.

Rainier nods to the mayor. "Geoffrey, thank you for coming."

Geoffrey's gaze travels around the room, taking in Gaëlle, pausing on me, then on Bastian, before sticking to Cadence. His stare lingers way too long, and not just on her face. It sweeps up and down her body. What the fuck? I clench my jaw and grip the icepack harder.

"I assume Adrien's gotten you up to speed?" Rainier asks.

The humanoid larvae nods and crouches down to take a peek under the sheet. "Unfortunate." He says this with zero emotion. "We should've prepared the town when the well overflowed. Delayed the new semester and come up with an excuse to keep the year-round residents locked up in their homes."

Rainier taps two fingers on the arm of his wheelchair. "We were handling it just fine." From his stiff countenance, I gather there's no love lost between him and the mayor.

"I see that." Geoffrey nods to the shrouded child.

Rainier's jaw ticks, and his eyes drift to the clean surface of his desk.

Geoffrey lets out a dramatic sigh. "I suppose I could put the town on lockdown. Tell them there's some kind of new viral infection that needs to be contained. Give them twenty-four hours to get out of Brume or stay tucked inside their houses." Geoffrey strokes the edge of his jaw. "This is a consequent request, though, Rainier. One that could jeopardize my political career."

Anger distends the pitchfork of veins on De Morel's hands. "What is it you want?"

Geoffrey's gaze settles on Cadence again.

If he even—

But he looks back at Rainier and says, "Once you've reinstated magic, I want to become a *diwaller*."

Gaëlle's forehead pleats. "You can't *become* a *diwaller*; you have to be born one."

"Actually, once the Quatrefoil is whole, one of you can concede your Council seat to me."

Since his gaze slides to me, I'm guessing it's mine he wants.

"There'll be a little blood exchange; nothing too outrageous." His attention shifts back to Cadence's father. "Thanks to Rainier's thorough research two decades ago, we learned how everything works."

A vein goes berserk beneath Rainier's temple and pulsates his silver-streaked hair.

"Not that he shared it with any of us, mind you. Amandine found out about it almost by chance. Thankfully, though, she brought it to Camille's attention, who brought it to mine since *my* wife trusted me."

Forget bad, the blood between those two is toxic.

"And you wonder why Maman chose my father over you, Monsieur Keene?"

Those two fought over Amandine de Morel? No wonder they loathe each other.

Cadence's posture has never been so straight, and her chin, so high. "She wasn't into petty men."

Geoffrey stares at her long and hard. There's anger there, but there's also something else . . . frustration, sadness. "I'm not here to discuss the past, Cadence. I'm here to discuss the future. *My* future."

"But Adrien is already on the Council," Gaëlle says, matter-of-factly.

"Last I checked, my son and I aren't conjoined twins, and I'm not a Mercier. Not even by name." That last part is a direct jab at Rainier.

A jab that streaks color across Cadence's cheekbones. "*Never.* We'll never make you a *diwaller*."

"Then I guess"—he gestures to the small shape beneath the white linen—"then I guess I'll call up my dear golf buddy, the chief of police." Geoffrey takes his phone from his pocket and touches the screen. "I'm sure after seeing the girl's body, Henri won't waste any time putting the lot of you behind bars."

"Dad!" Adrien gasps.

I think the mayor's bluffing. After all, he wants magic. Locking us up would be counterproductive. Unless he plans on locking Gaëlle and me up since we've already gotten our pieces . . .

272 | WILDENSTEIN & HAYOZ

"If we're behind bars, *Monsieur le maire*," I say calmly, "then you can kiss being a *diwaller* goodbye."

"Is that so? Because if I'm not mistaken, Roland, you've already gotten your piece."

Could the man be more predictable? I'm half tempted to force De Morel to unlock the safe so I can shove my piece at the tweed-wearing maggot. The expression on Rainier's face tells me he'd offer no objection.

"If you lock him up, Monsieur Keene . . . or *any* one of us"— Cadence's voice is as dark as that ink blot on the scroll behind her —"when my piece shows up, I'll sit back and watch it destroy our town."

If I didn't know her any better, if I didn't know she'd sooner doom herself than innocents, I'd worry she'd follow through. After all, she exhibits none of the usual tells a liar does: her lids don't twitch; her gaze doesn't shift; her skin doesn't turn blotchy.

"A seat to save a town. My offer isn't *terribly* wicked."

"Until the Quatrefoil's assembled, there is no Council. We can't promise you something we don't have," Gaëlle says.

He taps his phone's screen with a buffed fingernail. "Do you want more deaths on your conscience?"

"Dad, stop. This is hard enough."

I shove the icepack at Bastian, who jerks out of his stupor, then go toe-to-toe with the mayor. "I'm the only one responsible for Emilie's death. As for a seat, you can have mine. Magic killed my parents. Killed Cadence's mother. Killed this kid. When all of this is over, I'm out of here." I've got to get out. I'm done hurting people. "Just do your fucking job and protect the people of Brume from any further dangers."

"Slate!" Cadence gasps.

Geoffrey grins and slides the phone back into his jacket. "Deal. And don't renege on it, or I'll have you arrested." He pats his pocket. "I have our entire conversation recorded and have already sent it to my email accounts. Plural."

"And you wonder why Camille committed suicide." De Morel's smile is so vicious it douses Geoffrey's.

"Rainier, that was uncalled for," Adrien snaps.

"Apologies." De Morel doesn't sound apologetic. "Thank you for your visit and subordination, Geoffrey." His chair squeaks as he leans back into it.

The mayor doesn't smile. Not even cockily. For someone who got what he came for, he doesn't seem particularly victorious.

He stares down at Emilie, a muscle jumping in his jaw. "I'll let you dispose of the body. And don't tell me what you do with it."

"*Her*, not *it*," I grit out.

Geoffrey's eyes meet mine. "I don't want to know what you do with *her*." And then he turns and strides out of the study.

Once the front door clangs shut, Adrien asks, "So, what do we do with her?"

Gaëlle gnaws on her bottom lip. "The lake."

There's something inhumane about dumping a body into water. Especially a little girl's.

I want to do what they do in the fairy tales: cover her with flower petals and keep her in a glass coffin. "Dump her in the lake, and she'll be fish food. Not to mention that during spring melt, parts of her could resurface."

"Then what do you suggest, Roland? Incinerate her perhaps?" De Morel suggests.

"What if once the Quatrefoil's reassembled"—Cadence studies the framed photo on De Morel's desk, that of a woman holding an infant, a woman who looks a lot like Cadence—"what if it reverses the curse?"

I want to tell her that hope is dangerous, that it disappoints far more than it gratifies, but bite my tongue.

Gaëlle reaches out to Cadence and squeezes her hand. "Unless we succeed soon, her body will start to decay. There's a reason necromancy has always been considered a forbidden art."

"You mean, she'd rise a zombie?" These are the first words Bastian's said in almost an hour.

"It's just a hypothesis."

"A sound one." De Morel's gaze drifts to the frame on his desk, and I recall his wife's state of decay.

If only I could delete that sight from my mind. That entire night. Except the part when I stood next to Cadence during the countdown. I want to hold on to that.

"So, the crypt or the lake?" Adrien asks.

"The crypt's too easy to break into. Wouldn't want some drunk vagabond stumbling upon her body." Rainier's stare, although not as poisonous as the one he fired at Geoffrey, hits its mark: me.

I don't react, because I deserved that.

Adrien heaves a deep sigh. "So the lake it is." He crouches and bundles up Emilie, wincing every time his fingers graze her limbs.

I swallow down a painful ache in my throat. "I'll do it."

I shove Adrien away. He puts up no fight. I lean over and cradle the small body, trying desperately to get into the zone where nothing can touch me, a zone that saved me from losing my mind more than once in foster care. But she's so light . . . and the length of her hair that tumbles down over my forearm smells like kid: strawberry toothpaste, waxy crayons, and rainbows.

Cadence tucks the sheet tighter around Emilie's body. "I'll go with you."

"No."

"This wasn't me giving you a choice, Slate."

"I'm coming too," Bastian pipes in.

I grit my teeth, desperate to argue, to preserve their innocence just a while longer, but the set of Cadence's features and the determination in Bastian's eyes shut me up. The only way those two aren't coming with me is if I truss them up which I doubt either would appreciate, so I relent.

As we head out, De Morel pulls a set of keys from a drawer and hands them to Cadence. "Don't dump the sheet with her. And put some rocks in her clothes, so—"

"Enough," I say. "I know what to do."

Cadence blanches.

Rainier smirks. "I have no doubt you do, Roland."

Cadence is sweet, and I'm corrupt to the marrow. One more reason I need to leave this town . . .

I take the elevator down while Cadence and Bastian take the stairs. In the fancy gold-and-glass capsule, I blink like the time Bastian doused me with pepper spray, thinking I was a thief come to rob the apartment.

Hold it together, Slate.

I inhale slowly, sliding much needed oxygen into my lungs.

Cadence has put her coat back on by the time I reach the lobby, and she's already holding the front door open. She leads us around the house, down the steep, snow-covered lawn visible from Rainier's office. I don't look over my shoulder to see if he's staring at us. Not that I would see him considering how hard it's snowing.

Again.

Where did the earlier sun go?

Cadence clings to Bastian's arm while I tighten my hold on Emilie. As we get closer, the fog thickens. Soon, I can barely see more than a couple feet ahead of me.

When we reach De Morel's private dock, Bastian crouches down to collect stones from the pebbled shore.

"We're not weighing her down," I say.

"We're not?" Cadence's bare fingers are already red from the biting cold.

"Emilie's mother deserves closure. She deserves to know her daughter won't be coming home."

Cadence's thick lashes obscure her downturned eyes, but I catch her wiping them on the back of her hand. "I wish I could wake up and find out all of this was a nightmare."

And *I* wish I could make this come true.

Cadence unlocks the gate, and we trudge over the icy wooden boards of the dock. In the mist, the boat is nothing more than a shadowy mass until we're practically on top of it. After being in the *manoir*, I was expecting the boat to be a goliath navigational showcase. But, for once, Rainier seems to have reined in his ostentatious taste. A midsized walkaround bobs at the end of the dock, between a deicer and a specially-made ramp for wheelchair access.

I hug Emilie's body to my chest as I straddle the gunwale. Cadence is already unlocking the cabin door, and Bastian starts to lift the buoys and unlatch the ropes hooking the vessel to the dock. Above us, a crow stains the mist like an inkblot, dipping so low I swear I can feel the flap of its wings against my forehead. Its caws are loud and abrasive and raise the hairs on the back of my neck. Bastian swears and waves his arms at it. It carves back into the mist but leaves me with a fist of dread clenching my gut.

The motor starts, discharging a jet of exhaust. Cadence is at the

276 | WILDENSTEIN & HAYOZ

helm, brows furrowed in concentration. Any other time, I'd be going on about how sexy she looks in control. But right now, the only thing on my mind is the horror of the situation.

We cut through the fog, Cadence guided by the glowing screen of the GPS.

The din of the motor is muffled by the pounding of my heart. I remind myself to breathe, but when I take a breath, I smell Emilie.

"We're really doing this, huh?" Bastian asks.

"Have another suggestion?" It comes out sharper than necessary.

Bastian looks away and into the white cloud surrounding us. I should apologize but don't.

The boat shudders to a standstill, and Cadence turns her red-rimmed eyes to us. "This is the deepest part of the lake."

With the motor off and the mist suffocating us like a pillow, the only sound is our strained breaths. I've only been to church a few times in my life—foster mom number two dragged us there on Sundays to atone for her religious use of illegal substances—but kneeling on the cold floor of the stern throws me straight back to those wooden pews and silent stretches of prayer. No matter how many times I swallow, I can't get rid of the prickling in my throat.

I peel away the sheet, exposing the kid's moon-pale flesh. Emilie looks asleep, her eyes closed, her little rosebud mouth slightly parted. I lift her, cradling her against my pounding heart and lean over the gunwale. I hesitate, but then loosen my grip and her body rolls away and splashes into the steel gray water.

Her hair spreads and dances around her like dripping honey. Her pink pajamas create a bright, incongruous spot in the silver mist. But then the water grabs hold of her and tugs her under. We watch until the surface of the water is once again smooth and gray.

Cadence muffles her sobs in her coat collar as she starts the motor and makes a tight U-turn back toward the dock. None of us say a word.

The cold air slaps my face, coaxing tears from me. I squeeze the bridge of my nose and shut my eyes, but only manage to get myself under control when we're mooring the boat.

The three of us stare at the dock but don't make a move to get out.

Damp trails glitter on Cadence's cheeks. Even Bastian is bawling. I grip his shoulder and squeeze. Then I slide my arms around Cadence's waist and reel her in, inhaling her warmth, reveling in the sound of her beating heart. I hold her tight, to keep her, and myself, from shattering.

34

CADENCE

It's been five days since we fed Emilie to the lake. Five days
since we all retreated into our own heads, trying to deal with
the little girl's death, yet knowing we can't hide from the
Quatrefoil's dark magic forever.

Five quiet days.

Classes were canceled, and half the student body fled Brume
the moment Geoffrey announced the new viral outbreak. Those
who stayed have mostly remained indoors, holing themselves up
behind fogged windows, watching the cloud cover pour snow so
thick it looks like clumps of down.

Or at least, that's what I did.

I've been traveling between my bed, window seat, and kitchen,
trying not to think of the little girl floating among the fish.

The first three days, I managed to avoid Papa, but by the fourth
day, he found me scraping mayo onto a piece of bread and forced
me to talk. I told him how he treated Slate wasn't fair, that it was
shameful. He reminded me that Slate was an extortionist and that I
shouldn't trust a word that came out of his mouth.

"Stop it, Papa."

"Stop what? Protecting my little girl? I see the way he looks at
you, Cadence, and I don't like it one bit."

I'd gone back to slathering my bread in mayo, anger making
white globs of sauce splatter the countertop.

"I've had an eye on the boy for a long time now, *ma chérie*. I know all about his devious ways. He doesn't care about you. He sees you as prey. Do you know how many women he's charmed into his bed just to leave them hurting and alone when he runs off with their grandmother's engagement ring or their great aunt's pearls? He sleeps with women for their jewels and wallets."

"That's not true."

"Oh, Cadence. Think about it. What kind of man opens a sarcophagus to steal from a corpse? Not an honest one."

My skin prickled with annoyance. He was simply badmouthing Slate to keep me away. Well, it wouldn't work. Gritting my teeth, I slapped slivers of tomatoes and shredded smoked chicken between my bread slices, then crushed the sandwich together and left my father alone in the kitchen.

The sandwich remained on my nightstand untouched. The same way Slate's last two text messages—*Hey, how are you holding up? In the mood for dinner?*—remained unanswered.

In the back of my mind, I kept hearing Slate tell Geoffroy, *When all of this is over, I'm out of here.* And Papa's accusation sank deeper and deeper under my skin.

I phoned Alma, who'd trudged through knee-high snow to comfort me. The minute she'd arrived, I told her about my conversation with my father. From her ruffled brow, I sensed her hesitation to dismiss his claims.

"I don't know. I like him. He's funny. And hot. And certainly intriguing. But some people are good at hiding their game. And if he extorts people for a living . . . well, then, maybe your dad's right."

I'd called her over for comfort, not for her to gang up on me. But Alma thinks the world of Papa. His words hold weight for her. Enough weight for her to question her own opinions.

"You can take the boy off the streets, but you can't take the streets off the boy, sweetie."

I knew she was watching out for me, but that just made me simmer harder.

"Remember when he stole my ring at the New Year's Eve party?"

"He gave it right back."

"Because you told him to. It doesn't make him evil, but it definitely makes his motive to stick around Brume questionable."

"He's the son of the Rolands! That's why he's sticking around." I didn't mention the Bloodstone, which he *had* stolen from my mother. Oh, God, they were right . . . Still, I said, "He's not here to steal my inheritance. He's got one of his own."

"You can still have fun with him, just be careful." Alma tapped the charm bracelet I'd inherited from Maman. "Might want to take that off."

She and my father managed to plant a toxic seed that grew as the hours ticked by. He was a thief and a gigolo. He didn't fit in Brume.

On the fifth day, I needed to get out of my house. But to go where? The streets hadn't been cleared and the weather was bleak, like my mood. As though I'd broadcasted my desire for an escape, I received an offer in the form of a text message.

CHARLOTTE: *Surprise birthday party at Adrien's tonight. 7 p.m. I know you and him are close so come. And you can bring Slate. ;)*

ME: *I'll be there.*

I said nothing about Slate or *to* Slate. But I did call Alma.

I HUG the magnum of champagne I took from Papa's cellar to my chest as I slog through the snow to Third Kelc'h. The weather's awful, but I still wore a dress and packed a pair of heeled booties inside my fabric tote to replace my heavy-duty rubber snow boots.

"Cadence!" I turn to find Alma plowing toward me. "Look at you." She lets out a wolf whistle.

I'm tempted to roll my eyes. "I straightened my hair and put on mascara."

"And lipstick."

"Just gloss."

"Ugh. That's right. Your lips are already stupidly so red. You do know I hate you for that." She catches up to me, and we resume our walk. "How are you feeling today? About . . . you know . . . *him whom we shall not name.*"

I've come to terms with the fact that the kiss Slate and I shared was our last.

"Fine," I lie. My heart feels as crushed as the snow beneath my boots. I think of Emilie, and her fate puts my dilemma in perspective.

"You know what the best way to get over someone is?"

"No. What?"

"Getting under someone else." Alma waggles her eyebrows.

I sigh, because she's right. I got over my crush on Adrien by crushing on Slate. Now, I need to find someone else. Except I know everyone else in Brume, and considering our town is under fake-quarantine, there's no way Charlotte invited out-of-towners to her little party.

"I have the worst taste in men."

Alma bumps her shoulder into mine. "You don't. Brume just offers limited variety."

"You live here too, and you don't end up wanting all the wrong ones."

"Because I'm *way* less picky. Not to mention, I'm not looking for long-term."

"I don't want long-term."

Alma raises a single eyebrow. "Really?"

"Yes, really."

She lets out an eloquent snort. "Since when?"

"Since tonight. You know what? Tonight, I'm going to hook up with someone, and I'm going to have a one-night-stand."

Her eyes go very round and very wide. "Cadence de Morel, has a spirit possessed you?"

I grit my molars at the mention of spirits and possession. Why oh why did she have to mention the occult?

"No." My tone's as dry as the inside of my mouth. I wedge my arm more firmly around the champagne and trample the snow toward Adrien's two-story, gray stone house that glows like a beacon in the cold winter night.

"You okay?" Alma has to trot to keep up with me.

I expel a breath that clings to the air. "I've just realized life is short." Emilie's body floats up behind my lids. "And I don't want to die a virgin."

"Okay." I can tell she's still confused, because her eyebrows haven't leveled out yet. "In case you change your mind, let's come up with a safe word, and I'll whisk you away from any potential regrets. How about . . . *arctic fox*?"

"That's going to be easy to place in a conversation."

My sarcasm reboots Alma's good mood. As she brushes her wedged-heel boots against the bristly doormat, I stick the bottle in her arms to switch up my footwear, then clap my rubber boots together.

Two more people show up behind us: Liron and his older brother, a senior like Charlotte. If I'm not mistaken he used to date Charlotte's bestie, Jasmine.

"*Salut.*" Liron grins at us. "Caleb was worried there wouldn't be anyone at this party. Besides Jas, Char, and Adrien, that is."

Alma sucks in air. "God, I didn't even think about that."

I hadn't either. "That would've been . . ."

"Awkward?" Caleb supplies with a smile that doesn't curve his eyes or make them shine like Slate's.

Which is a good thing since I don't want a second Slate. I jam my finger into the doorbell. The door swings open, releasing a rush of warm air scented by cigarettes, weed, and melted cheese.

"Come in, come in!" Charlotte gushes over the loud music, her eyes so glossy I assume the drink in her hand isn't her first. As I step past her, she asks, "Where's Slate?"

I put my wet shoes down under the coat hanger by the door that's overflowing with wintry jackets and add mine to the pile. "He couldn't make it."

"Aw, man. Jas is going to be soooo disappointed," she slurs.

I know it's petty but I can't help thinking: *good.* "Where's Adrien?" I take the giant bottle of Amour de Deutz from Alma's hands.

"He's in the kitchen, trying to salvage the mini-quiches I over-cooked." She wrinkles her nose. "Anyway, grab a drink, or a blunt. Make yourselves comfortable. And do away with those hideous facemasks." Since neither Alma nor I nor the boys are wearing any, I imagine she's addressing another invitee. Sure enough two more people stand on the threshold of the house. "I have it on good authority that this virus isn't as contagious as we thought. Geoffrey told me." She adds a sloppy wink.

If I were Jasmine or Adrien, I'd forcibly remove her glass and make her drink some water. I mean, it's only 7:15 p.m.

I head through the living room to the open kitchen where Adrien hisses a string of expletives when his fingers connect to a sheet pan.

I smile. Can't help it. It's not that often I get to see cool and collected Adrien so domestically frazzled. "Want some help?"

He looks up from the burnt quiches. For half a second, he stares as though he doesn't recognize me, then he blinks and grunts, "Thanks for coming to my surprise party."

My smile grows. The fact that Charlotte didn't know he'd hate it increases my opinion about their lack of durability. "Not what you had in mind to celebrate the big 2-4?"

"Not even close." He stares past me at the crowd thickening like the snow on his windowsills. "In all honesty, I was hoping the fake outbreak would throw a wrench in her plan, but then my father had to go ahead and mention how this virus—"

"Isn't all that contagious. I heard." I prop the champagne bottle on the bar.

"Most of these kids are my students," he adds in a hushed voice.

"Your girlfriend is your student, Adrien."

"No. She *was* my student. I never crossed that line." He shoves a lock of gelled hair back with his bare forearm and reads the label on the golden bottle. His eyes snap back to mine. "That's much too good to drink tonight. I'll put it away for when we're done with the ... *puzzle*."

"Ah, the puzzle." I sigh as he sticks the bottle under the sink, next to a fire extinguisher and cleaning supplies. "I wish I'd already gotten my leaf."

He smiles, but it's wrought with tension. "I've been meaning to call and check how you were holding up after the other day."

I grab a metal spatula from the thick ceramic jug above the stove and start helping him slide the salvageable quiches from the blackened parchment paper onto the serving dish. "I'm okay. And you?"

He pauses. "I ran into her mother. She was visiting my dad."

I bite my lip, then release it to whisper, "Does she believe Emilie ran away?"

"No. She thinks someone kidnapped her. She hired a private investigator. Papa was trying to calm her down, but she told him to go screw himself and his virus. That if her daughter was out there, she would find her." He runs a hand down his face, getting a little smear of charred crust on his jaw. "It's so awful."

I'm about to tell him about the black smudge when Charlotte bustles in next to him, whining, "*Bébé*, you're missing out on your own party."

"Hardly. Cadence and I are having a grand old time making sure your guests don't start gnawing on my Tudor furniture."

"*Our* guests."

"Yes. Our guests."

She hooks one skinny arm around his neck and drags his face down to hers. I flick my gaze away, freezing when my eyes connect with a set of very, *very* dark ones. And I'm not just talking about their color.

Crap.

Slate ambles over to the kitchen, Bastian in tow, collecting quite a lot of attention on the way. I steel my spine and cross my arms, trying to quiet my ratcheting heart. I shouldn't feel guilty to have left his text messages unanswered or to have failed to extend Charlotte's invitation, and yet guilt is precisely the sentiment bubbling in me. That, and a little lust, because the boy cleans up much too well. Even the yellowing bruise on his forehead doesn't distract from his appeal.

"Aw, yay!" Charlotte spins away from Adrien and grins at Slate. "You managed to cancel your thing!" Her eyes go straight to the small crowd dangling off the carved walnut furniture Adrien inherited from his father's side of the family.

"Nice house," Bastian says, looking around before zeroing in on the floor. "Those tiles are amazing."

I study the deep blue arabesque motifs set against creamy white backgrounds. "Adrien brought them back from Marrakech." When I look back up, Slate's displeasure slams into me anew. Is he imagining me cementing them alongside Adrien? Probably . . .

"Cadence, can I talk to you?"

I want to say no but that would be childish, and I'm trying very hard to act like an adult, so I nod and walk toward the other end of the kitchen. "What?"

He frowns. "How are you?"

"Fine."

"I thought you might've missed my texts, but I'm guessing you chose not to answer them. The same way you chose not to invite me tonight." His voice has an unmistakable bite to it.

Instead of cowing me, it makes me stand straighter, taller.

His eyes don't stray off mine. "Is there a reason you've been avoiding me?"

The desire to come right out and ask him if he's truly a glorified gigolo hangs on the tip of my tongue, but he'll be gone in a week. Maybe sooner depending on the temperamental Quatrefoil. So instead I go with, "Look, I've thought about it and don't want to start anything that has no chance of going anywhere." Not the entire truth but entirely true.

"So you're going to shut me out until I leave?"

My pulse bangs against my tensed forearms, against my strained neck. I don't know how to respond so I keep quiet.

"Is this because of . . . what happened at the lake?" His voice breaks.

I may not want to be with him, but I can't have him thinking it has anything to do with little Emilie. The guilt would be too much. "No."

He's quiet a second, then his brows dip over his eyes, hooding them further. "Your father said something to you, didn't he?"

I swallow. How the heck did he guess?

"Can I at least know what I've been accused of? I'm no doubt guilty of it, but color me curious."

My nostrils flare in distress, and the scent of spice and black coffee leaps off his skin and streaks straight into my chest. "I don't think discussing it is necessary, Slate. Soon you'll be gone and—"

"Cadence, just rip the goddamn Band-Aid off."

"Fine." My arms stiffen some more. "I heard you seduce women to extort them. And when I say seduce, I mean . . ." I don't finish. I can't.

His pupils seem to spread although his irises are so dark and the kitchen lighting so weak, it could be my imagination. "Your father told you that?"

"Yes."

For a full minute, we both stay silent, even though, on the inside, I'm screaming, "Is it true?"

Behind Slate's squared shoulders, I catch Charlotte and her friend Jasmine trying to get past Bastian, who's doing a marvelous job at fencing them off with polite questions about their classes and degrees.

"Look, it doesn't matter. It's your life."

"It is my life. My business." He sounds annoyed but neither repentant nor stunned. "But it's also my *business*."

My lips pop around a shocked gasp. "So it's true?"

He clenches his jaw.

"Good to know." I go to sidestep him, but he shifts, blocking my escape.

"In case you're wondering if that's why I kissed you, Cadence, it's not."

I crane my neck. "The only thing I'd hate to lose is my bracelet." My bracelet, whose prongs are currently digging unpleasantly into my skin, whose emerald quatrefoil charm glitters quietly. "So if you do decide to take something before you leave, at least have the decency to leave me that."

And then I shove past him, heat engulfing my eyes, hating that Papa was actually right.

Hating that I kissed a mouth used on unsuspecting women to divest them of their prized possessions.

Alma catches up to me right as I reach the front door.

She shoots me a remorseful smile. "Arctic fox?"

"Yeah." I try to dig my jacket off the coat hanger, but all the fabrics blur together. Finally I spot silver and pull. Six coats fall. My jacket is among them. Alma gently tugs me away from creating a larger massacre, digs out my jacket, then gathers the fallen garments and lobs them back onto the coat hanger.

A tear trickles out just as a hand circles my bicep.

"Cadence. What happened? What did Slate do?" Adrien's hazel eyes are narrowed and murderous.

"N-nothing."

"Bullshit. What did the asshole do?"

I gape at Adrien, so unused to hearing him swear. "Really. It's nothing."

"You're crying, Cadence. What. Did. He. Do?"

"I'm overreacting."

"Cadence."

"I promise. I am. I swear he hasn't done anything. Not to me."

"But to someone else?"

"Adrien, please . . . not here. People are staring."

"I don't care about any of these people. The only person I care about is you."

And Charlotte.

I want to correct him but don't, because he obviously doesn't realize he's singled me out.

"Fine," he says. "Let's go outside, so you can—"

A shrill scream rents the living room, cutting him off. Only the music remains, thumping along with my pulse.

Our bodies go rigid as we spin around and see Charlotte's navel-baring pink angora sweater catch fire.

35

SLATE

C harlotte drops the champagne bottle she's fitted with a giant sparkler and starts swatting at her sweater. Brume has messed me up so much that, for a full five seconds, seeing a girl on fire doesn't strike me as odd.

My first reaction is, *Huh? This is entertaining.*

But then I'm like, *Oh, fuck!*

Adrien's reaction is instant. In a matter of seconds, he hurdles over his bulky, old-man furniture, skates through the champagne foam, and tackles Charlotte full-on yelling, "Cadence! Slate! It's my piece! Get everyone out of here, now!"

Putain de merde. That snaps me into action. "Out! Everybody out!" I shove Charlotte's friend away from Adrien and his lit-up, in every sense of the term, girlfriend, then extend my arms and rake through the crowd.

Cadence and Bastian are throwing coats and scarves at random to the students funneling out of the house. Charlotte's friend—can't remember her name, something with a G maybe—offers to help, but I signal Bastian who calmly escorts her out, barring me from shoving her into the snow. It's a goddamn circus, but a small one. In less than a minute, the party's over and the door's locked. No other guests are left except Alma, Cadence, Bastian, and me.

Shit. Alma. Should she be here?

I stare at Cadence, whose reddened eyes are wide with alarm. I hate that I did that. That I stood there and took the coward's way out of our doomed relationship by accepting my burglarizing Casanova reputation, because losing her respect beats breaking her heart.

Let her go. She's better off without you.

Everyone is.

Charlotte's friend bangs on the window. "Let me in!"

I ignore her. We all do.

"A little help!" Adrien yells, straddling Charlotte, batting at her sweater with his palms.

I grab the ice bucket on the coffee table and dump it, turning her into a sputtering, angry mess. The flames fizzle, leaving behind the mangy remains of her fuzzy sweater and patches of blistered skin. *Holy hell.* That's got to hurt. *Wait.* Does this mean she's cursed, or is this some fake-Charlotte? Emilie's listless body flashes behind my lids, and I stiffen like an ice-carving.

I glance at the ring on my middle finger. "Adrien, wait. The ring. It's not shining."

Adrien holds Charlotte to the ground, an arm shoved across her throat. "I'll kill you, *diaoul*," he growls. "Salt! I need salt!"

"Adrien . . ." I'm about to repeat my warning when the stone flares to life and a cramp shoots up my knuckles and tendons. I clench my jaw, breathing through the pain. *Putain de merde*, I was wrong. "Keep on doing whatever you're doing," I mutter through gritted teeth. "Bloodstone's aglowin'."

Charlotte's eyes bulge as she thrashes about, high heels and pale fists alternately banging the varnished wooden floorboards and Adrien's powder-blue sweater-vest.

Cadence snaps into action, sidestepping me and the pair writhing on the floor. A second later, she returns clutching a grinder filled with fancy pink flakes. Doesn't anyone own normal salt in this town?

Alma tugs at Adrien's sweater, stretching the collar. "Adrien, you're hurting her!"

Bastian steps up behind her and puts a palm on her shoulder, probably to haul her away before she can make contact with the piece and get cursed. *Sagacious kid.*

"She's a fire *diaoul*." A lock of hair flies into Adrien's slitted eyes.

"A demon!"

The stretched cashmere slips through Alma's fingers. "A d-demon?"

Bastian pulls her back, and she stumbles into him on those wedged stilts of hers.

"Something doesn't feel right," Cadence whispers beside me.

I glance down at her, my heart wadded inside my chest like chewed gum. She's right. The fire's out, and Charlotte's terrified. My *groac'h* was a lot of things, most of them nasty, but never panicked. There's no seductive magic or eerie evil.

Cadence darts a glance at the ring, which has stopped emitting light and random bolts of pain. I extend my palm in front of me, closer to Charlotte. The Bloodstone doesn't ghoulishly flare back, but a pin of bright scarlet remains in its center, and although my muscles are no longer seizing, they definitely feel a little crampy. But that could be due to the three-hundred pushups I did before coming to this rotten b-day party. I'd been trying to work out my excess . . . let's call it *energy*, and wine wasn't hitting the spot.

Adrien snatches the salt and sprinkles some on Charlotte anyway. Nothing happens. No smoke. No screaming. No melting. Nothing.

Charlotte's face is turning the same blue as his dainty kitchen tiles. Demons can't suffocate, can they? Can they even breathe?

"Adrien, get off her." When he doesn't, I grab a fistful of gelled locks and yank with such force that he yowls. That split-second of inattention is enough for Charlotte to slither away from his grip.

Cadence helps her sit.

"Don't touch her! She'll curse you, Cadence. Don't. Touch. Her." Adrien breaks away from me, but I grab him again, this time pinning him in a headlock. The dude turns feral, growling and clawing at my sleeve with his buffed fingernails.

I like this untamed side of Professor Prickhead, because it's got Cadence's upper lip hiked up in disgust. Yes, I pushed her away, but I most definitely don't want her to end up in Adrien's lap.

In any man's lap . . .

"She's not the piece, Adrien." Cadence's voice is firm, her limpid eyes radiating both sympathy and repugnance.

Charlotte's shaking and bawling. Through sobs, she shrieks,

"What the hell's wrong with you, Adrien?"

His body goes limp, the fight and conviction draining out of him. I release him, and he kneels on the wet floor beside Charlotte, who's clutching on to Cadence as though she were a lifeguard.

"*Merde.* Oh, *bébé*, I'm so sorry. I—"

"You're a fucking lunatic! A demon? *You're* the demon. I could press charges, you know? Assault. You weren't trying to put out the fire. You were trying to *hurt* me. Maybe even kill me." Charlotte's voice goes higher and higher with every word.

"No, I would never . . . I thought . . . I thought—"

Cadence helps her stand, then keeps an arm around her waist, because Charlotte's like a kid after their first-ever beer. Wobbly legs. Swaying body. No sense of depth perception. Her heels skid in the foamy puddle, and although Cadence's arm tightens, they both list and bump into the sideboard holding a hammered silver tajine dish. Adrien jumps back to his feet and reaches out to steady them, but Charlotte swats his hand away.

Cadence helps her toward the couch. "We need to get your burns treated—"

Charlotte's sudden glare halts Cadence mid-sentence. "I get it." She cackles, honest-to-goodness cackles. "You messed with the sparkler."

"Excuse me?"

"You've been pining over my boyfriend, so you messed with the sparkler."

"I was at the door when—"

"See. You're not even contradicting the first part of what I said. You little jailbait whore."

My gut tightens in time with my fists. "Watch your mouth," I snarl, low and menacing.

Charlotte watches Adrien, her body quaking with adrenaline and anger. "You fucking called out her name once when you were balls-deep inside me. Pretended you were thinking of class and grading papers."

"Char, that's not true." Adrien's voice is thin, oh-so-unconvincing.

Unfortunately, I can't see what the news is doing to Cadence, because her back is to me.

"Charlotte!" Her friend's voice is muffled by the windowpanes, yet it seems to blare across the quiet house. "The firemen are here! They're going to break down the door if you don't let them in."

Sure enough, there's loud banging.

"Bastian." I flick my chin toward the front door. He eases Alma onto a couch, then heads to the door.

Charlotte sniffs. "Maybe I should call the police. Or your daddy. I'm sure he'd love to hear about your little tryst."

"Nothing's going on between Adrien and me, Charlotte." Cadence's voice is unflinching.

"Yet."

My molars gnash.

"You're in shock, *bébé*."

"Don't you fucking call me baby. I am not your *bébé*. I am not your anything."

The same men who guarded the overflowing well last week are now standing in the living room, armed with fire-extinguishers and heavy-duty medical masks.

The friend snakes around them and latches on to Adrien's seething ex. And then the room breaks out in questions: What happened? Was the source of the blaze controlled? Did anyone retain physical injuries?

That last question wins them a barbed glare from Charlotte. "You think I painted boils on my fucking torso?"

"Besides you, mademoiselle," the fireman says.

"No. They were all spared. Just me."

"The paramedic will take a look at you." The chief clicks his fingers.

One of his men drapes a crinkling silver sheet around Charlotte's shoulders, the sort they hand out after marathons, then escorts her and her friend out of the house.

The chief pulls Adrien aside for a few more questions while Cadence heads to the kitchen and grabs a paper towel roll and the ice bucket I set aside. She crouches to collect the shards of glass, flinging them into the empty bucket. I go to help her, expecting her to charge into me and tell me to fuck off. She does neither. I'm not even sure she realizes I'm squatting next to her.

The noise level quiets down and then the door clicks shut.

Adrien stands facing it for a long time. His shoulders are stiff and yet tremors run down his arms. I almost feel bad for him. *Almost* because if what Charlotte said is true, then he's a fucking sleazebag.

I hear Alma and Bastian talk in low tones, the only other people who've stayed. Cadence stands and lugs the bucket to the kitchen where she empties it into the trash. And then she's balling paper towels and blotting the spilled champagne. I grab the roll from her and rip out some sheets, glancing at Adrien every few seconds. He still has his back to us but his hands are lifted, cradling his head. Shame rolls off him in thick waves.

Finally, he says, "I thought she was my piece."

After a beat of silence, Alma asks, "What does that even mean: your piece? What's going on?"

Cadence looks at her best friend. "I'll tell you later, honey."

Alma scoffs, "How about you tell me now, *honey*?"

Cadence turns to me. Is she seeking my counsel or my comfort? I want to give her both. "Bastian, why don't you explain what you know?"

After almost a week in this shithole, he's up to speed. Where I spent the last five days thinking about Emilie, retreating under the duvet, downing nothing but cheap madeleines and five-euro wine, he trudged up to Fifth Kelc'h to use the library, only to find it closed. So, he trudged back down and did a deep-dive into the internet instead. He's a total information sponge; every little tidbit sticks to his brain, no matter how insignificant it may be. And he can usually connect dots that no one else sees. On day five of my funk, he dragged my sorry-ass out of bed and got me to take a sorely-needed shower.

I watch him line up the discarded wine glasses on the coffee table with the half-drunk beers. He always fidgets when the spotlight's on him. When we were kids, and our foster parents would grill him on whether he cheated in class—his scores were too perfect—he'd tend to a sagging plant or color-code the canned food in the pantry closet.

As he walks Alma through the Quatrefoil and the curse, Adrien finally returns to the scene of the crime. "I can't believe I did that to Charlotte." He clasps the edge of his kitchen counter. "She'll never forgive me."

"For saying another girl's name during sex or calling her a demon?"

Cadence glares at me, color rising into her cheeks, into her eyes. I swear they're bluer. Yes, that was a dick move on my part, but do I regret it? Not even a little.

"Why did you call her a demon, Adrien?" Her searing eyes don't leave my face.

Adrien spears his hand through his mussed locks. "These past few days, I've been doing research on curses for the Fire piece. A *diaoul*—or demon—made of fire is one way the dark magic protects the Quatrefoil. When I saw her shirt in flames, I was sure it was a trick."

"This is so freaking insane!" Alma blurts out at Bastian's admission. "Magic is real. Curses are real. And you're the chosen ones! Wow." Excitement supplants her shock.

Cadence grimaces while I sigh and drop the last of the sopped paper towels into the ice bucket. "Adrien, do you have a mop? We need to rinse your floor, or it'll get sticky."

"I'll do it later. Don't worry." For the first time since the showdown, Adrien looks at Cadence, and she looks at him. "Cadence, I'm sorry. About what she said," he adds through lips that are so tightly wedged together I'm surprised he can produce any words.

She gives him a half-hearted smile. "Don't worry. I know it's not true."

The hell it isn't. I see the way he looks at her. It's the same way I do.

He tugs on the hem of his baby-blue vest, then readjusts his rolled shirtsleeves, as though to look like those nerdy teacher models on the covers of romance novels.

I ignore the pain sawing through my chest, through my arms, through my entire body. *Cadence thinks you're scum, Slate.* And I am. But, contrary to what Rainier told her, I empty pockets not hearts, and I don't bed the innocent. The women who end up wrapped in my sheets are just as heartless as I am—there for one reason. The same one as me. No-strings-attached gratification.

Cadence is different. She deserves better. Better than me.

Zero regrets, Slate.

But she also deserves better than Adrien.

I grab the bucket of soiled paper towels and dump everything in the garbage. And then I turn around, about to suggest walking the girls home, when my knuckles whiten around the metal bucket and the ring spits out so much red light, it actually tints the air around me.

Putain de bordel de merde.

The stone chimney breast, the mantel, even the hearth are expanding and retracting like the fireplace is . . . breathing. Tongues of fire lick the fire screen before writhing and pinwheeling, becoming one enormous sphere.

"Look out!" My arm cramps and cramps. I ball my fingers.

Bastian grabs Alma and ducks behind the couch while I chuck the bucket and crash into Cadence, knocking her to the floor just as the fireball streaks across the living room, its smoke and sparks inches from my back. I tense over Cadence, making sure every part of her body is securely tucked underneath me, her hip against my groin, her head in the crook of my neck.

Even though the Quatrefoil is back, I feel nothing but the press of her body against mine. I pick my head up to check on her. Her pupils are dilated, her cheeks flushed, and her glossy-red lips only inches from mine. Damn, even amidst all this chaos, the first thing I think is how much I want her.

"Slate, we need to get up."

I really don't want to. I'm going to bruise her hip by how much I don't want to.

Her eyes narrow, her palms flatten against my black button-down and then she shoves me. "We need to help Adrien."

Nostrils flaring, I rasp, "Fine. I'll go. You stay down."

"The hell I'm staying down."

"Cadence . . ." I growl.

"Slate," she growls right back, punching me with my own name.

I want to lick the sound from her lips, then make her scream it for a completely other reason.

Zero regrets, my ass. As soon as this is over, I'm taking back the reputation I allowed De Morel to tarnish and setting this girl straight. Cadence and I, we're probably going to crash and burn like Adrien's house, but I'd rather go up in flames with her than douse the hissing blaze.

36

CADENCE

A s I glower at Slate, a groan erupts from the kitchen where a fireball is ping-ponging against the painted blue cupboards and grid of windowpanes, whizzing around Adrien's head like a livid, sizzling bat. The sheers ignite, and then the fireball shoots back across the living room, slams into his thick walnut dining table before ricocheting against the oil portrait of his mother.

As flames chew through the canvas, melting Camille's face, I slam my gaze back on Adrien who stands in the middle of his narrow kitchen, unmoving and dazed.

"The fire extinguisher!" I shout at him. "Under the sink!"

He doesn't react, so I scramble to my feet. Slate grips my upper arms, and I think he's about to push me down, but he's actually helping me stand. His concern and protectiveness is muddying my focus, and I really need to stay alert, so I tear my gaze off his.

Alma peeks at me from behind Bastian's shoulder and a curtain of strawberry-blonde curls. Slate's brother can't begin to imagine how grateful I am for his presence tonight.

"Adrien, the fire extinguisher!" He still doesn't react to my screeching, so I streak into the kitchen, fling open the cupboard door, and grab the fire extinguisher before spraying the white goop over what's left of the kitchen curtains. The fireball hits the bookshelves bracketing the chimney and ignites the neat rows of spines before bouncing back into the fire screen and vanishing up the flue.

Crap, crap, crap.

Bastian has his head tilted back, his eyes closed, his nostrils flaring. "Brimstone."

"What?" Slate splutters as the cloud of smoke fattens and wood splinters.

Bastian levels his gaze on the chimney. "I think that fireball was the precursor to the main event."

"I really fucking hate this Quatrefoil," Slate mutters.

"What's a brimstone?" Alma whisper-asks.

"It's the biblical term for sulfur," Bastian explains. "Otherwise known as the smell of Hell."

Alma wrinkles her nose. "Lovely."

Smoke puffs from the fireplace, which begins to bloat again, and then the entire wall's trembling, and flaming books are falling off shelves.

"Bastian, get Alma out of here!" Slate roars. "And both of you stay out!"

"But—"

"Now!" Then he turns, hunting me down with his dark eyes. "Cadence, you too."

The portrait of Camille crashes to the floor, its wooden frame hitting the back of the brown suede couch. On his way to the front door, Bastian rips a folded woolen blanket from an armchair and tosses it over the blaze, effectively smothering it, but it seems so inconsequential considering the devastation.

To think that if Bastian's right, this is only the beginning.

As the front door claps shut behind our friends, Slate hollers at Adrien.

Adrien who's standing there like a lost child on a battlefield.

"What's the plan, Mercier?"

The house rumbles and then the stones lining the fireplace fly outward, crashing into the beige plaster ceiling and wainscoted walls. I cover my head, the hail of debris spraying us hard and fast, but the ensuing inhuman roar drags my arms right down.

Slate nods toward the scaled green beast breathing fire through saucer-sized nostrils. "I'm guessing *that's* your piece, Prof. A big-ass ugly snake with wings."

"A *guivre*," I breathe. We learned all about this kind of dragon in *Brumian Myths and Legends* last semester.

That startles Adrien out of his stupor. "Not just any *guivre*. A demonic *guivre*. It breathes hellfire."

Slate snorts. "Right. 'Cuz normal fire is for pussies."

Adrien's eyes are huge and shiny like marbles as he glances around the kitchen. "Salt. I need salt!"

"Planning on seasoning it, Prof?"

He finds the plastic grinder I left on the edge of the countertop, grabs it, and unscrews the lid, then shakes pink flakes into his palm and stuffs them inside his pockets before going for a second fistful. Finally, he upends the grinder's contents into his pockets.

The creature turns its head toward us, twin streams of steel smoke pulsing out of its nostrils, blurring the edges of its equine face and curled horns. I tighten my grip on the extinguisher, directing its nozzle toward the beast that hovers over the rubble, slitted eyes sunk on Adrien.

"Cadence, get out of here." Slate's standing beside me, his left arm flush against mine.

"No."

Even though Adrien doesn't look away from the *guivre*, he explains, "According to Gaëlle, the salt will immobilize my piece long enough for me to recite the incantation."

Incantation? He knows a spell against dragons?

I don't ask for fear of distracting him. I'm incredibly glad he has a plan, because my nifty fire extinguisher isn't going to do much against a *guivre* that could swallow both Slate and me, and still have room left for Adrien.

Something shatters, and I whirl around to find Slate running a sheet pan over the serrated edges of glass stuck inside the window frame above the kitchen sink.

"Cadence, I'll help him contain the piece. But get out. *Please.*"

"I'm not leaving him." *Or you.* I don't know why I don't utter that last part out loud. Because I'm mad and petty?

Slate's jaw gets a full workout from how unhappy my refusal makes him. I can tell he wants to argue some more, maybe even bundle me in his arms and toss me through the open window. But his eyes widen and then . . . and then he's throwing himself on me, and we slam down on the tiles, the momentum ripping the fire extinguisher from my hold. Although he cushions the back of my skull and tailbone with his palms, the impact jostles every bone in my body.

I blink, catching pale streaks of smoke whizzing past the pillar of bone, muscle, and warm skin shielding me. Were those . . . were those more fireballs?

Mon Dieu.

I try to wriggle out from underneath Slate, but not to get away, just to make sure he's okay. "Slate?"

He groans, his fingers curling into my hair. If he can move his fingers, then his knuckles didn't shatter, right?

Although tempered by my bodyguard's spicy scent, the reek of sulfur expands, and then the air fills with the flap of great wings.

The *guivre* is on the move.

37

SLATE

Everything hurts. *Again.*

But there's an upside—Cadence is under me, her body pressed against mine, her voice tinged with worry instead of hostility.

"Slate?"

"I think I'm dying. Give a man his last wish. Ravish me, Cadence." Even through my shut lids, I sense her eyeroll.

She presses against my chest gently. "You're not dying."

"Hmm . . ." When I finally draw my lids up, I catch the loveliest sight: pinked cheeks and tipped-up lips.

"Slate, the *guivre*. Come on." She slides out from underneath me like a car mechanic on a creeper.

Ah, yes. The dragon. Hence the horrid smell and ridiculously hot air in the room. Well, what's left of the room. Adrien's going to have a hell of a time redecorating.

The creature roars, and I feel its vibrations in the blue tiles.

I push back into a squat, and squint into the cloud of silver smoke. "Cadence, please," I try one last time. "Get to the window. I got—"

"I. Said. No." She stands but ducks as a giant wing nearly clips her head.

"Fuck." That gets me on my feet. "Prof?" I say into the smoke. Nothing. *Fuck.*

But then a grunted, *"Dragon de merde,"* reaches my ears, and I breathe a little easier.

Although there are some pros to this *dragon de merde* offing Mercier, the cons—such as, if he dies I die—outweigh any advantages.

"You sure about the salt, Prof?"

"Istor Breou talks about demons . . . taking all sorts of forms," he pant-mutters. "A *guivre* being one of them."

The smoke disperses. Instead of shapes and outlines, I can see everything clearly, especially since the beast managed to level Adrien's cluttered house. I'd joke about how nice and zen it looks, especially with its brand-new, unobstructed view of the fog and stars, but I suspect that would earn me a throat-punch from Cadence.

The dragon twists around like a cat whose tail got squashed and hisses a puff of fire at Adrien, blowing back his untidy blond strands and lighting them up like wicks. Howling, he palms his head. While I stand there, trying to decide how best to help, Cadence scoops up the fire extinguisher and squirts a rope of white foam at his smoldering, newfangled haircut.

Adrien blinks, then swipes at his eyes like a wild man.

Cadence grimaces. "Sorry. I, uh—"

"It's okay. I'm okay." Adrien does *not* look okay. He scrabbles for the salt he's stocked in his pockets, pinches some out, then flicks it at the beast.

The *guivre* snaps its head back, but then it lunges. Adrien dives out of the way, sliding over the whitened remains of calcinated wood, bumping into my boots. I grab his arm and heft him up.

"What about if we put a circle of salt around it? Like we did with that garlic mixture for Matthias?" Cadence suggests. "Not that it worked on him . . ."

"We'd have to get the damn thing to stay in one place first." On the wall beside the front door, which is surprisingly intact, I catch a glimpse of silver—two elaborate crisscrossed swords.

The sulfur must be making me giddy. I'm thinking of unhooking them to fight the dragon like one of Bastian's favorite fictional characters. Yeah. There's gotta be some hallucinogenic effect to the brimstone, because not only am I thinking of doing it, I actually feel like I could win and not get cursed. Before I can analyze my chances of becoming an epic hero or an epic piece of toast, I race across the open space and rip *Excalibur* down. Its heft takes me by surprise, and I nearly chop off my own foot.

Smooth.

I go to toss the sword Adrien's way when Cadence shrieks my name. I spin around in time to see the beast hack up a giant fireball. I swing like I'm playing cricket. The blade connects with the fiery orb, which glances off and sails straight through a smashed window.

Advantage, Slate.

I'm about to gloat about my backhand when Cadence yells my name again.

The creature snarls and flaps its fibrous wings once before lowering its head like a bull and charging me with its razor-tipped, obsidian horns.

"Don't make contact, Slate!" Cadence yells. "You'll get cursed! Please!"

Right.

I reel my arm back and toss the sword like a javelin, hoping to brain the beast. The blade meets flesh—not quite where I was aiming—with a loud, wet squelch. The dragon shakes its head, but *Excalibur* stays stuck, dangling from its left nostril like a giant piercing.

"Adrien! Cadence! The salt!"

They dash over. With trembling hands, Adrien digs the salt out of his pockets, dumps some in Cadence's palm, then reaches for more. Thank fuck he filled his pockets with the stuff because sifting salt out of this mess would've been impossible. Back to back, they draw arcs around the goth creature until they reach me.

"What do we do now?" Cadence asks.

"Gaëlle gave me a Sumerian demon burial bowl."

"Wouldn't happen to be in your pocket, Prof, 'cause—" I jut my chin to the surrounding rubble.

Cadence scans the wreckage, and then she's dashing toward where the couch used to be and leaning over, her black skirt riding up her ruined black tights. Too soon, she's straightening and flipping around, a hammered silver bowl tucked against her heaving chest. "This it, Adrien?"

He joggles his head as though his spine has turned into a spring.

Cadence strides back toward us, hair loose and whipping around her face, cheekbones blackened by soot. She looks like an avenging goddess come to defeat all evil. Badass and edible.

The dragon sneezes out the sword, the whizzing clank stealing my attention off the woman I almost passed on because of scruples. Fuck scruples. If Adrien's spell works, and I get to live another day, I'm going to make this girl mine.

The beast wheezes out a fireball aimed directly at Cadence. She holds out the bowl like a shield. My breath jams, and I lunge, my foot catching on something. I slam down on one knee just as the flaming sphere reaches Cadence. Noise vanishes as fear drills into my skull. I roar her name.

In slow-motion, the fireball thumps into the bowl, making Cadence stumble backward, then ricochets off and boomerangs toward the monster, whopping it square in its scaly chest. The odor of scorched reptile and rotten egg leaks out from the glowing crater.

"Holy hell." I climb to my feet. "It can't handle its own fire."

"That's it, Adrien!" Cadence yells excitedly. "That's how you defeat him. With fire! With its own fire."

Adrien's mouth is moving. I concentrate on his lips, discover he's speaking words that sound like Latin. The spell?

"*Mori. Ad inferos daemonium. Mori. Ad inferos daemonium.*"

The beast chuffs, its wings lifting as though readying to take off.

"Prof, I don't think your spell's—"

Something hisses, and it's not the dragon. The salt liquifies and binds together in a glowing, smoking circle. When the wispy veil drifts into the creature's face, its lids slam shut, then open, slitted pupils growing thinner. It rages, rolls its sinewy body, lowers its head, then charges straight for Cadence.

Her skin goes bone-white beneath her war paint.

"Run!" I yell.

She takes off, nimbly leaping over debris. I snap *Excalibur*'s sister off the wall and sprint toward the beast with my brandished weapon just as his curled horns slam into an invisible wall that sends it hurtling backward.

Cadence stumbles to a stop, lips parting around hectic breaths. "The salt worked!" Her chest lifts and falls almost as fast as my own.

Adrien speaks the incantation louder. The beast agitates its head as though the spell is causing it physical pain. It snarls and turns to Adrien, opening its mouth.

"Adrien, catch!" Cadence yells, frisbeeing the bowl at him.

Her aim is perfect and yet he fails to catch it. The bowl glances off his rigid body, spinning like a shiny top above the rubble.

"Fuck!" I dash toward him and pick it up.

The *guivre* spits out a jet of flames, arrowing straight at the professor.

I pop up in front of Adrien, shielding him with my body and the bowl. I lock my elbows and steady my gaze on the incoming fireball, praying for the Quatrefoil to have mercy.

The smoldering orb, like the dragon's horns earlier, pounds against the invisible salt barrier, before bouncing back and streaking toward the beast, chewing right through its right wing. The monster shrieks and thunders, then breathes out more fire, which knocks into the magical wall, before charging the beast's belly. And then his other wing. The smoke thickens and the place stinks like a prehistoric barbecue.

Bit by scaly bit, the *guivre* cremates itself. When the oily smoke clears, all that remains is a heap of ash.

I squint, trying to make out a glimmer. "Do you guys see the leaf?"

Cadence's eyebrows jolt together. "*Non.*"

"I think you have to go dig through the ash, Prof."

Wordlessly, Adrien seizes the bowl from my hands and crosses the ring of salt—perhaps because it's gone, or perhaps because the repellent magic doesn't affect the spellcaster. He kneels and sets the bowl down. Like a kid in a sandbox, he gathers the ashes and dumps them inside.

"The lid. There was a lid." He gazes around the bareboned house with the despondent look of a soldier who made it out of battle alive while his entire regiment was defeated. "I'm going to need it." His toneless voice fills me with pity.

"You mean this?" Cadence pulls a cone-shaped silver lid out of the rubble. It's adorned with runes and narrows into a chimney-like spout. He nods and Cadence walks over to him, but the wall, which hadn't affected Adrien, keeps her out.

Good. She shouldn't get too close to a piece that isn't hers.

Adrien gets up to retrieve the lid, his arm sliding right through the transparent boundary. He plucks it out of Cadence's hands, then returns to his bowl and plops it on top.

He whispers, "*Ad inferos daemonium,*" on a loop, until a thick ribbon of crimson smoke coils out of the pinhole-chimney.

The stench from that smoke is worse than brimstone. Worse than barbequed dragon. Worse than death. The bowl and lid shudder, and then something clinks inside. Adrien reaches down and removes the lid.

The Quatrefoil leaf glistens like pirate booty.

Three down.

One to go.

38

CADENCE

Drained. Hot. Cold. Dirty. Relieved.

I am swarmed by all of these feelings, and not one after the other, but all at once. They twist through me like a tornado, violent and exacting, harshening the beats of my heart.

We did it!

Or rather Adrien did it, and Slate and I managed to survive to see another sunrise. We faced a *guivre*. A real-life, fire-breathing beast. My new normal would drive a weaker girl to complete insanity. I'm halfway there myself.

To think the remaining piece of the Quatrefoil is mine to defeat. I shudder harder.

When the adrenaline fades, which happens as fast as a blown-out wick, my teeth chatter and a full-body shiver courses through me.

I cross my arms to ward off the chill and calm the tremors, but it does zilch.

"Did the *guivre* . . .?" Adrien stands, clutching his silver dish. "Did it touch you, Cadence?" His voice sounds like his cashmere vest—soft and half-charred.

I suck in a breath that momentarily calms my trembling and dart a glance at my legs. "I-I don't think so." Even though I'm covered in soot, and there are a dozen runs in my stockings, there are no visible burn marks. I untie my arms and dance my hands over the back of my dress, hoping not to feel any holes. Although, would the beast's fire have cursed us? As long as we didn't rub up against his scales, we should be fine . . .

Right?

"Slate?" Adrien asks.

I whip my attention toward the boy who protected my body but injured my heart, hoping to see him shake his head . . . *needing* to see him shake his head. I want him gone from my life and Brume but not from this world.

His gaze wanders off the Quatrefoil leaf at the bottom of Adrien's bowl and perches on my face. "Hope not," he says in that cool, careless tone of his.

He might try to act all stoic but he's not made of stone. Only of sin. He *steals* from innocents.

Correction.

He fornicates *then* steals.

I'm still not sure what I find more revolting: luring someone in before backstabbing them, or the larcenous act in and of itself.

Or the fact that I fell for him.

Banging on Adrien's door has my chest tightening. In the havoc of the moment, I'd forgotten there was a town beyond the walls of this house. A town that must've been privy to the nonsensical inferno.

Adrien blanches behind the veneer of blackened dust that coats his nose, cheeks, and jaw. His forehead is red and peppered with clear blisters, and the hair atop his head has been singed down to the roots. When he turns toward the door, his remaining blond locks flutter, dusty, chaotic but still there.

"Coming!" He hinges at the waist and pinches the lid off the floor, then replaces it on top of the bowl, sealing in the cursed artifact.

Slate steps in closer to me, the heat from his body rivaling the one coming off the carbonized entrails of the gutted house.

"You think they heard? You think they know?" I keep my voice extra low. Even though I dislike him on a personal level, we're still partners, so I attempt professionalism by discussing the situation.

"They didn't hear the *groac'h*. Or see the ghost. Maybe they didn't hear or see the dragon, either."

My teeth knock together, this time, because of the snowflakes drifting through Adrien's new skylight. Shivering, I scan the area next to where he's standing with his father, but just like everything else, my coat's disappeared in the fire.

"Cadence?" Slate's breath pulses against my temple.

My gaze travels between Geoffrey's fraught face and Adrien's pinched shoulder blades. "What?"

"It isn't true. What your father accused me of, it isn't true."

I narrow my eyes. "If you're expecting me to believe—"

"I'm no good for you. I know it. Your dad knows it. But somehow, you don't. Accepting what I was charged with felt like the honorable thing to do." Slate's lips twist. "*At the time*." He circles around me until we're face to face, until he's obstructing my line of sight. Surely his plan. "All this near-death shit is making me reconsider my resolve to keep you away."

"Keep me away?" I snort, which makes his eyebrows dip. "You make me sound like some desperate stalker."

"That's not—I didn't mean—" A sigh, long, low, brimming with frustration, rumbles from him. "I like you, Cadence de Morel. A lot. Too much. Okay?" He growls his declaration.

My heart swerves into my lungs before managing to brake its crazed careening and righting itself. Slate's a liar.

Li-ar.

I *need* to remember this.

I *need* to stop falling for him.

"Okay," I finally say, injecting my reply with a strong dose of nonchalance, then sidestep him and start toward the front door.

"Okay?" This time, his voice isn't low.

I can't help the small smile that curls one corner of my lips. He can't see it since I have my back to him. "Good evening, Mr. Keene."

"Mademoiselle de Morel." The mayor's eyes travel over my face, then lower. He is so repulsively sleazy that I almost wish he'd fought off the *guivre* with us. I might've just pushed him into its path.

"Cadence!" Papa's snowmobile sits at the bottom of the steps. His features are tensed and his skin pale as fresh snow.

I clamber down the two steps, bend over, and sling an arm around his neck. "Oh, Papa." I release a wobbly breath, then inhale his fragrance of home and safety. "Oh, Papa." I repeat softly. "It was so awful."

"*Ma chérie.*" He smooths back my hair over and over. "Did it—did you . . . touch it?"

"Only its ashes, never the flames or the piece."

He releases the king of all sighs. "*Dieu merci.*"

God had little to do with it. Slate, though . . .

I push away from Papa, sighing also, but not for the same reasons. I sigh because Slate is so darn confusing.

In the snowmobile's beam, I catch two figures hurrying over—one with springy curls, the other with big glasses. While Bastian, like me, looks as though he's been dropped down a chimney flue that hasn't been swept in over a decade, Alma's all clean and neat, barely a smudge of ash on her tear-stained face.

She hurls herself at me, squeezing me so hard it makes a cloud of soot bloom off my black dress. "Oh *mon Dieu, mon Dieu.* You're alive!" Her shrieked relief almost blows my eardrums.

I pat her rattling spine. "Did you think one little dragon would kill me?" I murmur so that the thin crowd of bundled-up rubber-neckers circling us can't overhear.

I'm imagining they're racked with curiosity and concern even though their expressions are difficult to decipher between the surgical masks and the faint light dribbling off the quarter moon.

"Dragon?" Alma breathes.

I nod.

Her eyes grow wide. "Holy shit."

"Your coat, *ma chérie,*" Papa says. "Where is it?"

"The fire got it." I'm surprisingly not cold, though. Maybe my skin absorbed the fiery-demonic heat and stocked it. Or maybe there's just so much going on inside me that my body can't process the outside world.

A wall of pulsing warmth appears at my back. A wall that smells of smoke but also of spice. "De Morel." A wall that sounds exceedingly incensed. If my father shared fallacious rumors about Slate, I suppose he would have every right to be mad.

But I'm not so quick to dismiss Papa's report and trust Slate. Just because I want it to be false doesn't mean it is. Does it matter, though? I'm not planning on getting back with Slate. He might not be a lowlife gigolo, but that doesn't erase the fact that he hates Brume and wants out.

"Roland. Glad to see you made it out in one piece."

"Are you?"

I don't say anything. Just keep my eyes on Papa and my back to Slate.

Under his breath, he adds, "I suppose you are glad. After all, I'm the glue to your precious clover."

I sigh. "Stop it, Slate."

I sense him tensing even though our bodies don't connect anywhere. It's something in the shifting of the air between us, or the way his breaths palpitating against the back of my head have turned shallower, swifter. How I wish the Bloodstone could double as a lie detector. I'd really love to know who's speaking the truth.

"Adrien!" Papa calls out.

I look over my shoulder, careful not to cross Slate's tenebrous scowl. Adrien, still gripping his silver tajine dish, makes his father take a couple steps back and then circles him, giving him a wide berth.

"We need to . . ." Papa tips his head in the direction of our house.

He doesn't mention the piece or the safe but we all get it. Well, except for Alma who's staring at the dish as though it contains the *guivre*'s bleeding heart.

"My father will stay here, deal with the . . . with the wreckage, and the firemen."

"You okay, son?"

"*Non*, Rainier."

Papa's forehead grooves. "Not that I ever doubted your strength and cunning, Adrien, but it brings me great comfort to see you standing before me."

"I bet," Slate mutters under his breath. "Would've put a real wrench in Operation Quatrefoil if he'd died."

Adrien cocks the patch of skin that used to house an eyebrow but now sits hairless on his blackened forehead.

"I like the new do, Prof. Party in the back. Churchy in the front."

"You're such an ass, Slate," Adrien says but smirks, so maybe he's not mad.

But I am. "You know, being a jerk's really off-putting."

I don't look to see what that does to Slate, but I see what it does to Adrien—makes his gaze, which had looked a little lost and wild, firm up. I don't know if what Charlotte insinuated is true. I don't know if Adrien actually harbors feelings for me. She probably said it out of spite.

"Papa has some hair clippers at home. I buzzed his hair once. Turned out fine. I'll gladly help you out. Unless you want to keep it—"

"No. Definitely not." Adrien runs his palm over his forehead then higher. "I definitely don't want to keep it this way. Thank you, Cadence. I appreciate your offer and will take you up on it."

"Cadence, Alma, I'll drive you home," Papa offers, but I shake my head.

"I need to walk, Papa."

Alma casts a longing glance at the snowmobile seat, but in the end, she hooks her arm through mine. Once the distance has grown between us and the four men, she says, "There are so many screwed-up parts about this evening, but right now, I need to know, do you still have feelings for Professor M, because—"

I pinch her arm and hiss, "Alma, he's right behind us."

Instead of dropping the subject she drops her voice. "He called out your freaking name while making love to his girlfriend, Cadence."

"I'm sure that happens to lots of people."

"Um, no. When you're doing it with someone, you're not thinking about *other* people. Or if you are, you're thinking about them silently. Totally silently."

"He was probably inebriated or something. But can we just not talk about it?" When she lets out a puff of breath, clearly annoyed I don't want to analyze every angle of Adrien's mishap, I add, "We can dissect it when it's just the two of us and everyone's gone, all right?"

She glances over her shoulder. "Why is everyone coming to your house by the way? And what's inside the metal pot? Please tell me it's not an organ."

How well do I know my bestie? Of course that's where her mind went.

"It's not an organ. It's a gold leaf. One of the Quatrefoil's."

Her mouth rounds in a perfect O.

"And they're all coming back to the manor so we can lock it inside the safe, because if anyone but Adrien touches it, that person becomes cursed."

"I was hoping to get some action tonight. Didn't realize just how much I'd get."

"You and I both. So much for losing my virginity . . ."

"There's still time. Plus you have two willing candidates."

My cheeks go so hot that I'm tempted to fan myself even though it's minus ninety-two degrees outside. "Oh my God, Alma, *shh*."

Her lips close around the wickedest smile that stays in place during our entire slog through the snowcapped circles of Brume, Papa's snowmobile rumbling softly behind us.

39

SLATE

I t's one giant slumber party, except it's all slumber and no party.

Adrien, Alma, Bastian, and I crash at the De Morel house. Alma with Cadence, Bastian with me, in the same room as last time, and Adrien in the suite off of Rainier's that apparently his nurse-slash-physical-therapist-slash-dominatrix Jaqueline uses sometimes.

The minute we arrived, Adrien and Rainier locked the piece in the safe. Then Cadence set off to give Prof a proper buzz-cut, while the rest of us retired to the bedrooms, too beat and shell-shocked to do much of anything else.

I scrub up four times in the shower, but the stink of barbequed dragon and soot still clings to me. I have no idea how I got out of that whole mess unscathed. I mean, yeah, I hurt like hell and there are plenty of scrapes and bruises all over my already scraped and bruised body, but for facing a demonic *guivre*, I'm in damn good shape.

For being in Brume, I'm in damn good shape.

This town's a killer.

I dress in the university-issued sweats and a T-shirt with the school logo De Morel's house elf left out on the bed.

"You should have seen me face the beast down with Adrien's sword," I tell Bastian as I step out of the bathroom, water spiraling down the nape of my neck from my waterlogged curls. "I'm getting a plaque with *Slate Ardoin, Dragon Slayer Extraordinaire* made for the house." I slash the air with an invisible sword to bring the picture to life.

Bastian snorts. He's taken over the bed, he, too, in U of B's gray uniform of sweats and T-shirt. "I'll have to take your word for it. All I saw was fire and smoke. And the roof caving in like it was made out of Legos." He straightens his glasses and runs a hand over his hair. "I was kind of busy comforting Alma."

I lift an eyebrow. "Oh, yeah?"

Color rises in his cheeks. "Don't get any ideas. I just put my arm around her and discussed magic." He adjusts his glasses again. "She's . . . nice."

Now it's my turn to snort. "Alma? Nice? I would put her more in the *naughty* category . . . Not that there's anything wrong with that. But you're—" I shrug. I'm not sure how to say it without getting his hackles up. He's a baby sparrow and she's a hawk who could rip his head off with one snap of her beak. "You're *too* nice."

"There's no such thing as too nice." He fluffs a pillow. "Enough about me, though. I'd much rather discuss you and Cadence."

My feet sink into the thick, ivory carpet. "Rainier told her I slept with women to steal their cash and jewels, so there really is no *me and Cadence.*"

He lifts his eyebrows.

"Yes, I've thieved, but I don't *screw* the women I've screwed over." I may be a conniving lowlife, but I'm not a complete jackass.

"Have you explained this distinction to Cadence?"

"I tried." I swallow a rawness in my throat. "But she's already made up her mind about me."

"She doesn't know you. Give her some time."

I rub the towel over my hair. "I'm not sure I have time."

Bastian shoots me a warning look, one that says: don't think like that, but how can I not? The new moon is in less than a week.

"Brume's changed you. You've never been the glass-half-empty sort, and you've *never* cared what people thought about you."

He's right. I normally don't give a shit about anyone's opinion of me.

"I mean, I knew you liked her, but you must *really* like her if you want to make such a great impression."

I sink onto the edge of the bed, still rubbing my head with the towel.

Bastian's gaze shifts toward the closed doors. "That Charlotte really reamed Adrien. Poor guy."

"*Poor guy*? Whose side are you on?"

"Oh, there are *sides* now?" Bastian smirks.

"Cadence is like a sister to him. Who the hell calls out his sister's name during sex?"

"Except she's not his sister."

"Except he's a decade older."

"Didn't he just turn twenty-four?"

I scowl at Bastian, who studies me like I'm an amoeba under a microscope. "What?"

He tilts his head to the side. "You got it bad for her, huh?"

I lunge and grab a pillow, then toss it at him. Even though my downy missile meets its mark, it doesn't wipe away the smile growing on Bastian's face.

He makes kissy noises. "Slate's in looooove."

"How old are you? Five?" I glance at the door to the Jack and Jill bathroom. "And I'm not fucking in love. I don't do love."

He sits up, laughing. "Look at you. You're all worked up. Over a girl."

"You asked for it." I spring to my feet and wrap an arm around his neck, grinding my knuckles against the top of his head.

Still laughing, he elbows me in the stomach, but I don't let go. His glasses topple onto the bed as I turn his hair into a rodent nest.

"Truce!" he wheezes between two deep chuckles.

I release him. "Weakling."

He plucks his glasses from the snow-white comforter. "I let you win."

"Sure ya did." Grinning, I retrieve my pillow, then yank the folded ivory and cream plaid blanket from the fat armchair in the corner. I toss both down on the carpet and lay back, eyes on the teardrop crystals of the chandelier. I've seen some fancy interiors, but a fucking crystal chandelier inside a bedroom . . .?

Ludicrous.

Once I get back to Marseille, I'm putting one of these up, but mine'll be double the size.

Bastian switches off the lights. "You know, there's room enough for two people in this king-size bed."

"I'm good, little brother." I shut my eyes and concentrate on the wind leaning against the windows. Sleeping on the floor grounds me; plus, you can't fall off the floor. Besides, the carpet's thicker than some of the pancake mattresses I've slept on over the years.

Dark little clouds smudge my thoughts at the memory of those homes. Horrible. All of them. No luck of the draw, there. Once I come into enough money that Bastian's grandkids never want for anything, I'll start a program to help orphaned youth. Maybe buy a castle . . . So many of those are dying in the French countryside because upkeep's too steep. I'll refurbish it and fill it with everything a kid could ever desire or need.

Yeah . . . that's what I'll do . . . once the ring comes off . . . and I have the money.

As sleep begins to haze my thoughts, Bastian murmurs, "I like who you are when you're with Cadence. You're the Slate I've always known, not the one you pretend to be." He pauses. "You're the good guy."

"Fuck you talking about. I've never been good." Just because I want to *do* good doesn't make me good. There's too much rot inside me. But his words nonetheless make my chest swell with warmth.

"Rémy Roland," he sounds my birth name quietly. "Maybe that's who you *really* are."

I think about that for way too long, wonder who I would've been if my parents were still alive, and I'd been raised in Brume. Would Cadence and I have been friends? More than friends?

I flip onto my side, punching my pillow to plump it up, then shut these thoughts down, because that kid died right along with his parents, and I'm the phoenix who rose from his ashes.

Besides with a name like Rémy I would've for sure been a wuss.

Not a go-getter.

Not a survivor.

A LOUD KNOCK on the bedroom door makes my lids snap up. Sunlight streams through the chink between the drapes. The sound of the shower running and Alma's stellar singing voice come from the bathroom, "Stayin' alive, stayin' alive . . . ah . . . ah . . . ah . . ."

Bastian sits up in bed, rubbing the sleep from his eyes, while I stumble over my blanket to open the door. Cadence is on the other side, dressed in a blue sweater and fluffy bunny slippers. Despite the circles purpling the delicate skin beneath her eyes, her expression is fierce.

I spear my hand through my hair, trying to put a little order in the chaos. "Hey."

"Papa wants to see you in his study."

Ah. Papa . . . Would it have been so much to ask that she'd sought me out because *she* wanted to see me?

"And what Papa wants, Papa gets."

She sighs. "Slate . . ."

I hold up my hands. "Sorry. Just give me a few minutes. I want to brush my teeth. Once Alma's done with her performance . . ."

A smile edges her lips. "She does like to sing."

"She does." I want to ask if she sings, too. I bet she has a beautiful singing voice considering how husky her speaking voice is.

She points down the hall. "There's a powder room down there. With new toothbrushes and disposable shaving kits. In case you wanted to shave."

I rub my day-old stubble, which makes a scratchy sound, like ripping Velcro.

Cadence trails my fingers' movement, black pupils beating against the clear blue.

"What do you think? Should I get rid of it?"

"I, uh . . . I think . . . unless it bothers you." Her cheeks pinken.

I'm taking her blush as a seal of approval. Stubble's staying.

Her throat moves with a swallow. "It's your face."

"Yeah, but I don't have to look at it. *You* do."

If possible, she grows more uncomfortable, and my ego gets a boost that I'm affecting her.

She clears her throat. "Anyway, Solange usually leaves everything in the drawers and stocks them up when they run empty."

Aha. "So, that's your house elf's name."

A hairline fracture of a smile touches her lips as I shut the door behind me to give Bastian privacy.

"How are you feeling by the way?"

"Like I faced off with a *guivre*," she deadpans.

"That's funny. I feel the same, exact way."

"Except you look like you won the fight."

"And you don't?" I take the opportunity to slide my gaze down the dark-gray leggings that hug her curves and then back up over the powder-blue sweater that offsets her eyes.

"My legs are *covered* in bruises."

"You mean, like my face? And hands?" I stretch out my digits. Three of my knuckles are a shade of eggplant-black that really makes the Bloodstone pop. "And torso? Care to see it?"

She lets out a soft snort. "We can compare bruises later."

"Your offer isn't falling on deaf ears."

Her eyes take on a slight shimmer. "It wasn't an offer."

"Sounded like one." I wink, then turn and disappear inside the pink and white powder room, which, at best, is large enough for a six-year-old girl.

I bang my elbows and knees against the walls as I brush my teeth and clean the night off my skin. I try to comb out the reek of cold smoke from my distraught curls, but it lingers. After tossing the used bamboo comb into the small vermeil bin, I pat the mess atop my head with some water until it's decent enough. Cadence is gone when I finally pop back into the hallway. I open the bedroom door to tell Bastian I'm off to a meeting with my favorite person, then clamber down a flight of stairs.

The study stinks of cigar smoke, and I spy a stub in the crystal ashtray on Rainier's desk. He sits behind it, thumbing through a manila folder. I catch the words ROLAND ESTATE on the tab. There's no chair for me to sit in, so I stand across from him, arms crossed. While me looming over him at his desk should make me feel empowered, it doesn't. Rainier somehow manages to look down his nose at people from the depths of his wheelchair.

"Let's skip the preamble." He pushes the folder toward me. "I've gotten all your financial records together and relinquished my hold on your accounts. All that's left for you to do is sign on the dotted line."

"Thinking I might survive this Quatrefoil gig after all, huh?" I open the file to a page bearing figures with an impressive number of zeroes.

A sigh whistles through his barely parted lips. "Slate, I know you believe me the devil incarnate, but I'm not betting against you." He leans farther back, the leather squeaking under his cream-colored cashmere turtleneck. "However, once this curse is defeated, I want you gone from Brume."

"What if I want to stay?"

"Why would you stay?"

To prove to your daughter I'm dependable. "To learn more about my heritage. I mean, if this works, I'll have magic. I'll probably need to figure out how to use it."

"I'm sure you'll be plenty capable of figuring everything out in Marseille."

My jaw aches from how hard I'm working it. "Why do you want me gone so badly?"

"You know *exactly* why." He doesn't utter his daughter's name, yet it dangles in the air between us like the reek of cold smoke.

"What exactly do you think I plan on doing to her?"

"The same thing you do to all the girls you keep company."

"You mean, extort them after repeatedly satisfying them sexually?"

His blue gaze turns positively lethal.

"I don't know where you picked up that information about me, but it's a lie. I don't screw over the women I *screw*."

"You're denying it?"

"Of course I'm denying it." My knuckles crack, sending little bolts of fire down the tendons. "I'm no saint, but I'm not some amoral gigolo. Have I ever let a woman buy me a meal or a gala ticket? Yeah. Have I ever helped a woman out of a bad marriage against material compensation? Guilty. But that doesn't make me the low-life asshole you depicted me as to Cadence." Because I'm feeling spiteful and petty, I add, "It's fresh, coming from you. A man who took his wife's last name and inherited all her assets. Who were you before becoming Monsieur de Morel, Rainier?"

If looks could kill, I wouldn't just be dead; I'd be buried six feet under solid concrete and a high-rise.

The door swings open, disturbing the coalescing tension.

"Am I interrupting?" Bastian asks.

I'm not sure whether he was eavesdropping or whether he sensed my morning meetup with De Morel wouldn't be pretty, but whatever his reasons for barging in, I'm grateful he's come. Then again, Bastian's the type of guy who shows up and sticks around, for better or worse.

De Morel growls, "yes" at the same time I answer, "no."

When Bastian has shuffled in beside me, I nod to the folder. "My financial records. Do your magic."

I'm expecting De Morel to clap his hand over the file, or start shredding the papers, but he keeps his fists on his armrests.

Bastian grabs the file, then begins leafing through it. As he squints at the legalese, I study the smudged upside-down triangles, statue-like sketches of people, and weird bugs littering the framed scroll above the filing cabinets. I'm so fucking angry that the small lines of illegible Breton blur, and a quatrefoil appears. Not by magic or anything, but the spaces in the text are arranged in a way that they align into four curved leaves.

I step in closer. "What's this?" When a minute passes and De Morel still hasn't answered, I hook a glance over my shoulder.

His skin's returned to its normal pasty shade of pale, but the hatred in his eyes burns darker than ever. "The *Kelouenn*, also known as the Scroll."

"Shouldn't it be stocked in that state-of-the-art archival room you got up in the Temple?"

"Cadence showed you the archival room?"

"She did."

Unhappiness wafts off him as potent as his fancy vetiver cologne.

"So what does this scroll say?"

"It explains how to assemble the Quatrefoil."

"You're fucking kidding me?" I whirl around. "And you didn't think to show us this blueprint before we faced the curses?"

"Adrien, Gaëlle, and Cadence all know what's on the *Kelouenn*. And technically, so do you. I explained what we've managed to gather from the translation the night you showed up wearing the ring."

"Mind if I take a look at the translation?"

"Why? Do you think I'm lying?"

I cross my arms. "No. Just curious."

"Trust isn't your forte, Monsieur Roland."

"Because you've given me so many reasons to trust you, De Morel?"

His mouth puckers as though he's chomped on a sour cherry. "The translation's in the library. In the archival room."

"Monsieur de Morel?" Bastian looks up from the file. "I have a question for you about Slate's assets?"

"You do, do you?"

Bastian pays his haughtiness no mind. "Can you explain the two payments that were made from Slate's inheritance four years ago for the amount of 50,000 euros to a *Marianne Shafir*?"

Little bro would make a fucking great lawyer.

Rainier's fists have loosened but not his fingers. All ten of them are gripping his armrests as though they were some whore's thighs. "Marianne was an elderly professor at the university, who had health problems, costly ones. Eugenia and Oscar were very fond of her. They would have wanted to help her." De Morel adds the last part as though to hammer in his donation's legitimacy.

"Hmm." Bastian slides his bottom lip between his slightly crooked teeth. I've offered him a full-ride to the orthodontist, but he insists it gives him character. "The state covers health care."

"Not every kind of cancer treatment."

"And you couldn't pitch in?" Bastian sweeps a hand around the room. "With all due respect, *you* don't seem to be strapped for cash, Monsieur de Morel."

De Morel rolls himself out from behind the desk. "Assets and cash are two very different things."

"So, you're saying you have no liquidities?" Bastian's eyebrows ruffle behind his glasses.

"Yes."

"So, you won't mind gifting some of those assets to Slate to compensate for the money transferred out of his account?"

"Compensate?" Rainier's eyes bulge. "He still has forty-two million euros in his name. And a house! Not to mention that once he has magic—"

"Slate?" Bastian turns to me. "Care to weigh in?"

I'm reeling from the number, but my priority remains ripping Rainier a new one. The vein on the side of his throat bloats and deflates, bloats and deflates. He may be a good father but he's a shitty human.

I narrow my eyes. "Tell your daughter the truth, that you lied about me sleeping with women and screwing them over, toss in the Gauguin graphite sketch in the foyer, and I won't press charges." Cadence may one day see the light on her own, but for now, she's still under his yoke.

"It's not mine to give. It belongs to my daughter. *Everything* belongs to my daughter."

I sense a bitterness there. As though he'd have preferred his wife to make *him* beneficiary. I have a serious itch to jab my finger on this sore spot—not to annoy the man, even though *Dieu sait* how much I enjoy doing so—but to understand what sort of woman Cadence's mother was. Did she transfer her estate to Cadence for tax reasons or because she didn't trust her husband?

"Why don't you ask her for the drawing?" There's a gloating quality to that question, a smugness, a challenge.

He knows I won't. "Just fucking fill her in on your *jackassness*, and I'll drop the subject of your 100K loan."

"*Jackassness* isn't a word, Slate," I hear Cadence say.

When I turn around, she's standing right there, leaning against the doorjamb, lips pressed so tightly together microscopic lines bracket her mouth.

"You may not be an unscrupulous libertine, but you are a black-mailing ass." A cyclone brews behind her lidded eyes. "Take the sketch. Draw up the papers, and I'll sign them. But after that, you leave my father alone."

Delight gusts off Rainier like smoke from the dragon. "*Merci, ma chérie.*"

She shoots her dad a glare that makes his shoulders twitch. "Slate may be a thief, but at least he isn't a liar."

De Morel goes whiter than his cozy sweater. "A . . . liar . . .?"

"You spread rumors about him. False rumors."

Slowly, his bleached cheeks fill back with color, as though relieved, which is strange.

"Please apologize, Papa."

De Morel sighs, but it sounds theatrical, like he's putting on a show for his beloved daughter. "I apologize, Roland. I wasn't aware the rumors I shared with Cadence were fabricated."

She pushes off the doorframe. "I'm going back to the dorms with Alma tonight, and I'll stay there for the foreseeable future." The sharpness of her voice stuns everyone into silence.

"Why?" De Morel stutters.

"Because I don't want to be here." The words *with you* hang in the air. Or maybe they're just suspended inside my mind.

Even though I don't want to ruin Cadence's relationship with her father, I do think it's important for her to see the man behind the expensive cashmere and neat smiles.

"*Ma chérie* . . . it's dangerous."

Who should appear behind her at that very moment, who should put his hand on her shoulder other than Prickhead, with his buzz-cut and blistered forehead. The cropped hair and burn marks change him, make him appear harder, more military officer than hoity-toity professor.

I study Cadence's reaction to his touch, hope to spot discomfort, but her muscles don't bunch. Is she unbothered or unaware?

"It's not the dorms that are dangerous, Papa; it's this whole damn town." She steps to the side, and Adrien's friendly hand slides down her arm and off her body. Little does she know that she's just spared Prof's fingers some accidental phalanx dislocations.

And Bastian thinks I'm a good guy . . .

I snort, which garners her attention.

Our eyes lock, stay locked, as her father says, "What if your piece shows up while you're alone?"

"I won't be alone. I'll be with Alma. And if my piece shows up, I'll do what the others did. I'll call everyone. Get the *squad* together." Her ponytail swishes as she flips around.

"Hey, Cadence?" I call out.

She stops next to Adrien, glances over her shoulder.

"Your father mentioned the translation of this scroll thing was in the basement of the library. Can I see it?"

It takes her a moment to answer.

Was she expecting a reminder about the Gauguin? I don't give a shit about it now that I have forty-two million dollars. I'd brought it up mostly to annoy De Morel, and because it's a fine piece of art that'd go extremely well on the black marble wall in front of my Toto toilet back home, but if it's Cadence's inheritance, I'm not touching it.

Finally, she nods. "I'll go pack a bag and meet you in the foyer in ten." And then she's out of sight. A minute later, a door slams somewhere in the gigantic house.

Rainier rolls himself toward the door. "See what you've done!"

"What *I've* done? All I did was ask you not to lie, De Morel."

He swings his chair around. "If anything happens to her, it's on you. Now, get out of my house."

"Is it your house?" I polish the Bloodstone on my sweatpants.

A cruel smile lights up his aristocratic features. "Oh, Slate . . ."

The way he says my name coupled with that smile gives me an actual chill. I swear my spine tingles. I knew this man had skeletons in his closet but now wonder if there are a couple non-metaphorical ones in there.

"These challenges have heightened both of your emotions, given you and Cadence shared experiences you wouldn't have had otherwise. Once this is over, my daughter will realize you two have nothing in common. And she'll finally see you for the man you really are."

I square my shoulders. "Who I really am?"

"You may carry the Roland name on your birth certificate, but you're still a nobody, Slate."

He's targeted the one wound I have that won't heal and pressed his dirty finger into it. It burns like hell.

"Somebody woke up on the wrong side of his wheelchair."

Adrien stares after De Morel as he rolls down the hall. In a quiet voice, he says, "You shouldn't goad him, Slate."

Is he warning me because he feels it, too? The old man's desire to do away with me?

Bastian tucks the folder under his arm.

"Did you think I had manners, Prof? Unlike you, I wasn't brought up with a silver spoon in my mouth."

Adrien shakes his head. "Now that you're rich, you no longer have to be a . . . *thug*."

OF WICKED BLOOD | 325

"Now that I'm rich?" I scoff. "I already was." Thanks to my salvaged Renoir.

"I'm guessing this is a whole new level of rich."

Yeah. It's a whole new level.

The Bloodstone casts a prick of red light on the manila folder as though it were aiming to shoot. The dot reminds me that the ring can and will destroy me if Cadence doesn't defeat the final curse. I have complete confidence in her, though.

"So, you wanted to see the translation of the *Kelouenn*?" Adrien nods to the framed scroll.

"Yep." I pluck my phone from my sweatpants' pocket and snap a few pics of the aged parchment. How the phone survived last night's arson show is beyond me, but I'm grateful it did. "Want to come with us, Prof?"

Adrien shrugs. "Why not? It beats combing through the rubble of my house."

A twinge of sympathy flickers in me. The same way I sense Rainier is rotten, I sense that Adrien isn't. If only he could get back with Charlotte. Or any other girl for that matter. I really don't give a rat's ass whom he beds as long as it isn't Cadence de Morel.

40

CADENCE

B efore a summer storm, the lake smooths to glass and every insect quiets. This is how I feel as I head downstairs, my overstuffed bag bouncing against my bruised ribs. Like a stillness has settled inside me, over me. A stillness that heralds something violent. One that sets my teeth on edge and makes swell after swell of chills dash themselves against my skin.

Alma's been darting worried glances my way. When I asked if I could stay with her in the dorms, she caught on that something was wrong. I suppose she guessed it had to do with Papa since I wanted out of my house.

When we reach the foyer, Slate, Bastian, and Adrien are already there, charred, ash-covered coats on. Adrien's the worse for wear with his blistered forehead, neck, hands, and back. Last night, I applied a soothing aloe gel to his burns while trying not to dwell on what Charlotte said, but her words wheeled around in my mind. Instead of filling my stomach with butterflies, they filled it with dread and confusion. I love Adrien but no longer romantically.

I've been realizing this a little every day since Slate smacked into me on New Year's Eve, but last night, after Charlotte said what she said, regardless of whether it was true, it hit me that my heart didn't quicken, my palms didn't moisten.

I felt *nothing*.

Well, nothing besides surprise. The only person who gets my

body thrumming these days is the infuriating boy with the chaotic black curls, the patchwork of bruises in various states of healing, and the scrim of stubble I long to feel scrape against my skin. The one standing so close to the Gauguin drawing that his breath's fogging up the protective glass.

I hate what Papa did to him. To us.

The thought of my father sours my mouth. I'm furious that he wrongfully slandered Slate, furious that I believed him, that I didn't even give Slate the benefit of the doubt, but there's something else bothering me. Something that has to do with Marianne Shafir.

Why didn't Papa tell me she had cancer? That she needed money for her treatment? Why take it out of Slate's account? I know Maman left everything in my name for tax purposes, but I would've given Papa access to any amount he needed. He must've known this. Sure, I was thirteen at the time, but I would've understood.

After I grab a jacket from the coat closet, an old red peacoat I haven't worn in a while because my silver puffer was my favorite, I walk over to where Slate stands, appreciating the Gauguin. "Admiring your new acquisition?"

He turns those dark, probing eyes of his on me. "No, Cadence. It's yours."

I put my bag down between my feet in order to pull on my coat. "Not anymore."

"I'm not taking it from you."

I frown. "My brain's a little sluggish, but didn't we go over this a few minutes ago? Papa borrowed money from you; I'm paying it back."

"When I thought it belonged to your father, I wanted it. I'm petty like that. I like to punish people for their regrettable decisions. *You*, however, have nothing to do with this and shouldn't be penalized for someone else's bad choices."

My fingers slide off the last button. "I'm sorry, Slate." I study the camber of his eyes, the downturned corners of his mouth, the roughness of his jaw. "I'm sorry I believed him."

Those words send a ripple of emotion across his face, softening all of his harsh angles and lighting up his dusky eyes.

I bend over to grab my bag, but Slate swipes it from between my legs and hooks it over his shoulder, dangling it from a single crooked finger.

"You don't have to—"

"I want to."

We're standing so close I can count each and every curled lash, can spot the faintest flutter of his pulse at his temple, can smell the warm soap on his skin beneath the scent of smoke that clings to him as doggedly as it clings to me. He leans in infinitesimally closer, and my lips unseal over a shallow breath.

I am outrageously and irrevocably attracted to this boy. So much so that I truly wonder if magic isn't involved. Yes, I'm young, but there's something about Slate that makes every nerve ending in my body clang, every inch of my skin heat, every muscle clench.

Before he can move any closer, I jerk my palm up and slap it against his warm T-shirt and the heart thundering beneath.

Easing him back, I whisper, a tad huskily, "I'm not done sorting through my jumbled feelings, Slate."

The fingers not holding my bag rise to my face and tuck back a lock of hair that's escaped my ponytail. "Take your time. I'm not going anywhere."

"You're not?"

He runs his fingertips along the side of my throat, down my arm, over my knuckles. "I'm not."

"I'd really like to believe you."

"Then do."

I stare into the conduits to his soul. "I don't know you well enough for that." I run the tip of my index over his knuckles, then down one finger, back up, down another. "But I'm willing to get to know you. You're just going to have to give me a little time."

His pupils bloat, and he swallows. Audibly.

"I want to hear about your past, Slate. All of it. The ugly parts too. But later. And in private." I tip my head toward our three-person audience.

When I pivot, they all avert their gazes. All except Adrien. He no longer has eyebrows, but the space where they used to be seems puffed up a little. I want so much for that look to mean nothing more than curiosity, but I'm so finetuned to his micro-expressions that I sense his perplexity. I don't know if it's because he feels protective of me or if it runs deeper. I don't care to dig, though.

I start to walk toward them when I hear the squeak of tires against marble. I tilt my head up, find Papa peering over the wrought-iron balustrade at me. My throat tightens because I love him. And I know he loves me. But I'm still angry at how he handled things with Slate.

Slate's hand drifts to my lower back. Papa's face becomes so distorted with rage that I have to look away because he's frightening. I shiver, which earns me a slow stroke of thumb against the base of my spine. Comforting heat trickles through the thick red wool and soothes the blaring tension locking up my vertebrae. Not bearing to look upon Papa's face any longer, I let Slate guide me away from him. Once the blue door clicks shut behind us, I drink in a breath and then another, the cold moisture sticking to my lungs, numbing the lining of my throat, scorching my palate.

"Get ready to be murdered, Slate," Alma singsongs.

"That's not funny, Alma." Papa lied to protect me from Slate. Murdering reputations is vastly different from cold-blooded killing.

Her smile fades in increments, like grime melting beneath pressurized water. "Um . . . it was a joke. I'm sorry."

Slate strums the base of my spine again as we walk. "Cadence, your dad can't hurt me."

"He has a lot of influence."

"In this town maybe, but—"

"As long as you're here, he *can* and *will* make your life hell."

He smiles at me as though it were the silliest thing he's ever heard.

I shake my head. "You don't believe me, do you?"

"I do." His smile doesn't decrease in intensity, though.

"Then why are you grinning?"

"Because I know Hell. Lived in that dimension for many, *many* years. Right, little bro?"

Bastian wrinkles his nose, which makes his glasses slide down. He presses them back up.

"Your papa can do his worst, Cadence. I guarantee I've already been there. Had it done to me. And *survived*."

Slate's confidence tempers my fear.

"Foster care was really that bad?" Adrien asks as we start up the stone stairs to Second Kelc'h.

Bastian joggles his head from side to side. "*Our* foster families were . . . not good. But I know there are some kind families out there. We just didn't land in the right spots."

As all three start discussing the system, I hang back with Slate. "Why do you want to see the translation of the *Kelouenn*?"

His gaze shifts off the back of Bastian's head and settles on me. "I noticed something when I was staring at it in your dad's office."

I frown. "Something?"

"In the middle of the scroll, when you let your eyes go blurry, a quatrefoil appears."

I come to a stop. "Really?"

"Yeah. It's the way the words are spaced out. Here let me show you." He removes his hand from my lower back to fish his phone out of his sweatpants, then flicks it on and opens up his photo app, bringing up a shot of the scroll. He squints at the screen as though to test out if he sees the shape again. "Here." He props the phone in my hands.

I stare at it, but nothing happens. "I don't see it."

"Relax your eyes."

This time, I fix the image until my vision goes hazy. Suddenly, the shape all but leaps out at me, and I clap a hand against my mouth. "*Mon Dieu!*"

The others stop walking and whirl around, already scanning the area for a threat.

"Guys, you have to see this." I stride up to where they're standing, phone flipped their way and quickly explain what Slate just told me, what he just showed me.

Adrien cups the back of his neck. "Incredible . . ."

"Whoa," Bastian says.

"Why is this so groundbreaking?" Alma asks. "I mean, it's cool, but—"

"Because the text has never made sense," Adrien says. "But perhaps, we're supposed to be reading it differently."

Bastian plucks the phone from my hand and blows up the image. "You think only the text contained in the quatrefoil should be read?"

"Or only the one around the shape." Slate rubs his jaw, and even though a torrent of vital things are going on at the present moment, I can't help but latch on to an incredibly insignificant one—the rough, sexy sound of his stubble. "Or maybe, I'm wrong about the entire thing. I don't want to get your hopes up for nothing."

"What do you think it'll tell you guys that you don't already know?" Alma stuffs her hands inside her coat pockets and shifts around on her wedge booties, surely freezing in her tiny dress and fresh pair of tights I lent her, which bunch at the knees considering our vast height difference.

"It's never made much sense." Adrien smooths a palm over his head. "Maybe now it will."

I exhale a deep breath. "Let's hope Slate's right, and there's something more on the scroll, because something more would be extremely welcomed."

I study the photo again. The ink is smudged in several places, but there's a large splotch in the middle. I zoom in. Something about it makes my brain tingle.

When I was young, the *Kelouenn* frightened me. Until Papa picked me up and held me in his arms so that the scroll was at eye level. "There's nothing to be afraid of, *ma chérie*. It's simply one big word search, like the ones we print out and do together, except in a different language."

Suddenly, it hits me. There'd been a big red dot ringed by tiny words at the heart of the scroll—the Bloodstone. Not a black splotch.

Although, maybe I'm mixing things up. I've studied so many texts about Brumian history that all of them have begun to bleed together.

I hand Slate his phone back, and he slides it into his pocket. He wraps his fingers around mine, and we resume carving through the thick fog all the way up to Fifth Kelc'h.

Even though this Quatrefoil quest is terrifying and brutal, at least I'm not in it alone.

41

SLATE

C adence pulls a fancy bronze skeleton key from her bag, its bow in the shape of a quatrefoil.

I lift an eyebrow. "Doesn't the university believe in modern security?"

"Not when the old ways work. Plus, it's a piece of history." She fits it into the embossed iron lock on the massive wooden doors. As she turns it, two filigreed latches pop up, allowing her to slide a long bolt to one side. "I think it's kind of cool."

I have to admit. It is. Feels like we're entering a medieval castle, not a 21st century university building. Although, it isn't really a 21st century building. It's a converted temple—once a place to worship magic; now a place to worship knowledge.

The ticking of the clock greets us as Cadence pushes the door open and hits the lights. We cross the threshold into the vast space paved by ochre and white floor tiles. For some reason, I hadn't noticed during my previous visits that many are festooned with inscriptions—names and dates. Some worn and near illegible, others newer and sharper. Like the one under my left boot: MARI-ANNE SHAFIR.

I stop and nudge Bastian. "Isn't that the woman named in my financial documents?"

He nods.

OF WICKED BLOOD | 333
OF WICKED BLOOD | 333
OF WICKED BLOOD | 333

"When did Rainier give her my money again?" I keep my voice low.

Bastian flicks through the folder, then peers back up at me. "Four years ago. Same year as on the tile."

"Huh." It didn't hit me when we were in De Morel's office, but it does now.

When I first met him, Rainier implied he'd saved me from my asshole foster father. Bastian and I were in Vincent's "care" four years ago.

I look up and catch Cadence frowning at me. "What's wrong, Slate?"

"Nothing." I keep my mouth shut about Rainier. I've got the money now. Whether he accessed my bank account before he found out I was alive or after doesn't matter.

Bastian crouches to examine Marianne's tile. "What's with the names and dates on these things?"

"They're for dedicated university staff who passed away." Cadence's eyes track the name of the professor beneath her feet. "The dates mark the year they left us."

"As in, retire?" Bastian asks.

"As in, die."

His eyebrows rise so high they overtake the top of his black frames.

"What?" Alma asks.

"Nothing." I step on the tile with Marianne's name, my marrow ringing with alarm. An alarm I don't want to sound, yet. Not until I'm sure of its reason for ringing.

Alma and Cadence exchange a look.

"Slate?" Cadence asks.

"It's Marianne's tile." Adrien, whose brows would've been knitted together had he not endured a wyvern-wax, narrows his eyes on my boot.

Alma looks confused. "Marianne?"

"You know, the art professor?" Cadence supplies. "The one who painted the evolution of handwriting throughout the ages?"

"I love that painting! It's one of my favorite art pieces. That and your mother's statue. What did that old woman call herself again? The graphologist artist? Or was it, graphartist?"

Adrien smiles. "Graphartist? I hadn't heard that one." He puts a hand to his head as though to thrust his fingers through hair. When he realizes he has none, he grimaces and rubs his palm over the burnt, buzz-cut instead.

"She died at the same time as your mom, didn't she?" Alma asks.

Cadence elbows her.

"Sorry. I didn't mean to sound so insensitive, Adrien."

"It's okay. And yes. Her funeral was the week after my mother's."

I can hear the grief in his voice, and despite myself, I feel for him.

"And your mother's was when exactly?" Bastian asks.

"June."

The word stokes the alarm. Cadence's jackass of a father knew I was alive when he "borrowed" my money since Vincent was out of my life on March 4th. I remember the date because I celebrate it each year without fault.

"Your parents have tiles here, too, Slate."

"Yeah?" My gut twists and twists. I put Rainier out of my mind —for now—and scan the floor.

"Their tiles are over by that bookcase." Cadence points to a cracked ochre tile bearing the names EUGENIA & OSCAR ROLAND. Underneath them, in smaller letters is RÉMY.

My knees go a little rubbery.

Well . . . fuck.

Bastian grips my upper arm to keep me from keeling over. "You all right, Slate?"

"Fucking fine," I grumble. I'm not the dead boy; I'm Slate Ardoin.

Bastian doesn't seem convinced. He keeps glancing between the tile and me.

I shrug him off and then shrug off the little zaps bursting along my spine. *This isn't a headstone or an omen, Slate.*

Cadence must sense where my mind has gone, because she says, "It's proof that you have roots in this town." Her teeth dent her lip. "That you have every right to be here. To stay here, if you want, no matter what anyone else says. That you belong in Brume."

Between the revelation about Rainier and my honorific tile, I'm incapable of stringing two words together. I hope she doesn't interpret my silence as reticence about belonging to her town. It may not feel like home, but I'm willing to stick around for a while.

After sifting through my expression for something—confirmation that telling her I was staying wasn't just a trick to get her to trust me again—she turns on her heels and heads toward the trapdoor on the opposite side of the temple. As though the shelves of books release a collective exhale, I'm struck by wafts of dust, mildewed paper, and old incense that makes my nostrils twitch.

Bastian cinches my wrist as the others patter away, their footsteps resonating against the curved walls. "He knew. When he *borrowed*"—he air-quotes the word—"the money, he knew about you."

"Were you really expecting he didn't?"

"You should tell Cadence."

It's impossible that she's heard her name considering she's on the other side of the temple, yet she turns, one eyebrow peaked.

"Not yet. Not until I understand why he lied."

Bastian's fingers slide off my wrist as we go after the others. He walks with his head tipped so far back I expect to hear the cartilage of his trachea crack.

"Here I thought you'd be salivating over the books."

"Trust me, I—" He comes to a violent halt by the recessed centerpiece: the clock. "Whoa. It's massive. Way bigger than I thought it would be." He doesn't move for a long time, and then he's lunging around the guardrail, eyes sparkling behind glasses that keep slipping down his nose.

Last time I came here, I didn't pay close attention to it, too worried about my finger falling off. Now, I take the time to absorb each detail—the four elemental signs carved into the thick gold band, the golden quatrefoil outline that spans the entire enameled face, the larger of the two dials that runs from white to navy and the smaller one embedded with diamond-like constellations. Last but not least, the hands fastened to the smooth golden disk at the heart of the clock, one tipped with a star and the other with a crescent moon.

"The *dihuner!*" Bastian eyes the golden crescent tip on the longer hand. "I thought it was out of order."

I knew there was something I forgot to tell him.

"All thanks to this baby." I hold up my ringed finger.

He glances at it, then back at the crescent resting atop a sliver of blue veering toward navy. "That's the moon phase dial, right?"

"Right," Cadence says, chewing her lip.

"Five days until the new moon," Adrien announces.

Five days . . .

Bastian shakes his head. "I was expecting religious symbolism, but there's none."

Adrien's peering down at the clock as though it were a wish-granting well. My spine jams up. *Yeah.* I don't want to be thinking about wells right now. Or ever, for that matter.

"Because it isn't a religious temple. At least, not the sort of religion that's popular in the world," Adrien explains. "During the inquisition, the zealots labeled it the devil's playground and forbade people from entering."

"Brume holds the record for most witch trials and convictions in all of France. Some even called it the Salem of the East." Cadence is studying one of the elements: a triangle with a bar running through it. Earth? Air?

Thanks to Bastian, I'm up to date on my elemental symbolism.

Alma whirls, looking around her at the temple of magic. "To think you told me it was all lore." She shivers and rubs her arms. "Am I the only one getting chills?"

Bastian eyes the cupola. "Why didn't they burn it in the era of witch hunts?"

"They tried, but apparently the fire wouldn't take." Adrien's clutching the top of the glass guardrail. "They also tried to rip apart the clock, but they couldn't even dent the enamel, so they boarded up the entire temple."

Cadence tips her head toward the trapdoor. "Guys, the translation. We can admire the clock and discuss history later."

As she heaves the basement door open, I tell Bastian, "You're going to weep in awe when you see what's below."

That makes him move.

Sure enough, when I get down there, Bastian's mouth is wide, *wide* open. Forget flies, he could trap bats. The ancient mechanical lacework of cogs is impressive. Its sheer size alone would make anyone gawp.

"Come on." Alma holds open the door of the chilled tank that contains the precious documents of Brume.

Cadence is already pulling on her special gloves to take out the huge tome filled with the Quatrefoil history, which she sets on one of the tables. As the door suctions shut behind us, she removes the gloves, laying them on the leather cover, and heads toward another shelving unit.

When I see her push up on tiptoe, trying to inch a big white box her way, I stride over and pluck it off the shelf. "You know, asking for assistance isn't a sign of weakness."

"I would've gotten it. Eventually."

"I have no doubt about that. Just reminding you that I'm here. For an indeterminate amount of time," I add quietly, handing over the archival box.

Without looking away from my eyes, she takes it from me, her fingers brushing over mine, feather-soft. She lets them linger, the coolness of her skin seeping into the warmness of mine. My entire body goes still, still and hard. Very hard. I angle myself toward the shelving unit, because I'm tenting my sweatpants, and although I don't mind if Cadence sees what her touch does to me, I'd rather not scar the others.

I concentrate on a moldy book spine.

I think moldy thoughts.

I must look like I'm in pain, because she gasps, "Is it the ring? Is my piece—"

"It's not the ring," I reassure her, then repeat it louder, because the others have stopped talking, so I imagine they're staring.

"Then what is it?" Her voice is full of concern.

I look at her, then at my crotch. She follows my line of sight. When our eyes meet again, her cheeks brighten, but so do her eyes. And then she smiles. And since that's not kryptonite enough, she bites her lip.

"Are you trying to make it worse?" I grumble.

She pushes up on her toes again, this time to whisper, "Think of the Quatrefoil, Slate. Of all those monsters we faced."

Her minty breath warms the shell of my ear.

338 | WILDENSTEIN & HAYOZ

"Better?" She rocks back onto her heels, but not before grazing the edge of my jaw with her pillowy lips.

I shut my eyes, trying desperately to summon up Matthias's ugly face. If only the others hadn't been here. I would've pushed Cadence against the stacks, or laid her out on the table, and—

She gasps, and I think I may have spoken my dirty designs for her out loud when I realize her attention isn't on me but on the archival box, which she's nudged open.

It's empty.

42

CADENCE

"T he translations!" I whisper-shout. "The translations are gone!"

Slate's pupils go from distended to pin-sized, along with his erection.

Yes, my eyes went there. How could they not? But now my eyes are back on the empty beige lining of the box.

For the barest of seconds, I wonder if I might've grabbed the wrong one, and my gaze flies to the top shelf, but there aren't any other boxes.

"Are you sure?" Adrien's by my side now, peering into the empty container.

It shouldn't piss me off that he doesn't believe me, but it does, so I none too gently shove it into his arms. "Check for yourself."

Slate's hand lands on my shaking one and envelops my fingers. I don't pull away. Instead I lean into him until more than our hands touch.

"Do you guys have a logbook down here?" Bastian asks.

"No." My teeth chatter and not from the cold. Although it is *really* cold. "Why would someone t-take them?"

Slate squeezes my hand, then lets go and grips my hip, dragging me into him. Adrien's gaze flicks off the box to the point of contact between Slate's protective, possessive fingers and the waistband of my gray leggings.

"Could they have been misplaced?" Bastian suggests.

I look around the small, sterile room. "I d-don't think so. I mean, there were close to a hundred sheets in there. That's a lot of p-paper to misplace." Slate's thumb slides beneath the hem of my sweater and sets on my chilled skin, then starts small, slow strokes.

"When did you see them last?" Adrien's voice is as harsh as the lighting.

I have to rack my brain. Did I pull the box down the day I showed Slate *Istor Breou*? No. I'd thought about it but hadn't trusted him enough. Feeling a groove form between my eyebrows, I say, "The last time I looked at them was with your mother, Adrien. I was helping her type them." It feels like yesterday and yet four years have passed.

Alma spins on a stool. "How many people have access to this room?"

"Not many. Adrien, Papa, me, and one of the librarians. But Papa never comes here. Because. You know, his wheelchair."

Adrien sets the empty box on the table.

"When was the last time you looked at them, Prof?" Slate's thumb is still moving, still coaxing goose bumps from my skin.

"Not since my thesis two years ago." One of his eyes closes a little as though he's remembering something.

"What?" I ask.

"There were a couple pages missing back then. I asked your father about it, and he said I should check Mom's computer. That they might be backed-up on there. Except her computer was never retrieved after . . ." He swallows, and I feel the pain of his loss echo in my bones.

"Could she have saved the file on the Cloud?" Bastian asks.

Adrien shakes his head. "No. The information was too sensitive."

Alma blows into her palms. "Why would anyone steal transla-tions anyway?"

"Because something's written on that scroll someone doesn't want us to discover," Slate mutters.

Alma freezes, and her hands fall into her lap. "That would mean someone knows about the Quatrefoil outside of you four. Well, six with Rainier and Geoffrey."

"Nolwenn and Juda know about it." I remember Papa telling us the night after the well. "He said they were scared of the curses."

Adrien stares steadily at me. I know what he's thinking because I'm thinking the very same thing: one of them destroyed the papers, hoping to deter us from this wild hunt. But does Nolwenn have access to this room? It's not impossible . . .

"Does the keypad store the imprint of who goes in and out?" Bastian asks.

"No." I loop the tip of my ponytail around my slightly bobbing finger. "It's just an electronic lock. Nothing more."

"Are there any cameras?"

"There's an alarm system."

Slate's ribcage inflates with a sigh and his thumb stills. "Doesn't matter. We have the original scroll. We need to move on. Move forward. You and Cadence speak Breton, right, Adrien?"

I peer up at the boy holding me, at his dark eyes that seem black in the surrounding whiteness. "I know some, but hardly enough to translate the *Kelouenn*."

"I can do it," Adrien says on a breath. "It's going to take time, but I can do it."

Time isn't the commodity we have the most of, but wasting it trying to figure out who did away with Camille's hard work won't help us.

Adrien drums his fingers against his thigh. "There's a printer upstairs, right?"

I nod.

"We need to blow up the picture Slate took, then print out a few sets. If it's illegible, we head back to your house." He holds out his palm that bobs like my own hand, both of us strung out on stress and adrenaline. "Your phone, Slate?"

Slate unlocks the phone and hands it to Adrien, who streaks toward the door.

"What about the history book?" Bastian asks. "Can it be taken out of here?"

I bite my lip. "It's better not to."

"Mind if I read it?" Bastian, who's sitting on the stool beside Alma's, rubs his palms on his thighs. "If you don't trust me—"

"I trust you."

"I'll stay with him," Alma suggests. "I'm an awesome note taker."

I shoot my friend a grateful smile, because I know she's hanging down here to put my mind at ease while Adrien, Slate, and I are upstairs.

Technically, Slate isn't needed to transcribe the scroll since his knowledge of Breton is zilch, but I want to keep him at my side. I feel safer when he's around. And since my piece still hasn't shown up—

"Don't try to leave me behind." He slots his fingers through mine.

My heart fires off a fierce thump. "I wasn't."

"Good." He holds the door open for me. "Like I always say, little bro, don't do anything I would do." He winks at Bastian, who mutters something that makes Alma laugh.

As the spring-loaded, mechanical arm closes the door, I shake my head at Slate. "You're terrible."

"Unarguably so." He sweeps his arm toward the stairs. "After you, milady."

I smile in spite of the crappy day it's been, then begin to ascend, but stop midway to look at Slate. Really look at him. We wield no magic and yet this boy has managed to bewitch me with his charisma and humor . . . with his light. He could've let the darkness consume him. Consume me. Consume Brume. But he didn't. He fights his battles and everyone else's.

I take a step down, then another, until our faces are aligned. And then I do something uncharacteristically-Cadence-like. I grip his shoulders and kiss him. He's not expecting it. I can tell because his mouth is sealed shut, and the tendons running under his skin are stiff as steel beams. But soon, he snaps out of his daze and flips me sideways, backing me up into the rough stone wall, lips opening, tongue dancing against mine. His hand lands on the back of my skull, winds through my hair, ruining my ponytail.

Not that I give a crap about my ponytail.

All I care about is deepening our connection.

Maybe it's the adrenaline, or days of pent-up anger, or fear for what is to come, or just lust, but I want this boy so badly it hurts. My pulse drills my veins, muscles I didn't even know I possessed clench, and the bruises and soreness from last night's battle awaken, turning my sensitive skin into a minefield of tiny explosions.

But that doesn't slow me down, because what I feel more deeply than any aches and pains is this welling affection for this lost boy who's found his way home.

43

SLATE

"Slate, we should go—"

"Fuck that." I nuzzle her neck which is soft as silk and smells so sweet I find myself suckling it. "We've defeated three curses without any fucking translations."

"Fuck's your favorite word, isn't it?"

I comb away a lock of her hair stuck to her swollen lips. "I apologize for being crass, Cadence. Never did make it into finishing school."

"Don't apologize for how you talk. Or think. I don't care what comes out of your mouth as long as it isn't a lie." She presses a kiss to the edge of my jaw. "I like you just the way you are. Foul tongue and all. But we really need to go upstairs and help Adrien."

I really don't feel like deciphering a worm-eaten scroll. "I'm sure he's loving it." I splay my palm on the small of her back and drag her tight body into my groin. "Besides, my brain's been deprived of blood for so long that I'd be useless up there."

On a huff of laughter, she levers her body off mine. "Perhaps, but now's really not a good time to do away with my virginity, Slate Ardoin."

Wait . . . *what?* My fingers don't spring off her back, but they definitely turn flaccid. Unlike another part of my anatomy. I don't think there's any chance of that happening as long as I'm pressed up against Cadence de Morel.

"You've never . . .?"

"No." She swallows, and then her cheek dimples as though she's biting the inside of it.

I sweep my thumb over her intensifying blush, trying to smooth away her nerves, but thumbs aren't magical, and since I still haven't said anything, she's growing more antsy. "And here I thought librarians were supposed to be a promiscuous bunch."

She bestows a smile upon me, one of her most radiant ones yet, and damn if it doesn't make the entire staircase shine. "You're not scared of me now are you?"

"Scared. Pfff. I faced down a busty incarnation of Jaws in a pitch-black tunnel. Trust me, your wholesomeness does *not* scare me." I slide my thumb over her lips. "I just hope you're not too attached to it."

"Not attached to it at all." Her breathing has sped up considerably.

I put a hand against the wall and pry my body off hers. However badly I want her, I'm not going to corrupt her in a stairwell with my brother and her best friend sitting a couple feet away and Adrien Mercier upstairs. No. I'm going to corrupt her nice and slow, in a bedroom, with not another soul around.

"Go. I need to cool down. Don't want to make Prof feel underwhelming."

Her eyebrows scrunch and then jerk up, and she swats my bicep.

I tsk. "So violent, Mademoiselle de Morel."

"So arrogant, Monsieur Ardoin."

I grin at her, which makes her respond in kind with another one of her glorious smiles.

"Okay." She steps away from me, her smile falling, the glitter in her eyes dimming. As she climbs the stairs, she tugs the elastic out of her hair, finger-combs it, then reties it. Is it me or are her hands shaking?

I don't think I imagined her edginess, and it chills my pounding blood. When I start picturing her piece showing up and me not being there, I climb the stairs two at a time. I find her sitting at a big square table with Adrien, head bent over a copy of the *Kelouenn*, pencil already poised and scratching at her paper. I watch them discuss possible meanings of a Breton word.

I try not to feel jealous that they share something. Remind myself of all we shared downstairs. I square my shoulders and head over.

I can be useful.

I'll find a way to be useful.

I END up being useful by getting food and making photocopies. Cadence and Adrien squint at the damn scroll all day, and even when Alma and Bastian join them, things don't speed up. We hit the sheets late and are back at the library again in the morning. Early afternoon, I grab the food Adrien ordered at the tavern and bring it back to the squad. Bastian and Alma sit with Adrien and Cadence, trying to consolidate their notes from the history book with the words from the translated scroll.

"In the book downstairs, it says the *dihuner* had a heart of blood." Alma bites the tip of her pencil. "Does the scroll mention it?"

"I didn't see anything about that in the text, but there's still pieces Cadence and I haven't been able to translate."

"I mean, there's the Bloodstone." Cadence gestures to my hand, which is presently pulling the lids off containers of charcuterie and cheese. "Could the stone have been on the clock?"

Adrien joggles his head.

I filch two cubes of Emmental cheese. "Have you figured out how the creepy-ass drawings factor into the text?"

"They correlate to the text outside the quatrefoil shape," Adrien says.

Apparently, they made progress while I was being a good delivery boy.

"They're examples of curses," he says, as I examine an unannotated copy.

Between the ink smudges and words that look scrawled by an epileptic in the middle of a seizure, I'm surprised they managed to decipher a thing.

Alma flips over the drawing of a splayed corpse. "Can't eat with that in my face."

Bastian studies a fanged insect, or is it a body part? I've taken part in some twisted treasure hunts, but this one takes the cake for most insanity-inducing.

He leans over and grabs one of Cadence's papers, and then they're exchanging notes. She claps excitedly, which makes Bastian grin and jot something down. Apparently, some people are enjoying the task.

Freaks.

My freaks.

When I hear Adrien mumbling to himself, I glance his way.

I'm glad to see him reading over his notes, because I was momentarily worried he'd lost his mind, and since he's already lost all of his hair . . .

"Anything, Prof?" I roll my neck from side to side.

"I think I got something. I'm not sure exactly what it means, but—"

"Lay it on us."

"Like I said, the passage outside the quatrefoil is a list of plagues and curses. Insects, the undead, something about stone and dust. I'm guessing it's an explanation of the dark magic that went on before the Quatrefoil was broken apart. I'd need more time to figure it out."

"And the passage inside?" Cadence coils her ponytail into some sort of knot at the nape of her neck.

Adrien sighs. "Well, there's this big ink spot that covers part of the text."

"I noticed that earlier." Cadence frowns. "It's odd. I would swear it wasn't always there."

I eye the print-out of the scroll. "Ink's a different color. Closer to black, while the rest is dark brown, so it probably wasn't."

Everyone gapes at me.

"What? I'm not fucking colorblind."

Bastian's eyebrows lift. "The difference is really subtle, but Slate's right. It doesn't look like an original spill."

Cadence turns to Adrien. "You think we can scrape it off, or use a light to see through it?"

"Maybe, but we'd have to remove it from the frame, which could damage it."

The quiet patter of snow falling against the stained-glass cupola becomes the only sound apart from the constant ticking in the temple of knowledge.

I approach Cadence's chair and lean my head over her shoulder, grazing her cheek with my jaw. To anyone watching, I'm feigning interest in the scribbled text. But quickly, my interest is unfeigned. "What do you guys make of this: *The new moon will abscond with the leaves unless cradled in Brume's beating heart at eventide?*"

"Unfortunately, it's nothing groundbreaking or new." Adrien sighs. "If the Quatrefoil isn't assembled, the leaves disappear with the new moon."

Alma nibbles on her pinkie nail. "What's eventide again?"

"An older word for twilight," Adrien explains.

Bastian's eyes spark. "But twilight's broken up into three phases, so I'm guessing, since the clock is astronomical, it would mean astronomical twilight: when it feels dark, but you can't observe stars with the naked eye."

"Not sure how that helps, considering the fog." Alma points to the cupola. "Not much star-gazing happening in Brume during winter."

"You don't actually need to see the sky. All you have to do is calculate the solar depression angle . . ." Bastian lets his sentence slide away when he notices our collective bafflement. "I'll just calculate it and get you the number."

Alma grins. "What did they feed you when you were a kid? Wikipedia bytes?"

"You'd have to ask Slate. He was the provider."

"I made sure he got all the good stuff. I needed one of us to be smart enough to get us off the streets."

Cadence tips her head to the side to look at me and wraps her fingers around my wrist, squeezing it gently.

"Since eventide happens every day, does that mean you guys could somehow lock the leaves in every day?" Bastian asks, back on track.

Cadence's attention jerks back to the others. "You mean, individually?"

I read the last part of the sentence out loud again: "*Unless cradled in Brume's beating heart at eventide.* Seems to say there's a way to lock them in."

Adrien sits up. "Which would mean that if we somehow failed to get the last leaf—"

"—which we won't." I shoot him a glare.

"Which we won't," he repeats slowly. "All wouldn't be lost."

I tap the Bloodstone against the table. "You'll be able to pry the ring from my cold, dead hand and finish the wicked hunt."

Adrien has the decency to blanch. "Slate, sorry. I didn't mean—"

"It's fine, Prof." I press away from the table and straighten.

"Why dead?" Alma asks.

"The ring can only come off once the four leaves are reunited, and this has to be done before the new moon," Cadence explains.

Alma cocks her head to the side, her long curls sliding over her shoulder. "Still don't get why Slate would die."

"'Cause the Bloodstone will leak dark magic into my veins and cripple me, thus making me die a slow, excruciatingly painful death."

The minute the words leave my mouth, Cadence gasps, and I freeze. *Shit.* Rainier had sworn me to secrecy. He hadn't wanted Cadence to know how much her mother had suffered on her way out of this wretched world.

Silence settles over the library, silence interrupted by the steady tolling of the astronomical clock.

Bastian shifts on his chair, tugs on his hoodie strings, shifts some more. "Slate's going to be fine."

I want to believe this, but I've seen what the curses can do. Little Emilie's tiny body rises into my mind. I shut my eyes but the image of her pink pajamas sharpens, so I pry my lids up and focus on the page Cadence is clutching.

"Any guesses on that cradle?" I want to focus on something other than the limp body of the child whom I failed.

Cadence tilts her head up, and I feel her clear blue gaze hunt my face. I don't meet her eyes; I don't want to subject her to my anger and intensifying negativity.

"The history book said the forest was the birthplace of the Quatrefoil. And since this hill used to be a part of it before it became a town, maybe that's its beating heart? See, I listen in class, Professor M." Alma winks at Adrien.

"Or it's inside the actual forest," Cadence says.

Bastian releases his hoodie strings. "It's a big forest."

Adrien slides Cadence's pad toward him. "*The new moon will abscond with the leaves unless cradled in Brume's beating heart at eventide.*"

"What about Merlin's tomb?" *Yes, I'm starting to believe Merlin was real. It's worrying.*

"We don't know where it is," Adrien says. "If it even exists . . ."

Bastian drums his fingers. "I saw it on the tourist map."

Adrien shakes his head. "That one's just for lore-seekers."

My eyebrows knit together. "Cadence has a painting of it in her house."

"That's true!" She lets out a startled gasp that flutters a lock of her hair. "The shape of the Quatrefoil's imprinted on the stone."

"It could be allegorical," Adrien says.

"But it could also be real," Cadence counters.

"Except stones don't beat," Adrien, forever the spoilsport, declares.

"Maybe magical ones do," I say.

"Look, I've canvased that forest and never come across his burial site or anything remotely resembling a quatrefoil-stamped burial stone, let alone a *beating* stone."

"You're such a killjoy, Prof."

"I'm sorry, Slate, but the new moon's in four days. I just don't want us to go on a wild goose chase." He shoves a hand through the air in exasperation. "A *wilder* goose chase."

Bastian pulls off his hoodie. His hair is flat in some places and sticking straight up in others. "The clock beats. Well, it ticks. But that's pretty much the same thing."

Adrien blinks, then slams a hand on the table. We all jump.

Waggling his finger at Bastian, he jerks to his feet. "You're a genius."

I admit it makes more sense than a stone, but I don't discard my hypothesis. I mean, we are talking about a *magical* hunt. What's more magical than an old wizard?

Bastian follows after Adrien, who's already rounded the shelving unit.

Alma stretches her arms over her head. "Wait up, B." Her heels clack on the tiles as she trots after them.

"How sweet." I smile as I scoot Cadence's chair back. "They have nicknames for each other."

She rises and faces me. "You don't actually think you aren't smart, right?"

I frown. "Where did that come from?"

"Earlier, you said Bastian was the smart one."

I tuck a fugitive brown strand behind her ear. "I'm street-smart. That's good enough for me."

"You're way more than street-smart, Slate."

"I wasn't much help these past few days." My self-esteem's fine, but the truth's the truth.

"Because you can't sit still long enough."

"Yeah. I think I've got ADD." Undiagnosed because it isn't like I ever consulted a medical professional when I was a kid. "Unless, I'm looking at you. Then I can sit and stare. And stare."

"Not creepy at all." She laughs softly, then presses her lips to mine.

The kiss is chaste but reaches deep and pumps up my ego.

The first time I bumped into Cadence de Morel, I thought her naïve and spoiled, interesting and the owner of a great ass, sure, but two-dimensional. Was I ever wrong. The girl's deeper and mightier than the Verdon Gorge.

If only I had time to take her there . . .

"Come on. Let's go check out Brume's beating heart."

I stow away my lancing glumness. "I'd rather check out your beating heart."

She smiles and shakes her head as she tows me around the stacks toward the infamous *dihuner*.

44

CADENCE

S late's fingers stay laced with mine as we circle the *dihuner*, proving to me he's the boy I thought he was and not the one Papa wanted me to see. A boy with a kind and steadfast heart.

Speaking of hearts, Alma's words skitter back into my mind. I squint to make out the middle of the clock-face from where I stand. Even though it's recessed, between the waning sunlight and breadth of the magical antiquity, I can't see much of anything.

"We need to get closer," Adrien says, climbing over the guardrail.

Bastian follows suit. Once he's on the other side, he carefully sticks to the meter-wide section of tiles ringing the wide, golden rim.

"I can't get over how big this thing is." He palms the nape of his neck, eyes sparkling as ardently as the constellation dial's inlaid white topazes.

"Cadence, can you turn on some more lights?" Adrien asks.

Leaving Slate by the guardrail, I head toward the panel near the door and flick on the remaining switches. The bright beams aimed at the clock catch on the golden accents, making them glimmer like the lake at sunset. I've always found the seven-century-old relic majestic and mysterious, but now, knowing that the Quatrefoil is real, that magic is real, it has taken on a whole new allure.

"Hey, Slate, can you help me over?" Alma nods to the guardrail. "Short legs. Tall barrier."

He hoists her up as though she weighs less than little Emilie.

Grief swallows me like the water swallowed the child mere days ago, and I shudder. I may be in awe of the Quatrefoil, but I am also deeply disgusted by its power.

"Need a leg up?" Slate asks, putting an end to my dark thoughts.

I nod. He picks me up and delicately places me on the other side, and then he leaps over.

"Anyone spot any cradles?" I scan the clockface, then the four elements sculpted on the exterior edge.

The crown wheel advances notch by notch, trickling a slow *tick, tick, tick* that echoes around the library.

Bastian crouches. "Maybe the cradles are the elements?"

"Or in the Quatrefoil loops, or petals, or whatever they're called?" Alma stares at the gold outline that extends from one edge of the clock to the next.

"Alma may have a point. Perhaps we're supposed to place our pieces in the leaves aligned with our element." Adrien gestures to one of the triangles—either his or Slate's, since there's no bar through it.

The Air and Earth triangles are both slashed to indicate the separation between the ground and the sky. Mine should be upside-down, but all the triangles are pointing out, making the *dihuner* resemble a giant compass.

Alma squints at the element closest to her. "How can you tell whose element is whose? They all sort of look the same."

Bastian points to mine and Gaëlle's. "Two have bars through them. Earth and Air."

"Okay . . . but how can you tell which one is which?"

"The one that's upside-down is Earth. The other is Air."

"And how do you know which one's upside-down?"

"Oh." Bastian rubs the back of his head. "I'm not sure. Adrien?"

Adrien touches the triangle that could potentially be his. When he's not struck down by a freakish bolt of lightning, I lean forward and run my fingertips over the one that could theoretically be mine. The slashed triangle emits a pulse of neon green light that sends me stumbling back. My tailbone whacks the tiles.

"Cadence!" Slate yells, racing across the clock instead of around it.

I want to tell him not to tread on it, but by the time I shake off my surprise, he's already kneeling beside me, flipping my hands over as though checking for burn marks. "I'm okay. I was just surprised and slipped."

Slate's dark eyes narrow. "So, the element didn't send you hurtling back?"

"No."

He's still checking over my fingers.

"I promise."

"It's true, Slate. Look." Adrien's walked around to the opposite side of where he was standing when I fell, and his hand rests on the second plain triangle.

The shape glows crimson.

"How cool!" Alma claps her hands.

"Wow." Bastian presses his glasses up the bridge of his nose.

A new noise, a grinding of sorts, sounds over the steady ticking.

"What is that?" I whisper. Or maybe I yell it. My blood pounds so loudly against my eardrums it's hard for me to gauge the volume of my voice.

Although he doesn't let go of my hands, Slate finally looks away from them and over his shoulder.

"*That* would be the cradles," Adrien whispers reverently.

I tear my hands from Slate's and push myself up. Sure enough, in the middle of the leaf aligned with the fire element, a recess has appeared in the exact shape and size of the leaf he collected after he defeated the *guivre*.

I blink and stare, then blink some more. And then I lean over and press my fingertips to my shape. It ignites, sending my pulse into orbit. I tip my head back, find Slate looming over me, arms crossed, chin dipped into his neck, black eyes painted a vivid emerald-green and narrowed on the point of contact between my body and the clock.

"We need to call Gaëlle," I whisper, my voice husky with wonder. "And Papa."

"You also need to get the pieces and see if they fit," Alma adds. "And Bastian needs to calculate perfect twilight."

I straighten. "Do you think we're the first to figure this out?" When my hand lifts off the element, the light snuffs out right away, and the cradle grinds back up, smoothing until its outline melts into the dark enamel.

Adrien releases his hold on his element and presses himself up. "Our parents definitely didn't know, because if they had, we wouldn't be starting from scratch."

"Unless they can't be cradled individually . . ." I hold on to the hope that this isn't true, though. That the last generation didn't uncover the cradles. "Papa never talked about it, so they probably didn't know."

The mention of my father seems to make Slate's biceps bulge under the athletic T-shirt.

"So, astronomical twilight starts at six fifty-three tonight and ends at seven-thirty." Bastian flashes us the screen on his phone. Not that I can see it from where I stand all the way across from him.

Adrien glances toward his wristwatch. "That's in two hours."

I stare at the loop of the Quatrefoil that swoops toward my element. I stare at the spot where the enamel dipped in preparation to receive my leaf.

A leaf that has yet to show itself.

A leaf I have yet to earn.

A battle that will determine whether Slate lives or dies.

45

SLATE

Adrien, Gaëlle, and I each hold our wrapped pieces like they're made of glass as we climb the hill. The wind is bitter tonight, made even more so by the clinging fog. Cadence is at the head of our snail-paced procession, beaming a flashlight she grabbed from the tavern where she waited with Alma and Bastian while we retrieved our pieces.

She hadn't wanted to bump into her father. Claimed she wasn't ready to see him yet. She'll forgive him eventually I suppose, even though I won't.

"Six forty-seven," Alma chimes from below. Far below.

The same way Cadence is several steps ahead of me.

I hadn't wanted her, Alma, and Bastian to come at all, but they proved a bunch of stubborn asses. As long as they don't brush up against us, they should be fine, but the stairs are slippery as fuck. My heart has stopped twice already. Once, when we hit the top of Third Kelc'h and Cadence skidded, thankfully falling forward, on her knees. If she'd hurtled down the stairs, I'm not sure what I would've done. The second time I almost had a heart attack was when I heard Gaëlle squeak, "My leaf!" It had slipped from her gloved hand and glided down two steps, falling inches from Bastian's feet. I don't usually yell at women, but I roared at her, told her to take off her damn gloves. And then I'd apologized, blaming my nerves, which were firing like a plug plunged into water.

The last time I felt this way, like my body was buried inside an ant farm, was in the well. I focus on that as I climb the circles.

Focus on how I defeated the siren.

When we reach Fifth, I expel a tight breath. "Cadence, get farther away," I order, forgoing any pleases.

She nods, her skin moon-white in the wisps of fog curling around her body, and backs up, flashlight splashing the carpet of snow underneath her boots. She's been pale since the tavern. She got even paler after she stepped out of the kitchen with Nolwenn. When I asked her what was wrong, she passed off her anxiety as dread, dread for the battle she still had to wage, dread for what might happen when we lock our leaves into the clock.

Yes, it's crossed my mind that it might set forth a bunch of bad things. I said as much to Adrien on our way to the De Morel manor. It made him so skittish he suggested holding off until Cadence got her piece. And we almost did, but then I looked at the ring and told him that I, at least, needed to lock my piece in.

In case . . .

When we rang the doorbell, Rainier had seemed about ready to spring out of his wheelchair and clobber me. But Adrien stepped between us and explained our discovery. That had quieted the old man, who confessed to not knowing about the cradles. Although a liar, his gaping-fish mouth told me he really had no clue about the *dihuner*'s role in the hunt.

Lost in thought, I don't realize Cadence has fallen into step beside me. I stop so suddenly that she halts, too.

"Do you have a death wish? Get away from me," I growl.

At first, she looks offended. Then her eyes flare with anger. "Fine." She stalks off toward the library.

I don't care if I piss her off right now. I need her to be safe.

As I start up again, I sweep the obscurity around me to map out everyone else's locations. Thankfully, they're all satisfactorily social distancing. When we reach the library, Cadence is fitting the key into the lock. Her hands shake, which makes it jangle. Soon, though, she has the door open and the lights on.

Bastian treads closer to Cadence and leans his weight into the great door to widen the opening.

"Six fifty-two," Alma announces.

"One minute to go," Gaëlle whispers, her light brown skin as ashen as the foggy air.

She slips through first, then Adrien. Before I follow them, I say to the others, "You guys stay out here."

"What?" Cadence's eyebrows jolt up. "No! Don't be ridiculous."

"We don't know what's about to happen," I say.

"I've been with you guys during every curse. I don't see how this is any more dangerous."

"We were contending with one leaf at a time. There are three now. When we put them in, hell could rain down upon us." I want to go over to her and touch her, but until I've gotten rid of the golden, palm-sized frond, I barely dare breathe in her direction. "Please, I can't see you get hurt." Just the thought sends a sawing pain through my chest.

"He's right, Cadence." Adrien's blistered forehead pleats. "Wait for us out here with Alma and Bastian."

Cadence's eyes widen. "I want to be there. I want to—"

"Six fifty-four," Alma announces.

"We have to go," Adrien says. "Come on, Slate."

I set my teeth. "I won't go anywhere until Cadence swears she'll stay out here."

I shift my gaze to Bastian, and he nods in silent understanding. He may be skinny, but he's bigger than Cadence, so he can hold her back if she tries anything.

"Fine!" Anger rolls off her like the mist forever cloaking this damn town. "Fine!" She lurches away from the door and whirls on her heels, the beam of her flashlight zigzagging over the white expanse.

"We'll take care of her," Alma adds, already running after her.

Bastian stares at me as I finally walk past him. His lips press together, Adam's apple bobbing and bobbing. I sense he wants to say something, but either he's not sure what, or fear's got his tongue.

"It'll be fine, little bro. All will be fine." Maybe if I say it enough, I'll start believing it.

He releases the door once I've stepped over the threshold. It bangs shut, locking me in with three fragments of a maleficent relic and a ticking clock. I steel my spine, swallow hard, and head over to seal my leaf in its cradle, and quite possibly my fate with the Quatrefoil's.

No.

That's not true.

My fate was sealed the day I read the spell on the inside of the band and put on the ring.

46

CADENCE

B etween my talk with Nolwenn and the others all but booting me out of the library, my blood zings. I understand their reasons for keeping me out, and quite possibly, if I hadn't been a ball of stress and anger, I would've placidly agreed that I had no added value in there.

"What is going on with you?" Alma asks, once she catches up to me. "You do realize they're trying to protect us?"

"I know."

"Then why are we storming off?"

"Because, Alma!" I growl.

"Because what?" she growls back.

"Because I'm pissed!"

"They're—"

"Not at them!" I toss my arms in the air, the beam of my flashlight catching on the wisps of fog, and then beyond that, on gray limestone.

Her brow furrows. "Did I do something wrong?"

"No. No, it's not at you either."

"Then who are you pissed at?"

"At Papa."

She cinches my upper arm to hold me in place. "You have to forgive him. He was just trying to protect you. You're his little girl."

"I'm not mad at him because of what he said about Slate"—I

mean, it still definitely rankles—"I'm mad because of what he did to him."

She frowns. "Did to him? What did he do?"

"He stole money from him."

Her fingers jerk away from my arm. "Stole?"

"In the trust fund file, Bastian noticed there were two wire transfers made out to Marianne Shafir to help cover her medical bills. Apparently, she had cancer." My gaze strays to the gray façade of the Beaux-Arts building where her scroll hangs. I can just see the corner of framed vellum through one of the windows.

"Really? Geez. I didn't know."

"I didn't either, so I asked Nolwenn about it." My gaze is pulled farther, to Maman's terracotta war god enclosed in the glass veranda that juts out of the art center like a translucent bug eye.

"And?"

"And Nolwenn asked where I'd picked up that heinous information. She said Marianne didn't have cancer." My nose prickles. "Papa lied, Alma."

"Maybe she needed money for an embarrassing reason."

"Like what?"

"A full-body lift? She was getting pretty saggy by the end."

"Alma!"

"What? It's true."

"You think she did a hundred thousand euros worth of plastic surgery?"

She bites her lip, then releases it. "Probably not. She looked pretty saggy on her deathbed, too. But I'm sure there's a perfectly logical explanation." Alma's devotion to my father blinds her to any faults he might have. Papa could kill someone, and my friend would find him a valid excuse. "Actually, you know what?"

"No. What?"

"Maybe he lent her the money to have herself committed. Do you remember how loopy she acted at Camille's funeral, when Geoffrey insisted his wife didn't commit suicide and said she was murdered? Marianne started laughing hysterically. The police chief had to physically remove her from the cemetery."

A bone-deep shudder shoots up my legs. "I remember that. I also remember Adrien holding his father."

It had been the single-most devastating spectacle of my life—a son holding up his father, trying to soothe his despair. It was the only time where I'd felt something other than revulsion for Geoffrey Keene. Perhaps he'd loved my mother, but he'd also loved his wife.

Maybe it was possible to love two people the same.

Another tremor goes through me. "Come to think of it, would you trust a crazy person to have themselves committed? You'd probably send the money straight to the psychiatric hospital . . ."

Alma frowns.

I wrap my arms around myself, feeling unbearably cold. And jumpy. God, I'm jumpy. My knees wobble so hard they almost buckle.

"Cadence . . . is it me, or is the ground shaking?"

My skin becomes as slick as the cobbled square around the *Puits Fleuri* the night it overflowed.

47

SLATE

I'm used to seeing the clock bathed in colored light from the glass cupola. But under the fluorescent tubing, the monstrosity looks menacing, like a mechanical bomb from a steampunk horror movie. The ticking is just as sluggish as it was earlier, but it echoes through the space, its pace setting my teeth on edge. I can't help but notice how close to the end of the lunar cycle that damn clock hand is.

I calm my nerves by reminding myself that Bastian, Cadence and Alma aren't here. No matter what happens with the clock, at least those three will be safe.

We climb over the plexiglass guardrail. Gaëlle struggles a bit, the pocket of her coat catching on the edge of the barrier, but I can't help her since touching her body is a direct conduit for the dark magic. Still, when she wobbles, I reflexively reach out.

"Don't, Slate. I've got it." She tugs on her coat.

We each take our place around the *dihuner*—Gaëlle at the top with Air, Adrien and I across from each other with Fire and Water.

Adrien unwraps his piece. Like good little students, Gaëlle and I follow suit. The Bloodstone lights up, and liquid fire shoots through my veins. I grit my teeth to avoid growling.

Gaëlle's knuckles go white, like she's strangling her piece. I wonder if she feels something, too.

"With your free hand, touch the symbol at the edge of the dial."

Adrien crouches and rests his fingers on the triangle representing fire. Like earlier, a red glow leaks from the symbol.

Gaëlle presses hers to the barred triangle in front of her and is immediately bathed in white light. She gasps in surprise.

My skin itches even before I touch the water symbol. I hesitate for a second, but then drive my hand down. Blue light ignites and outlines my arm.

The clock gears screech, and the recesses for the Quatrefoil leaves grind down.

Another rushed exhale escapes from Gaëlle's parted lips. "Do we put them all in at the same time or separately?"

"I don't know that it matters," Adrien murmurs.

"I think we should do it together." Gaëlle's voice is thin.

Adrien nods. "On the count of three."

Tick ... tick ...

"One ..." he says. "Two ..."

I swallow, ignoring how both the ring and the leaf feel like they're charring through my flesh even though no flames engulf my palms.

"Three!"

Like a synchronized dance crew, Adrien, Gaëlle, and I each reach forward with our pieces. As the distance between them and the grooves decreases, a magnetic pull sets in, towing my fingers faster than I'd like. My leaf snaps into its cradle with an audible clank. Gaëlle's and Adrien's, too. The lowest leaf of the Quatrefoil—Earth—stays empty.

We all recoil, breathing as hard as when we faced our curses.

48

CADENCE

My gaze lurches off the shifting snow and vaults toward the temple.

There'd been tremors the night Slate slid on the ring and jumpstarted the clock. Maybe that's the source of the earthquake.

"Bastian?" I yell.

He turns in my direction but doesn't move away from his post near the library's entrance which he's guarding like Cerberus.

"Get the door open! It's the clock!"

"The clock?" Alma says at the same time, as he yells back, "What?"

"The door! Open the door!"

He jerks around and lunges for the handle, but before he can grab it, the ground gives a violent shudder, and his head smashes into the door. His body bounces backward and crumples.

"Oh *mon Dieu*!" Alma gasps, flying off toward him.

I'm tearing across the snow after her, when the sound of glass shattering followed by an inhuman roar pins my boots to the throbbing earth.

Papa said the ground shook when my mother's piece showed up. In slow motion, I turn. My heart, which had been stampeding, holds perfectly still.

Shards of glass burst away from the Beaux-Arts veranda, glinting in the thin wash of moonlight before sinking into the thick carpet of snow.

It's not the clock.

It's my leaf.

49

SLATE

T he clock sputters, a whoosh of air followed by a metallic clang resounding behind the dials.

I jump back, my muscles cramping, my veins filling with acid heat. Makes sense considering I'm near three-fourths of the Quatrefoil.

The gears emit a scraping and winding sound, as the enamel swallows the golden leaves, and our elemental symbols blaze anew. Suddenly, the slow tick of the clock speeds up like it just snorted a shitload of cocaine.

"Watch out!" Adrien whips out his right arm like he's wielding a magic wand and can protect me and Gaëlle from whatever chaos is brewing.

For a bunch of frenzied heartbeats, nothing new happens—the clock goes back to ticking an even pace while my insides keep spasming, as though my bones were becoming soft tissue. But then the ring flares, giving off more light than the symbols, and a distant rumble strikes the stone walls enclosing us.

The library begins to shake with the force of a Richter-scale-defying earthquake. Dust and books fall from the shelves like shrapnel. A cracking sound comes from the cupola. I look up and see fissures zippering along the glass.

"Look out!" I shout, hopping over the guardrail. I extend my hand to help them over, but it's too late. The cupola shatters, blades of stained glass raining down.

Gaëlle and Adrien drop to their knees, curling into a fetal position with their hands cradled over the back of their heads.

Another shudder goes through the temple, disintegrates the guardrail, loosens the remaining pieces of the cupola that plummet like incisors. I lurch forward and yank Gaëlle's arm, sliding her across the glass-littered tiles before she gets impaled.

"We've got to get out of here!" Adrien yells, sprinting toward the door.

"Gaëlle, get up!" I shout over the din.

I see her mouth form words but don't hear them over the splintering of bookshelves.

"Come on!"

I think she says, "I can't."

I'm about to remind her that she defeated a ghost, so she can do anything, when I notice the massive sliver of yellow glass poking out of her leg. Blood stains the denim black.

"Fuck!" I turn around and holler, "Adrien!"

Miraculously, he hears me and doubles back.

I pull off my scarf and knot it hard around her thigh. "Pull it out."

Adrien winces but does as I ask. When blood squirts out along with the glass, his hairless head turns a sickening shade of yellow-green.

I scoop Gaëlle up and then scram for the exit, Adrien on my tail.

Another tremor rocks the building, tipping an oak bookcase. With a loud thud, it slams into the door, wedging it closed.

That was our way out.

50

CADENCE

Maman's terracotta war god releases a thunderous roar as he bursts through the broken glass wall and whirls, his dull eyes settling on me.

"What the hell's that?" Alma screeches.

"That's my piece," I say but then whip my attention off Ares and look toward Alma who stands halfway between me and Bastian's prostrate body. "You can see him?"

"Well, duh. He's a behemoth, and he's standing right there!" She carves up the air with a jerky hand movement.

Yet, she hadn't seen the dragon. Can she see my piece because it breathed life into something that already existed? Why am I wasting time pondering this? It's a good thing she can see him. At least, she won't run into him by mistake.

The statue takes a step and then another before stopping and letting out a cry so fierce the force of it rips out my hair tie.

"Alma, help Bastian, and get the others! And whatever you do, stay away from the statue, okay? Under no circumstance do you touch him. He's only after me."

When he steps in my direction again, which is also Alma's direction, I take off sideways, leading him toward the Humanities building. As expected, he follows. For some reason, he doesn't run, but he's so inhumanly huge, that his strides are giant, and soon, he's closing in on me.

Weapon. I need a weapon. I try the door but it's locked.

When I look over my shoulder, Ares is right there, sword brandished, ready to pin me against the door like a butterfly.

I thought I'd felt fear before but apparently not. The icy claws tearing through my body are a brand-new sensation.

Ares's arm flexes, and he plunges his terracotta sword forward, straight toward my head.

51

SLATE

"I t's solid oak. There's no way we can move it by ourselves." Adrien uselessly shoves the bookshelf blocking the library door.

"What about a fire exit?" I venture.

He gazes across the room, where more thousand-pound bookshelves have fallen like dominoes. "This is a magical temple. There is no fire exit."

"You've got to be kidding me." Thank fuck Cadence and Bastian and Alma aren't here. Thank fuck they're safe.

The room shudders, and books tumble down. The sharp corner of one knocks into my skull. *Great.* I was all out of head lumps.

Gaëlle sucks in a breath as a book lands on her leg.

"There should be a first-aid kit behind the reference desk," Adrien tells me.

"And where is this reference desk?" I nod to the wreckage.

He weaves through the jungle of fallen bookshelves, smashed tables, and swinging light fixtures, then ducks, coming up with a zippered pack adorned with a red cross which he waves like a beacon.

I rip the soaking denim to expose the wound as he dashes back toward us. "We'll fix you right up."

"I've given birth," she rasps. "This is like a bug bite."

While Adrien goes to work squirting antiseptic ointment over

Gaëlle's leg, we get a moment of respite. A moment that stretches on and on.

The shaking's stopped, yet the fire in my veins hasn't quelled. I slide my phone from my pocket and dial Cadence before I remember her phone went the way of her silver jacket—up in flames.

Adrien starts wrapping a long bandage around Gaëlle's leg as I dial Bastian.

It rings. And rings. And rings.

Come the fuck on! Pick up, little bro!

I hear fumbling and muffled swearing then finally, "Oh, my God!"

It's not Bastian.

Dread pools in my belly. "Alma?"

"Slate! Oh, God." Her voice wavers like she's crying. "Bastian slipped and smacked his head. He's out cold and—"

"*What?*" I roar.

Another tremor shakes me so violently my ribcage hurts. Or maybe it's no tremor. Maybe it's just me.

"And Cadence ran off after her statue."

"After her *what*?" I shout.

"The statue her mom sculpted. She says it's her piece. It came to life like a cursed Golem."

"No! *Fuck!*" The words come out of me like a keening yowl.

Adrien and Gaëlle are now studying me, eyes narrowed.

My muscles cramp again, and the ring flares brighter. Oh, no. No, no, no. I should've known it was Cadence's piece burning my blood. Not the goddamn clock.

I made her stay out there . . .

I want to shred something. I settle for a hard punch against wood that splits my knuckles.

All of this is my fault.

I should've kept her by my side. Instead . . . instead she's out there, fighting alone.

"Bastian needs help and so does Cadence." Alma's voice gives me something to focus on besides my sharpening ire. "You guys, please help," she whimpers.

"We fucking can't!" I punch the bookcase again, leaving a smear of blood behind. "We're fucking stuck in here. Call an ambulance for Bastian!"

"We don't have ambulances in Brume. But I'll call Sylvie—"

"Call the police. And the fire department. And the freaking Girl Scouts!"

"Okay, but Cadence said no one else can touch the piece."

"I don't fucking care!" I hang up and start scrolling through past calls to find Rainier's number. Vaguely, I hear Gaëlle say my name, but I focus on the phone. My hand is shaking so hard I accidentally call my lawyer. Then Bastian's number again.

I thought I was scared when I was fourteen and Vincent came at me with a knife. I thought I was scared when they hauled me into juvie and my cellmate tried to chew my fucking ear off. I thought I was scared when that *groac'h* had me in her talons. I thought I was scared when I let go of little Emilie's hand.

"Slate?" All of a sudden, Adrien's right beside me. He rips the phone from my hands. "What's going on?"

"Call Rainier." I shove the bookcase keeping me away from Cadence with every ounce of strength I have. It doesn't even slide an inch.

"What do I tell him?"

I shoulder the solid oak again, drive my boots into the tiles, push.

"Slate? What do I tell Rainier?"

All those times I thought I was scared? They were nothing. Nothing compared to the terror that grips me now.

My eyes meet Adrien's. His face blurs as I say, "Bastian's knocked out and Cadence is fighting for her piece . . . alone."

52

CADENCE

I fall into a crouch, and the sword whispers above my head. It hits the door with a deafening thwack. And then pellets of something—splintered wood?—rain down on me. Before one can knock me out, I lurch away, ducking under Ares's still raised arm.

My opponent howls his discontentment as I scramble upright and whirl around, backing away without taking my eyes off him. He turns, and though there is little light, I notice the blade of his sword is gone. What bombarded me wasn't bits of wood but fragments of dry clay.

The man can crumble. This is how I defeat him! The realization injects vigor and hope where there was only fear and despair.

He takes a step in my direction, then another. I pray the others are on their way even though I need to fight like they aren't coming. Make my own luck, as Slate told me the first night we met.

Would Ares charge me into another wall? Maybe. But would my organs survive being body-checked by a man made of hardened clay? Probably not.

No. I really do need a weapon. For a fleeting moment, as I prance backward, my gaze zooms onto the temple. The doors are still sealed shut, and although the crescent moon spits out the faintest trickle of light, I can see the outline of a body hunched over another.

My bones chafe against one another as fear wads up in my throat. Why aren't they out? Why are the doors closed? If anything happened to them . . . I wheeze in a breath, tears stinging.

I can't go there. I need to focus.

So I do.

On the growling warlord advancing toward me.

SLATE

P lease, God. Please.
      I'll do anything.
         Fucking anything.
Stop thieving.
Stop swearing.
Give up drinking and madeleines.
Give up everything I own.
Go back to living off scraps and handouts.
Just keep Bastian and Cadence safe.

CADENCE

T hink, Cadence. Think. Where can you get a weapon? If the Humanities building and temple are locked, then so will—

The answer slams into me so hard I almost trip on my own feet. I twist around, recover my balance, and sprint toward the Beaux-Arts edifice, toward the shattered veranda. I only glance over my shoulder once my boots crunch on more than icy snow. I grab a shard of glass and hurl it at the giant who's closing in on me.

He blocks the missile with his shield. The glass explodes against it without even leaving a dent.

Wood. I need wood. Or metal. Something harder than glass.

I look around the trampled snow, but nothing remotely useful jumps out at me.

And then Ares is three paces away. If I don't haul ass, he's going to crush me.

I spin and run, the blood pounding in time with my footfalls.

I know this building.

I know every nook and cranny.

Every object inside.

I know there's something I'll be able to use.

I hang tight to this confidence that's keeping me from stopping and surrendering.

I will win this. Just like the others did.

I can do this.

The walls and columns swim in and out of focus as I streak past them. The art displays blur. The lines of text on Marianne's scroll smudge into one long strip of ink. Slow footfalls ring out behind me, distant enough for me to slow my frantic race and glance backward. The warrior still doesn't run. Maybe the impact of his boots against the ground would make him crumble. Whatever the reason for his unhurried pace, I am freaking thankful. I wouldn't have stood a chance if he'd moved any quicker.

Although I keep his hulking figure in the corner of my eye, I scan the dark hallway for something . . . anything. The sheen of a marble bust makes me lurch toward it and haul it off its pedestal. The weight drags my arms down, making me stagger forward.

I grit my teeth, plant my feet wide, and heave the bust up. My elbows scream as I raise it like a tennis racket. Sweat running down the sides of my face, I wait for Maman's god to come closer, wishing she'd been into miniatures instead of larger-than-life men.

When he's too close for comfort, hopefully close enough for me to reach, I twirl, creating the momentum I desperately need considering how my arms shake. When I spin back, I let the bust fly. It hits him, but nowhere near the place I was aiming for.

It crashes into his ankle, which immobilizes the giant. His huge, pinkish-brown head bows to stare at what I've done, which is blow off his foot. He sways, but before he can tip over, which would've been quite ideal, he releases his broken sword and drapes a massive arm around one of the columns holding up the vaulted ceiling. The clay hilt, that had once held a long blade, shatters into chunks at his remaining sandaled foot.

The building shakes, and flecks of sky-colored plaster drizzle down. And then larger pieces, one so big it bears the entire body of a cherub, halo, cloud, and all.

If the roof caves in, he might die, but so will I.

He releases an indignant rumble that makes the marble tremble underfoot. I lock my knees, but when the shaking gets too violent, I lurch toward another column and hug it.

As the plexiglass case filled with kindling falls with a jarring crunch, I map out all the exits: the broken veranda, the emergency fire door at the end of the East hallway, the window behind the suit of armor. It hasn't blown out but with a punch of the sword—

The sword!

I pitch myself toward the armor, slamming into it so violently I go down with it. As I land, my eyeballs feel like they touch the back of my skull. Body rattling, I pry the sword loose before flipping onto my backside and scuttling like a cockroach, scanning the hall for any changes, but the giant's still cuddling the column.

Thank freaking all that is magical that my bust blasted his foot off.

I straighten, feeling braver now that I'm armed and the warlord is immobilized. As I advance toward him, the ground stops shaking, but the plaster's still peeling off the ceiling and drifting down like sheets of snow during an avalanche.

"Not feeling so proud now, Ares, huh?"

Under the lip of his helmet, his eyes rove over me. They don't glitter like real eyes, because they aren't real.

He isn't real.

And yet, when I'm going to plunge this sword inside his chest, I'm going to feel real satisfaction.

He growls, and then in one surprisingly fluid stroke for someone made of clay, he rips his shield off his vambrace and frisbees it toward me.

I dive sideways. My head ricochets off the marble, crackling the edge of my vision. I blink and blink, then heave myself onto all fours, knuckles of the hand clutching the sword smarting from where they met stone. Something wet and warm drips over my lids, then down the sides of my nose.

Crap.

As I force myself to stand, I wipe it away, knowing it's blood without needing to see the crimson stain.

Doesn't matter.

It's just a flesh wound.

The shield lays smashed a body's breadth from where I fell. The ochre chunks poking out from underneath the kindling Slate had mistaken for wands when I'd given him a tour of this building.

Thinking of Slate steels my rattling spine.

I roll my shoulders back and face the warrior again.

SLATE

"Stop it, you two. Stop!" The way Gaëlle speaks, with such desperation, makes me think this isn't the first time she's tried to get boys to stop acting like boys.

Sweat drips into my eyes. Warmth and pain radiates through my upper body. My sweater's stained a deep scarlet. I've been beating myself bloody trying to move the damn bookcase.

Adrien, too, has open wounds on his hands, and a sheen of sweat across his blistered forehead. He closes his eyes and sags against the massive piece of furniture, looking utterly defeated.

The clock is still ticking. The ground still shaking.

Bastian's cell phone died fifteen minutes ago, so I have no idea what's going on out there. All I know is that Rainier was sending the whole freaking fire brigade up to Fifth.

A dull thud comes from the other side of the bookcase.

"Stay away from the doors!" yells a muffled voice. "We're coming in!"

Relief and impatience flood through me in equal parts. "About fucking time."

CADENCE

Ares's mouth opens around another roar, displaying toothless gums. I guess that if my mother didn't sculpt it, it doesn't exist. He reaches to his head and pops off his helmet like a Lego hat, then bowls it at me. I duck.

"You're getting predictable, Ares." I scan the rest of his attire. Besides a toga, and one sandal, he's weaponless.

Before he decides to strip and strangle me with his clay dress, I launch myself at him, sword pointed straight at his chest. He swats the air, the back of his hand catching the blade, sending it and me flying sideways. I go down on one knee, speckling blood all over the pale stone. My joint feels like it's popped out of its socket, and yet I manage to stand, so it must have stayed put.

I hobble toward the monster, rethinking my strategy of going for his chest. It's not like he has a heart to pierce. I circle him. There is no way I can reach his head to saw through his neck. He twists around the column, hopping on one foot. The column chips from his weight, but astonishingly, it holds up.

My gaze locks on his remaining foot. Clutching the sword with both hands, I run at the giant and swing the sword into his calf. The impact rattles my wrists and makes me utter a string of obscenities, but I hold on. Hold strong.

The clay fissures and then his ankle snaps off.

Ares's livid howl reverberates through the cavernous building as he slithers like a snail down the column, spiderweb cracks shooting up his shins when they connect with stone.

He crumbles and crumbles.

I did it.

I defeated the Quatrefoil!

I did it.

Tears stream down my eyes, mix with the blood still gushing from my forehead. I want an unobstructed view of my victory, so I wipe them away, smearing my cheeks, pasting my hair to my throbbing skull.

The leaf glistens and falls with a clank amidst the debris of clay. I step toward it and then lean over and clasp the warm, smooth metal. I want to kiss it. I want to spit on it. I want to stomp it under my boots. I want to hug it.

In the end, I just hold it with both hands.

A thunderous crack sounds next to me. The column breaks in half along with every other column balancing the vaulted ceiling. And the ceiling . . . the beautiful ceiling painted with cherubs and clouds collapses over me.

I waged a battle against a monster and won.

I will not lose to plaster.

I run toward the window just as it explodes, thankfully, outward.

Before I can reach my escape hatch, something glances against the back of my skull.

I stumble. My ears ring, and my tongue tastes leaden.

I press my palms into the shuddering ground.

My leaf?

Where's my leaf?

I crawl, my palms scraping through the debris. Before I can spot my prize, something heavy slams into the base of my spine, flattens me. I try to get up, but the world spins, and spins.

Quiet and dark.

Flecked by pinpricks of light.

Stars.

I see stars.

And then I see nothing.

57

SLATE

I turn off my phone. All is in order.

Bastian will receive everything I own when I die at moon-set, which according to him, is at 4:43 p.m.

Thing is, I don't even give a fuck about dying. Because it's been almost four days, and Cadence is still in a coma. Her face is covered in cuts and scratches. She's got a black eye and a gash through her right eyebrow.

Miraculously, no broken bones. But hell, I'd beg for broken bones over this unconscious shit. A clear bag of IV fluid hangs above her, and countless machines beep, their pattern never changing. She's breathing, yet she barely seems alive.

There might not be a hospital in Brume, but the fancy university clinic more than makes up for its absence. The rooms are so new they sparkle, and the bathrooms . . . they rival mine back in Marseille. If the University's short on funds, this place is why. If only they'd allocated ten euros of the cash spent on decorating this joint to replace the hairy soap-on-a-stick in my dorm's *toilettes hommes* with liquid soap dispensers.

Two hours and thirty-six minutes.

You deserve to die, Rainier told me when Cadence was transported in here.

I didn't disagree. No matter what kind of weird shit he did with my money, no matter how easily he left me to the sharks in the system, no matter how often he's lied, it doesn't matter.

I put on the ring. *I* started this whole mess.

And then *the one time* I needed to be by Cadence's side, I forced her to go off on her own. And she ended up here.

When the fire brigade broke down the temple door, I set out like a doped-up racehorse leaping out of a starting gate. On the temple steps, a paramedic was shining a pen light into Bastian's eyes and asking him questions. He was conscious and answering accurately.

Still, I asked him to list the foster parents we'd had. Once he'd spoken all their hateful names, I'd raced across the quad toward a site of such destruction that my heart didn't beat once on the way there.

The Beaux-Arts veranda was gone, thousands of shards of glass glinting like diamonds on the snow as the firefighters swept over the area with their flashlights. The building itself had caved in, now resembling a Roman ruin with its smashed pillars, uneven sections of gray limestone walls, and arches of tenacious ceiling.

Two men grunted as they lifted a slab of slate roofing.

"We have something!" one of them yelled.

I ran toward where they stood. When I reached them, reached *her*, my breaths stopped short in my lungs. For an eternity, I stared down at her unmoving body. And then something in me snapped, and I lunged. Before my fingers could brush over her bloodied cheek, seek out her pulse, Adrien and one of the firemen cuffed my arms and hauled me back to let the paramedic do his job. I spit obscenities at them, roared to be released.

"Slate, calm down. Cadence would want you to calm down."

"Calm down? Are you fucking kidding me? How am I supposed to fucking calm down, Prof?"

"I have a pulse," the man kneeling beside her exclaimed.

I stopped fighting and gulped back the jagged lump stuck in my throat.

"Should he be touching her?" Adrien asked.

I was about to go off on him when I understood what he meant. If she was clutching her piece, he'd be cursed.

"Too late now," I murmured.

They dug out her legs, then brought over a stretcher and laid her unresponsive body out. Her red coat was white with powdered plaster, her leggings dark with blood, and her fingers limp, devoid of any golden leaf.

"Could she have put it inside her pockets?" Adrien asked.

I grazed both. Empty.

I wanted to accompany the firemen wherever they were taking Cadence, but Adrien tipped his head to the rubble of glass, snow, and stone. "We need to find it."

We spent hours, Adrien and I, on our knees. At some point, Bastian and Alma joined, and even though I growled at them to get the fuck away, they didn't.

The sun was rising when we finally gave up, my death warrant signed and sealed.

But, like I said, doesn't matter.

As long as Cadence lives . . .

Rainier rolls up to me now, an odd gentleness to his voice. "There's rooftop access in this building. Gives onto the rocks below."

His blue eyes, so many shades darker than his daughter's, stray to the bay window with a panorama of the mist-cloaked, icy lake. It's such a different view than the one from his office. Perhaps because the clinic's perched on Fourth, and his manor—*Cadence's* manor—sits on the lowest circle of this town.

"If I were you, I'd go up there and jump."

I take a serrated breath in. "The world will be rid of me soon enough, De Morel."

His eyes flash. "Oh, it's never soon enough."

He's not wrong.

His voice grows soft again, soothing. "I'd do it now, Roland, while you're still in control. Because later, when the poison's in your system, and you're writhing in pain, you'll wish you had."

He's got a point. There's nothing worse than losing control.

I take the stairs, the slap of my boots echoing on the concrete, and push open the heavy door to the roof. Snow curls about in the wind, whirlpools of powdered sugar at my feet. The air whips through my hair as I make my way across the frozen tar. I hold my breath until I reach the edge.

The mist unspools like windblown clouds, offering a glimpse of the jagged rocks on the sandy shore below. It would be easy to step off. It would mean I decide what my last moments look like, not some evil poison in my blood. It would mean no more pain. No more anything.

I lean forward.

But then I step back, too much of a coward to take my own life. Or maybe I'm too much of a fighter. And I know Bastian will never forgive me if I don't stick around until the very last second.

Bones cold as icicles, I return to Cadence's side.

Rainier's gone.

I sit in the transparent plastic chair next to her bed, accidentally banging the finger with the ring against the armrest. Pain lances up my arm from my newest injury. The one Bastian gave me yesterday.

The day after Cadence . . . after she . . . lost consciousness, Bastian, along with Adrien, Alma, and Gaëlle pored through the salvaged documents in the library. The temple had taken a beating, but it still stood, proud and cupola-less at the heart of Brume.

The following day, Bastian crawled around the astronomical clock like a bug, on the hunt for something. I wasn't sure what. Maybe a bottle-opener made to pop Bloodstones off rings. He found nothing.

And yesterday, he came at me with industrial-sized bolt-cutters that didn't even dent the golden band. In a last desperate attempt, he closed the cutters around my finger. Let's just say it felt like the *groac'h*'s needle-sharp teeth had made babies with the *guivre*'s noxious fire. Blood had spewed everywhere. Bone had crunched like crispy crackers. And then, because even the nastiest messes need a cherry on top, Bastian had vomited. Definitely rated in the *Top 5 Weirdest Moments of Slate Ardoin's Miserable Life.*

Anticlimactically, my goddamn finger didn't come off.

Instead, before our very stunned eyes, my skin and bone knitted together. What should've been a savage amputation became nothing more than an ugly bruise.

The ring has cursed me, and cursed me good.

Gripping the handrail of her medicalized bed, I study Cadence's beautiful face, so still, so pale. An angel's face. I reach out and wrap my warm fingers around her frosty ones.

"Come back," I whisper. "Please, princess, come back."

The machines beep in the same constant rhythm they've done since she was plugged into them.

"Come back to me, Cadence."

Her eyelids flutter but stay closed. They've done that a lot so I don't hold my breath.

I tug on my sweater collar.

I need air.

I stride out of the room, almost smack into Nolwenn.

Her face is lined with a hundred more wrinkles than the last time I saw her.

I gesture to Cadence's room. "She's . . . she's the same."

Nolwenn nods. "It's you I came to see, Marseille."

"Me?"

She takes a step closer and whispers, "It's important."

I sigh and run a hand through my hair. "Okay."

There's no one in the waiting area on this floor, just a handful of empty armchairs. A student nurse is working behind the desk, earbuds in, head bopping. She looks up when we enter the room, but Nolwenn waves her away. We walk to the farthest corner from the desk. Nolwenn sits, crosses her legs, pats her puffy blonde hair, and clears her throat. She gives me a quick smile, and I see she's got lipstick on her teeth.

I'm debating whether to tell her or not but am brutally interrupted by a confession that pins my lips shut.

"I'm the one who sent you away from Brume."

I don't know what I was expecting her to say but not this.

I find my voice. "So, the mystery of how I ended up in foster care's finally solved." The irony that I get closure minutes before I'm set to die isn't lost on me. "Do you know how fucking awful it was?"

She flinches as though I'd slapped her. "I'm sorry, Marseille. Back then, we thought anything would be better than you being here. We had no idea what you might endure. I'm truly sorry." Between the purple smudging her eyes and the red rimming them, she looks it.

A flash of anger sparks through me, then settles into cold indifference. It doesn't matter anymore. Nothing fucking matters anymore.

Still, I ask, "Why?"

"Amandine asked me to."

My whole body feels hollowed out. "Amandine de Morel? Cadence's mother?"

"Yes." She puts a hand to her helmet of hair again.

"So Rainier knew the whole fucking time where I was . . ."

It's not a question, but she must think it is because she shakes her head and says, "No."

I grip my knees, and pain radiates up my bruised phalanx. "I don't understand."

She plays with the rectangular catch on her purse, flipping it open, then closed. "You were only a toddler. But also the only Roland left. If you'd stayed in town, Amandine was convinced . . ." Her gaze flitters to every inch of deserted space. "She was convinced he would try to get the Quatrefoil together again, no matter your age."

"Who's *he*?"

She lifts a penciled-in eyebrow.

"You said *he* would have tried to get the Quatrefoil together again. Who's he?" I want to hear her say it.

She snaps the golden clasp shut and hugs her purse to her chest, her gaze flitting around the empty waiting room again.

"Rainier," she whispers.

His name echoes like a gunshot inside my throbbing skull. I roll my fingers into fists, relax them, roll them back in. "Amandine asked you to hide me from him?"

"Yes."

Glad to see my gut hasn't deceived me yet. "Why tell me now?"

She eyes the Bloodstone. "I've lived with this secret for seventeen years. And then I lived with the guilt of having lost track of you. I don't know if the others told you, but my son was cursed. When it happened, when he started acting—" A tear snakes down her cheek, gets lost in one of her wrinkles. "He consumed my every thought. My every minute. After I sent him away, I tried locating you, but you'd vanished . . . without a trace." Her voice grows thinner, her grief heavier. "I hope you can forgive me."

I don't answer her, too busy planning how I will take De Morel down with me when I go. I might be scum, but a man feared by his own wife . . . there's no word to describe that sort of person. I stand and pace, back and forth, back and forth.

Nolwenn sniffs, following my frantic marching with her shiny eyes. "Marseille?"

"I knew I couldn't trust him."

"Him? It was my fault."

"You did it to save me. To get me away from *him*."

"And I failed." She inhales deeply, as though to quiet her sorrow, but more tears stream out. She squeezes her eyes shut. "You found your way back home."

"No. He found me."

It hits me then that although he claimed to have gotten me out of Vincent's clutches, he might've had no hand in it. That when he loaned my money to that Marianne-chick, he might not have known I was alive. Not that either is consequential at the moment.

Nolwenn grabs my sleeve, effectively halting me. "Marseille, you cannot tell him you know. You cannot say a thing. I have grand-children."

Holy shit. Does she think he'd hurt those kids?

"And he's got a daughter who worships the ground he stands on," she adds in a small voice.

"Doesn't do much standing if you ask me. Unless he's faking his handicap."

"No. It's real." She wipes one cheek, then the other. "Do you promise to keep my secret?"

Going down without a fight goes against every fiber of my being, but there's so much terror in Nolwenn's brown eyes. And I don't want to be the cause of it.

I scrub my hands down my face and heave out a sigh. "Fine. But once I'm gone, you have to swear you're going to take care of Cadence as though she was your grandkid, Nolwenn."

"I swear upon the Quatrefoil that I will."

Is this some sick joke? "The Quatrefoil?"

"Sorry. It's . . . the saying's so ingrained in me."

Taking Rainier's wrongdoings to my grave better earn me some damned angel wings.

WHEN I RETURN from my walk a half hour before moonset, Cadence's clinic room is crowded. Adrien stands at the window, fogging up the glass with his slow breathing, staring out into the darkening grayness. Gaëlle leans against the wall under the mounted TV set, head back, eyes closed. Alma sits on the bed, cheek resting upon Cadence's shoulder. Bastian occupies the Kartell ghost chair in the corner, punching his phone's screen.

They all turn when I enter, their faces carved in granite.

I avert my gaze.

"I miscalculated, Slate. The new moon sets at 4:47."

Whoopedy-woo. I get four extra minutes.

"Maybe that'll give us time to—"

"To what, Bastian?" I don't mean to sound like an ass.

He swallows, his Adam's apple bobbing in his throat. "Maybe we could—"

"Just let it go. Just fucking let it go."

The door swings inward, and the doc strides in. She lifts an eyebrow at the amount of people in the room but doesn't ask any of us to leave. Then she zeroes in on me and smiles. "Ah! You're due for a rabies shot, Monsieur Ardoin. I was worried you were trying to avoid me."

There's no way in hell I am getting a shot before I die. No. Fucking. Way. "I'll come in tomorrow."

"Did they ever find that dog?" She looks from me to Adrien. "The . . . what was it again?"

"A German Shepherd-pug," I answer tonelessly. Doesn't even make me smile anymore . . .

Adrien crosses his arms. "We found it. And we put it down."

"Good." Doc bobs her head, her silver braid settling over her white lab coat. "I've been meaning to call you, Adrien. About that puppy."

Adrien begins to shift on a pair of loafers so shiny they must be from his post-*quivre* closet.

"I'd really love your thoughts on breeds, and—"

"Doc?" I cut her off. "Can you just tell us if anything's new with Cadence?"

Her cheeks brighten. She gently shoos Alma off the mattress, eyes the machines and scrolls through some information on a tablet she pulls from the foot of the bed. She shines a pen light into Cadence's eyes and taps something onto the tablet screen. "For now, no change. But, like I said a couple of days ago, she's breathing on her own, shows no signs of brain damage, and no signs of infection."

Also, no signs of life.

"She's a strong girl. She's going to come back from this." Doc puts the tablet back into the pocket at the foot of the bed. "I need to go check on a few other patients, and then I'll head home. If anything of note happens, one of the nurses will contact me immediately, and I will contact you."

"Thank you, Sylvie," Adrien says quietly.

She smiles as she walks out, and then the room falls silent except for the *beep-beep-beep* of the machines.

I glance at my Daytona: 4:25 pm. Twenty-two minutes to go before Slate Ardoin is no more.

"Can you all give me a bit of privacy with Cadence?" I study the wrinkled plastic IV sack, refusing to look at any of them. Refusing to see the pity in their eyes.

They all reluctantly shuffle out.

I sit on Cadence's bed, lace my fingers through hers, and say for the hundredth time, "I'm so sorry."

She doesn't respond.

I set my gaze on the darkening sky, but all I see is my reflection in the glass. I'm pale and drawn and pretty damn pathetic-looking. Grief has pooled into my eyes and dragged the corners of my mouth down.

Grief at losing Cadence. At abandoning Bastian. At leaving this life.

So much for making my own luck.

Cadence's chest rises and falls quietly. Steadily.

"You know, princess, I'd feel a hell of a lot better about tonight if you'd pop those beautiful eyes of yours open and give me a kiss goodbye."

Her lids flutter. I want to hope they'll do more than that, but I know miracles don't happen.

I part my lips to speak again when her fingers twitch.

The words I was about to utter die on my rushed inhale.

Her eyelids quiver, and then they lift, and I get to look upon the most priceless jewels—Cadence de Morel's aquamarine eyes.

"Slate?" Her voice is broken, hoarse.

My heart expands so suddenly I think it might injure my ribs. My dying wish came true. Not only is she awake, but she remembers me. I lean over, thread my arms between the wires and tubes and take her face in my hands. "Thank fucking God."

She raises a hand, knuckles my week-old stubble.

I swallow the rawness that's gripped my throat. "How I've missed you, Mademoiselle de Morel."

"I would hope so." Her smile ignites something in me. Something that hurts, because it's about to burn out.

I lean forward and graze her bruised, pale skin with my lips— her forehead, her cheeks, her chin, her nose—before finishing with a soft kiss on her mouth.

The machines beep out of time as though hooked to my own pulse.

Suddenly, the door of the room flies open, and the student nurse hurries to the bedside. "Mademoiselle de Morel!" When she sees Cadence is awake, her eyes grow wide with relief. "Welcome back. How are you feeling?"

"Okay." Cadence smiles at me, and the sight fucking takes my breath away. "More than okay."

The nurse resets the machines. "Let me call the doctor. She'll want to see you."

When the door closes, Cadence's grin turns fiercer. "We did it. We defeated the Quatrefoil."

I swallow down a sharp prickle in my throat. Do I go with it, or set her straight? I don't want to upset her.

I don't have a chance to decide, because her gaze falls on the Bloodstone, and her face goes from pale to bone-white.

"Slate, why are you still wearing the ring?"

I clear my throat. "It . . . well . . . it doesn't matter. All that matters is that you're alive and your brain's working."

"Take it off. We defeated the Quatrefoil. Take it off."

"Cadence—"

She sits up, her breaths coming faster and faster, making the machines go wild. "Ares crumbled. I got the leaf. I *got* it."

"Cadence, it's okay—"

"I got my piece, Slate. I won it!"

The machines bleat anew.

"We looked for it." I avert my gaze, smooth a crease in the sheet that covers her body.

The door swings open again.

"Can you give us a fucking minute!" I snap.

The nurse freezes midway to Cadence's bed. "I was just going to switch off the machines."

"Okay. Switch them off."

She does it, then rolls the equipment against the wall. "If you're upsetting the patient, then I'm going to have to ask you to leave."

Cadence's eyes flash. "He's not upsetting me!"

The nurse blinks before trundling out. She's probably going to phone up Rainier. Fucking Rainier, who's going to have a lifetime with Cadence while I get a handful of seconds. My tongue itches to reveal all Nolwenn said, but I think of Gaëlle's twins, whom I have yet to meet, of her stepson, whom I have met. I won't betray her or them, but she better hold up her end of the bargain or I will fucking haunt her ass like Matthias haunted her daughter-in-law.

"Slate, how long have I been in the clinic? How much longer before the new moon?"

Before I can answer that it's already risen and will soon set, the whole Quatrefoil crew piles into the room—Adrien, Gaëlle, Alma, Bastian.

"Alma!" She yanks the IV out of her arm and scoots off the bed to give her best friend a one-armed hug before returning to my side. "I had the leaf before . . . before . . ." She puts a hand on her rumpled hair. "We have to go find it. It must still be there." She twists her neck left and right, most likely looking for her shoes. "I remember where I dropped it."

"We searched everywhere." Adrien rubs his chin, eyes downcast.

"You mustn't have searched *everywhere*," she snaps.

My eyes slide to my watch. For once, I hope Bastian's calculations are wrong. But they never are.

He glances at me, his eyes bloodshot and swollen behind his glasses. Ever since our botched attempt at removing my finger yesterday, he's been bawling on and off like a freaking baby. "The moon sets in eight minutes, Cadence."

"The moon sets? I don't—" Her eyes go to the window, to the drab, dark sky, then to my hand, and finally to my face. "I had the leaf. I had it. This can't be happening."

"Princess," I start.

A sob splinters out of her. I kiss her forehead.

Eight fucking minutes.

Maybe seven now.

This feels like the first night we met. When they counted down the seconds to the new year. Now, we're counting down the minutes to the new moon.

"I . . ." I clear my throat. "I need to leave." I clear my throat again and then get to my feet.

Although I want to go to Bastian, so I can give him one final hug and a pep talk, and then to Cadence, so I can bruise her mouth with mine, I don't deviate from my outbound trajectory.

I don't want anyone to see me suffer.

I don't want their last memory of me to be tainted by me begging for mercy.

I stop on the threshold. Without turning, I utter Bastian's name followed by the words I've told him so many times he'll probably have them inscribed on my headstone: "Don't do anything I would do."

Shit. Will I have a headstone or will the date of Rémy Roland's death be altered to fit my new narrative?

I tear out of the room, my boots clapping the linoleum. I nearly plow into the doc as I round the corner and barrel into the stairwell. I take the stairs two at a time until I'm on the ground floor, shoving the fire door open and tumbling forward into the hoary darkness.

Squeezing my eyes shut, I grit my teeth and wait for the torturous burning Rainier assured me would come.

Snow falls onto my clasped lids. An owl hoots in a not so distant tree. A motor rumbles.

"Slate?" De Morel's voice echoes through the frigid air.

"Come to watch me writhe in pain, De Morel?" I turn to where he sits like a fucking incapacitated king on his snowmobile, revving it up, even though the headlight is off.

I really don't want the last thing I see to be his smug face, so I turn around and shut my eyes, and wait for the pain.

And wait for it.

And wait for it.

It doesn't come.

I crack open an eyelid to see if I died without realizing it.

The stone wall of the clinic's still there, a pale blemish against the night, and so is the pile of cigarette butts in the standing chrome ashtray beside the door, and so is the rumble of the snowmobile.

It's hard to believe, but Bastian must've been off his game.

I lift my hand to swear at the cursed Bloodstone for dragging this out. The ruby gem is a dull burgundy, the color of the wine bottle I left behind in Amandine's crypt.

Amandine, who tried to save me.

"You foiled a lot of things, Slate." The motor revs louder.

I swallow thickly, fingers cold, numbed by fear and frost.

Molars gritted, I turn back to face Rainier. I want to push him off his snowmobile, drag his limp ass to the roof, and shove him off there. But I think of Cadence. I can't do that to her.

"She just woke up. Your daughter just woke up."

He freezes, his thumb slackening on the throttle. The motor still rumbles, but no longer as though Rainier was about to ram his sleek black ride into me.

My knuckles feel stiff. I spread my fingers to stretch them out and get the blood flowing, however pointless that might be. The band dips on my finger, and then the heavy stone drags it down.

Over the knuckle.

Over the nail.

And into the snow.

EPILOGUE
CADENCE

"**S**late!" I screech as I shove the clinic door open. "Slate!"

It takes my eyes a second to adjust to the darkness, to spot his broad body, his hunched shoulders, his bowed neck, his downturned face. Next to him sits Papa on his snowmobile.

"Slate!" I leap into the snow, barefoot, my thin hospital gown flapping. Six quick strides, and I reach them. "How dare you leave like that!" I shove his shoulder. "How dare you, Slate Ardoin."

I don't want to cry, but tears roll down my cheeks. I'm about to lose a boy I care so much about that I can't imagine him not existing. Not being part of my life.

His hands sweep across my wet cheeks. "Cadence . . ." His voice is soft. The tone of someone about to apologize. About to say goodbye.

"We'll find a way, Slate. I'll find a way to save you," I croak. "Right, Papa? We'll find a way."

My father remains as mute and still as my mother's statue before the Quatrefoil animated it.

"Cadence . . ." Slate wipes my tears away again before resting his palms on either side of my face and tugging me so close our noses bump.

"You said we have to make our own luck. Running off to die

OF WICKED BLOOD | 397

alone—well, with Papa—is not making your own luck. That's called giving up. I'm not letting you give up. I'm going to—"

"Cadence," he says my name more forcibly.

I sniff. "What?"

"The ring came off."

I blink. "What?"

"The ring came off."

I jerk my head back. "What?"

"The ring came off."

"I heard you the first time around."

"Then why do you keep saying *what*?"

I want to swat him for being so wickedly insolent. I want to kiss him for being so wickedly beautiful, inside and out. "*How* did the ring come off?"

"I put my hand down like this." He pivots his wrist until his fingers point to the snow. "And *voilà.*"

My heartbeats quiet, then thunder when I spot a dark stain on the trampled white expanse. I don't crouch to pick it up. Don't dare touch it.

I raise my gaze to Slate, brushing every inch of his face and neck and torso with my fingertips. "Does anything hurt?"

"For once, not a damn thing."

"Papa! Did you hear that? The ring came off." New tears spring into my eyes. "Does that mean he won't be poisoned? Does that mean he'll live?"

Slate slants my father a serrated glare which my father reciprocates. I need to get those two to like each other. Or at the very least, to stand each other.

My name's called. Slate's name, too. And then the others are crowding us. When they spot Slate's bare finger, their mouths part.

"*How?*" Gaëlle touches the base of her neck as though seeking out the comfort of her scarf. "How did you get it off?"

"It just slid off," Slate explains.

"Without killing you . . ." Bastian marvels, his eyes so red and puffy they almost touch his glass lenses.

Adrien stares at the cursed ring smudging the snow. "You think it came off because we locked the leaves into their cradles, Rainier?"

Papa's palms drift off the snowmobile's handles and perch on his lap. "Why, yes." His forehead smooths. "*That* must be the reason." His relief is so strong it's palpable.

I grin at him, then at Slate, who's watching Papa again. "You're going to live." I tow Slate's face down. "You're going to live!"

His eyes lock on mine, and their camber grows. "Hear that, De Morel? I'm going to live."

"I heard."

Adrien releases a rigid sigh. "We need to grab the ring before anyone else does."

"It won't adhere to anyone's fingers but ours. And none of us will be putting it back on, right?" Gaëlle levels a pointed stare at Slate.

He raises his palms in the air. "Fuck no."

"We still can't leave it here." Adrien leans over and fishes it out of the snow. After he pockets it, he rubs his palms on his pants as though to rid his fingers of any residual, sordid magic.

I press my lips against Slate's before whispering, "You're alive," because I can still hardly believe it.

"I am. And you know what? I think I'm going to stick around." He scoops me up so suddenly I let out a shrill squeal.

Or maybe Alma does. She's grinning from ear to ear while Bastian keeps weeping. The poor guy's probably in shock.

I hook an arm around Slate's neck as he walks me back to the clinic.

"Even though I like the outfit, princess, it's highly unsuitable for wintertime in Brume."

My wet cheeks ache from smiling. "You're really staying?"

He leans over until the milky cloud of his exhales warms my lips. "I really am."

AFTERWORD

DIVE INTO OUR QUATREFOIL CREW'S NEXT ADVENTURE:

OF
TAINTED
HEART

ACKNOWLEDGMENTS

KATIE:

I am extremely lucky to have some of the most amazing writing friends on the planet—the best critique partners, the best book buddies, the best friends all around. I want to thank each and every one of you, for caring enough to be honest even when it hurt and for never allowing me to give up.

But when it comes to *Of Wicked Blood*, the person I want to thank most is my co-author, Olivia: Thank you for having faith in me and my writing. Thank you for your patience and understanding when I slowed things down. Thank you for always bringing enthusiasm to this project, even at its most muddled moments. Thank you for never once making me feel I wasn't up to the job. Thank you for making writing feel like an adventure again. It was wild, messy, and crazy. But so much fun. I am honored to have my name next to yours on this book. I am so ready do it again!

OLIVIA:

I love reaching this part in a book, because it means I've accomplished what I set out to do: complete a new novel.

I have many people to thank for helping me get the job done. First our fabulous editor, Krystal, who is nitpicky to the trillionth degree—we love you for it, I promise. Second our talented cover designer Monika, whose design of a quatrefoil spurred our witchy tale. Third, Karen Thompson from my Facebook reader group (Olivia's Darling Readers), who came up with the name for our quaint, mist-cloaked town, BRUME (in French, the word translates as "mist," which made it perfect for our story setting).

However, there is one person who deserves my entire gratitude, and that is none other than my extraordinary co-author and dear friend, Katie.

Thank you for putting up with me and my OCE (Obsessive Compulsive Editing).

Thank you for writing scenes that made me laugh so hard my computer screen blurred.

Thank you for our endless, and I really do mean endless, brainstorming sessions that led to all those twists you, dear reader, might not have seen coming, because we, authors, definitely didn't.

OF WICKED BLOOD was such a fun project thanks to you, and hopefully, the first of many together.

Dear reader, thank you for tagging along with our ragtag Quatrefoil crew. I hope you've enjoyed their wild adventures as much as we've enjoyed concocting them.

Want to talk more about Slate and Cadence? Join our shared Facebook reader group: **The O. K. Crew.**

By popular demand, we've decided to share the process of co-writing. Without further ado, the making of OF WICKED BLOOD . . .

THE MAKING OF . . .

STEP 1: Discuss haircuts in order to avoid inconsistencies in character development.

STEP 2: Illustrate! And be as accurate as possible.

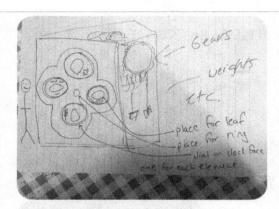

Told you I couldn't draw.

I find it beautiful. WE'll auction it off once our book hits all the bestseller lists. 😊

Lol. Can you at least understand it?

Yes 😊

Good. That's Slate standing there, btw

You forgot to put his ring so I couldn't tell

STEP 3: WORD SEARCHES. THEY'RE NOT ONLY FUN, OR FOR KIDS.

> Two things: First, I am in awe of how you can take my rough draft of a chapter and turn it into something amazing. Seriously, woman. Really good. Second, you're evil! Sending the dragon back to me! 😅 Just kidding. I will tangle with it this week.

Tue, May 19, 14:53

> Did a word search for "fuck" in the ms. 205 times. 😳 Ahem. Think on the next full read through I will try to reduce that by 80%. Eep.

> I do enjoy swearing...

Hahaha

> I need some new expletives.

Check the urban dictionary or use more merdes

> Lol! Yeah! French swearing!

STEP 4: PAT EACH OTHER ON THE BACK DURING THE PROCESS AND TOSS IN WORDS THAT DON'T EXIST BUT REALLY SHOULD. (I MEAN, hookier...).

Sitting down to rewrite the end of my chapter and reading what you edited of mine. I have three words for you: You complete me. 😍

I feel like co-writing is magic. I sit in front of my computer and so many great new words pop up ;)

Can I please send you everything I've written ever so you can work that magic on it? 😇

I only have like five novels for you...lol

But I'm all seriousness, do you want me to end the chapter with Gaëlle stopping him from going into the well or while he still is trying to go in

Sorry was at the gym.

Your other books are fab!

Whatever feels like a hookier ending!

OTHER WORKS BY THESE AUTHORS

KATIE HAYOZ

The Clockwork Siren series

IMMERSED

SUBMERGED

SURFACED

ENSNARED (spinoff novella)

The Devil of Roanoke series

THE CURSE THAT BINDS US

The Quatrefoil Chronicles series

OF WICKED BLOOD

OF TAINTED HEART

Standalone

UNTETHERED

OLIVIA WILDENSTEIN

The Lost Clan series

ROSE PETAL GRAVES

ROWAN WOOD LEGENDS

RISING SILVER MIST

RAGING RIVAL HEARTS

RECKLESS CRUEL HEIRS

The Boulder Wolves series

A PACK OF BLOOD AND LIES

A PACK OF VOWS AND TEARS

A PACK OF LOVE AND HATE

A PACK OF STORMS AND STARS

Angels of Elysium series

FEATHER

CELESTIAL

STARLIGHT

The Quatrefoil Chronicles series

OF WICKED BLOOD

OF TAINTED HEART

Standalones

GHOSTBOY, CHAMELEON & THE DUKE OF GRAFFITI

NOT ANOTHER LOVE SONG

Masterful series

THE MASTERKEY

THE MASTERPIECERS

THE MASTERMINDS